KISSING JOY AS IT FLIES

LIVING IN ETERNITY'S SUNRISE

THE LIFE STORY OF FRANK KING KELLY

AN ORAL HISTORY

EDITED BY DAVID E. RUSSELL

Library of Congress Control Number: 2008910797

Kelly, Frank K.

Kissing Joy as it Flies—Living in Eternity's Sunrise

ISBN 978-0-615-26002-0

"Eternity" – by William Blake (1757-1827)

DEDICATION

TO ALL THE INSPIRING PEOPLE who have guided me, chided me, taught me, delighted me, encouraged me, amazed me, shocked me, thrilled me, debated me, aroused me, forgiven me, shaken me, startled me, and shaped me as I have leaped from place to place, from world to world, in a long and wonderful life:

My beloved wife, Barbara Mandigo Kelly;

My parents, Francis Michael Kelly and Martha King Kelly;

My sons, Terry and Stephen Kelly;

My daughters-in-law, Mary and Misa Kelly;

My beloved friend, Christine Boesch;

My therapist, Fabio Duran;

My Celtic ancestors, with love and gratitude from here to eternity;

And a wonderful soprano named Carolyn Manzi, who lifted me to the heights with her great voice, who soared to the skies and made me aware of the hope of heaven.

ACKNOWLEDGEMENTS

Oral history is a collaborative literary form. Although the list of those who played a role in producing *Kissing Joy as It Flies—Living in Eternity's Sunrise* is long, most of the credit is owed to the narrator: Frank King Kelly. His gift as a storyteller is unparalleled. No subject was off limits, and the ease and willingness he exhibited in telling his life story made the tasks associated with going from audiotape to printed page a joy. His story captivated the student assistants who helped prepare the oral history for publication, without whose help the oral history program would not exist.

Jennifer Mundy Johnson, a history major, transcribed the interviews and proofread the first draft of the oral history. She also played a major role in copy editing the final edition, and scanned and prepared the photographs used to illustrate the book. Her contributions are greatly appreciated, as are those of two additional student assistants: Sarah Schulman and Amanda McAdam. They produced the second half of the oral history: *Selected Works of Frank King Kelly*, a process that involved locating the articles and books, many of which are out of print, and preparing electronic files for each.

Deb McCue, Executive Assistant for Frank's son Terry Kelly, designed the cover, fact checked the oral history, placed the photographs in the text, established the layout, and coordinated the project.

Terry and Mary Kelly, as publishers, managed the publication of Frank's oral history.

While their contributions, as well as those of the others mentioned above, made this book possible, the authors are responsible for any errors or omissions.

David E. Russell is Director of the University of California, Santa Barbara, Oral History Program. *Kissing Joy as it Flies—Living in Eternity's Sunrise* is part of an ongoing project dealing with authors and publishers in California. Among the authors included in this series are: Robert Olney Easton, *Life and Work*; Carl Rogers, *The Quiet Revolutionary*; James F.T. Bugental, *A Twentieth Century Life*; and George Leonard, *Author and Editor of Look Magazine*. The most recent oral history in the series is *Lou Cannon: Reporter and Presidential Historian*.

Eternity

He who binds to himself a joy
Does the winged life destroy;
But he who kisses the joy as it flies
Lives in eternity's sun rise

— William Blake

KISSING JOY AS IT FLIES

LIVING IN ETERNITY'S SUNRISE

THE LIFE STORY OF FRANK KING KELLY

Contents

PROLOGUE

ORAL HISTORY is neither biography nor autobiography. It is more drama, than studied reflection, as it contains the spontaneity of an unrehearsed conversation. The life story is told to a historian, whose role is to help shape and direct the dialogue, through questions that delve deeper into the story line, and by simply being present and bearing witness. In its purist form, it is the ancient art of story telling. It is thoughtful speech that spirals out from the center, to clarify and illuminate, and then returns anew, and in so doing captures the essence of life at a particular time and place. It is not measured and weighed, as a biographer would in the confines of his or her own study, where the search for verification governs what remains on the printed page. And yet in many respects oral history goes beyond biography and the measured picture it provides, by also including insights not found in the historical record—the inner feelings, the regrets, the private agreements and understandings between associates and family members that color and shed light on one's life.

As there is a natural rhythm to the life cycle—a natural progression—the same can be said for the telling of one's own life story. No hard rule exists, but for most, the time for reflection occurs after retirement, when life's journey turns inward, as death claims family and friends, and health problems slow one's vitality. Although one's memory is not as sharp, and names and exact dates fade, the inner tracings of one's personal history become clearer. And this was the case for Frank Kelly as he told his life story.

The following autobiographical history is based on a series of taped interviews. The setting for the interviews was informal and the atmosphere relaxed. Talk was wide ranging, often revealing new subject matter which led to revision of agendas for past and future sessions, while adhering generally to the outline for that day. The completed tapes were then transcribed and printouts extensively edited and revised.

It is important to recognize that oral history does not represent the written word, but rather, thoughtful speech with its usual false starts, pauses, and incomplete trains of thought, and without the body language and voice inflections that breathe life into dialogue. And, in making the cuts and welding them into a coherent piece, a major effort was made to preserve the conversational tone at the expense of perfect syntax and grammar.

The tapes, transcripts, and original manuscript of *Kissing Joy As It Flies—Living in Eternity's Sunrise*, are open to researchers in the Davidson Library's Department of Special Collections.

David E. Russell, Director
Davidson Library Oral History Program
University of California, Santa Barbara

PART I
LIFE STORY

Emergence in a Storm

Frank King Kelly, c. 1918

DISTANT VOICES

"Thunder and lightning filled the sky the night of your birth," my mother would tell me whenever my life took an exciting turn. It was a story she loved to tell. "You were born during a thunder storm," she would say, "and just as I was about to give birth I raised my head and saw a flash of lightning through the upstairs bedroom window of your grandparents' house, where your father and I were living at the time." So I came into the world with lightning and thunder. It was very dramatic. And in later years whenever she retold the story, she would always say, "Frank's always had a lot of dramatic events in his life." And she was right; I have experienced many unexpected events. And to this day, when I hear thunder, and see flashes of lightning, I think of her, and can hear and see her retelling my story.

The tracing runs deep. And her story is never far from my mind, but its meaning was never deeper—or more in-tune with my early remembrances—than years later when I read the opening lines of Sean O'Casey's autobiography, *I Knock at the Door—Swift Glances Back At Things That Made Me*. There he recounts the events of his birth as "…a mother in child-pain clenched her teeth, dug her knees home into the bed, sweated and panted and grunted, became a tense living mass of agony and effort, groaned and pressed and groaned and pressed and pressed a little boy out of her womb into a world where white horses and black horses and brown horses and white and black horses and brown and white horses trotted tap-tap-tap tap-tap-tappety-tap over cobble stones."

But unlike O'Casey's horses, who labored in the duty of commerce and transportation, mine were fire horses, magnificent beasts that charged out into the streets pulling fire wagons in search of citizens in distress. I was born in a house next to one of the main firehouses in Kansas City. My father was a fireman. And it must have been on one of these missions of mercy that my mother noticed him. They met, courted and married, and the first few years of my life were spent in my grandparents' home.

We lived on Harrison Street, in a large house next to the fire station where my father worked. And as I look back on my formative years, one of the strongest images I have is of the fire horses, magnificent beasts that pulled big wagons belching smoke. I never tired of watching my father, Francis Kelly. I still see him atop the engine, his massive arms straining to guide the horses as they turned, gathered speed and thundered down the street. Just as vivid are the tracings left by family—father, mother, grandparents, and my Aunt Mamie—who now reside in the recesses of my mind; voices silent in the here and now, but so alive in later years as I tell my life story.

The Kelly clan is Irish. Our story is no different than many of those forced from Ireland during the hard times of the potato famine in the 1840's. The first generation forged a

Frank's Mother – Martha King Kelly

lasting bond handed down from parent to child through stories retold at wakes, and in public houses of OUR EXODUS, the potato famine, and the dreaded NINA, No Irish Need Apply, an admonishment that dogged their every step in search of employment. Undaunted, they pursued the American dream. From Ellis Island they found refuge in New York, Boston, Chicago, New Orleans, Kansas City and throughout the west.

No job was too hard. They joined the long line of immigrant groups who built America: subway systems, high-rise buildings, and the westward span of the transcontinental railroad. We Irish did our parts. We fought to preserve the federal union against the confederate rebels. And gradually we erased the stigma of the Mick: a brawling lowlife, who lived to drink, and filled the slums of urban America. Each generation climbed a rung of the ladder. And my generation stood on the shoulders of our parents who had won respectability; they were firemen, policemen, politicians and men and women of letters. The ghosts of our past were relegated to the fictional voice of Mr. Dooley, who held a mirror to authority. His sayings lessened the sting of bigotry, as we learned to laugh at ourselves.

By 1914, the year of my birth, my family had settled in Kansas City; little is known—at least to me—of my family's journey west. I was the first-born. After my birth, we moved up on 2912 Charlotte, which was a quite different neighborhood, more quiet and residential than where my grandparents lived. And the Kellys had a house up there.

THE KELLYS AND THE KINGS

My grandfather's name was Alf King; he was a detective on the Kansas City Police Force. And Mr. and Mrs. King and their daughter, Martha, lived in a house almost next door to the fire station. And my mother got to meet my father because, you know, living next to a fire station is a fascinating place.

Mother told me jokingly that she liked the way he slid down the fire pole to go to the fires. When I was a little boy I remember seeing him riding forth, driving the huge fire horses. It made me feel he was an awesome figure. Of course, fathers are generally that to little boys. One day my father had an accident with a streetcar—the streetcars were pulled by horses, too—and I'm told that he managed to collide with the horses pulling the streetcar. It took them quite a while to get the horses to stop kicking each other.

He stayed at the firehouse when his shift was on, I guess. I am sure I was allowed to go and see him; I don't remember any of the details about it, but I'm sure I did.

GREAT WHITE FLEET—MY FATHER'S TRIP AROUND THE WORLD

As a boy, my father had served in the US Navy. He ran away from home when he was 15 or 16. He was big and tall. Roosevelt decided to send this big fleet that he had built up, called the Great White Fleet. They were going on a trip around the world. So my dad made the trip, and began to

Father with shipmates from the
Great White Fleet, Japan

understand how large and complicated the world was. He talked to me about it all the time. I don't remember the name of his ship. I do know that his most delightful time was in Yokohama. He said the Japanese people there were just wonderful; their hospitality was great. I have a picture of him somewhere wearing a Japanese kimono, sitting with his Japanese friends. That was a big event in my dad's life. And, you know, when World War II began he couldn't understand why we were fighting the Japanese. They'd been so cordial and so receptive to the American sailors. Well, of course, they were probably scared too; they wanted our friendship, and they felt we had become antagonistic toward them in the 1930's.

The Navy went around the world in 1906, and my father was on that great trip. He was no longer just a fireman. And he saw so much of the world. When I came along, my dad was a man with worldwide experience already. He told me stories about that cruise; nothing like it ever occurred again.

THE WAR TO END ALL WARS

My father got involved in World War I when Woodrow Wilson called for a declaration of war in 1917. He rushed out and enlisted right away. He went up to Camp Funston, an officers' training camp, and he later became a captain in the Infantry. He went off to war, and came back badly wounded; there was a big hole on the side of his neck from a piece of German shrapnel. You know with the Infantry, he had to lead men over the top. He said, "You couldn't imagine." General

Sherman said, "War is hell." But with shells bursting overhead, he had to tell a group of frightened men in a trench, "C'mon, boys, we're going over the top," and some of them couldn't go. Some of them went into a panic, the other soldiers tied ropes around their feet, and dragged the frightened ones with them over the top of the trench because they weren't going to let them stay there and not go out into the battle.

My father never got over his nightmares of World War I, so I say my life has been very much affected by the experience of having to try to get my father to wake up from these horrible dreams. He'd be fighting with a German in a trench; it was a hand-to-hand combat, and he had a bayonet and the German had a bayonet and they were trying to stab each other to death. And he would scream; he'd wake the whole house night after night. He never got over that as long as he lived.

— Did he tell you stories of what it was like in the trenches, and the horrible conditions they faced?

— Yeah, about how terrible it was, to be face-to-face with another person, and know that you had to kill that person or be killed. That's primitive warfare isn't it?

— Yes, very much.

DECISION TO GO TO WAR

I've been very much opposed to war all my life and I think it's a part of my heritage. When my dad went off to the

Francis Michael Kelly c. 1918
Camp Funston

Army in 1917, I was three years old. My mother and I were crushed by that because we thought he was deserting us. He rushed out the day after Woodrow Wilson made his speech and ran down to the recruiting office and signed up. We felt he was abandoning us.

He used to tell me that, "I believed that the first war was going to end war and make the world safe for democracy." And my poor dad was so disillusioned, when he came back from France with a big hole in his neck, badly wounded, and with a peace that didn't lead to anything.

He was treated over in France in a French hospital, in a military hospital at first. "They had good care," he said. And he recovered enough to take part in the occupation of the Rhineland.

He commanded an American unit there. He was an officer, but he had enlisted first as a private. He did so well in the officers' training camp, they commissioned him as a captain. The other guys became lieutenants. But he was noted as outstanding, made a captain. Because of that he commanded a company in France. I think he served in the 89th Infantry Division.

He never met Truman, but I have a picture of my dad in that Army uniform and he looks exactly like Truman with a big Army hat on, and with the tight suit and all that. He even had me dressed up in a little soldier suit, while he was in training camp. I was three or four years old. My dad was super-patriotic at that time. He changed; he got disillusioned after he came back.

Going over the Top

When he came back he looked so horrible that I was frightened of him. I'd hide behind a chair. I didn't want to see him. I didn't believe that was my father. My mother told me his face was warped; the right side was pulled down in an ugly way, when he got hit by a shell. He went over the top leading his company and ran into a terrific German barrage. He was knocked into a shell hole; he told me this himself. And he was lying there and he thought, "Oh, it's raining. How could that be? It wasn't raining when we left the trenches." And he realized that the fountain that was coming up and down on him was his own blood.

He was lying on his side and the blood was pouring up and then coming down on his face. He thought, "Oh my God, I'm going to die if I can't plug that hole." And his hand scrabbled around in the mud in the shell hole and found a piece of shrapnel and some mud and jammed it in. When the medics came, the bleeding had stopped. They pulled him out of the shell hole and said: "Ah, this guy's alive. He's got a plug in his wound." And they thought it'd get infected and everything, but it never did.

He told me that the experience of dying was wonderful. "Don't worry about dying," he said. "As I was lying there I had the most great, ecstatic feeling that I was connected with everything in the universe and I was sort of floating on a big feather bed." And he said, "Oh, it was marvelous." I don't know if he got any special medals, but he should have. He saved his own life.

After he was wounded he went to Paris. He went to a military hospital, and then he was sent to a convalescent camp or something.

I don't know how they treated his wound, but he wrote to us from France. I used to have some of his letters. Uh, one was a picture of him with some French hospital orderlies. And he said, "These are the men who fixed your dad's French fried potatoes in the morning." That was his sense of humor. But when he came back, that was a shock. See, when he got back it was 1918, 1919 because he was in the occupation of Germany. I was then five years old, and intensely aware of everything. A strange looking man came home. He didn't seem to be the father who had rushed off to war.

Last Meeting—K.C. Train Station

I remember when my father went overseas; my mother had a psychic vision about it. She saw that a train was going through the Kansas City Union Station, and my dad was on it. And if we wanted to bid him farewell we'd better get down there. So I remember going down there with my mother, at least I remember she constantly reminded me of it, all through my childhood. And we went up to the stationmaster and my mother said, "What time is the troop-train coming through?"

Frank Kelly with his mother, Martha King Kelly,
before father's shipment overseas

"Troop-train, lady?" He said, looking at us. "We don't have any troop-trains coming through here today. Where in the world did you get that idea?"

My mother said, "There's a train coming through." And she mentioned, "I think it's going to be early in the afternoon. And I'm going to go down and wait by the tracks."

"Lady, you can do that," he says, "I haven't any information about it"

She said, "My husband's going to be on that train. This is my little boy and we want to see his dad go off to war."

And the stationmaster said, "Well that's all secret. You know, I can't tell you one way or another but I can tell you I don't have any trains scheduled. Anyway," he said, "I'll let you go down there, lady." He said, "You're married to a captain in the Infantry, and this is his little boy." So we got down, stood by the tracks. Lo and behold, at the time my mother mentioned, here comes this train. Crammed with soldiers. And they were all leaping out, walking up and down the platform. My dad saw us, and came over and picked me up, gave me a big hug and said, "You take care of your mother while I'm gone, son." I remember him saying that. My mother was weeping and hugging him. And he hopped back on the train and away it went. She knew that was going to happen. And I remember it happening. My mother always had psychic visions.

COMBAT FATIGUE

So he got over to France of course and he was thrown into the first battle. Many men were slaughtered or wounded. When he got home and he talked to me about it, his descriptions went into me like sharp swords. Those became visions that never left me.

After the Armistice he was sent to Germany as an officer in the Allied Occupation Force. He was sent back into Germany to command a village. I don't remember the name of the village, and if he did mention it I don't remember. But he said it was such a beautiful village. You know how clean the Germans keep everything. And he never forgot how shocked his men were, these soldiers, American soldiers. He never forgot that. And I never did either. He discovered that many Germans would not face the reality of their defeat. Many of the American soldiers found the Germans more likeable than the French.

He told me when he came home, "Son, you know, when I was in charge of a German village, it was such a beautiful place. The streets were so clean and everything was kept well and my men came to me and said, "Captain, why didn't we fight the French? Their towns were sloppy and dirty. Why did we fight these wonderful Germans? And I had to try to explain it to them." And then I would talk to the Germans, and they said, "Of course we were not defeated. You don't believe that you defeated us. Nobody defeated the German Army. And there will come a time when our Army will be great again." My father said to me, even then, "Son, you're going to be in another war. They're going to try it again, and I'm sorry, you'll probably be involved. We couldn't do the job." He said, "They blamed their defeat on the Jews, on secret enemies, subversives in their government, which surrendered while the great German Army was still capable of fighting on."

FATHER'S DRINKING AND OTHER ITEMS

My father was sort of a Dr. Jekyll and Mr. Hyde. He was a wonderful man when he was sober. But when he drank heavily, he was very different, very negative, and very punishing. When he was drunk he was awful. So I never knew what I would have to face. There would be six months of wonderful times in the family and then my mother would say, "We've got to go over to grandma King's because your dad's on a rampage." And she'd pick us up in the middle of the night and we'd go over to my grandmother's house. I was frightened but my father always came back, loving and strong. And once I got accustomed to facing that fact, I felt better about things.

But he always encouraged me to write, and I thought that was great. He liked to read books of all kinds. He read mostly history. He was a very well educated man, in the same way that Truman was. They were very much alike, my father and Harry Truman. And I even remarked on that later, and Truman laughed. "Well your dad was in the same outfit I was,

I think." I don't know if he was but Truman was in the same division.

MAIL ORDER BUSINESS

My father didn't return to the fire department after coming home. He got a job with Sears-Roebuck and that came about in a strange way too. He read an ad in the paper saying that General Robert E. Wood, the new chairman of Sears-Roebuck & Co., would offer an executive job to any officer of the U.S. Army who had been in combat. And my dad wrote to him and so he went to Chicago and General Wood liked him and gave him a job. And he became an executive with Sears in Kansas City. Wood wrote a letter to the general manager. Sears had a plant in Kansas City, so that took my dad into a different atmosphere all together from the firemen's atmosphere.

He stayed there a long time. For a while he worked for a company called the National Coat & Suit Company, and then in the Depression he lost his job and we had to move to Indianapolis where one of his lieutenants was a veteran's administration director; he gave my father a job on the VA staff there. But he was in the mail order business most of his life. I guess he could have gone back to the Fire Department, but he didn't. Although he only had a grade school education, he'd been a captain, and it was through General Wood that he was able to land an executive position with Sears-Roebuck. And so that changed life for my mother and me.

The way he got his job at Sears was interesting. He was in a public toilet and he looked down and there was a newspaper that somebody had used for private purposes floating around in the toilet bowl. And he caught a glimpse of a headline in the paper: "General Wood Offers Jobs to Officers." Anyway, that's the story my dad told me. He said, "I found out, son, that General Wood of Sears-Roebuck had offered an executive job to any officer who had been in combat in World War I."

So my dad went to Chicago with no preparation, no appointment, walked in and was told, by the secretary, that he couldn't see General Wood without an appointment. My dad said, "No, I don't have an appointment but I would certainly enjoy talking with the General, just five minutes." The girl said, "Well, I'll check." So she went in and came out and said, "The General says he will see you." Dad got in, and they got to talking about World War I and, you know, General Wood had been in the war too. So he said, "Well, I'll give you a job in the Kansas City branch of Sears." So he appointed my dad to a good executive job with good pay.

Later, during World War II, I don't recall receiving any letters from him before going overseas, but I know he was sorry I had to go. He said, "If I look back on it, I wouldn't have volunteered. That was crazy; I was a crazy young man." Maybe I was a wild young man, too, in a different way.

MOTHER: MARTHA ONEITA KING

My mother's name was King, Martha Oneita King. Her middle name, Oneita, had some relationship to an Indian name. I always heard in the family that one of her mother's friends or somebody was very close to an Indian maiden named Oneita in Nebraska. I've forgotten what the tribe is up there but I've always been proud of my mother's name. I also wanted to have a connection with an Indian background. And my mother insisted on naming me, putting her last name as my middle name, so I was named Francis King Kelly. Her mother and father were from Nebraska. They lived in Nebraska and then they moved to Kansas City. Then my grandmother married a man named Alf King, who was a detective on the Kansas City police force. He was the grandfather I spent much of my time with as a boy.

My mother was a person who had to put up with a lot, because my father was a brilliant but unstable man; when he was sober he was loving and generous, and gave presents to his sons. He was just great. But when he got drunk, he was belligerent. My mother coped with that. She always kept us from being too frightened. She would gather us up and say we were going to my grandmother's house. So we would go over to her mother's house, which was not too far away, and we'd stay there until my dad came to himself again. And he'd come around and apologize, and we would all go back to our house.

My mother also encouraged me in my writing; she was a very loving person. She encouraged everybody. And she took care of my poor father, who was depressed in his later years. She never got angry with him, as far as I can remember. Never threatened to leave him, or anything like that. She really held the family together. If I hadn't had that strong mother I would have been unable to function. I know friends of mine who say that they just can never forgive their fathers for what happened in their childhood. I forgave mine and I was rewarded by him.

SIBLINGS: VINCENT AND KITTY KELLY

My brother is gone now. He was much younger than I, nine years younger. I was the only boy in the family for quite a while, so I was very bossy and dominating of course. I had a wonderful sister, who was born in 1920. She was six years younger than I.

My brother Vincent was the last born in the family. He never felt a lot of self-confidence. He didn't know what he wanted to do. He didn't like his given name. My parents had given him the name of Vincent, but he wanted us to call him Bud. And none of us wanted to do it. He was just kind of a sad man. He died of lung cancer from heavy smoking at the age of 61. He worked for a bank in Kansas City, as a teller, and fell in love with a girl in the next cage over. And he thought she encouraged him and then she ran off and married another man. He was gravely stricken by that, and he never married.

My sister was a powerful, wonderful person who had a great impact on my life. When I got the job with the Fund for the Republic, and we decided to move to California (as the Center for the Study of Democratic Institutions), my secretary in New York came to me and she said, "Mr. Kelly. As you know, I am from Mississippi, and I wanted to get up here to New York and go to all these glamorous places and meet all these wonderful men; now you want me to go out to some little town in California. I won't go! I am quitting." She was the one who told me how thrilled she was when she saw Mrs. Roosevelt in the women's room at the Fund.

I said, "Well, Penny, I'm sorry to hear that."

She said, "I wanted to give plenty of warning for you to get out there and find another secretary." She had been very good; I really enjoyed her presence on the staff.

So I told Bob Hutchins that I had a wild idea, and asked him what he'd think if I offered my sister Kitty, who was then an executive with Prudential Insurance Company in Kansas City, a job as my secretary. She wanted to work with me.

He said, "Fine with me. It's up to you to appoint your own secretary.

So I called Kitty up, and she was thrilled. She quit her job, and came out to Santa Barbara. She became a very active staff member at the Center. Hutchins liked her; everybody liked her. And she dealt with all sorts of excited people who wanted to see me or wanted to see Hutchins. She was a very important member of our staff. I remember someone said, "That Frank Kelly is a square! His secretary is good looking, but she's his sister. So he can't fool around with her." She kept all the files for me. She knew everything that I really should know. Somebody would come in and I would say, "What do we have on so-and-so?" And she'd have a folder on almost anybody who came through the Center. Executive secretaries were very important, and we really relied on them. Hutchins had one, Leslie Donnelly. She was like my sister, absolutely devoted to him. These were dedicated women.

GRANDFATHER: ALF KING

Grandfather King—my mother's father—was a powerful person in my life. Alf King was a police officer, a detective—a plain-clothes man.

He told me all kinds of stories about catching the bad guys. I remember him telling me about his partner. My memory is his partner was an Italian, named Olivera, or something like that, and they were engaged in some investigation. They knew it was dangerous, and that their lives were in danger. They were walking down the street one day, and Olivera suddenly said to him, "Alf! Get down!" He shoved my grandfather to the pavement. And just then, from behind a fence, a gangster opened fire and killed Olivera. My grandfather never forgot that. And that burned into me the idea that if you are a friend, you must be ready to lay down your life for your friend.

He used to take me down to the police station with him. It was scary. Very grim, you know. Because they were bringing in mostly the poor old bums, the homeless people, and there was some police brutality. I remember, after I became a reporter, hearing them beating up guys. And I finally went to the city editor and I said, "Shouldn't we have some articles on what happens to these poor old bums downtown?"

"Nah!" He said, "We have got to stay in with the cops. They give us a lot of news. So we're not going to write anything about that." So they never got in the paper.

But my fondest memories of my Grandfather King are going to the movies together to see William S. Hart in *Tumbleweeds*. He'd pick me up during the day and we'd go off to the theater, and Kansas City had some pretty good movie theaters, big ones. And I think movies cost a nickel in those days. Hart was a cowboy star before Tom Mix. And he had a beautiful horse he'd ride across the plains. And I remember seeing these tumbleweeds rolling in the wind; it was kind of a symbol of western life. You're just rolling along from one horizon to another.

I worried about my grandfather. And I got a lot of worries from my poor mother, who was a wonderful protective Irish mother. She didn't want to see me go out of the house for fear that someone might hurt us. I don't know if there was a fear of kidnappers then or what, but I had to be careful, and not talk to strangers.

My Grandfather King had an English name. Not Alfred, but Alf. Everyone said I looked like him. Unlike my father, he was very, very careful not to drink too much. He hardly ever touched a drink. He said, "You can't do your best work if you have drinks." I imagine he was a pretty good detective, from what I heard.

I had gone to New York when he retired. He lived to be 70 something, 72. But he was pretty active when I was there. I would see him from time to time, and we'd have lunch and dinner, and he'd tell me some tales. Sometimes he helped me on covering some stories for the *Star*. He'd tell me what to look for in covering a story.

He was a very handsome man. What you'd call portly today. He had a bit of a frontage, but was very well dressed. He was something of a dandy. He always told me, "Francis, you keep your shoes shined, and your pants pressed and you will be all right." He always wore a tie, and a felt fedora.

Everyone told me he looked like me. He had a big bold dome, with a big face, a very open face. And he was mostly Irish. He never served in the military. He was a little too old. He was just at the age where he couldn't have been drafted I don't think. So he wasn't involved in either war. I assume he went to Catholic school, but I don't know if he did or not.

GRANDMOTHER: GRAM KING

While we were in Indianapolis, my grandmother became terribly ill. The family decided that since I was the one most available, I would go to Kansas City and look after her in her last illness. So I had to get on a bus from Indianapolis. Went all night long to Kansas City to be with my dear Grandmother King. I loved her, and she loved me very much. She made fabulous cookies and she taught me how to play cards.

When I got back to Kansas City to stay with her, I found she was in terrible shape. Mamie said that she was shocked when she came home one night and I was guiding grandma to the bathroom. I was holding her with one hand, and reading a book I held in my other hand. And I didn't know anything about the caring for a person like that, and my Aunt Mamie, who worked for the Western Union, she helped as much as she could.

Grandma had a heart condition. So she died a few months later. I was in the house when she died. I wasn't in the room. That was a great blow; she was a great person. She had a wonderful house in Kansas City with a big cherry tree in the backyard and would make wonderful cherry pies.

Grandmother King was also very sharp. I remember her saying to me, "Francis, you might get involved in a poker game someday. So let me tell you how to do it. You don't want the other boys to take advantage of you." She taught me all right. But then when I got married my wife would never let me go out and play poker. She thought the other guys would beat me. Because she said, "You can't bluff. Anybody could read your mind. If you get four aces; your face would give it away." She said, "You'd lose all our money if you get in a poker game." And she was right. I went to a couple of them but I stopped after a while.

We talked about everything during that time of her illness, my grandmother and me. I wish I could remember more, but I can't, except that she was very loving, and she had a deep faith and she was sure that God would take care of her. She never seemed to yield to despair. I think that did have a major impact on my outlook on life. I tell people and I really mean it, all through my life there have been these wonderful, strong, brave women. People ask me, "How can you be optimistic about the human race? Can't you see what monsters men are? They slaughter each other all over the place." And I say, "Yeah, I know that but there are some wonderful people in this world and I know it personally. And I had a great mother and a great grandmother and a wonderful sister, all of whom never gave up on anything. Then I worked for Harry Truman, the man that everybody said was sure to lose, and he won." So I said, "I know miracles can happen." When I tell people this they stop calling me a wild-eyed optimist.

Grandmother King was a smiling, indomitable person. She was sort of mad at my grandfather because she thought he was chasing girls, or they were chasing him. I don't know which was correct. But she ran things pretty much by herself in her house. Alf King, the detective, he was out a lot of the time on mysterious projects. I never knew what was going on except that grandpa was doing some secret thing for the cops.

My grandmother maintained a big house; she loved to play poker; she had a weekly poker club. As I mentioned, she taught me how to play poker. She was a little bit doubtful about how well I learned. She said, "Don't get in any big games! You can't bluff. With that face of yours, they'll know exactly how many aces you have or how many deuces." And my wife said the same thing to me when I wanted to go out at night to go with my friends to play poker. My wife even tried to practice with me. "You just can't hide what you feel Frank! You are not a good poker player and you don't have the poker face." How do you get a poker face?

My Grandmother King was important to me because my mother, who was born a King of course, used to take us over to her mother's house when my father was having what we called an episode.

GRANDFATHER: MICHAEL KELLY

— I'd like to turn to your father's family now. What was your father's name?

— Frank Kelly. Francis M. Kelly. He came from a long line of Irishmen. My grandfather, Michael Kelly, came over from a town called Croom near Limerick in Ireland in the 1840's during the potato famine.

— And they settled where?

— In Kansas City, Missouri. And my grandfather got a job there and eventually worked for the Pendergast political machine in Kansas City. And all my family was associated with Democratic politics, but I never thought of getting into politics myself, so that's a different story.

— Was your grandfather part of the Pendergast political machine?

— Well, in a minor sense. He was one of the many Irish immigrants who were given jobs by the Pendergast. Tom and

Jim Pendergast, of course, were Irish themselves. But they had difficulties getting some other jobs so they found jobs at the city.

— What was your grandfather's occupation?

— I don't know exactly what it was. I know he had some sort of position with the city. I can't remember now. My Grandfather Kelly, Grandfather Michael, was a very formidable old Irishman with a big white mustache and he didn't hesitate to intimidate his grandson by taking out his false teeth and snapping them at me. It really scared the wits out of me. Can you imagine your grandpa reaches up and pulls out his teeth and snaps them at you? That's a terrible early memory.

— Yes it is.

— My Grandpa Mike was kind of a distant person. I gave him a copy of my first stories. I started writing science fiction in my teens, I guess I was thirteen or fourteen when I wrote the story, and I gave it to Grandpa Mike. And he read it and he handed back, chewing on his mustache he says, "Well Francis, it's a good story but it's got too goddamn many superfluous words." That taught me a lot about literary criticism, to cut out the "goddamn superfluous words." I cut them out after that.

— Your best critic?

— Yeah, he was a good critic.

Grandfather Kelly worked for the Pendergast organization in the water department. He went around inspecting fireplugs; it was some kind of a political job.

— But he wasn't the character that your Grandfather King was?

— Oh yeah, he was a character too, with the white mustache, and the way he would take out his false teeth and snap them at me. That was Grandfather Kelly.

GRANDMOTHER: MRS. MICHAEL KELLY

— What about your Grandmother Kelly?

— All that I know about her is the memory that she was a musician. She played the piano, and maybe that accounts for the talents both of my sons have in music. Particularly Stephen. He is a concert pianist.

But my Grandmother Kelly was not very vivid in my life.

AUNT MAMIE: MARY M. KING

My Aunt Mamie was very concerned with me when I was born because I had such a large head. She said, "I think he's got water on the brain. Why don't they open it up and drain a little of the water out?" The doctor wouldn't do it. Aunt Mamie was my mother's sister. She was a "flaming Mame," we used to call her. Her name was Mary Marguerite King. And she was a Western Union telegraph operator for about fifty years before she retired. She had bright red hair and we called her "Flamin' Mame!"

She was my mother's sister; she lived with my grandmother, Constance King at 2912 Charlotte Street. She didn't have any children. She couldn't find a man that was fit to marry, she said. And she kind of adopted me, and made over me. I was known in the family as Mamie's pet. She taught me what to avoid, and all about girls. She was a great person. I remember she came out to Santa Barbara in her last years, retired out here. We found a place for her to live, not far from my house.

She worked at Western Union, as a telegraph operator, sending messages. She always had the latest jokes from all over the country. Some were racy and saucy.

I'd say, "Mamie, where do you get those terrible jokes?" And she'd say, "You know, when we are not busy on the wires sending messages for people, we send jokes around the country. That's how jokes get circulated on the Western Union wires." I thought that was kind of funny.

She had red hair, long flaming red hair. Very good looking. Very sparkly. She had a bright smile and lots of jokes, and was always full of laughter.

DANCING LESSONS

— Did your aunt teach you to dance?

— No, I went to a dance school for a week or so. Maybe two weeks.

— Whose idea was that?

— I don't know. I think it was mine, I think I wanted to dance. I don't think it happened until I got into college when there were girls to dance with.

— That is a good way, to learn how to do it.

— Yeah. Oh some friend of mine must have said, "Why don't you try it!" Most of the guys, you know how kids are, boys particularly, are ashamed to go to a dance school, but this guy persuaded me to go. That's how I learned ballroom dancing; the waltz and a couple of other dances. So when I got to college that was very useful...or maybe I was in college when I learned it. Maybe some girl I dated said, "Why, you've got to learn to dance!" After that I became a free-lance dancer; I'd dance with anybody and make up steps, and I remember we would have dances in the basketball auditorium at the University of Kansas City. And the best dancer was Isabelle Bash. I remember her name vividly, beautiful gal and a marvelous dancer. She was the sheriff's daughter, and it was always fun to dance with the sheriff's daughter. Boy she could spin around; we'd spin backwards and forwards. We'd dance until we were exhausted. We danced for hours at a time.

EDUCATION: ST. VINCENT SCHOOL

— Where did you attend school?

— I went to parochial schools, first, St. Vincent school in Kansas City. I went there from the first grade until the seventh. The nuns were wonderful. I don't remember the order but I remember their names; Sister Mary Alacoque and other sisters. Sister Mary Alacoque was very close to my family and very close to me. And she encouraged me when I started writing these wild science fiction stories. She said, "Well, God has given you an imagination, you should use it, don't be afraid of it." Other people scoffed at me. (I don't remember an awful lot about grade school.)

St. Vincent Catholic School

DISCOVERING SCIENCE FICTION

— When did you start writing science fiction? Had you seen a movie or read a story that sparked your interest in trying to do a story of your own?

— No, it was simpler than that. I was walking home from school one day, St. Vincent's school, and stopped in a drug store, and I saw this magazine with a big cover on it: *The War of the Worlds*, by H.G. Wells. It had pictures of the Martians advancing on tall tripods. So I got that magazine and I read it and I decided that I would try to write. I don't know why, but the stars have always fascinated me. When I was a kid I'd walk out in the backyard and look up and think that someday human beings were going to leap to the stars and explore the heavens. I didn't worry about monsters or aliens from outer space coming here and conquering the earth. My stories were about going out there and human beings gradually exploring the whole universe.

— Did you see any of the early films about space exploration?

— Oh yeah. I loved them!

— Were those part of it, part of this too?

— And one of the early pictures was about people who landed on the moon, and the people in the film and the sets looked exactly like a drawing and illustration of one of my stories. They were wearing the same kinds of helmets, and spacesuits that I had had in my stories. Only I was quite a few years ahead of that.

— Do you remember your first story?

— Yeah, the first one was called, *The Light Bender.* I have a copy of it somewhere upstairs. It was about some scientists, who learn how to bend light so they can go into other universes. I was interested in the idea that there were parallel universes existing. Later on this became quite fashionable among some scientists. And I also was probably one of the first ones to write about black holes. One of my stories was about a black hole.

— At what age? How old were you when your first story was published?

— Oh, my teens, somewhere in my teens. I stopped writing science fiction when I was twenty or twenty-one.

— But up to that time, that was your main thrust as far as writing is concerned? And were they just science fiction stories?

— Yeah. There's a book out called *Pioneers of Wonder,* that's about the young science fiction writers of the United States and there is a chapter in there about me.

— Were all your stories published?

— They were all published, every story I wrote. My parents had given me a typewriter for my birthday. That's what I begged them for and I wrote these things as fast I could go, and mailed them off to *Astounding Stories, Amazing Stories, Wonder Stories,* and they printed them without changing a word! And I don't know where the ideas came from; I never to this day can tell you where they came from.

— Now you had to be making some money?

— Well they paid you a penny a word. So I wrote long stories of fifteen to twenty thousand words but at most I would get a couple hundred dollars per story.

— But that was pretty good at that time.

— It was good in those times. But anyway, then I…

— What did your parents think of your writing?

— Oh they didn't know what to make of it at all. My brother, Vincent, said to my mother once, "Have you read Frank's latest story in *Amazing Stories*?" And my mother said, "No, I haven't had time to do it." And my brother said, "You better read it, mom, he's crazy." I suppose they thought I was crazy. He said, "He's got people exploding other people with disintegration rays and he's got people blowing other planets to…" I don't know where all these ideas came from.

— We've talked about Einstein on several occasions.

— I admired him very much. And I suppose when I started writing science fiction, people referred to Einstein and his theories and that led me to read a lot of things about him and things that he wrote.

— Did you ever use any of his concepts or ideas in your stories?

— Oh I probably did unconsciously, you know.

— So you were going to the library and picking up science books or articles that he'd written. That's fascinating.

— And there were other scientists that I liked and admired, but Einstein was the main one.

Even as a child I was thinking about what was going to come over the horizon. One world has never been enough for me. Because it seemed to me that the whole universe was open for human exploration. And so I wrote these science fiction stories in the 1930's and some of them are still circulating in anthologies.

The principal work of mine was a story called, *Star Ship Invincible*. It's about a spaceship that is designed to go through a black hole. In the story a great black hole had opened in space between Earth and Jupiter, which cut people on Earth from their relatives and friends and the colonists on Jupiter. They wanted to figure out a way to get across this black hole in space. So they built this tremendous ship, the *Starship Invincible*, with every scientific device to enable it to go through this black hole. So a lot of the people whose relatives were on Jupiter got on board and I characterized some of them: wives who were seeking to get in touch with their husbands, parents, or children and so on. They go on this great ship and it plunges into the hole. But instead of going through the hole and coming out close to Jupiter, it comes out in another world, where everything is changed. All the people are almost unrecognizable. A different dimension, you know. And those who disappeared in that ship were not heard from again. The moral of the story was that the humans found out that it was impossible to build a ship that was invincible. I was 19, I think, or 20 when I wrote that story. It was published in 1934.

— Who did you send your first story to?

— I just sent it to the editor, and they accepted it, never changed a word. David Lasser was the editor for Hugo

Gernsback, the founder of *Amazing Stories*, and a founder of science fiction in the United States. One day I got a letter from Lasser saying, "We love your stories and we're going to print them all, but do you have to keep on making up new words all the time? What the hell do these words mean?" But I just thought, when I was describing some kind of scientific gizmo that might exist in the year 2100, I had to have different words. When I explained it to them they accepted it.

— Did they know how old you were?

— No, they didn't realize at first. Some readers wrote in and complained about my earliest stories, that they were very grim and pessimistic, and had unhappy endings. So the readers wrote in and said, "Who is this Frank Kelly? It must be a bitter old man who's writing these stories with horrible endings."

I had to say I was a teenager, 16 or 17 at the time. But I sounded like a bitter old man. It's one of the paradoxes of my life, I started out in life, feeling like it was a terrible existence and I read too much apocalyptic literature; the early science tales which were all pretty grim. I'd hammer all day long at my typewriter, churning out fifteen, twenty thousand words in one day, and mail the story off. Now, when I am writing more focused tales, I spend days on every paragraph and every sentence.

THE LIBRARY

I spent a lot of time in the library. Not the large public library, but a small library that was connected with a women's organization. It was small but it had a lot of good collections. The librarian and I got acquainted, and she let me use a little room in the back where I could have any book that I wanted.

— Was it a lending library?

— No, it wasn't a lending library; I may have done some of my writing in that library. I started studying some of the writers I was reading, how they wrote their novels. The library had a lot of stuff like that.

— Do you remember any of the writers?

— Hemingway, and H. G. Wells. Those two. I read Jules Verne but I wasn't too high on him. It seemed to me his style was too strained, but Wells was a real writer in my view, with real literary value. Verne struck me as just putting out fantasies, very roughly written, but not Wells. *The War of the Worlds*, which I first read in a science fiction magazine, launched my career as a writer. I have never forgotten that cover, with the tripods, and the Martians on top. I can see it now. When I saw those strange monsters, I thought, "Is it really that way on Mars?" Are they unfriendly? Or what if they are friendly? Or maybe we will be the ones who will go out and make war on them. That's how my imagination grew.

HIGH SCHOOL: DE LA SALLE ACADEMY

— Where did you attend high school?

— High school was at De La Salle Academy in Kansas City. I graduated in the top of the class. It was a very strict Christian Brothers high school. If you got out of line, they'd beat you with a ruler. We studied four years of Latin, which I enjoyed. I don't remember being close friends with anybody there. In fact the kids that went to that school were so tough, I used to tell my father, "Come and get me after school because if I don't run faster, I'll get beaten up." So he would come and pick me up. There were a lot of bullies there. I guess a lot of kids have had that experience.

And my father promised me that if I got all A's, he would buy me a ticket to the baseball game in the summer. That was my favorite sport so I went out there every summer and watched the Kansas City Blues, a minor league team.

— What year did you graduate?

— I graduated in 1930. I was 16 years old, a very young graduate. And I got all sorts of awards and things. I was a bookworm, studied hard, because I hardly had any friends in my teenage years. I was so introverted that most of the other kids thought I was kind of a nut, I guess. I was always reading. And writing. My baptismal name was Francis, so they'd say, "Francis is in one of his trances." They used to kid the hell out of you. That was my father's name too: Francis, but he changed it to Frank. So did I, finally.

De La Salle Academy was downtown in sort of a little bit of a run-down neighborhood; it was on the lower part of the Paseo Boulevard, and there was a park nearby. But the Christian Brothers didn't have much money. The school's classrooms were very bare, and there was no special equipment or anything like that. Most of what you did was go to the blackboard, and prove that you had read what they told you to read the night before.

— Was there corporal punishment if you didn't?

— If you didn't, you got a smack on the hand with an eraser sometimes, or a heavy ruler that really hurt your skin.

— Do you remember any of the Brothers?

— I remember them vividly, but I can't attach the names. I remember one older Brother, who wore some kind of tattered habit, and he was really down on the British. He taught the history of Europe and the British were "Perfidious Albion". He liked that phrase. Of course coming from Ireland, he told us all about the terrible things the British had done. Conquering most of the world, especially oppressing our ancestors in Ireland, taking away our Gaelic language and all that. Boy, he could ride a horse on the British. Did that come out of Shakespeare? Perfidious Albion. We had a lot of Shakespeare; we had a pretty amazing education. Four years of Latin: Caesar's Gallic Wars. I think the study of Latin helped my writing, gave me some sentence structure. That was almost 80 years ago.

— You mentioned you had problems with people in the neighborhood beating you up or fighting with you?

— Some of the kids in the school regarded me somewhat as a sissy; and I was, because my mother sort of pampered me. I was the oldest son in the family, and my father was very protective. Some of the guys in my class were much bigger than I was, and they wanted to dominate all the new boys in school.

— Is that when your father decided to take you to school?

— I guess I could have gone on a bus, but I was kind of protected, everyone thought I never learned how to fight, and things like that. So I told him that if I went on the bus I had to run like hell to get out of school or one of the boys would give me a cuffing around or something. So he decided he would take me. And that was very unusual for the rest of the class. They laughed at me. Particularly because my father, who was not excessively affectionate, always wanted me to kiss him when I got out of the car. I kissed him on the cheek, and he kissed me. I guess he had a lot of affection for me. More than I realized at the time.

— Of course the kids saw that.

— Yes, and they started joking about how the guy's father brought him to school, and he had to kiss his dad. It was big joke for some of them. But I think it was really a nice experience.

Baseball: "Boost the Blues"

— Kansas City had a great black baseball team, too.

— The Kansas City Monarchs. Satchel Paige was a great pitcher for them. We all knew his sayings. And he went on to play in the major leagues after Jackie Robinson finally broke the color barrier.

— Did you ever watch any of their ballgames?

— Oh yeah. They were a great team, great team. They had better baseball players than the white teams had in those days, but a black couldn't play in the major leagues. They all had separate leagues. And it was kind of sad when the barriers were broken and the black leagues broke up even though they had some terrific teams. Satchel Paige was an incredible athlete. He was a great pitcher. He had a great saying, too. "Don't look back, someone might be gaining on you. Don't eat fried foods, they angry up your blood." We all knew what Satchel had to say about life; his philosophy was very well spread.

— How often did you get to go to the games?

— My father said, "Get all A's, and I'll buy you a ticket for the whole season at the ballpark." My father thought baseball was the best sport in the world.

— And he did?

— Yes.

— Was that during your high school years?

— I was in my teens. The Kansas City Blues were in the old American Association and they played at Muehlebach Field. It was built in 1923. Yeah. Yeah, the Kansas City Blues, "Boost the Blues." There was direct streetcar service to the ball park.

One time we had a torrential rain. My Aunt Mamie got worried about me being at the ballpark. The storm came up during the game. And the streets around the park were flooded. And Aunt Mamie came down to rescue me and got stuck in her car in a whole stream of water on one of those streets.

— Did you ever go to any of the Monarchs games, the black team?

— I think I saw Satchel Paige pitch; that may be wishful thinking, but I think I did. They also played at Muehlebach Field. That was unusual at that time. I used to sit down near the dugout, right behind the box seats, because there was only a handful there most of the time. In those days, people who bought box seats didn't always come to the games and they'd let me go down to the dugout, and talk to the guys. How big they were, but of course I was a small boy at the time, and they were huge beefy ball players. They had good crowds. One year they had a winning team, and they won the minor league pennant.

The Kansas City Blues…"Boost the Blues." I love that. I had to get home by dark. They played in the afternoon usually; four o'clock or something like that. But all the other kids thought I was a lucky stiff. All summer long I was out there at the ballpark. I learned the lingo of the game and the strategy.

— Did you keep box score?

— No. I was not that meticulous in those days.

— Did you follow the team in the newspaper?

— Oh yeah. The *Star* wrote it up and the Kansas City Journal, *Journal-Post*. I liked those old Blues players. Now it's the Kansas City Royals. A lot of them went on to play in the majors, and became big name stars.

THE GREAT DEPRESSION

We listened to Father Coughlin on the radio every Sunday. My father was a great fan of his until Father

Coughlin broke with President Roosevelt and announced he would not support Roosevelt anymore. My father went over and turned off the radio. He said, "We'll never listen to him again." So the issue came when Roosevelt or Coughlin had to go, and my father chose Roosevelt. My father was a very intelligent man. I think he got very skeptical about Coughlin, who was a demagogue. But he fooled a lot of Catholics. He had a big following for a while.

I've lived more than ninety years. I lived through two World Wars, the Vietnam War, the Korean War, I lived through the terrible Depression of the 1930's when millions of people lost their jobs, thousands committed suicide, and our country was supposed to be on the verge of collapse. We had a president in there; I remember my mother and father, my sister and my brother, and we were sitting in the living room listening to Mr. Roosevelt. I heard my mother saying in a whisper to my father, "Well, the banks closed. How are we going to get groceries?"

He said, "Well, what about our grocery man, Mr. Nall? He'll carry us for a few weeks."

"What are we going to do unless the banks open?"

Then the president's voice comes out of the radio: "We have nothing to fear but fear itself."

And that one act gave us courage. I mean here was Franklin Roosevelt, he hadn't done anything yet really, but he gave people the courage to feel that things would open up. Our grocery man carried us for months, I don't remember how long, for food. But you know we could eat. Think how close we were to starvation!

When I turned 21 I immediately registered as a Democrat. My father and my grandfather were. My uncle was assistant postmaster of Kansas City, which was a political job he got through the Democratic Party. I was very interested in Roosevelt and his New Deal. We all were. He was our hero, our leader! We never thought about the fact that he was paralyzed and in a wheelchair. The media didn't bring it out at all. It was only later that I found out that Roosevelt couldn't get out of bed by himself. They had to lift him out and put him in his wheelchair. He was a great phenomenon, but the media did not bring that out, his full heroism.

MOVE TO INDIANAPOLIS

We lived in a better house and my dad started doing very well until the Depression came and then one day he came home as white as that wall over there and told us he'd been fired. The company was letting fifty percent of their workforce go. My dad was an efficiency expert, and they kept praising him and giving him raises and bonuses and he never dreamed he'd be on the list of those fired. It was shocking. It struck terror in my heart because here was my dad, this strong man, pale as a sheet, and just almost crying. I think he did cry.

My mother cried too. Losing your job was unthinkable for a good middle-class American. But he couldn't find one. And we had Veterans' Administration benefits so we were living in a nice house with a big mortgage. The government interest for VA loans was held at only four percent, something like that. We could use the house for rental income. But we had to live elsewhere. So dad wrote to one of his lieutenants who'd served under him in the Infantry, a man named Lee, John Lee, I think. And Lee had become director of the Veterans' Administration office in Indiana. He wrote back to dad and said, "I don't have any job fitting your background and your abilities, but what I've got is a minor job on the staff in my headquarters in Indianapolis. We'd be glad to give you that, but it doesn't pay very much." My dad grabbed it. So we went to Indianapolis and that's when I had to go work in a box factory because dad's salary was very meager.

— Do you remember your father telling you that you were going to have to find a job after the move to Indianapolis?

— He said, "You know, son, Lieutenant Lee" or whatever his name, I think it was Lee, "can't pay me very much but it's a job and I've got to have a job. And we can rent our house in Kansas City." Pretty nice house; and we got a good rent. "We'll find a small house in Indianapolis, but you're going to have to help the family." There was a great family spirit, and that's why I went to be with my grandmother when she became ill, because my dad said, "You know, son, you need to do this because I've got to stay at my job."

THE BOX FACTORY

— Had you graduated from high school before you moved?

— Yes, I had graduated.

— Did you take the train?

— We must have gone there in a car; we had a car, I know that.

My first job there was in a box factory. I had to stack up these boxes for shipping. When I came home the first few nights, my arms were black and blue from the shoulders down. I worked twelve hours a day, for twenty-five cents an hour. Can you imagine that? Six days a week, 72 hours a week!

— How many days a week?

— Six days a week. There were no child labor laws in those days.

— How old were you at that time?

— In my teens, I think I was about sixteen or seventeen. And I sold my first story, and that gave me the light at the end of the tunnel. But I still wonder how people could get through that drudgery? But in those days there were no child labor laws, so an employer could work you twelve hours or more and pay you as little as he wanted.

And I would come home so exhausted I would just fall into bed, and not know anything until my father woke me up in the morning.

Six days a week I did that. Meanwhile, one of my stories I hadn't heard anything about, I sent it into *Astounding* or *Amazing,* and they finally wrote back and sent a check. So I said to my father, "Look, I can make a little more money writing these stories." So he agreed that I could quit that job. That saved me. I tell you, though, I've always sympathized with people in hard labor jobs.

— Do you remember the name of the factory?

— No I don't. Then later I worked for Real Silk Hosiery for a short time but then we moved back to Kansas City. My father got a job with Sears again, I think he started out with another mail order company, but he got this job with Sears-Roebuck. We moved back to Kansas City and that was the end of my days in the box factories, but I have never forgotten them.

— What were conditions like in the factory?

— It was awful. The obscenity! Everybody used a stream of obscenities. And the girls who worked there, the men would chase them into corners and grab them. They had no protection from sexual advances. It was kind of a hellhole, I thought.

— Do you remember the name of the factory?

— Yes, but I wouldn't want to mention it. It would be libelous.

— Were you making the boxes, or loading them?

— Oh, I wasn't making them. They were made, and as they'd come off of the assembly line, I'd take them, and stack them up on a dock where the trucks would back up, and we'd load all these boxes on to the truck.

— How big were the boxes?

— They were too big for me, I'll tell you that. I don't remember, but they bruised my arms when I picked them up.

— Do you remember what they would hold?

— No, I don't remember that either, I just remember the boxes. I was there for just a few months, but long enough. I thought, "How can people do this kind of work?" And I don't remember anybody.

— Did the experience creep into the stories you were writing at that time?

— I imagine it did, because as I read my stories again now I referred to those who were for the underdogs, and helping people to face up to the oppression of the poor and all that. I must have got those feelings working in the factory.

Then for a while before I went to the university I worked for the Real Silk Hosiery Company, in their shipping department. That job was much easier, not so physical. But again I felt sorry for the girls, because there were no laws then against sexual provocation, or the laws were ignored. They had a lot of girls working there. And guys were constantly shouting at them. "How about it, baby? Let's go in the corner." I was sensing how the girls were defenseless, and I had a wonderful sister and I wouldn't want her treated that way.

— No one seemed to stand up for those girls?

— No, the orders were coming in, and you were filling orders. You couldn't help anybody. I guess I was scared, too.

— Did you start writing while you worked there?

— I'd written some things before we went to Indianapolis, but I was so exhausted there I couldn't write. But after I worked in the box factory and I sold the first story, my dad said I could think about going to the university.

BUTLER UNIVERSITY

— Why did you decide to go to Butler?

— It was the only big school in Indianapolis, and somebody recommended it to me. Somebody I knew in Kansas City said it was a pretty good school. And I enjoyed the short time I was there. I made friends with a very nice guy. He had a beautiful convertible, and we got dates with girls. He was a rich guy. He had everything as far as I could see. One day I heard he went home and shot himself. I was utterly horrified by that.

— How long were you at Butler?

— Only a few months; it was a short time.

— Did you pick a major?

— No, I don't recall any major. But I guess it was probably English or Literature if I had. But then when I got back to Kansas City, the new University of Kansas City had opened up. I wanted to go there, but my mother didn't want me to go because she thought it would ruin my religion and turn me into a cynic. She was right!

UNIVERSITY OF KANSAS CITY

The University of Kansas City was a private university started by a man named William Volker, a furniture manufacturer, who made a lot of money and he wanted to help Kansas City have its own university. It's now a part of the University of Missouri system; it's called the University of Missouri at Kansas City, UMKC. It only had 300 students when I was there and I made a lot of friends.

— Did the Christian Brothers talk to you about going to college?

— Yeah, they encouraged me. But they saw it was going to be very tough. I'd have to get a scholarship or I'd have to get a job either working for the university or being a clean-up man or something, or delivering groceries or something in the city so I could pay my own way. I didn't have a dime.

— Didn't you receive a scholarship?

— Yes, from Mr. Volker. He established a scholarship program. He was deeply interested in young people, a nice man, but he was very shy. He hardly said a word to me during my interview for the scholarship. When I arrived for my interview, I was told to take a seat in one of rocking chairs that had been lined up outside his office, and wait my turn. Miss Juanita Forgey was staff director of the scholarship program. She was a very eccentric social worker. And each applicant had to pass her approval test: you had to be a very nice young man, well behaved, and not a heavy drinker. When your turn came, Miss Forgey would escort you into the office, and introduce you to Mr. Volker; you'd sit down. Then Miss Forgey gave her report. "I've talked to Mr. Kelly's parents," she said. "They are nice people. He's graduated from high school, and he knows some Latin."

Mr. Volker didn't say a word. So I said, "I've always wanted to go to college, Mr. Volker."

And he said, "Well, I'm glad you think that's so important."

I said, "I know a lot of things I'd like to do, but if I don't go to college, they won't even give you a chance."

He said, "You're right, my boy, you're right."

— That was it?

— No, he said, "Give this boy full scholarship."

Each year, Mr. Volker gave scholarships to a number of students. He sort of adopted us. We received a monthly allowance just as if we were his children. I remember we got twelve dollars a month. And I thought that was great. I knew I could take girls out on twelve dollars a month. My mother didn't charge me anything for room and board and Mr. Volker paid my tuition. I had a good deal going. And he never changed it; he paid everything, and never asked any questions.

National Recognition: *With Some Gaiety and Laughter*

— Who was the professor who entered your story into the national contest, the one that discouraged you from writing science fiction? What was his name?

— His name was H. Robinson Shipherd. He was an Englishman. See in the days of the 1930's, jobs at the universities were scarce like everywhere else so I don't know how the University of Kansas City got him, but he had been educated at Oxford. He was quite an impressive figure, with an Oxford accent and all that. He kind of looked down on most of the Midwest stuff.

— I can imagine.

— Well, he was interested in writing, and he sent my story, *With Some Gaiety and Laughter*, to *Story Magazine*, and I won a prize that made a big impression on the *Star*. They had an article about me. Then the story was picked up in the *Best American Short Stories*, a book edited by Edward O'Brien, an anthology that came out every year. So my story was in there and it was read on the National Broadcasting Company Network, so that story moved me into a different atmosphere from science fiction.

— What was the story about, the one that won the prize?

— It was about a man, a starving veteran of World War I, whose last possession was a record playing human laughter. And he goes into this pawnshop to try to sell the only thing that keeps him from committing suicide, which is this phonograph record. And the pawnbroker thought, what could he do with that? It really wasn't worth anything. "Well, I'll let you play it." So he puts it on the machine and the story describes the impact of human laughter in the midst of all the darkness of the Depression, and how it was affecting people and this poor man that came in. Even the pawnbroker was moved by it and he offered him five bucks for the record. And even though the man was starving, he hadn't eaten anything, he said, "No." He couldn't sell it, finally. This was the thing that was keeping him alive, and it was a very cold snowy day and he'd come into the shop, and so he picked it up and he went out. In the end the war veteran walks off into the winter's day still holding his record. That was the end of the story.

— How much did you get for that?

— What did I get? $25, or something like that.

— It was still a little bit of money then wasn't it?

— Yeah. That story really had a lot of repercussions; it was reprinted in Sweden and Germany and various places because it showed the depths of the Depression and how it affected people you know.

— And what about your father? He was a World War I veteran. Did he read it?

— Yeah. Oh yeah, he was very touched by it. He always encouraged me to write.

After the story was published in *Best Short Stories of 1936*, I got a letter from the Writer's Conference at the University of Colorado in Boulder, asking me if I wanted to come to their summer meeting and saying that I would have all my expenses paid. They were inviting three or four young writers to come as guests. So I said, "Oh yeah." So I got there and who was the star there but Thomas Wolfe, who was one of my heroes.

One night I remember up on the Boulder mountain, we had this party and, uh, everybody had a little too much to drink and so somebody said to Thomas Wolfe, um, "Let's play the story of 'The Three Little Pigs'". So they got up on this flat rock and these three young writers pretended to be pigs and Wolfe was rushing at them and growling like a wolf and one of them fell off the rock and landed on his back and Wolfe jumped down and picked the guy up, just like he was a toy. Wolfe was so huge.

— He was a big man, wasn't he?

— Oh yeah, six feet six, or something like that. He said, "Where are you hurt? Let's take care of this man." And, "Oh I'm so sorry." And the guy said, "Oh, I just fell on my back, I'm all right." But seeing Thomas Wolfe playing 'The Three Little Pigs.' He was the Big Bad Wolf. I've never forgotten that.

And I heard him give his famous talk at that conference: how he started writing in Brooklyn. He had this refrigerator and he stood in the kitchen and wrote on top of the refrigerator. He told a lot about his life. It was a wonderful experience to be there. For a while I was really obsessed with Thomas Wolfe. He gave you that impression that he knew what we were going through in that age. It was a great experience being in that writers' conference.

— Did you have an opportunity to socialize with him?

— Yes, I remember on one of the nights of the conference, Wolfe was walking on the campus. And I was with a young writer named Alfred Grimwood—I don't know what became of him—but we went up and told him how much we admired him and so on. Wolfe said, "I'm just going down the mountain to get some hamburgers. Come on down. Have a burger with me." We said, "Fine." So we went down to the shop and Wolfe ordered six of these huge burgers. Had them laid out. And he ate them, just like nothing, you know. He said, "Come on boys, have some hamburgers." The way he put away that food.

— He was a big man in many ways.

— His appetite and he drank quite a bit. I thought it was a tragedy that he died at 38. I'm just awed by the fact that I've had 94 years of life and I'm still going, and a man like Thomas Wolfe dies at 38.

REPORTING—FROM THE STAR AND AP TO WAR CORRESPONDENT

Since my life has been partly devoted to journalism, I've always been fascinated by the role of the journalist himself in shaping the history that he covers. So I suggested to the *Atlantic Monthly Press* and they bought the idea that I'd do a book about reporters, and their adventures around the world. And so I wrote this book, *Reporters Around the World*, and they published it. It starts out with Daniel Dafoe, who was put in the pillory for writing unpopular things back in his time. There are chapters about a number of journalists, including: Doctor Samuel Johnson; Charles Dickens, finding his father in prison; Stanley Livingston; Mark Twain's long march in the wilderness; Stephen Crane, hunting the truth about courage; the capture and escape of Winston Churchill in the Boer War; and Hemingway under fire, finding that he is mortal.

— How did the idea for the book come to you?

— Once I started working with the *Kansas City Star*, I heard stories about journalists themselves. We'd sit around and talk about the big guys in the field like Hemingway,

Richard Harding Davis, and Stephen Crane. So I just thought: well, maybe I'll try to have a short chapter about each one illuminating what kind of person he was and maybe a situation in which he risked his life. So that's the book.

— Do you have a favorite chapter?

— Putting aside Hal Boyle, I think in many ways my favorite in the book is the chapter about Daniel Dafoe being put in the pillory for writing something that was contrary to the views of powerful people in his day. It could happen to anyone of us now in the age of the Patriot Act.

DECISION TO BECOME A JOURNALIST

— How did you decide to become a reporter?

— One of my professors at University of Kansas City, even while I was writing science fiction, said, "Oh, you don't want to write that stuff." He said, "That's just pulp fiction. You're a really good writer." He said, "I want to enter one of your stories in a contest." *Story Magazine* had a competition for short stories by college people. So he entered my story, "With Some Gaiety and Laughter," and it won a prize and was printed in *Story*.

So then he said, "What are you going to do when you graduate?"

I said, "I don't know."

He said, "You can't make a living out of science fiction. Why don't you go into journalism?"

I said, "I never thought about journalism. And I've never taken a course in journalism."

He said, "Well I know an editor on the *Kansas City Star*. They don't seem to care whether you have had a course in journalism or not. I'll talk to Pete Wellington." And when my story came out in *The Best American Short Stories*, the *Star* gave it a big review, "Local Author's Story is Contained in an International Anthology."

So he made the appointment for me to go down and see Mr. Wellington. And that's how I got into journalism. I told him, "I don't know anything about journalism."

And he said, "That's fine. We want writers and we admire your writing and the *Kansas City Star* has a reputation for literary quality and we want you to use your talents as a writer. Only you have to confine yourself more or less to the facts as a journalist."

I said, "I think I might be able to do that, Mr. Wellington." And he said, "But there's one thing about it."

He said, "Mr. Kelly, I want to hire you. I know you've got the gift and all that, and several of my editors admired what you'd written. But," he said, "I'm afraid you'll do what another young man did that I hired back in 1916." He said, "This fellow was a wonderful reporter. We were training him to be a *Star* Man." That's what Wellington wanted; the editor wanted you to be a *Star* Man. "And then he ran off to Europe and he wrote a lot of stuff and he never came back."

I said, "What was his name?"

He said, "Ernest Hemingway." Isn't that a great story? Wellington didn't want me to be another Ernest Hemingway. I was supposed to be a *Star* Man.

He said, "We'll give you a job, but I bet three or four years from now, you're going to come to me and say, 'Mr. Wellington, I want a leave of absence. I'm going to New York to write.' Just the way that Hemingway fellow did."

And I did it. I was on the *Star* about three and a half years I guess. I started in 1937 and left for New York in early '41.

— Did you write any science fiction?

— No, I stopped. When I got into journalism I stopped writing science fiction. My last published science fiction story was 1935, I think.

— Do you remember the first story you wrote for the *Star*?

— Yes. The *Star* asked me to cover my own graduation from the University. They said, "That'd be an interesting idea," because I was graduating from the University of Kansas City. It was a brand new university started with private money. This was the first class, so I was sent to cover the festivities, and to pick up my degree on the way. There I was, covering it as a story. I had a great time, and my story for the *Star* was accepted and I had a story on the front page.

THE STAR: FIRST IMPRESSIONS

— Describe the newsroom on your first day at the *Star*? What impressed you? Did you see an editor?

— Well, he looked me over. At that time, every reporter at the *Star* had a spittoon because a lot of them chewed tobacco. And I saw reporters spitting tobacco and hitting a spittoon. But I didn't chew tobacco, and I didn't know if I'd fit in or not. The *Star* had a long row of telephone booths and the whole newsroom was a block long, one great big room with all the divisions: the foreign news, the city news. It was all on one floor.

The city editor at that time was named Charles Blood. He always signed his expense accounts in red ink—blood. So he was a very gruff old boy and he said, "Sit down over there Mr. Kelly, I'll think of some things for you to do."

Charles Blood had been there thirty years. He was a heavyset man. Gray hair. Ruddy face. And he liked to sit back in his chair at the city desk, flipping a pencil in the air. It would go up and turn over and come back and he'd catch it. And he didn't have things get too close to him. He'd like to turn around in his chair, see some reporter, "Mr. Kelly, catch a fire on six." Telephone booth 6. You know. That's the way he liked to handle it.

We had this row of telephones with numbers on them, in glassed-in booths. You'd go in there, and somebody from the *Star* would give you the story. You'd take it down, then rush to your typewriter and bang away.

Sometimes the assistant city editor, a very tough character named Ray Lyle, who was always spitting tobacco juice, would come and lean over your shoulder and look at your copy and then whoosh! The tobacco would go over your shoulder and land in a spittoon. I had a spittoon too; but I never used it.

Ray Lyle would yell, "Bring it over to the city desk." So you'd beat your typewriter, as fast as you could go, and then you'd call for a copy boy who would come and rip the paper out of your typewriter and take it over to the city desk. And he'd, Lyle would, go over it and then he'd say, "Mr. Kelly, come over here. We've got a question." And then he'd ask, "What about this? Where did you get this statement? Can you verify that?" Verification was a big deal, and I see the *New York Times* is in trouble now because some of their reporters didn't bother to verify. Well that was the heart of journalism when I worked for the *Star*. You had to write "VER" on each piece of copy you wrote, "VER" meaning verified. You'd have to check with one other person. That was verification. You didn't have time to do more than that.

Ray Lyle was incredible. He never shaved and he had a racy vocabulary, and was skeptical of everybody. He reminded me of the rude guys in the movie *Front Page*: cynical, tough, and a strong influence on all of us. There was no particular style; he wanted it kept short, and very concentrated. "Don't go off on tangents."

FIRST ASSIGNMENT: GENERAL HOSPITAL

I went to the General Hospital and rode in the ambulances to the scenes of murders, of shootings, and car crashes and all that. Then I was on general assignment interviewing people, prominent people who came to town, and writing feature stories. I wrote all kinds of editorial page features on every subject under the sun.

So after three or four years I went over to Mr. Wellington and I said, "Well, Mr. Wellington, you were right after all. I want to go to New York, I want to write a book."

"Why can't you write a book right here in Kansas City?"

I said, "It's tough here and I just want to see what it's like in New York."

And he said, "All right, we'll give you a leave of absence but you'll never come back, just like that fellow Hemingway."

There was a police beat, hospital beat, and the nightclub beat. I went on that voluntarily. When you were out covering a story, there was a guy down at the *Star* in a booth. I was at the other end a lot of the time too. If I wasn't out on the ambulance, if I was down there in what you call the newsroom, they had a small booth. And Mr. Blood, the senior editor, would whirl around and say, "Mr. Kelly, catch a death on five." And you had to catch somebody. Or "Mr. Kelly, there's a fire downtown. Joe's calling in from the fire department."

— Who got the byline?

— In those days you didn't get bylines on the *Star* very often. You were a reporter for the *Kansas City Star.* I did get some bylines later on some special work. Sometimes you were the guy who was phoning in from a scene of a murder or an accident, sometimes you were the person answering the phone and writing it down, and then there was another person, who would listen to the guy on the phone and would say, "Now wait a minute, calm down Joe, that doesn't make sense. Tell me some of the other things that happened?" If it was a complicated story—like a murder—you'd have to sort of act as an editor for the reporter out in the field. It was very collaborative.

Most people had no idea about what went on in the newsroom. They got their paper in the morning and they looked for the death notices first. I found out that the obits were often the first thing people would read. They wanted to find out if any of their friends had died and then they read the rest of the paper.

— Did having to make a deadline affect your writing?

— Well it harms it and it helps it in a way. A deadline doesn't give you a chance to meditate on turning out good prose. But, on the other hand, it intensifies your focus. You know that you've got this one thing that you've got to try to describe, and I learned that. I took journalism too lightly. It's a very difficult art. Learning how to describe a terrible scene that you went to in the ambulance, do it accurately, and do it so that the reader at home will have some idea what's going on. It gave you an intensity of effort, which no other kind of writing does.

— What about the length of a story, were restrictions placed on the amount of space you were allowed, would the editor limit a story to, say, two hundred words?

— The editor wouldn't usually say that, but once in a while he would because some of the reporters went on and on and he didn't want them to type too long. But usually he'd leave it up to you as to how long the story was going to be, unless you kept sending copies over to the desk. Mr. Lyle would come over and say, "That's enough! Kelly, we don't need anymore. Don't write a book about it."

— What were working conditions like at the *Star*?

— Well, they didn't pay very well. They started me off at $100 a month. And then after two years they gave me a raise to $125. But I wrote a lot of editorial page features, which is what they called them then. I wrote articles on every subject under the sun and they would print them on Sundays in their editorial section.

— Could you pick the topic?

— Yes, they agreed to almost anything I suggested. And it was those articles that I wrote for the *Star* that helped me get my name, and get the Nieman Fellowship I applied for after I left the *Star* for New York.

— Did you have a byline?

— Oh yeah, I got bylines on all of those.

— What other newspapers existed in Kansas City when you started at the *Star*?

— The *Journal, Kansas City Journal-Post*, and there was a black newspaper, the *Kansas City Call*.

— I don't imagine there were any people of color working at the *Star*?

— I think we had some black copy boys, but none of the staff members were black.

— How has the art of reporting shaped writers like Dickens and Hemingway, who were journalists at one time in their careers?

— They were bigger. They were not confined to being reporters. I don't think any journalist really is just simply a reporter. I say this because one of the things I was struck by when I went to work at the *Kansas City Star* was the editor's response to my admission I had never had a course in journalism. I was very forthright about my lack of experience. And he said, "We don't care. Reporters have come here who've had been taught journalism as a science, and they go out and try to cover things according to formula. We don't want any formulas. We want you as a sensitive, intelligent, feeling person to go out into the world and experience what's happening, and then bring it back to us." That's what these people do.

FEATURE ARTICLES FOR THE STAR

— You mentioned that you also wrote a number of editorial or feature articles on a wide range of subjects.

— They were feature articles on a wide variety of topics, which the *Star* printed usually on its editorial page, usually written by staff members, or freelance writers. I wrote a lot of those.

— Did they pay you when you did it?

— They paid me $15 for each one. That's why I wrote so many; my pay at the *Star* was so small. If I could write five or six of those for 15 bucks apiece, I had $60 more a month. I often did that, too. I banged them out pretty fast. I had the *Star's* library right next to where I was sitting, and I drew a lot of resources it had already available. Somebody would pop up in the news, and they'd want me to write something about what kind of person they were.

— Were those pieces edited?

— They edited them pretty lightly, not very much. Bill Reddig, the editor of that section, got to be a good friend of mine, and he liked the way I wrote, so on almost any subject under the sun he'd ask me, "Want to do a piece for me?" And of course I did. Fifteen dollars was big money in those days.

— How many words?

— I think they were relatively short, 1000 words or 1200, maybe less. I remember one that I wrote about Confucius; at one time there was this talk about the Chinese scholar. People were going around saying, "Confucius says..." So I said, "Who was Confucius?" I think that was my take off for it, and they published it. So I had complete range; it was fun. And I heard from all kinds of people, because I wrote about everything under the sun.

WRITING OBITUARY NOTICES

At first I was assigned to the "glooms." That was the death notices. One booth in the newsroom had gloomy poems about death and dying. You would go there and call up all the undertakers. And I've never forgotten, sometimes there'd be chiming bells when the phone would ring. Newcomer's was one of the big mortuaries. "Frank Kelly at the *Kansas City Star*, do you have any items for us?" I'd say. "Oh, yes, we have four good ones, famous people who have died, and we have all the details." And they'd give me all the information and I'd write it up. I found out that everybody in Kansas City read the death notices, more than anything else in the paper. Mr. Blood told me that; he said, "If you make a mistake, you're going to catch it because people read those things."

— Did you take the information down shorthand?

— No, I didn't. Never took any courses for that. I wrote in long hand. It made me realize how important every life is to the people who are living and involved in it. Most of these people were not famous people even though the Newcomer's staff might have thought so. But the obits were among the most interesting and difficult stories to write, because when you talked to people about the life of their father or mother or their uncle or somebody who was a relative, they all had different slants and all had different stories.

It was just fascinating to talk to the relatives and friends to try to determine what a person's life added up to, and what impressed each one, and what did that person care about? Was he religious or not religious? Was he generous or stingy? And so on. What impact did a person have on the community?

GENERAL HOSPITAL

After about ten months of writing what we called "the glooms," I was ordered to go to the General Hospital, which gave me a tremendous change of atmosphere. The pressroom up there had a couple of desks and a couple of telephones, right next to the emergency room in the hospital. When they got a call for an ambulance up there, the ambulance driver, who was right across the hall, would come in and yell, "Come on Kelly, shooting downtown. We're going." So I'd run after him and jump in the ambulance. I'd get in the back and lie down on the gurney. These crazy drivers scared me to death, scared the wits out of me, because every now and then I'd lift my head and see a street car coming and the driver would turn and pass it on the wrong side—on two wheels usually. We'd get to the scenes of accidents and murders, fires and shootings and suicides. And it was just overwhelming, the stream of painful life that you encountered as an ambulance rider. I suppose in any city, when you went out from the general hospital you'd encounter pain and death and horrible suffering. It was hard for me to cope with, but I had been brought up as a very religious person who thought that God was good and all you had to do was to say your prayers and do what was right and then nothing bad would happen to you. But I saw bad things happening to good people, and those events went deep into my assessment of life, and what it was like and what you had to get through and what was the value of suffering and what was the meaning of suffering.

When you're writing a short story, creating characters and creating a scene of your own, that's a different type of creativity. When you're out at the scene of a shooting or a bloody accident or something ghastly, having arrived on an ambulance, you hop out of the ambulance with a doctor and attendants. They're picking people up off the streets and you're trying to figure out what happened by hurling questions at people there.

"Tell me what happened." And they're going from one to the other. You have to go to the police usually, because they probably got there ahead of you and they had the authority to question people while they're lying on the pavement bleeding. So you get it hot from the people who were there when it just happened. They tell you their version and you have to rush to a telephone and put together what they said to you, what the police said to you, and what you saw yourself: that's a news story.

— Were you assigned evenings?

— I was on the night side, as they called it. The *Kansas City Star* had two shifts. The night side; we wrote for the morning paper, the *Times*, and our stories were printed in the morning. And there was a morning shift that came in and worked for the daily paper, the one that came out in the afternoon. That was a big paper. The *Star* had three hundred and some forty thousand circulation, with a big staff—lots of people.

I started work at about four o'clock in the afternoon. And I'd work until midnight, sometimes one o'clock, or longer if a story was breaking. I remember covering some suicides, where people were living in dire poverty. We'd go down and find somebody who had been living in a littered apartment, and had just given up on life. And you saw what could happen to human beings, who had lost contact with their friends and everything else. Those stories really got to me. It was very depressing. They made me think about everything I saw, and wondered why the upper classes were so fortunate. We had good schools and we had all kinds of opportunities, but there were a lot of people who were just boxed in like animals. They led an animal life really, and that struck me as very hard—and unjust too.

Lifestyle of a Cub Reporter

When I wasn't in an ambulance or police cruiser, I drove a car. I bought my first car in 1938, a brand new wonderful Plymouth, for $650. That was the price for a new Plymouth in those days. I think that today it's about $20,000. I saved up the money and I paid for it. Drove it home and thought, "Oh boy." That was freedom because before that I didn't have a car of my own. So once I got it I began to follow the ambulance in my car. I didn't have to worry about those crazy ambulance drivers. And that gave me more maneuverability. I could get to a phone more easily, and didn't have to wait for the drivers and the cops to give me the names of the people who were involved in these tragedies. Once in a while I'd talk to somebody. But usually if somebody had been at the scene of a shooting or a terrible accident they're so dazed you can't get much out of them anyway. So we had to rely pretty heavily on the cops and the ambulance people. They were very cooperative with us. They liked to have their names in the paper, and you'd mention them sometimes.

The General Hospital assignment revealed to me the fragile nature of life, and the way so many people live without any security or any protection from the dangers that surround us, conditions you can only imagine when you're middle class. My folks had a home in the nice district, where you'd get up in the morning and the sun was shining and everybody was pretty well off, and you didn't hear people screaming. It's a totally different feeling to live in misery.

General Assignment Reporter

— From the hospital you moved to…?

— General assignment, which meant I went back to the main newsroom on Eighteenth and Grant, and I'd sit at a desk and Mr. Blood, our city editor, would turn around and say, "Mr. Kelly, catch a death on telephone 4." And I'd go and catch a death. Or, "Mr. Kelly, go over to the Chamber of Commerce. I want you to go on over there; they've got a big meeting today. Give us 100 words, or 200 words on it." As a general assignment reporter, I'd go down to the Union Station and interview people who were coming through on the Santa Fe Chief going to Hollywood. Norma Shearer, and all the different Hollywood stars and well-known people, including Myrna Loy—boy, was she beautiful. I fell in love with her. This train would stop on the way to the West Coast, and if you knew she was on board, you'd go up to the stateroom and knock on the door. Quite often they would get off the train and go in to buy a book, and of course you'd recognize them and you'd go up and say, "I'm with the *Star*, can I do a little interview?" And they were always very nice and cooperative. Often I had a photographer with me; we took pictures. That was a lot of fun.

One time Mr. Blood assigned me to cover dance performers, Martha Graham and her company. And I said, "I don't know anything about modern dance." He said, "Nobody else does around here, Mr. Kelly, you're supposed to be able to cover anything. Get over there." So I got over there. I loved it, and I wrote a glowing review. I didn't know a thing about the techniques of dance. But my rave notice got in the paper. I don't know if it got on the front page or not but Martha Graham and her company liked it all right.

Another time I was assigned to interview Rosita Royce, the dove dancer. All she wore during her performance was doves: one would land on one shoulder and she'd shrug it off and one would land on one breast and then fly on to a gleaming hip. It was stimulating to see how the birds feasted on her. I wished I could be a bird too!

— Was she performing in one of the burlesque theaters?

— Yes. The burlesque theater was a part of American life then. Most people don't realize burlesque was really a big form of entertainment. A lot of people went. Especially men. And they had some charming, beautiful girls dancing around. Some of the big-named comedians that we know today—like Jackie Gleason, Red Buttons, W. C. Fields, Phil Silver and Bob Hope—also got their start in burlesque.

THE PENDERGAST MACHINE

— How did your family react to the *Star's* investigation and ultimate exposure of Tom Pendergast?

— It was quite a shock to me to go to work on the *Kansas City Star,* because all my family were Democrats. To them Tom Pendergast was the leader of the Democratic Party organization, and not a man who spent most of his money on gambling, but supposedly the person who helped Irish people get jobs when they came to Kansas City. My grandfather had been helped by one of the Pendergasts; and Harry Truman was helped by one of them. So when I was offered the job on the *Star,* which was called a Republican paper, and always investigating the Democrats, and claiming that Pendergast had a machine and there was something wrong with it, these were accusations my family took very skeptically because we thought it was Republican bias. It wasn't until I worked on the *Star* that I thought there was something more to it than that. Of course it all came out later on, but the early atmosphere in Kansas City was that if you were Irish and you came to Kansas City and needed a job, Tom Pendergast or his brother Jim would help you get one. That was tremendously important to the people in my family circle.

— Were you part of the *Star's* investigation of Tom Pendergast?

— I was not assigned to the main investigation, but I sort of covered some of the fringe activity. The poverty was just incredible then. And also there were open red light districts in Kansas City too. Tom Pendergast permitted that. When I went home at night, I drove through the red light section and there'd be row after row of these houses with big windows, bay windows, and girls sitting in the windows, with lights on them. They would rap on the windows with nickels and dimes. "Come on in, come on in." Some of them would come out and jump on the running board. And I'd say, "Oh no, get off, I don't want you to get hurt. I'm not, I'm not going to go anywhere with you."

Most of these girls were farm girls, who got caught up in this life and didn't know anything better. The district was in the downtown area, close to the black district. I've forgotten the exact street numbers now. It was all downtown mostly near what we called the North End. But it was quite an experience to drive home at two or three in the morning and have girls jumping on your running board.

— How would you characterize the Pendergast investigation? It must have been very large?

— It was large, but I didn't have much of a part in that to tell you the truth. Older reporters who'd been covering politics headed up the investigation; as a young man I didn't cover politics, the assignment fell to reporters who had been around a long time.

— What part did you play though? You said it was on the periphery.

— I was told one time to go to a certain bar and wait there and see if certain other people connected with the Pendergast machine would be having a meeting there with some of the men who were accused of stuffing the ballot boxes. And that's all I did. I watched to make sure that they came and reported that they were there. The meeting was held, and that's about all I did.

— Did you file a story?

— No, I turned that over to the editor. But I was shocked when it came out about the amount of money Pendergast wasted at the racetrack. We had wonderful racetracks just north of Kansas City. And everybody used to go there. Riverside Racetrack was one. Pendergast would bet hundreds of thousands of dollars. He had a company called Ready Mix Concrete and he paved most of the streets and all of the alleys of Kansas City at a high price. That's where he made a lot of money. And that's where most of the jobs I guess were too, from that standpoint.

— As part of a long line of political bosses—Tweed in New York, Curley in Boston, and, more recently Daley in Chicago—how would you describe Tom Pendergast?

— If you met him he was a very friendly, ebullient sort of man. Greeted everybody warmly. They said he was moody but I never saw that side of him. I only met him a few times.

ERNEST HEMINGWAY

One night while I was on the *Star's* staff, Ernest Hemingway came in with his latest wife, a beautiful blonde named Martha Gellhorn. She was wearing a mink coat. They came striding in exuding glamour and success and all that. Hemingway had just finished writing *For Whom the Bell Tolls*.

So he comes into the room with Gellhorn on his side and he says, "C'mon, let's close the place down. Let the office boy handle it if the city blows up or something. Let's go down to Al & Sully's." That was a saloon where everybody went. So the whole staff abandoned the newsroom to sit at the feet of Hemingway. I did get one chance to talk to him a little bit and I said, "You know, I'm writing a novel and it's hard going to write a book."

"Yeah," he said, "I know it is. I just had a hell of a struggle with *For Whom the Bell Tolls*."

I said, "Could you give me any advice?"

He looked at me and said, "Listen, kid, I'll tell you one thing. Quit when you're going good."

And I said, "What does that mean?"

He said, "You know how tough it is, you sit down in the morning with a blank piece of paper?"

I said, "Oh yeah, it's terrible."

"All right, you struggle and then you finally get started and then all of a sudden the thoughts are flowing and words are coming and everything's just pouring out," he said. "Quit right there."

I said, "Why?"

He said, "So the next day when you look at that last sheet, those words will be alive and they'll encourage you to go on."

And I tried it. It worked too. It worked very well for me. I wrote a number of books after that. And I acted on another piece of advice he gave me. He said, "If you really want to be a writer, you've got to do what I did: get the hell out of town. Don't stay in Kansas City."

— How did Hemingway's writing influence you?

— He made me feel that the writer's life was glamorous. I did leave Kansas City, searching for exciting experiences. And my life had a wider horizon.

— Did he talk about persistence and the idea of writing everyday?

— He said that it was very important to do it everyday. And I knew that already, of course. He was in a great mood that night. He had this new wife, Martha Gellhorn. She was wearing a big mink coat, and he was showing her off to all of us young reporters, basking in our admiration. And it was a great evening for us, too. He had a lot of good stories. I didn't see any of the signs that led to his suicide, though. He didn't seem to be moody or anything like that, but of course he wouldn't have shown his deeper feelings to a group of young reporters. He was there to show us, "Boys, I made it, and if you want to make it you've got to get out in this big world." And that's what enchanted me: that big world out there.

— What impressed you about his writing? Was it his style; his use of short crisp sentences?

— No, I think what impressed me was that the feeling was strong. He wasn't writing abstractly. He was reacting very strongly to life and telling you about the deepest problems you face and how to cope with them or not cope with them. Hemingway had a way of charging his words with intense feeling. You just felt there was tension. That's what appealed to me. It wasn't the style necessarily, but the feeling behind it.

Writing itself is a mystery to me. I don't mean journalism, but creative writing. When you write a story and it comes out of you and it goes on and on you don't know where it's coming from. It's a very exciting, serious feeling you have, and I felt that Hemingway and I were on the same wavelength.

Rachel Maddux and the Bohemian Group

— What was it like for a young single reporter in Kansas City at that time?

— We had this little group with Rachel Maddux. She was a beautiful red-headed woman who was a writer. Wrote some good stuff. We had a love affair. She had an apartment on the top floor of an old building in Kansas City. We used to gather there for drinking parties and bohemian style discussions.

— Where did you meet her?

— What happened was that Edward J. O'Brien came out with a collection of best American short stories and I had a story in it, and the *Star* gave it a glowing review. And Rachel Maddux had just moved to Kansas City and she'd written a story for *Story Magazine* called "Turnip's Blood." I thought it was a wonderful story, and one of the reporters on the *Star*, a friend of mine named Harry Kaufman, came to see me. He says, "Hey, there's a beautiful dame who wants to see you." He did a little article about her when her story came out and it got good reviews too. Kaufman said, "She asked me if I knew you; she would like to have you come out to her apartment one night. She has parties out there." So that's how it happened. I went out there and we hit it off very well. Had a great time together. One time, I went to her apartment after getting off at about 12 o'clock. She was standing at the top of the stairs and this light was pouring over her. She was absolutely naked, with this beautiful red hair cascading down over her shoulders. She wore red shoes and nothing else!

— What happened to the group?

— What happened was that all members of her group were inspired. They included Bill Kalis, another close friend of mine from the University of Kansas City, Shelby Storck, and Harry Kaufman. We all resolved that we would help one guy to get out and get to New York, and we would send him a little money, each one of us, a few bucks a month, so that he could survive there until he got a job. And then when he got a job, he was supposed to help the next man get to New York.

Bill Kalis was first to go. He went there and he finally got a job. I was second in line and so he called up and said, "Come on. I've got an apartment and you can room with me. There're two rooms here." So that's how I got away from Kansas City, by a kind of group method with each one of us helping another guy get away.

— Who came up with the idea?

— I think it was Bill Kalis. I'm not sure.

Rachel encouraged us in this, and I got very despairing because even though we had some wonderful times together, she refused to marry me. She said she just didn't think it would work. I got so despairing one night at a party at her apartment that I decided to throw myself off her balcony. I was running toward the balcony, yelling, "I'm going to take the big jump!" One of my friends, Shelby Storck, tackled me like a football player and sat on my chest. He said: "I am not going to let you do this. You've got a lot ahead of you. You'll have a great life. You can't end it now." So he saved me! And I'm glad he did.

Her apartment was what, three or four stories up; it covered the top floor of an old building. She had that balcony where you could go and stand and look at the city, and I was going to dive off her balcony. Thank God I didn't, because I would have missed a lot of interesting things.

She told me later that she was very angry with me. She eventually married a stockbroker and moved away from Kansas City. I was crazy about her, though. You know how love is. I felt that was the end of the world when she wasn't going to marry me. But she always was encouraging to me, saying, "You're going to do wonderful things. You'll realize someday that you and I wouldn't have been the right partners for life. And you'll find another girl before long." And I did. About two years after that I met Barbara and we had our whirlwind romance. Rachel was right. If I had married her, it wouldn't have worked. Barbara was the right one for me.

— How did Rachel's literary career develop?

— She went on to write several novels. *The Green Kingdom* was about a mythical place on earth where everything was in perfect harmony and perfect ecology. Wonderful book. And then she wrote another one called *A Walk in the Spring Rain* that was made into a movie. So Rachel Maddux did pretty well as a writer.

— Who else was in the group?

— Let me tell you more about Rachel. She was an interior decorator when I met her. I worked nights and she worked days, so I would go to her apartment at night and then in the morning I'd have to get up and drive her around to her decorating appointments. I'd be driving this car and I'd keep falling asleep. I thought, "Oh, I'm going to hit something or somebody." I never did, but I was exhausted. I was going 18 hours a day and my parents said, "You're losing weight. You're obsessed with this girl and driving her around town." But, I don't know, I got through it.

FRIENDS FROM UNIVERSITY OF KANSAS CITY

— Who else was there?

— Oh, there was Bill Kalis. There was Shelby Storck. He was in radio. Shelby was a big, tall, handsome, blond guy who led demonstrations. You know, in the 30's students demonstrated on the campus. Shelby was the firebrand, and we marched across the campus carrying signs saying "Mussolini is a murderer." He had invaded Ethiopia, and we yelled, "Let's have peace," and all that as we marched across campus. Of course the other students thought we were crazy, but Shelby was one of these very crusading types. He would ride around the country on freight trains to get material for stories, and talk to these bums who were on the freight trains. He had a lot of wonderful stories to tell. After the war we all belonged to the American Veterans Committee.

— Did such political activities shape your views?

— To some extent. Shelby and I had a lot of long talks together and he was very radical because he rode around the country on these freight cars during the Depression. He'd told me about these camps where thousands of homeless men lived, what did they call them?...Hoovervilles. When Shelby would come back, we'd get together and he'd tell me all these terrible stories about how grim life was in America and then along came Roosevelt and changed everything.

— Was Shelby working?

— He did get a job with the *Kansas City Star* radio station. I think the trips were his attempt to try and find out what was going on in the country. Shelby rode the rails, and he made me think of John Steinbeck and his wanting to go out and find out what was happening. He wanted to write too.

— Did you read any of his work?

— Yeah. But he never could get published. I don't know what happened. I read some. There wasn't any organization; he just put down impressions and ideas. But he was great on the radio; he had a wonderful voice, a deep, baritone voice. While he was at the university he floated out around the country, but he'd come back to class. And he led the student strike at one time. We wanted to close down the university, I forget why, but he mobilized the students. He was a good organizer.

— Did you take part?

— I took part in it, but I don't know for the life of me what it was about. Except I remember the march against Mussolini. That was well justified and a good thing to do.

Another friend was Kenny Birkhead, whose father, Leon Birkhead, started an organization called Friends of Democracy. I don't know if you remember, but in the 30's you had Gerald L. K. Smith, and all kinds of neo-fascist movements and Huey Long. Actually, President Roosevelt said once that he was quite afraid that one of these groups would try to overthrow our government.

During the pre-war period, the tensions got terribly high between the people who didn't want to get in the war, many of them were isolationists or Nazis, and others, like the Committee to Defend America by Aiding the Allies, which was headed by William Allen Smith, who was an editor of the *Emporia Gazette*, I think.

— You were in that group?

— I was in that group, because I didn't see how we could stay out of the war. Isolationism didn't make sense. But Kenny Birkhead was part of the group that came to Rachel's apartment, almost two or three nights a week. Kenny was a tall, heavyset guy, and very gentle and very thoughtful. He always had an optimistic viewpoint, which I liked. Kenny was the man who recommended me for a place on President Truman's speechwriting staff in the 1948 campaign.

— Was he a writer?

— He was writing articles about what was happening in the fascist movement. And, as I just mentioned, he went to New York with his father and they founded a group called Friends of Democracy; they put out liberal reports on civil liberties. Kenny was one of our most active members.

Joseph Guilfoyle was another friend who came into our picture. I was sitting in the cafeteria at the University of Kansas City one day, with Shelby Storck, I think, and maybe Kenny Birkhead. And this young man came in and looked around and said, "I'm trying to find a man named Frank Kelly." And they brought him over to the table, and he says, "I'm Joe Guilfoyle." He said, "I read your story in *Story Magazine* and I was so impressed, I thought if the University of Kansas City has students like that, that's where I want to go." Joe became one of my closest friends. He later went to law school and he worked for Truman when Truman was a senator. He also entered the Justice Department and became Assistant Attorney General under Bobby Kennedy. Joe was terribly Irish, and remained close to his Gaelic side.

— Was he a hard drinker?

— We were all drinkers.

LITERARY GROUP

— To pick up that New York thread, Frank. So you were the second to make it to New York City. What about the others?

— I don't know if the others ever got there. No, Shelby decided to stay in Kansas City and became a newscaster for the *Star*'s station, WDAF. I think Kalis and I were the only ones who made it of the group. No, Kenny Birkhead also made it.

— And the others? How did their lives play out?

— Let's see. Bill Kalis eventually became public relations director for the Republic of the Bahamas. Had a wonderful job, entertaining the queen when she came to the Bahamas and all that. He was a great PR man. And Shelby Storck became a newscaster, and then he got into the war as a pilot in the Navy. Several of my friends were killed. They all went off to be pilots. After the war, Shelby went back to Kansas City and continued his career in television. And let's see. Joe Guilfoyle, as I told you, went to Washington, and got a job with Senator Truman, and then later in the Justice Department.

I kept in touch with another girl I knew in Kansas City, a girl named Barbara Middendorf who married a Dr. Rosen, a dentist. She was a gifted artist—a glorious being with many admirers. I went to see her on a visit to Kansas City in 2007.

JAZZ IN KANSAS CITY

Sometimes our group would go down to Twelfth Street where we'd hear some of the great jazz musicians of the century: Pete Johnson, Duke Ellington, and Cab Calloway. I love Cab Calloway. I remember Cab's song:

Hi-de-ho
Blood, sweat & tears
Hi-de-ho Hi-de-hi
Gonna get me a piece of the sky
Gonna get me some o' that old sweet roll,
I'm singin' Hi-de-hi-de-hi-de-hi-de-ho

We'd go down there, with maybe a friend from the *Star*, and we'd sit around and listen to that jazz and get home about three or four in the morning. I still lived at home then and my mother and dad were shocked by the bohemian life that I was leading. But whenever they talked to me about it I said, "Well, I can move out." But they didn't want me to move out.

Kansas City was an exciting and dangerous town when I was there. There were a lot of gang shootings, a lot of fights, and the nightlong songs of wild music. It prepared me for life in New York when I finally went there.

Even in New York, I didn't find what I heard on Twelfth Street in Kansas City. It was a long street, with smoky little bars on it. Most of them, you went down a few steps into a basement and most of the musicians were black and most of the people who came there were a bit eccentric in terms of the middle class of Kansas City. But there was camaraderie between those of us who came to listen and the ones who played. And we got to know them and we'd sit and listen to them play. Pete Johnson was the best of the bunch. And I don't think he ever got internationally famous. I loved to hear him play the *Empty Bed Blues*. It was our favorite. And we loved to hear Johnson play it. Bessie Smith originally recorded that song:

I woke up this morning with a awful aching head
My new man had left me, just a room and a empty bed
Bought me a coffee grinder that's the best one I could find
Oh, he could grind my coffee, 'cause he had a brand new grind
He's a deep sea diver with a stroke that can't go wrong
He can stay at the bottom and his wind holds out so long
Oh, he knows how to thrill me, he thrills me night and day
He's got a new way of loving, almost takes my breath away ...

It's my favorite. I can hear that throbbing voice of Bessie even in my 90's.

— Kansas City was the Paris of the Plains, but it was racially divided. We still had segregation.

— As a reporter I was shocked to find out that ambulances didn't stop for accidents involving blacks. We'd see an accident but we'd keep going with the sirens screaming. I'd say, "Wait, what about picking up those people?" "Oh, those are black people, they have their own ambulances, and they have their own hospital. We don't stop to pick up black people."

I think this was the first time that the deep brutality of segregation came home to me. My family didn't have any idea of how terrible life was for the black people of Kansas City. They were mostly segregated into a ghetto, the black section of town. And white people rarely had any contact with them. And so they had to have their own ambulance, their own doctors, and we never had contact with them, except to see them as maids and servants.

— Except when you wanted to listen to jazz.

— Yeah, except when you got into these nightclubs. Those of us who went to black nightclubs were regarded as being pretty eccentric, and we were, I guess, in those days. Kansas City was a very high bound city, very uptight, and very middle class.

— Did you keep journals at that time?

— No. I've never kept a journal. I wish I had, but I didn't. I got to know some of these black musicians and respected them very much, and it was just such a shock when I'd go in white circles and hear white people talk with contempt of the blacks. "Oh, those people," or, "They just don't understand anything and they're not very bright and they don't have it up here. They don't have much culture. They're sort of good for being servants and bartenders and waiters and things like that." I found it very troubling, but I didn't try to do anything about it.

Kansas City was a wonderful town to grow up in, and to spend my early manhood years. It was a rich atmosphere, you know, because people came there from all over, and the recordings made there were heard in many places.

MOVE TO NEW YORK CITY

— How did your parents react to your decision to go to New York? It must have been very difficult for them.

— Yeah, it was. But I thought I had to do it, because Hemingway said, "Kid, if you're going to amount to anything as a writer, you've got to get out of Kansas City. You can't stay here." That's what I realized. "You've got to get into a wider world than that." And Hemingway really had an enormous impact on me. I admired his writing and when he told me that, I even told my folks. "I'm a writer; I've got to go places!"

They wondered why I wouldn't stay. I had a good job on the *Kansas City Star*, and I was getting known in Kansas City. My mother and dad just couldn't comprehend why I wanted to quit that and go to New York and take my chances in that wild city, where my mother feared I would get in with bad people and be drinking heavily and chasing girls and my morality would be gone. She even thought I'd lose my religion, and of course it all happened too. She was right to be concerned.

— Did you ever have any misgivings about going to New York?

— Well, I've never been in the habit of looking back and saying, "Well, maybe I wish I'd done this or that." I just went from one thing to another: life just flowed. And I loved those days and I enjoyed Kansas City but then I went to New York. It was just great. I moved on to something with more scope.

NEW YORK CITY: FIRST IMPRESSIONS

— What were your first impressions of New York?

— It was kind of overwhelming: the noise and the number of people. Kansas City was a pretty big city, but New York was another dimension. I think Bill Kalis met me at the train and took me to this apartment that he had rented on Seventeenth Street. It was a real dark and dreary looking apartment. And I thought, "Oh God, why did I leave Kansas City for this?" But anyway I was only in that apartment for about a year; let's see…January '41. In September of that year I went back to Kansas City for my sister's wedding, and that's when I met Barbara, so then I asked her to marry me, and she came and we got married in December. So I was only in that dark apartment for a few months. But my first impression was that New York was a pretty tough town.

I told the folks I was leaving. My mother cried. She said I was too young to be leaving home. I was 26 years old! I remember they all went down to the railroad station with me, to see me off. And they acted as though I was going off to the other side of the earth. When I went to Bill's apartment it seemed to be the darkest pit I'd ever seen. I'd left my parents' nice house in Kansas City, and here I was in this New York City tenement! I'd descended into a pit!

— What part of New York?

— Seventeenth Street. I don't know what the intersection was; I remember Seventeenth and Seventh Avenue or something. Oh, subways were rattling underneath us all the time. I was there; the plan had worked, but I didn't have a job, and I was in a dark tenement.

FREELANCE WRITING

I sold some stories. *Liberty* was flourishing then, as was *True Stories*, and they bought some of my stuff and gave me a market.

— So you wrote for those?

— So I wrote *True Stories* out of my imagination. In fact I wrote a book about girls in Washington D.C, which was featured in the anthology, *True Stories of 1941*. Washington was swarming with young women, far more women than men, so I went down there. My friends asked me to come down and spend some time talking with these girls, and I got a pretty lurid novelette out of it. So that went over pretty well.

— Did you have an agent?

— Not at first. But there was a friend of a professor at the University of Kansas City who knew the editor of *True Story Magazine*. I think his name was Bill Rapp. My professor friend wrote and told him that I was a good writer, so Rapp got in touch with me and he liked what I wrote so I had a built-in market. But I didn't want to make a career writing for *True Story*.

— Did you write any science fiction?

— No, I didn't have ideas then for such stories. Bill Rapp thought I could do a lot of good using people's real experiences for stories. So I wrote one. I went to Washington and talked to some of the girls down there, the city was dominated by girls without men. So I wrote their stories, which Bill put into *True Story Magazine,* and one of them was also in a collection, *Best True Stories of 1941*. It was based on the true experiences of girls in Washington DC, trying to make their way down there.

I spent a week in Washington. I had friends there. And they introduced me to a lot of people. I went down there several times. The story came out in the magazine under a different name of course. I used a pseudonym, but I can't remember the name I used. It was a manufactured true story. I wrote several "true" stories in that magazine. He bought all my stories, which helped to keep me alive while I was waiting.

— How much were they paying for something like that?

— I can't remember now...couple hundred dollars, three hundred dollars, but it was pretty good for those days.

Literary Agent: Jacques Chambrun

— Did you ever get an agent?

— Yeah. Jacques Chambrun. I received a letter from him after I had a story published in *Story Magazine*. "You come to New York, and you want an agent, we must get together." So he went after the young writers. He'd been around the literary world for quite a while, and he had a lot of good writers.

— Where was his office?

— On Fifth Avenue. I didn't know that he sold some of my stories and he didn't give me all the money he got from them. He was one of those agents who could do that in those days. But he did sell some stories, but I knew that Boyle was right. I was not going to make a living as a freelance writer.

And my agent thought I was making a mistake by going to work for the AP. He said, "You have to give it a year or two, Kelly," but I didn't know that he sold stories for me to *Esquire* and *Liberty Magazine*.

And uh, they pay pretty well. But what I didn't realize was, he would get 1000 bucks from *Esquire* for my story and give me 500 instead. Taking more than his ten percent agent's fee.

— How did you find that out?

— I just found out about it someway. Somebody told me that Jacques Chambrun wasn't giving me the full amount. He was notorious for that. But he could sell these stories. He knew the editors. I was glad to get what I got. *Esquire* paid very well. I had a number of stories in there.

True Story Magazine paid pretty well, but I didn't like to pretend to be a girl. But the other ones were under my byline. My stories in *Esquire* had bylines. I liked that.

— How many did you write for *Esquire*?

— I don't know, two or three. Not too many. But they paid well.

— Did Chambrun ever talk to you about changing style or suggest topics for stories or anything of that nature?

— No. He just let me write what I wanted to write, and he'd say, "Oh, I think I can sell this. Let's try *Esquire*." And I was surprised when he was able to do it. But he encouraged me to write serious books, and he got Simon and Shuster interested in offering me a possible contract if I'd just write a few chapters of a book.

— What were you going to write about? Did you have any ideas for a book?

— Well, I didn't try it. I just decided not to do it.

THE ASSOCIATED PRESS

Hal Boyle, another Irish friend of mine who I met in Kansas City, was working at the Associated Press. He had a good job there as one of the New York bureau editors and he said, "How about coming to work for the AP?"

And I said, "Oh no, I didn't want to do that. That wasn't literary enough."

He said, "You can write anything you want." And he just pestered a guy named Gardner Bridge who was the bureau chief until finally one day Bridge called me and said, "We want you to come to work. Boyle is driving me crazy. We'll give you a job, just to shut him up." So I got on the AP that way. And I loved it, and I did well.

When Boyle got me the job on the AP things opened up. New York was quite different then. I could go to the Stork Club and do all these things. When I first got there it was overwhelming.

NEW YORK OFFICES FOR THE ASSOCIATED PRESS

— How would you describe the AP office in New York just before the war? What was it like?

— Well the Associated Press had its own building at Rockefeller Center, right next to the RCA building, as I recall. It was twelve or fifteen stories high. But the main newsroom was a whole city block with pillars all over the place and with clocks that would tell what time it was in Tokyo, Moscow, Paris, and London. So I was working in the New York bureau, which had one corner of this huge room. But we were close to the A-wire. The A-wire was the place where all the news from all over the world came through the various bureaus, and then the editors there took it and decided what would be good on the main wire, that was the A-wire, through Washington and London and all those places. So I was working in the New York bureau for a while.

And then I'll never forget one time I was at work—this was in June 1941—and all the bells began to ring on the A-wire. When there was big news coming in, these bells would ring and you knew something big from Washington or London was *coming across*. So I went over there and I saw this message: High American Military Authority Made the Following Statement, which we want to [send out] on all channels. You were not allowed to use his name but it came from General George C. Marshall. So I read it: This military authority said that the Germans had just attacked Russia in June of 1941, predicted that the Soviet Army would collapse within six weeks, and that the United States would have to face Nazi Germany as the only major power. That was Marshall's prediction.

He was right, except that the Russians kept on fighting. He said the Soviets were not prepared. There was no stopping the German advance until they got to Stalingrad.

I was surprised by the coverage given to General Marshall's statement by the big journals like the *New York Times* and others. Nobody asked to have his statement supported by a statement from another source. He was an "authority" and that made his words treated as authoritative.

AP ASSIGNMENTS: THE JOE LOUIS AND BILLY CONN FIGHT

One of my most exciting experiences with the AP was the night Joe Louis fought Billy Conn. And Louis was losing, from the first reports. So the editor at the AP said, "Kelly, get a cab and get up to the Hotel Theresa. That's where the black leaders hang out. Give us some local color of what the reaction will be in Harlem if Joe Louis loses."

So I went out and got a cab just right outside of the AP building.

"Where to?" the driver asked.

"The hotel Theresa in Harlem," I said.

And he said, "You're going up to Harlem tonight? That could be dangerous."

I said, "But why?"

He said, "Well, hell man, if Joe Louis loses they'll tear white people apart. They're not going to stand for it."

"Oh yeah, come on." I didn't believe him.

We arrived at the Hotel Theresa, which was the main place for Joe Louis and his people to hang out. As we got there, a mob of black people closed in on the cab. One of them looked at us and said, "There's a honky in there." And they started to rock the cab back and forth. "Let's tip this damn thing over," one black guy said.

And the doorman at the Hotel Theresa came running over and said, "Let that guy alone, he's with the AP." And they finally backed off. But I was scared to death. The doorman said, "Come on in here, boy, get out of that cab." And we ran into the lobby of the Hotel Theresa, and I stayed there until morning. When finally Joe Louis did win, of course, everybody was friendly as they could be. But I could feel this feeling of, you know, if our hero gets beaten, we're really going to take it out on the honkies.

— Did you file a story for the AP?

— I think I wrote something for the AP about the incident and what it was like being in Harlem the night of the fight. Anyway I stayed the night. I tried to go out, and the doorman said, "You can. But we've got a big couch over here, you can sleep on that if you want to." So I just stayed there until it was daylight, when I could go outside safely.

New York City Jazz Clubs

— Did you go to any of the jazz clubs in Harlem, like you did in Kansas City?

— The Cotton Club was one of the best spots in New York for jazz. And I went to some of the dance halls up in Harlem too at various times just to see what they were like. The Savoy Ballroom was great. I've never seen such dancing in my life. These guys would throw the girls up in the air and they'd spin around and then catch them and then dance some more.

— It's great, you know.

— Yeah, I tried to date a beautiful young woman up there. She said, "I don't go out with white guys." She wouldn't have anything to do with me. I thought, "Oh race prejudice is terrible." It was her prejudice against white guys. I was hurt by it. I realized again what insults were inflicted on black people who were as prejudiced as that beautiful black girl.

AP CORRESPONDENTS: NEW YORK CITY DESK

— Who were some of reporters you worked with in the New York office of the AP?

— Hal Boyle was a very close friend of mine. He became one of the best-known war correspondents in World War II for the AP. He had grown up in Kansas City, too. We used to go out together a lot. And, uh, he was a very moody Irish guy and used to go and get pretty loaded at McSorley's Old Ale House. And later on they gave him a column right after World War II. I also had a New York column for a while for the AP but I didn't want to stay with it.

— What was Boyle like?

— Boyle looked a lot like Jimmy Cagney, you know. Irish face. There is something you can call an Irish face, very ebullient when he was in a good mood, and very down on life when he was in a bad mood, like me and like a lot of the Irish.

First Byline: The Stork Club

I got a byline in the *Kansas City Star* after I went to New York and worked for the AP.

— Did you hear about it from home?

— My friends in Kansas City were amazed. When I got to New York one of the first stories I was asked to cover by the AP was the party for Miss Debutante of 1941. Her name was Brenda Frazier or something like that. It was held at the Stork Club and I went over there and I wrote the story and it went on the AP wire and, uh, the next thing I know my mother says, "Oh, you're on the front page of the *Star*, your name is on the front page. All about dancing with this debutante." It was the first time I had a byline. I did get to dance with her, but I didn't try to take her home. She was a sexy girl but far above me, I thought.

— Was the AP newsroom anything like what you had experienced at the *Star*?

— Except at the AP you ordinarily didn't go out into the city. The AP had so much news coming at it from all over the world. You had to sit at the desk and you had all this copy piled up and you picked out the stories that you wanted to send on the A-wire or the B-wire or wherever you wanted them to go. In effect we were all editors, and occasionally we'd get an assignment outside like the one I got for the Stork Club and that was a lot of fun.

I've got a picture taken of me in the Stork Club with a friend, and it was the ultimate sophistication. You saw a lot of show business people at the Stork Club, and some gangsters. The waiters said: "So-and-so is in the mob." But he was accepted. You'd just hope that he wouldn't start any shooting while you were there.

COURTSHIP AND MARRIAGE

I was only at the AP for a short while when my sister Kitty announced that she was going to get married to a Kansas City man. So I went back home for her wedding, went to a party at the home of my college friend, Shelby Storck, one of my closest friends, and he'd been telling me for years that "my wife has a friend named Barbara Mandigo who's just right for you. If you ever meet her, you'll fall in love with her." So I met her that night and I took her home. We had two dates. I went back to New York, called her up, and I said, "Will you marry me?" And she said she would. She came to New York and we were married on December 5th, two days before Pearl Harbor.

— St. Patrick's Cathedral? Were you married there?

— We were married in the Episcopal Cathedral of St. John the Divine. She knew the dean. He married us in the St. Ambrose Chapel on the fifth of December. So we had a big party on the night of December 6th, with all the newspaper people in New York it seemed to me. Boyle had the party at his apartment and I remember correspondents talking about the Japanese threat, and one of them was saying, "Ah, those guys will never attack us. They're no damn good at flying airplanes. There's something wrong with their balance in their ears or something." This was the very morning of Pearl Harbor!

My wife and I woke up on the second morning of our honeymoon, we turned on the radio to get the New York Philharmonic, listening to this wonderful music, and all of a sudden this frantic voice comes on and says, "The White House has just announced that Japanese planes have bombed Pearl Harbor. We're at war." Just like that. I'd seen how war affected my father, and I didn't want to get involved in it.

— Her mother and father?

— Her father was of Portuguese background; his name was Clark Mandigo. I had never heard of the name before. And her mother was a DAR, from one of the Allens of New England. Gladys Allen Mandigo. That was her family background.

So anyway, I said to her on the second date we had, "I love you and I want to marry you."

And she said, "My goodness."

I said, "Don't rule it out."

She said, "Oh, I won't."

I said: "On the train going to New York, if I can find a place to send a telegram from Harrisburg, Pennsylvania—the train stops there—I'll send you a telegram and you'll know my wish to marry you is genuine."

She said, "Oh all right. If I get that telegram that'll be a signal."

So the train did stop at Harrisburg, Pennsylvania. As I looked from the train window, I thought: Where am I going

Wedding Picture – December 5, 1941

to find a place to send a telegram? All of a sudden, there appeared before me, this little Western Union boy and he walked right up to me and he said, "Want to send a telegram, Mister? Telegram?" I said, "Oh yeah I do." So I wrote off this message. And he got off the train.

I got to New York and I called her up and I said, "Did you get my telegram?"

She said, "I did."

And I said, "Well what's the answer to my question?"

She said, "I'll do it, I'll marry you." Isn't that a funny story?

— It's a great story.

— This was September 1941. She had to make some arrangements in Kansas City. She was a social worker at that time. And I said, "I'd like to marry you on your birthday. That way I'll save money for anniversary presents."

— And that date was?

— December 5th, 1941. Her birthday was December fifth. So I said, "Let's make it December the fifth. She said, "Fine." So she came to New York. And my friends at the AP said, "How many dates did you have with this girl?"

And I said, "Two."

And they said, "Was it dark both times?"

"Oh, it was night you know."

"If you want us to go down to the station with you, we'll have you stand against a pillar and we will move along the train and say, 'Frank Kelly is standing by pillar 26 so you can recognize him'".

But I recognized her as soon as I saw her get off the train. That was just a gag, a newspaperman's gag. So anyway, with such good luck, I thought: now where are we going to live? I had been living with my friend from Kansas City in an apartment in New York. I told all my friends about this romance and they were all delighted. One of my friends came up to me and said, "You know, I've got an apartment in Patchin Place in Greenwich Village, a perfectly romantic place, but my wife and I are going to Peru." I don't know why he was going; I think he was doing a book or something. "So you can have it for as long as we're away. We'll be gone all year, so we'll give you the lease tonight." and he said, "The furniture we have there is not much, just a few sticks and stuff." And I said, "Well, I don't have much money." And I went down and looked at the place and offered him $65 for the furniture. And he took it, so we had a place to move into. It was small with a living room, bedroom, and a kitchen about the size of oh, four by four, with just a tiny stove. And we were right across the street from E. E. Cummings, the poet. Patchin Place was known as a street of poets, famous poets. Anais Nin was a few doors down. You probably know some of her work. And I also was told that John Masefield once lived in the apartment below where we were when he was in New York. Patchin Place was a blind alley with a lamp at the end and there was one tree. It was called the tree of heaven. Just imagine coming home. Walking by the lamp and the tree, turning right, and going up the stairs to our apartment. It was a very romantic setting.

— Did Barbara write any poems when she was there?

— Oh yes. She was writing all the time. I'll give you a copy of her collection. I remember several of them. One was about one of the first dinners we had, and I brought her two red roses for the second month of our anniversary. We went out to a French restaurant on Sixth Avenue. So I gave her these two red roses and she wrote a poem. Then we had two glasses of wine. And the poem was:

> Two red roses
> Two glasses of wine
> Dinner Français with that husband of mine...

It goes like that.

— Where were you, Frank, when you heard about Pearl Harbor? Were you at home?

— Well the next morning Barbara and I woke up on the second morning of our honeymoon, we turned on the radio we had by the bed to get the New York Philharmonic, and the beautiful music was pouring out appropriate for a honeymoon. And then all of a sudden we heard this voice say, "The White House has just announced that Japanese planes have bombed Pearl Harbor." So Barbara and I clutched each other and said, "We're at war. We're at war." It's the second day of our honeymoon. I got so concerned about whether or not maybe I was needed at the AP office at Rockefeller Center. You know war is news. So after a while I said, "Do you mind if I call the AP?"

And she said, "Well, it's the second day of our honeymoon."

I said, "I've got to call them." And I called up the AP and talked to the editor on duty, his name was Norm Lodge. He was a veteran of World War I, a very down-to-earth guy, and he had been at our party. And he said, "What the hell, Kelly! You just got married. It's just another goddamn war. Go back to bed."

I said, "Well, Barbara, he hung up on me, so our honeymoon goes on." In those days the newsboys sold papers on the streets. So that night I heard this crying in the street, "War, war, war." There were six newspapers in New York at that time. I bought copies of the editions. (I didn't save them but I wish I had.) Barbara was kind of shocked. She said, "On our honeymoon you are reading all these old New York papers." I guess that's a newspaperman for you. But she was loving, and sweet, and she forgave me.

The first week I got a call from a friend of mine, who had worked in another news agency, and he said, "Hey Frank, we got a tip and I want to call you. German planes are on their way to New York. You and Barbara should get under some kind of shelter. Got anything you can cover yourselves with in that apartment?" We looked at this little coffee table about so big. I said, "Bill, the only thing we've got is this coffee table, where our feet would stick out on the sides, so I guess there's no use for our trying to get under cover."

And then one night there was an air raid alarm and the whole city lit up, the worst thing to do in a real air raid. I went to Fifth Avenue, which wasn't far from Patchin Place. I looked up and down this avenue and all the buildings were lighting up. This was just the worst thing in the world to do: making themselves targets. You were supposed to put the lights out in that scenario. But nobody knew. Nobody expected the United States to be threatened. And of course it was a lot of nonsense. Hitler didn't have any planes that could reach New York but it created a kind of hysteria, and then one day one of our artillery on Staten Island went off accidentally and some shells hit the Empire State Building. That shook everybody up. At first it was thought to have been enemy fire but of course it was an accidental firing of anti-aircraft defense.

— Did you see any of the American Nazi parades?

— Oh, the German-American Bund? They had a big demonstration in Madison Square Garden. A friend of mine worked for an organization called Friends of Democracy that exposed a lot of these rightwing fascist groups. They were flourishing in those days.

PATCHIN PLACE

— How would you describe Patchin Place? Were there great restaurants nearby?

— It was wonderful. There were all kinds of good restaurants. There was Peter's Backyard; there was Charles', this French place, on Sixth Avenue I think it was. One thing about our life at that time, which prevented us from going to some of the places we wanted to, was that all of our friends worked nights. I worked nights at the AP and they worked for the *Herald Tribune* and the *Times*. And we all had our parties starting at about 2:30 in the morning. The parties would go until daylight. So Barbara and I would be walking home from a party and everybody else was going to work.

Even though the parties broke up before dawn, and it'd still be dark, we never had the slightest hesitation about walking through the streets of New York. Nobody ever heard of anyone being mugged or attacked or anything. That's the way it was in the 40's. New York was a wonderful town in those days.

— You said E. E. Cummings was living across the street from your apartment?

— Yeah. He had a beautiful, long-legged wife, Marion Morehouse, a fashion model and photographer; I remember her. She was gorgeous. But we never saw very much of him. He was very reclusive. We never got to talk with him or anything. But my wife admired E.E. Cummings' poetry very much. So she was thrilled to be living across the street from him.

Patchin Place was such a delightful spot. It's been declared a New York State historical site. And it's still the same. My son was in New York, many years later, and he sent me a picture of it, and it's just the way it was when we were there in 1941. Patchin Place. We were on the second floor.

HARVARD UNIVERSITY AND NIEMAN FELLOWSHIP

— When did you decide to apply for a Nieman Fellowship?

— I read that Harvard University was offering fellowships for outstanding journalists, Nieman Fellowships. So I said to my wife, "Gee, it would be great if I could get one of those but I don't have a chance."

She said, "Why don't you put together some of your articles for the *Star* and the AP and I'll send in the application."

"Oh," I said, "I don't have a chance."

But she insisted and then I heard from Louis Lyons, the curator at the Nieman Foundation. He said, "I want you to meet with two or three of our professors." I had to go over to the Harvard Club on Fifth Avenue, sit down with Arthur Schlesinger Jr., and two other famous professors. I was so nervous that I really wasn't in very good form talking with them. I went back to my wife and I said, "Well, I guess I killed my chances."

So then Louis Lyons called up Barbara and said, "What got into Frank?" He said, "His articles are wonderful, but Schlesinger and the others said he seems to be a cold stiff, he seemed to be frightened. But we're going to give him a fellowship anyway." It was just that I was nervous, but I did get it.

In October of 1942, we left New York. We kept our apartment, and we sublet it. We kept that apartment all through the war at Patchin Place and we went up to Harvard, and had a wonderful time up there.

— Do you remember any of the questions they asked?

— They mainly asked about my views on the history of the American character and then they went back and reported that I was obviously a brilliant fellow but I was so stiff. I didn't make any jokes, and they wondered if I had a sense of humor. So later when I get up there and I became known as the [comedian] of the Nieman Fellows, Louis Lyons said, "Why were you concealing your sense of humor?" I told him I was nervous about that interview: a boy from Kansas City being interviewed by three Harvard professors at the Harvard.

The club has an awesome, stuffy atmosphere. I was really in a state of shock during the whole interview. I don't even remember what we talked about very well.

HARVARD UNIVERSITY

So we went up to Harvard in October of 1942. I got a leave from the AP to go up there. And while I was there, we had some great experiences at Harvard. We had weekly seminars with people like Walter Lippmann. One session I'll never forget, was with Heinrich Brüning, who was the last chancellor of the German Democratic Republic. And he told us how Hitler really got into power. Franz von Papen put a document in front of old man Hindenburg, who had been elected President of Germany in 1932. He said, "The general had gone around the bend." I guess he had what we call Alzheimer's. He didn't know what he was signing, that he was making Hitler Chancellor of Germany. But they slipped it in and he signed it. And Brüning said that the aristocrats and the wealthy people put Hitler into power. And a lot of them got killed as a result too. Isn't that a tragic story?

— What was Harvard like during the years leading up to war?

— Well, there was an atmosphere of great freedom, wonderful freedom. I really enjoyed that.

— Were you given a desk?

— No. The Nieman Foundation was housed in a couple of small rooms in one of the old buildings right off Harvard Square. It was in an old house. But we were just free, absolutely free, to go to any class we wanted to and to write whatever we thought was stimulating about the Nieman year. It was just wonderful. I got acquainted with Arthur Schlesinger Sr. and Jr. They were very impressive, very helpful to me. We would have dinners every Thursday night at the Signet Society Clubhouse, which was off Harvard Square. And these well-known people like Lippmann and Brüning and others would come and meet with us. They'd have dinner with us and then we'd have a "no holds barred" discussion. I remember somebody told me, "If you want to get there in time to get a cocktail, they put out a table loaded with martinis and manhattans, a big table, better get there early because the Harvard faculty will drink all the martinis before you get there." So I took that to heart.

— Was he right?

— Yeah. Some of the faculty was always invited to come and join us. We had some wonderful sessions. Except my wife complained, she said, "You come home from those

Nieman meetings smelling like antifreeze." Also they passed out free cigars. I'd never smoked a cigar before so I thought boy, this is the life, sitting here smoking a free cigar, and talking to people like Heinrich Brüning. It was a good life.

— So you were there for one year?

— No, I was drafted in the second semester. And I'm the only man who had two Nieman Fellowships, and the oldest living Neiman Fellow now. They want to do a little article on me for the *Nieman Reports*.

— All the Nieman Fellows have their fellowship divided into two classes. I was in the class of 1942-1943, but I didn't finish then because I went into the Army in January '43. I got out of the Army in December '45 and Louis Lyons said, "Do you want to come back and finish your Nieman Fellowship?" So I went back for four and a half more months, so I'm a member of two classes and I knew a lot of guys in both classes.

— Do you know anything about the history of the Nieman family?

— Mrs. Agnes Wahl Nieman wanted to give money to Harvard. She was the owner of the *Milwaukee Journal*. She, or one of her advisors, wanted to do something for American journalism. She didn't want to set up a journalism school, so she offered this money to Harvard. I think it was President James Conant who also had a hand in establishing the Nieman Foundation at Harvard. Their purpose was not to create a journalism school, but to create fellowships for outstanding journalists, who were already working and out in the field. So you got a year at Harvard, with a good income, an opportunity to take any class you wanted, membership to the faculty club, all that and we weren't even required to write a report or anything. Complete freedom. You're scheduled to go up to Harvard, and once you are part of the program you have really carte blanche as far as what you want to do there.

— Did you have any personal goals or objectives for that year?

— Well, I wanted to get better informed about modern European history, and I was interested in the origins of Nazism and fascism.

— Do you remember any of the courses?

— No, not specifically. I wasn't required to take exams or anything. We just sat in the background unobtrusively. While I was a Nieman Fellow, I met the editors at the *Atlantic Monthly Press*. They got interested in my writing, and printed some of my articles while I was at Harvard, and asked me if I wanted to do a book. So I said I did. So I wrote a book for them, which was based on my experiences at the AP as one of the correspondents at the first sessions of the United Nations. It's all about the crisis with the Soviet Union over Iran. The Soviets refused to get their troops out of Northern Iran, and Truman told them they had to do it or else. It was much more serious than anybody ever realized. We were thinking it was another war. Truman didn't really want to go to war, but he put the heat on Stalin. It made a good background for a book.

NIEMAN CLASSMATES

— Who were some of your classmates at Harvard?

— Oh let's see. Tom Griffith, who later became an editor of *TIME* magazine; Leon Savirsky, who wrote a lot of books; Bob Manning, who later became Assistant Secretary of State; they had quite a group of journalists in the Nieman Fellowship.

Fred Neal and I had gotten to be very close friends when he was a Nieman and I was too. He was from the *Wall Street Journal.* Later on he became very radical, but then he was a hot Republican writer and he and I used to argue about politics and the New Deal. His wife, Virginia, and Barbara and I, we all had great times together as close friends. Developing new friendships is one of the values of the Nieman Fellowship; all these journalists came from very different backgrounds and you got to know them and we'd have some pretty lively dialogues. But Fred and I got to be close, although I became good friends with a number of them. They're all gone now.

— Were there any others you'd like to mention?

— Oh yes, John Day. He and I were close friends. He became the managing editor of the *Louisville Courier Journal* for a while; then he worked for CBS. He was just a delightful Southern guy. We knocked around a lot together.

— Do you remember any of the establishments you frequented?

— I can't remember them all; there were a lot of pubs. Of course we went to a lot of things in the Harvard halls, and had classes together.

— The faculty club? How often were you there?

— We went to lunch there all the time, we all had memberships there. The food was good, and we got to know a number of the Harvard faculty by going to lunch with them at the club.

— Have you remained in contact with the Foundation?

— They have Nieman reunions from time to time, since we are all scattered across the country. They are usually held at Harvard. I've been back for a few of them. I am a member of two classes. I remember reminding Louis Lyons at one of the reunions, that I was a member of two classes. He said, "Officially you are a member of the class of 1942-43."

President James Bryant Conant

— Did President Conant spend much time with the Nieman Fellows?

— I was very impressed with President Conant. He had weekly dinners at his house for the Nieman Fellows. We'd go over to his house and he'd bring in some people from the faculty and we'd sit around the fireplace and talk and have a drink or two. It was really wonderful. I'd read a lot of books on the English tutorial at Cambridge and Oxford, and I thought how wonderful that would be to have informal access to the brilliant men who made up the core. And that's exactly what we had as Nieman Fellows.

I don't recall one-on-one tutorials, but we had two weekly seminars, two of them; dinner with President Conant and one for the Signet Society, which was the literary society at Harvard.

— What was Conant like during these seminars? Was he approachable?

— He was very down-to-earth and friendly. He even laughed at my puns. He was wonderful, and very open. Having grown up in Kansas City, Missouri, I thought of Harvard as being composed of men with stuffed shirts, and guys who were very conscious of their importance, and some of them were but not Conant. I remember one dinner he invited a Thomas Reed Powell, who was professor at the Harvard Law School, and a wonderful character. Powell brought his old grade books to the dinner. Three of his former students were on the U.S. Supreme Court, and Powell read from the books. He graded the Supreme Court that evening.

Nieman Fellows also had the privilege of sitting in the press box at the Harvard football games, which nobody competed for because the Harvard teams hardly ever won, so we'd sit out there in the press box. We invited Professor Powell to come with us one day and he showed up in the biggest, most moth-eaten raccoon coat I've ever seen. It was right out of Scott Fitzgerald: gray, big, furry coat with all these holes in it. And during the game we got excited and we all jumped and cheered some play and Powell said, "Anybody suffering from snake bite down there?" And he pulled out the biggest bottle of Old Forrester bourbon, and hurled it down the line. We were all sitting in a row, and somebody leaped up and caught the bottle or it would've landed on somebody's head. I thought: well, he's a pretty informal guy for a Harvard professor. You didn't expect professors to jump up and throw bottles of bourbon during a game. He was so funny. He used to get drunk and drive around in his funny old car and run into trees in the Harvard yard. What a character!

The Nieman Fellowship had many impacts on my life, and led to my connection with the Center for the Study of Democratic Institutions.

HEINRICH BRÜNING

— How would you describe Heinrich Brüning?

— I was surprised by what a gentle person he was. He was a professorial type. I'm not sure, was he a professor in Germany?

— Yes. He had his doctorate from a German university. Were you impressed with him?

— Yes, I was impressed with his quiet acceptance of what had happened and his willingness to look at the whole picture. He was deeply wounded by what happened to his country, you know. He said that people think that German people are really supportive of the Nazis, but you look at their election in 1932 when President Hindenburg ran against Hitler. Hitler was badly defeated. The public's perception seemed to worry him a lot, the fact that people thought that Germany really supported Hitler. And he talked of Hitlerism as a monstrous evil, and he spent quite a long time on that, but emphasized that this was his view. He also said that the German aristocrats and the industrialists, who had decided that Hitler would make a good stooge for them, were the ones who put the document in front of General von Hindenburg. Apparently by then he would sign anything his assistants placed before him. Brüning said, "They brought Hindenburg into his office, sat him at his desk and he signed the act that made Adolf Hitler Chancellor of Germany.

Brüning never seemed to have gotten over that fact that here was this great country with all the culture of Germany and the history of Germany and music and art was turned over to this monster, Hitler, through an act of plotters who thought that they could control this man, that they could manipulate him, he would be easy in their hands. Of course it turned out that he destroyed I think every one of them once he came to power.

— Were you surprised about what Brüning said?

— Well, you know, after the Versailles Treaty, the Chancellor of Germany was only a dim figure to most Americans. We didn't know he was there, and we thought that the Weimar Republic had fallen apart because of the weakness of the leaders and they hadn't done this or that. Maybe Brüning was making a case for himself and his administration, but he insisted that all this plotting was going on by these extreme right-wing people who wanted to capture the government and turn Germany over to Hitler.

— Was his talk given at Conant's house?

— No. This was during our special seminars, at Eliot House or one of the houses. He talked for about two hours. Brüning was a man who was trying to figure out how could this terrible thing have happened to his country, to his people, and to our civilization, because you know there's never been anything quite as monstrous as Hitler in American history or in Europe as far as I know.

Walter Lippmann

— Who were some of the other presenters?

— I particularly remember Walter Lippmann, the great columnist from the *New York Herald-Tribune*.

— What did you think of him as a newspaper columnist before he arrived?

— I was very impressed with him. I thought he was very intelligent and very thoughtful.

— Did you read him?

— We all read him. He was sort of the guru of journalism at that time. Walter Lippmann, he was the top columnist, sort of a pundit really. So he came and we had a lunch. I remember that. And he wanted a special kind of coffee or something like that. Anyway in the course of the luncheon—this was in September or October 1942, right after I arrived at Harvard—he was talking about the war and it was going pretty badly then you know. So Walter Lippmann at the luncheon looks around and says, "The war is going to take a change for the better." He said, "Don't worry. We are going to have a landing at North Africa, and it's going to take the Germans by surprise. Now keep this confidential." I was surprised that he could talk about it. But that was true and he knew all about it, and how it was going to go. And he thought it would be very successful and turn the tide of war in the favor of the allies at that point. Of course he was predicting the landing that happened I think in November of '42.

— That's right.

— And we did knock the Germans out of North Africa but nobody expected that. So I said later to Louis Lyons, the Nieman curator, "How in the world did Walter Lippmann know all of this? He talked about how he knew about their strategy."

He says, "Well he's a pundit. Everybody in Washington confides in Walter Lippmann: the president, the chiefs of staff."

I don't think a journalist has that stature anymore. But I've never forgotten that one.

— And from the standpoint of his writing?

— Lippmann was just somebody you had to read; he was in the paper five times a week. He was a high quality man I thought. Later that night Fred Neal, his wife, and my wife, we all had dinner and I told him what Lippmann had said at lunch. I said, "He shouldn't have told us about this coming attack." Neal said, "I don't know any German spies." But I wonder if we didn't kind of break some rules. What do you think?

— That's a touchy question isn't it?

— I think he wanted to impress us—being that we were Nieman Fellows, which carried a certain amount of prestige too—and show us that he, Walter Lippmann, was on the inside. But I thought in a way it was kind of dangerous for him to do that. That was a great session with Walter Lippmann.

CAMBRIDGE ON THE EVE OF WAR

— What was it like being in Cambridge before the war? Where were you living?

— Chauncey Street. It was a nice apartment building except it was freezing cold because the Germans were sinking our oil tankers right off the shore, right off the Massachusetts seashore. You could watch them sinking if you wanted to. So we couldn't get any heat for our apartment. We almost froze that way too. When I went up to Fort Devens for basic training, I was warm up there, but poor Barbara froze all through the winter. It was terrible.

— So she stayed in Boston?

— Yeah, she got a job with the Red Cross.

— Did you do any writing during your fellowship?

— When I came back for the second round I was writing the chapter. The first time around though, we were so busy going to seminars. I was soaking up the Harvard experience, and I don't think I wrote much.

— How important was the experience for you? The ability to take a year away from the daily activities of being a journalist and to simply have time to reflect your career?

— I think it is very important. I found it to be very valuable to me and all the Nieman Fellows who I have talked to thought it was very worthwhile. Some of my friends at the AP laughed when they heard I'd gotten a Neiman Fellowship. "Why are you going to go back there and hang around with those academic types, when you could be out here covering the world, man! You're going off there with the haughty ivory tower people, double domes, and think tank guys. They really made fun of me. I hadn't realized that so many newspapermen have this latent feeling about academics. But apparently it exists.

You know, I was kind of a naive kid from Kansas City, really; my wife's mother was so thrilled because her husband had gone to Harvard, and she insisted that one of my sons must go to Harvard. There was no other university equal to it; she convinced us that Harvard was practically like going to the Vatican or something, a holy place. But it really was a wonderful place.

James Bryant Conant was president then and he was very friendly with the Neiman Fellows. Later that had an effect when he offered me a job on his Committee on the Present Danger. One thing I found about being a Neiman fellow was that no matter what some people said about us scornfully, a lot of other people felt any Neiman Fellow must be pretty bright.

— It opened doors?

— I could get recommended. Louis Lyons was always recommending me for various jobs. And people said, "How do you get all those damn jobs?" I said, "I guess it's Louis Lyons up there in Boston." A lot of people consulted him as the curator of the Nieman Foundation.

— Did he correspond with you?

— Yes, he kept a correspondence with a lot of us.

DRAFTED: UNITED STATES ARMY

— When did you get drafted?

— In December of '42, my draft board in Kansas City notified me. I had been deferred after they found out I got married. By pure chance, if you got married before Pearl Harbor, the draft board accepted it as a valid marriage because they thought, you know, nobody would rush into marriage after Pearl Harbor. Since we'd been married two days before Pearl Harbor that kept me out of the Army for several months and saved my life. But I was drafted finally in 1942, the end of '42.

The Neiman Fellows gave me a big party. All the Harvard people came. The next day, I went to the draft office at Harvard, one of those little offices with a little old man with his steel-rimmed glasses. I went over there and reported for duty. And he just looked at me and said, "Oh, Mr. Kelly," he says, "Oh dear, we didn't finish processing your papers. Come back in a month." The war was on and I had told everybody I was entering the Army. I said, "What am I going to do?" I walked across the Harvard courtyard and I went to see the Nieman curator, Louis Lyons. And he said, "Oh don't worry about it Frank." But he laughed. He said, "We could have another party when you really go away." Then he said, "We'll put you back on the Nieman payroll." So I went home and told Barbara and she was happy. We had another month together.

BASIC TRAINING: FORT DEVENS, MASSACHUSETTS

In January of '43 they sent me a notice that I had to go. So I went over, went down to take the exam, and just barely passed the physical tests, especially on my eyesight. I was very near sighted. So they finally decided they would accept me for limited service and I said to this lieutenant, "What does that mean?" He said, "Well," he said, "we won't let you fire a machine gun but we'll let you wipe the sweat off of the brow of the machine gun operator."

— How was basic training?

— Fort Devens almost killed me. One night I was sitting in the Nieman dinner, smoking cigars, and fraternizing with famous people and the next day I was at Fort Devens and a soldier was flashing a light in my eyes and saying, "Get up, Kelly, you're on KP." So I had to go out and clean garbage cans. What a change, I'll tell you. And we marched. The snow and the air were terrible up at Devens, but we marched through the snow fifteen to twenty miles. Later, I never felt so good in my life. I got into perfect physical condition because I had to do calisthenics, and long marches. I never thought I could survive it, but I did. Most of the other guys there were much younger than I. I was in my twenties and most of them were teenagers.

I finished my training, learned how to shoot a rifle I hoped I'd never use, and I went to a battle-conditioning course. There was barbed wire stretched over you, you crawled on your hands and knees, you're just flat. Meanwhile they're firing machine guns over your head, you could hear the bullets going by. If you stuck your head up you were killed. Anyway, I got stuck in the barbed wire. Two of my friends said, "Oh, damn it. Our Kelly is stuck again." They went back, got me loose from the wire, and pulled me over to the end of the training course. If I didn't have friends, I never would have survived the Army. I was the oldest man in the unit—27 or 28 before they finally got me in the Army.

I was in the Infantry. Then as we were coming to the end of our training, word came that the Army had created a specialized training program, ASTP, for people who were in colleges. They wanted to keep the colleges open. So the sergeant in charge of my unit at Fort Devens said: "Oh Kelly," he said, "I'll put you down for Harvard again. You want to go back to Harvard?" I said, "Sure, why not?" So then I got on the Army specialized training program and they sent me back to Harvard. So I am the only Nieman fellow who had all this time at Harvard. I was in uniform. We were all marching and doing calisthenics, firing rifles, but meanwhile we were going to classes at Harvard. So that saved me, for a while.

EUROPEAN THEATER: MARCH 1944

It was another six months before I went on active duty. I was sent overseas in March of 1944, and I was trembling when I went up that gangplank into the ship. On the way over our convoy was jumped by German submarines; the ship next to ours was sunk and I thought my life was coming to an end. I was standing on a life raft, looking down at the water, and we saw this torpedo coming and hissing along; it just missed our ship. All the ships were turning in the fog. The Nazi submarines had been in the fog and our convoy just went right through it, and we didn't know they were there. But the ship next to ours was blown up. It was an oil tanker and I never forgot those men burning up alive. I could see their faces, just like pieces of paper. I thought: my God, why was I spared? Why were those on the other ship lost? Why did that torpedo miss us and hit the oil tanker? You can't answer questions like that, can you?

— No, no, not at all. So you made it to England?

— When we got to England, we landed at Liverpool and there were all sorts of lights in the sky and, coming down the gangplank, I said to this British soldier, "Boy, you sure gave us a big welcome." And he said, "Welcome to hell, Yank, it's an air raid, get under cover!" They were shooting anti-aircraft fire at these German planes. But the war to me was like being in a movie. It was just a fantastic experience. I never felt somehow or other I was going to get killed but I saw a lot of people wounded and killed and I escaped.

— Where were you assigned?

— First I was in a replacement depot in Bristol, England. They sent me from Liverpool down to Bristol, a huge place where they parked a lot of soldiers who'd been trained in the Infantry. We were going to be thrown in after the first wave landed on the beaches of Normandy. We knew a lot of people were going to get killed and wounded. We were what were called replacements.

We were training there, and one day an officer came from General Eisenhower's headquarters saying they were looking for soldiers with journalistic experience to interview the wounded for hometown newspapers. And the colonel in charge of the base said, "Oh, there's a man here who's been with the AP." I had gotten acquainted with him because I'd had the nerve to go in and say to him, "You know we got all these guys sitting around here, Colonel, they don't even know what's going on in the war. Why don't you let me put on a news program once a week with some latest developments?"

He said, "I like that." So we started doing the news program; that's how he became aware that I was a journalist. So that led to my getting into the Army Correspondents Corps. That's what I was with.

— How did you prepare for these shows? Were the programs based on newspaper accounts about the war?

— Yeah, and radio reports and the *Stars and Stripes*. We would just project pictures of what was in the *Stars and Stripes*.

— And then you talked about the stories?

— I would talk about what was happening in Italy or what was happening in the Pacific and all that. And the guys enjoyed it because we were cut off. We weren't allowed to buy any British newspapers. Although we did, we smuggled them on base. I was lucky in having a good colonel who was really interested in keeping us informed. He knew we were just there to replace other guys—to keep the war going.

So they pulled me out, and decided to make me a war correspondent. And most of the guys there, I think, got killed on a beach. But I didn't land with them. I was given credentials as an Army correspondent so I didn't land on the beach until weeks after they did. It was still covered with wreckage. Horrifying sight. They had these strips of illuminated wire that you had to watch out for because there were land mines on each side. We climbed up the cliffs, got on these trucks, started down the road in Normandy. And we went into these French villages, one after another. We saw they were just smashed up. We believed the allies had precision bombing but then we saw those villages, churches, schools—everything just blasted. The people crawled out of the wreckage and shook their fists at us, as we passed them. We thought we were liberators but the French saw that we had blown up their villages. That's war, you know—hellish madness.

— Who were some of the journalists with you?

— I didn't see any at first. I was really still in the Army. I rode in an Army truck.

— So you went from there to the Correspondents Corps. What was that duty like?

— I was told I was going to go to Normandy with this unit called the Channel Base Corps. And we landed near Calais; eventually we were assigned to go with General Patton, when he was ordered by Eisenhower to lead the liberation of Paris. So we found ourselves riding right behind the general! That was pure luck.

— So you were part of the force that went into Paris.

— Oh yeah. I took part in the liberation of Paris and we came in and Germans were running down the street and the free French were shooting at them, even though people were sitting at tables, drinking their cocktails. They never budged. They didn't run away! I'd have ducked under the table, but they didn't. Finally then we got hugged and kissed by a lot of the girls and some of the men, you know. We'd push the men away. We went into a bar, my friend Joe Pihodna and I; there was a big mural over the bar, and we ordered beer, wine or whatever, and were just getting our drinks when some of these girls, who had been part of the welcoming crowd, entered the bar and came up behind us. And they slipped their arms around our necks. They smelled real good too! They said, "Suckie suckie? Want a little suckie suckie?"

I said, "No, thanks. Not today."

Pihodna said, "Girls, you're pretty and you're very enticing, but we're married men!"

They just giggled and laughed, "What difference does that make?"

Joseph Pihodna came from a Czechoslovakian background, and he'd gotten into the Army the way I did. I think he'd been with the *Herald Tribune* in New York. I don't know what became of him. We kept in touch for a while after the war. We were in Paris for about ten days, and I ran into Hemingway's ex-wife. I said, "Where's Papa?"

She said, "I don't know where he is! And I hope he breaks his goddamned neck!" So I knew their marriage was over.

— Did you run into Hemingway?

— I saw him, but I didn't say anything to him about what Martha said. She was furious, because he had so many girls.

— Was he writing for a newspaper at that time?

— Yeah, he was a correspondent. He had two pistols, like Patton. He wasn't supposed to carry guns, but he did.

— Patton was a character.

— With his silver mounted pistols, General Patton was a cowboy, very flamboyant; but he got in trouble for slapping a soldier.

— That's right, in Italy wasn't it?

— Yes, it was at an aid station, and the soldier didn't want to go back to the front. The general whacked him. "You coward!" He apologized later, at the insistence of Eisenhower, who said, "You'd better apologize! The folks back home are demanding I send you home!" Patton and Ike were good friends, but Ike couldn't overlook what Patton had done.

— Where were you assigned after Paris?

— We were sent to Lille, a town up on the Belgian border; we had nice quarters there. It was a vacated apartment building, and we had good beds.

— What was your assignment?

— The Battle of the Bulge had started. We covered the wounded. We were on the edge of the battle. The Germans struck through Belgium and into Northern France to try and reach the ports on the channel. If they got control of those ports, they could bring in more supplies. But they didn't quite make it; our forces were mobilized just in time to cut them off. I remember our commanding officer gathered us and said, "Sorry to tell you, boys, you're doing good work here, but headquarters says 'any man under 30 is going to be sent to the front.'" Lucky for me, I'd just had my 30th birthday a few weeks before!

— Luck of the Irish.

— Some of those guys who were rushed to the front never got home. They sent them right up to the front, and they got killed. Meanwhile I was back there praying.

I remained in Lille, where I was attached to a field hospital. I was interviewing all these poor guys who were brought in. They'd bring them in; they were bleeding and screaming for their mothers. They never screamed for their fathers. I don't know why. Some of them had lost eyes, legs; I don't want to think about it. You were writing for home newspapers. You didn't want to emphasize the bloody side of war. I'd find out where a wounded soldier came from, and then we'd write a story, for his local paper, "Corporal So-and-so was wounded in battle today. He showed extraordinary bravery." The Army gave all of the wounded medals before they died. The stories were sent to the hometown paper; some of them appeared in *Stars and Stripes*. Anyway, I published stories about people in the Infantry, the artillery. God, some of the wounds those guys had. Terrible.

— These must have been very difficult years for your parents?

— My father thought I was going to get killed. He didn't want me to go. He'd been so badly wounded, you know. He had nightmares all his life.

— What were your views on the war? Were you in favor of the United States entering the war before Pearl Harbor?

— I was opposed to our getting into it. But as the war went on, and also things were brought out by people like Harry Truman, I saw that Hitler had to be stopped. Truman made a speech in 1943, using information made available to him as a senator, calling on all the countries to open up their free lands for Jewish immigrants from Germany. He said, "I have enough information to know that terrible things are going on there. They are building camps. They are going to destroy many thousands of the Jewish people." He made the speech in Chicago. It got no reaction from the White House, and this has always baffled me. Franklin D. Roosevelt was a humanitarian, obviously cared about the poor and all that. Why was it he didn't act when Truman and others begged him to? He must have known about it. It's one of the mysteries of history. Many of his friends were Jewish. Jews had helped him get into the White House. Yet he seemed to ignore the reports of the slaughter there.

Truman was one of the early ones to call for action, as early as '43. I suppose it's one of the reasons why he always had strong Jewish support.

THE HOME FRONT

— How long did Barbara stay in Cambridge?

— She stayed in Boston for that winter, and when I went overseas in the Army, she returned to New York, and got another job at the Red Cross, and moved back to our New York apartment and stayed there until I came home in June of '45. She went through all that rationing, but she never talked about that very much. She was so eager to get back to our normal life.

She was living with a friend of hers, named Margery Hanson, who she knew from Kansas City, while I was away overseas in the Army. One night she woke up and she saw a man on the fire escape. She lived on the second floor. New York apartments had these new fire escapes in front of their windows. And she called to the man: "Get down from there! What are you doing here?"

And he said, "Oh well, lady, I'm drunk. I just want to come through your apartment."

She said, "You're not going to come through my apartment." There was a merchant seaman, who lived in the apartment above us in Patchin Place. And Barbara got up, went up to the apartment of the seaman and knocked on the door and told him there was a burglar outside on the fire escape.

"Ah, you're just imagining things." So he and his wife went to the window. "By God, there is." He said, "Yeah I'll get my gun." He said to the man on the fire escape, "I got a bead on you. You better get the hell out of my sight." This guy went rapidly down the fire escape. That was the only adventure she had while I was away.

— Did Barbara save any of your letters?

— I've got a bag full of letters from her somewhere. We wrote a lot. She wrote me a lot of V-mail. You know those little mails that we got while overseas?

— What happened to your friends from Kansas City?

— Shelby volunteered. He went in the Navy and became a pilot. Bill Kalis also became a Navy pilot. Joe Guilfoyle went into the Navy as a regular Naval officer. Dick Barnes was killed in training to be a pilot down in Florida. So we felt the war in that way.

COMING HOME

— Did you return home by troopship?

— No. I got to fly home because my mother was injured in a fall and my father had a heart attack on V-E Day. And the Red Cross put in a word for me. I was in France at the time. Otherwise it would've taken me I don't know how long to get home.

— Do you know the date or the time when you got word of your father's death?

— It was V-E Day. My father was listening to the radio and when he heard that the Germans had surrendered. He got up and yelled, fell over, and died.

— Heart attack?

— Yes. He'd been very afraid that I was going to be killed over there because he heard that the fighting had gotten more intense and Hitler was throwing his last troops into battle. He knew I was on the edge of the Battle of the Bulge. Mother was worried, too. My mother was a worry wort. "We haven't heard from Frank for weeks!" Then they got a little V-mail and it had red spots on it and my mother said, "Oh my God! That's blood!" Of course, it wasn't blood.

— Amazing that your father died on V-E Day!

— Yes, on V-E Day, at the hour of victory! My mother tried to pick him up. He wasn't as heavy as I am, but she thought she had to get him up and get a doctor. And she slipped and fell. I don't know whether she had a hemorrhage or what, but she broke something. My sister just came home and my sister said, "Oh God, let's call an ambulance for both of them." And then my sister got in touch with the Red Cross and she said, "Both Frank's father and mother had a terrible thing on V-E Day. His father died and his mother suffered some kind of a heart collapse and she's out in the research hospital." So then the Red Cross came in and told my commander that I should be given compassionate leave.

— Then you managed to come home?

— I got home right away; a lot of the guys didn't get back for months. I was one of those who had the privilege of flying across the Atlantic on a DC-4. I was sitting next to this Infantryman, who had been wounded and he'd never been in a plane before, a huge muscular guy, he almost choked me to death.

"Hey guy, is this all right? Is this all right? I'm scared to death," he kept saying.

I said, "Listen man, you've been in combat. You've gone through things that would scare me. It's fine."

"Have you ever been in a plane before?"

I said, "Yeah, once, it was wonderful."

"Sure it's all right?"

I said, "Yeah."

And then we had to make an emergency landing. We landed in Newfoundland. He survived it. So I had a little adventure coming home from Europe, too. Then we got on another plane, and landed, I guess it was, on Long Island. I got into town, and surprised my wife in Patchin Place.

— Were you able to get back in time for the funeral?

— No. It took a week or so to go through the red tape, and by the time I made it back my father had already been buried. It was around the seventh or eighth of May 1945.

DROPPING OF THE ATOMIC BOMB

— Where were you when the atomic bomb was dropped?

— I was in Jefferson Barracks, in Saint Louis, Missouri. I'd come back from the European phase of the war, and I was in the Jefferson Barracks, a huge military installation. There were thousands of us there, having been brought back from Europe. The word that we were given was that we were being prepared to go to the Pacific. The fighting was still going on fiercely, and we were all very depressed and sad about the idea. So we cheered when Truman announced that the Japanese were going to surrender.

My wife was in St. Louis. We were allowed to have our wives living near the barracks, and I thought, oh God I don't want to leave her for another year and a half, and go over to the Pacific. Nobody did. So then out of the blue came this announcement, that President Truman had ordered the dropping of the atomic bomb on Japan. Two days later the Japanese surrendered, and we were thrilled, we thought it was great. Nobody in that barracks said, "Oh he shouldn't have done that. Or why did he do it?" We just said, the war is over!

When I talked to Truman later, in the White House, I asked him about how he could bring himself to use such a horrible weapon. He said he put in many nights of painful thought about it and came to the conclusion he had to do it. We were in hell and he wanted to get us out of hell, which was kind of a naive assumption. But I never heard anybody talk about the atomic bomb decision the way Truman did.

When I interviewed him in 1949, he made it evident that he felt God had enabled the United States to develop atomic weapons ahead of all the other countries. He was the

Commander-in-Chief of the American armed forces. Therefore, he thought he had the freedom and responsibility to decide what to do with those awesome weapons. He called it, "the most terrible decision that any man in the history of the world has had to make."

I was on active duty when Truman made the decision. I do not regret the fact that I joined in the cheers that came from the soldiers at Jefferson Barracks. Like Truman, we had learned that war is hell—and a war with nuclear weapons might lead to the end of life on earth. As soldiers with personal experiences of war, we knew we had to devote our postwar lives to peace and justice.

NEIMAN FELLOWSHIP—CLASS OF '46

— What do you remember about your return to Harvard for the completion of your Neiman Fellowship?

— In the Neiman class of 1946, there was one man who had quite an impact on me: Leon Svirsky. He was an editor of *TIME* magazine. When he got to Harvard, he persuaded the Fellows to do a book on the "American Newspaper", and how it was covering the big issues of the time, and how it was failing. When I came there, he asked me to write one of those chapters, and contribute to it. So I was listed as one of the contributors, or co-editors. Macmillan published the book, and it was called, *Your Newspaper.* It was a really strong critique of the whole American newspaper business. And I am very proud that I took part in that.

—Which chapter did you write?

— I don't remember. I contributed ideas to all of them. *Your Newspaper* was published in 1947 or '48. And that, in a way, also had an impact on my life because when the time came for the International Press Institute in Geneva, when they got a big grant from the Ford Foundation to do a study of the flow of world news, my friend McNeil Lowry, a former correspondent for the *Dayton Ohio News*, called me up. I was just at the end of the Harriman Campaign, and he said, "Frank, if Harriman doesn't get the nomination, would you consider going to work for the International Press Institute, and be our United States director, and coordinate the studies of all the major American Newspapers?" That appealed to me a great deal. I think he had read *Your Newspaper*, so it just shows you how one thing leads to another. It's amazing.

CIVIL COURAGE:
THE PUBLIC SQUARE

— When did you return to the Associated Press after the war? Do you remember the date?

— In December 1945, I got an Honorable Discharge at Jefferson Barracks. And I got on a train with my wife and we went to New York and I started work for the Associated Press sometime around the middle of December 1945. I stayed with the Associated Press until early in 1946, when I was offered a job as an information specialist for the United States Housing Agency.

DANCER FITZGERALD SAMPLE

I stayed with the Housing Agency about a year, from '46 to '47. In 1947, the 80th Congress came into power, a Republican dominated Congress. They abolished the National Housing Agency. All of us were out of jobs. Then I was offered a place at a big public relations agency—Dancer Fitzgerald Sample. I was with the agency from 1947 to the spring of 1948.

The agency had some interesting clients, like the Creole Petroleum Company, one of the biggest oil companies. They were located in Venezuela, and I had actually gone down to

Venezuela to write a book for the company based on operations at an oil field there. We also had the Pennsylvania Railroad, which was a delightful client to have too, but I got awfully tired of writing out little booklets about the company.

— When were you asked to join the 1948 Truman campaign as a speechwriter? It must have been about this time.

— I was in Boston when I received a call from the White House. It's all included in my book on Truman, *Harry Truman and the Human Family*. It's right over there. If you'd hand it to me, I'll read the passage where I got the phone call. Lets see, here it is:

> …The ringing of the telephone close to my bed aroused me from a troubled dream. When I opened my eyes, brilliant sunlight dazzled me. I seized the receiver. "This is the White House calling," a strong feminine voice informed me. "We want to talk to Frank Kelly. Is he there?"
>
> In my days as a reporter for the Associated Press and the *Kansas City Star* I had made many calls to disturb people, and I had received calls of many kinds. But the mention of the White House shook me. I didn't have any connection with the incumbent president, although I had seen him several times in Kansas City. The book I had just finished for the *Atlantic Monthly Press* dealt with Truman's drive to compel Joseph Stalin to remove Soviet troops from Iran or risk a war. But I didn't think anybody on Truman's staff had heard about the book.
>
> "What kind of a gag is this?" I said, sitting up in the bed. "Is it not a gag, sir," the telephone operator said sharply. "Am I speaking to Mr. Kelly?" "You are," I answered. "What do you

want?" "Just a moment," she said. Then a hearty masculine voice boomed into the receiver. "Frank, this is Bill Batt. I'm calling you from Clark Clifford's office. President Truman is going to make two or three hundred speeches this year and he needs some writers. We've been told that you're a good one. A friend of yours has informed us that you've just done a book about Truman's handling of the crisis in Iran, and he thought you might be available." That's how the invitation came.

It turns out that Kenny Birkhead, an old friend from Kansas City, had been asked by the Truman campaign to help staff what was to be a Research Division at the Democratic National Committee, and he had recommended me.

THE 1948 PRESIDENTIAL CAMPAIGN

— Did you have any misgiving about going to work for Truman as a speechwriter, given that his reelection looked like an uphill battle?

— When I was offered the job, I asked my friends, "Should I take the job with Truman?"

"Oh no, he's a dead duck, Frank." One friend said if I worked for Truman, I'd be regarded as subnormal mentally the rest of my life. Truman was dead! Every political expert unanimously said that Dewey would beat him and Truman won. After living through that campaign, I can have a lot of hope that experts can be wrong.

— What was it like being a speechwriter for Truman?

— He was making many speeches a day. We turned them out as fast as we could go. That's a lot of speeches to do, and all together I wrote a large number of speeches. I wrote on so many different topics. It's amazing.

— What were his strengths as a politician?

— Truman knew who he was, what kind of position he was in, and he was going to stand on it. His mother told him that. "Harry, do what's right." When Truman got the word that his mother was very ill, he got on the plane, and he laid down to take a nap during the flight, and she appeared to him in a dream. This is about the same time she died and in the dream she was saying to him, "Harry, you be good. There you go. That's Harry. Harry, you be good." He tried to be good, because he felt his mother was watching over him.

— In *Truman*, David McCullough establishes just how little Truman knew about what FDR was doing—including the Manhattan Project. Do you agree?

— Yes. When Roosevelt died Truman didn't know much of anything.

— How much did he lean on Mrs. Roosevelt during those first few months following FDR's death?

— A lot. When he went down to the White House, Mrs. Roosevelt greeted him and said, "Yes, the president is dead." And then she said to Truman, "Now you're the one who needs help. You have the burden of the presidency. What can we do to help you?" And that touched Truman a great deal. He said, "I'll want all the help you can give me, Mrs. Roosevelt. I want your advice and your assistance." And she said, "Everything I can give, I will give to help you."

JOSEPH STALIN

— Did you ever talk to Truman about Stalin?

— Oh, a little bit. He said that he thought Old Joe, as he called him, reminded him of Tom Pendergast. I said, "Oh, he does?"

He said, "He's a tough guy, doesn't talk very much, but he expects his orders to be carried out just the way Tom did."

And I said, "Did you tell Stalin about the atom bomb when you were at Potsdam?" It was after the successful test.

"Well, I didn't use those words because it was still a secret, Frank. I said, 'We have a new weapon that's the greatest in the world; with enough fire power to bring about victory in the war'".

I said, "What did Old Joe say to that?"

He said "He never showed any change of expression, he just said, 'That's fine. I hope you will use it as soon as possible'". Of course Stalin knew all about it. But Truman didn't know Stalin knew. That's about all I remember about Truman and Stalin.

— How open was Truman to reporters' questions? Was he scripted, and on message?

— Oh, very open. Well see, we felt right at home because we were both born in Missouri, we both were in combat zones in wars; we both were from Kansas City in a way. So I just always felt, whenever I was talking to Truman, it wasn't like talking to a stranger. He knew my Uncle Joe. My Uncle Joe was active in the Democratic Party in Kansas City.

And he said this to Charlie Ross, his press secretary. Charlie scolded him for telling me a lot of stuff about the atomic bomb, which was top secret.

"Mr. President, you told Frank all these things. What kind of a clearance does he have?"

Truman looked at him and said, "Oh, come on Charlie, I know his family in Kansas City. I'll give him top clearance." Isn't that incredible?

— It is, and very human. It's what we're missing today.

— Whenever I talked with Truman, it was always man-to-man, person-to-person. That's the way he was.

— Did you ever go for a walk with him in the morning?

— No. I wish I had. The secret service men told me about it. It was incredible. He'd be walking down the street, waving at people and people would come over to him and say, "Mr. President, how are you doing?" "I'm doing pretty well. How about you?" Everybody would talk to him and he'd talk to them.

— Down-to-earth.

— Yeah. And he put his own letters in the mailboxes on the street. He'd write letters to people expressing his views; like the letter he wrote to Paul Hume, the music critic, denouncing him for writing a bad review of Margaret's recital. He had his own little package of stamps that he put on the letters and popped them in the mailbox. The secret service men sometimes asked him about these letters, and he'd say, "Nothing to worry about, boys, nothing for you to worry about."

The staff didn't even know what he was doing. When those senators got those letters, they'd hit the ceiling.

— But he had substance to him.

— Oh did he, my! And he had a prayer, which is in my book, "Lord, make me honest, keep me honest, don't let me say anything that isn't really true just to make myself sound important." Not many public people pray like that.

— What about his sign: "The Buck Stops Here"?

— I saw it, but then everybody did within the Oval Office. I don't know who gave him that. Anyway he did take me over there. Eisenhower gave him a globe, a big globe he had in the Oval Office, and Truman said to me one day: "Let me show you something." He turned this globe and pointed out all these countries and said, "In every one of those countries, Frank, people are living in terrible poverty. They're practically starving. Now, with my Point Four Plan we're going to bring all those people up out of poverty. The whole world is going to have enough to eat and clothes to wear, and shelter. We're going to do it." That was his dream.

— Having served on both sides of Pennsylvania Avenue, how would you rate his ability to get programs—like his Point Four program—through Congress?

— He wasn't good at that. No. And part of it was the political reality of the time. When he was elected he didn't carry with him a liberal Congress. The coalition, they called it, of Southern Democrats and Republicans, dominated Congress most of the time even when Roosevelt was president. They could block Roosevelt, too.

So when he came up with a plan for national health care and women's equal rights, the boys on the hill could block it! And I got so frustrated working for the Senate and watching this happen that I decided I'd leave. After four years I just had to leave. It just wasn't going to change.

Here we are—59 years after Truman proposed national health care—still trying to forge ahead on this issue. Why haven't we found enough political capital to defeat the opposition? Why is there such resistance to meeting such a basic need, as universal health care?

It's the lobbies. The lobbies are so powerful in Washington; the medical insurance lobbies, doctor's lobbies, of course the American Medical Association, which was the richest lobby when I was there, all oppose any change to the status quo. When I worked for Senator Lucas, who stood for reelection from Illinois for the Senate in 1950, we were beaten by Everett Dirksen, and the fact was that in every town, the doctors gave out booklets against him. Lucas voted for Truman's socialist healthcare plan; that really hurt him. And the doctors paid for the negative ads. I don't know how Lyndon Johnson got a health care plan—Medicare—through a few years later.

— Who was the author of Truman's health plan? Do you remember?

— I don't remember. I don't know. In a president's office there are so many people going out, so many people working on the president's legislative programs that it's hard to single out one individual as the author. As Truman said,

"The American people expect so much of a president that no one man can do the job." And you're crazy even to think you can do it because you're expected to be the foreign policy maker, the chief legislator, the man who controls the judicial system; it's an enormous job. It's beyond human capacity. And yet, I think it was actually Truman who said, "The American people have one lobby and that lobby is the President of the United States." He was put on the ticket in 1944 by Roosevelt's advisers, because of the Truman Committee. Truman's investigation of the war effort had exposed countless examples of graft, and saved the taxpayers billions of dollars. Truman became so popular the Democratic bosses decided that it was time to get Henry Wallace off the nomination for vice president, and to bring in a man like Truman who had a reputation, in the eyes of the public, of somebody who was going to save them a lot of money because he was honest.

— Did he ever talk about how difficult the transition was to Commander-in-Chief in the middle of a war, having to deal with General Marshall and the diplomatic decisions he now faced?

— Oh yeah, he was really floundering at first. He told me that, "When somebody would say, 'The president is here.' I'd look around and say, 'Oh! I'm the president.'" Or that FDR had come back or something. So for the first year or two I think he was not a strong president. He made some mistakes in the first couple of years.

— Did you ever talk to him about Potsdam?

— Oh yeah a little bit, in more than one conversation.

— What did he think of Stalin?

— I asked him if he told Stalin about our having the atom bomb. And he said, "Yes, I told Marshal Stalin that we had this new weapon with tremendous power, but I didn't say it was an atomic weapon, because I didn't want to give away any secrets." And, I said, "Uh, what did Stalin say?" He said, "You know, to me he said, 'Mr. President, I hope you will use it as soon as possible to get the war over.' And that's what I planned to do. But Stalin encouraged me to use it." Of course Stalin knew more about it than he admitted, but Truman didn't know that. He liked Stalin. He told me that at the meetings at Potsdam, Stalin was a very impressive—very quick mind—and very good in the meetings at responding to points that were brought up. He thought he was a brilliant person. He said that Stalin reminded him of Tom Pendergast, the boss of Kansas City.

— What a comparison. Tom must be turning in his grave right now, and Stalin would shudder at the thought.

— That was Harry's way of describing people, "Oh he reminds me of old so-and-so."

— Much is made of his reading habits, and perhaps one of the most repeated stories about him is that he had read every book in the library as a boy growing up in Missouri. Did you get a glimpse into just how well read he actually was?

— Oh, in the campaign he had a book and somebody asked him about it, "What's that you're reading, Mr. President? *How to Beat Tom Dewey*?" He said, "Oh no. I'm reading a new book on the French Revolution." That's the kind of mind he had. He was constantly reading. He'd probably read as much as any man who ever sat in the White House. And you know he only finished grade school. Just an avid reader. Read everything. Someone said, "Aren't you studying the issues of the campaign?" "No, I already know those." He was relaxed and open, and down-to-earth. He was one of the people, and it came across.

I felt a great kinship with him because I'd been the same kind of kid he was. Truman said to me, "You know, Frank, as a boy, I wasn't very good at baseball or any of these games, so I spent a lot of time in the library." I said, "I did too, Mr. President. I was always down there reading and reading and reading." He said, "That's the way I was too, because nobody wanted me to play on the soccer team or the baseball team." I said, "Same with me." So we had a kinship there.

THE 1948 CAMPAIGN

— You mentioned that the speeches he gave during his whistle stop campaign were typed on cards for Truman.

— They were put on cards for delivery from the back end of the train at each of the stops that were made along the way.

— So those speeches were more spontaneous then?

— A lot of it was spontaneous. We gave him certain themes and we gave a lot of material that we had gathered about the town, and we called it in to the staff on the train ahead of each stop. We talked to everybody we could in the towns that were on the route. So when Truman was going through Illinois, he was going to stop at five or six towns. We would talk to the mayor and we'd talk to the newspaper editors, and women leaders. We asked all kinds of people:

"What's going on in your town? What are you worried about? What's the exciting thing? Good thing?" So we worked those items into these little whistle stop speeches. And he'd come out at the end of the train and talk about world affairs, you know, dealings with Stalin and all that. And then he'd say, "By the way, I hear you have some good news in your town here." And he'd mention them. People would say, "Good God, the president knows what's going on in our town!" I think that was one of the secrets to how he won.

— Who came up with that idea?

— I've forgotten, but it was probably Charlie Murphy, maybe Clark Clifford, or one of the people close to him.

— Were you ever on the train with him?

— No. We were supplying the stuff that was put on the train.

— So this was all done by Teletype?

— Some Teletype, and some by sending a plane ahead of the train, with a load on board of enough speeches for the next three or four weeks. All together, he delivered hundreds of speeches that year. I was with him up in Boston. My first book was coming out with *Atlantic Monthly Press*, and I went up there to get a copy, so I told George Elsey on the White House staff, that, "I hope to join the Truman party there."

He said, "Sure. I'll give you a note for the Secret Service."

So I got up there and after I had gone over to the *Atlantic Monthly Press* and picked up the first copy of my book, I went over to the hotel where Truman was staying, and got in there; he was playing the piano and having a good time.

He said, "Time to go, boys." And we went down to get into the waiting cars. I knew Dr. Graham, who was there in the crowd of course. He always was with the president because there's always a danger of an attack on the president, and a need for a doctor.

So I said, "What car am I supposed to ride in?"

Dr. Graham said, "Ride with me."

So I get in the car right behind the president and we started off and I've never seen such a mob in my life. The streets of Boston were absolutely packed and people were screaming and throwing confetti, I don't know what it was, but some kind of paper. So I said to this beefy Irish cop, when we had to stop, I said, "How does this crowd compare with the number of people who came out to see Roosevelt during his campaigns?"

The cop looked at me and said, "Roosevelt never drew a crowd half as big as this. We like Harry up here."

So we get to this conference hall where he was going to speak, a big auditorium in downtown Boston, so we get out of the car, and the president went on the platform. Then came the press guys. As they were coming in I said, "What do you make of this crowd, boys?"

"Oh, Kelly, you know they like him; everybody likes Truman but they're not going to vote for him."

I said, "Really? They turn out like this and they're not going to vote for him?" That's how wrong they were. There were people denying what was right in front of their eyes, and they did it all the way through. The pollsters were wrong, too.

Truman gave a rip-snorting speech in Boston that night against communism, about how the Republicans accused him of being soft on communism. He really tore that to shreds. Truman was not an orator in the sense that Franklin Roosevelt was, but once he got going, he could deliver a pretty good speech.

Here is an excerpt from that Boston Speech:

President Truman...

THANK YOU, thank you very much. I can't tell you how very much I appreciate that magnificent reception. And the reception on the street this afternoon was something out of this world.

Thank you, my good friends and fellow citizens.

Twenty years ago another Democratic candidate for president came to Boston. He was that great, outstanding American, Alfred E. Smith.

You gave him a tremendous reception. And when the cheers had subsided, he took all of you to his heart with one phrase. He said, "It's good to come home."

I know just how Al Smith felt. For Massachusetts is home to every American who loves freedom and trusts the people.

From the first days of our Nation, the spirit of the men and women of the Bay State has impressed upon American life the love of freedom and the hatred of tyranny.

Even before the end of the Revolutionary War, Massachusetts freed her slaves—all of them—because the people held that liberty was not for any one race or creed.

Here in Boston, you still stand among the Nation's foremost fighters for freedom and against intolerance.

Now, many of you recall that campaign of 1928, when Al Smith ran for president against that well-known engineer, Herbert Hoover. He was one engineer who really did a job of running things backward.

That campaign of 1928 was one of the most shameful political campaigns in our history.

A vile whispering campaign was spearheaded by the Ku Klux Klan and by Klan-minded people to discredit Al Smith. The Republican appeal was based on religious prejudice because of Al Smith's Catholic faith.

The leaders of the Republican Party served notice on America then and there that they would stop at nothing in order to gain power.

Don't think that the elephant has changed his habits in the last 20 years. This Republican elephant is not that kind of elephant. They're trying to make you believe he has that new look, but he hasn't.

That Al Smith campaign of 1928 was fought with different arguments from those we hear today. But, fundamentally, the issue was the same—that is, the rights of all the people against special privilege for the few.

I have often thought what a different and better world we would have had if Al Smith had been elected president.

But that didn't happen. And the great engineer we elected backed the train all the way into the waiting room and brought us to panic, depression, and despair.

Here at home, we had boom and bust.

In our dealings with other countries, we had Republican high tariffs, political isolation, and economic confusion—forces that helped to bring on World War II.

I say to you people of Boston that if Al Smith—and not Herbert Hoover—had been chosen president in 1928, we and the world would have been spared untold misery and suffering.

Unfortunately, there was no mechanical Republican substitute for Al Smith's great heart. No engineering equivalent could be found for his moral courage, his passion for justice, and his love of humanity.

After the Republicans had made such a mess of our domestic welfare and world security, we brought to the presidency a Democrat—that courageous leader and great humanitarian, Franklin D. Roosevelt.

Under Roosevelt's leadership, we licked the Hoover depression, we rebuilt a strong America, and we won the greatest war in all history.

I am proud to have been a part in Roosevelt's great fight for the rights and liberties of humanity.

At the end of the war, in 1945, the people of this country were more prosperous than ever before in their history. The Democrats planned it that way. And in spite of the scorn and derision which the Republicans in Congress expressed about government planning, that planning paid off.

Labor was stronger than ever before. The farmers were more secure than ever before. Business was making more money than ever before. Our homes and our earnings were protected against inflation and rising prices.

We seemed to be headed for a period of safe and wholesome progress in this country.

But in November 1946 we suffered a misfortune which now threatens to destroy our hopes and our safety with a new wave of blind and selfish reaction. Two years ago, when it was the responsibility of the people to elect a new Congress, millions of Americans failed to vote. Almost two-thirds of those entitled to vote did not vote. And the result was the notorious "do-nothing" Republican Congress—the Congress that owes its election to Democrats who didn't bother to vote.

You know the record of that Congress.

You know how it refused to deal with inflation and how it let prices keep on rising.

You know how it failed to provide low-rent housing and how it remained faithful to the slogan of "Two families in every garage."

You know how it played the game of big business lobbies at Washington and how it shackled labor with that awful Taft-Hartley law.

And now the Republicans tell us that they stand for unity. In the old days, Al Smith would have said, "That's baloney." Today, I think he would say, "That's a lot of hooey." And if that rhymes with anything, it is not my fault.

They made their great mistake when they decided that the election of 1946 was a mandate—a mandate, mind you—to destroy the New Deal.

Two years ago the people lost control of the Congress. Control passed to big business—to special privilege—to the owners of the Republican Party. Big business and special privilege have only one idea—to charge all that traffic will bear. Through the action of the 80th Congress they have given you warning of worse things to come.

But less than a week from now you will have a chance to regain control of your government. You can elect a Democratic Congress and a Democratic president.

My friends, there will never be a time in your life when you can spend two hours to better advantage than by voting on this election day, November the 2nd. For more than your prosperity hangs on the result of that decision.

The peace and freedom of the entire world depend on the courage and imagination of a people's government at Washington.

Yesterday, the free peoples of the world were threatened by the black menace of fascism. The American people helped to save them. Today, the free peoples of the world are threatened by the red menace of communism.

And again, the American people are helping to save them.

I think that I speak for every loyal American—Democrat and Republican alike—when I say that we detest what Communists stand for, and what they have done to the free peoples under their control.

If the people of some other country freely choose a Communist form of government, that is their own business. But we don't want any Communist government in the United States of America.

And if the people of other countries don't want communism, we don't want to see it imposed upon them against their will.

We have been taking positive and successful action, everywhere in the world, to halt the threat of communism.

There are some Republicans who have been trying to make you believe that your government is endangered by Communist infiltration. That is just a plain, malicious lie.

But that is not a new form of attack. The Republican candidate for president in 1944, who is trying again this year, said here in Boston—now listen to this—he said, right here in Boston—that Franklin Roosevelt was soliciting the support of Communists. He said that the Communists were seizing control of the New Deal.

Those statements were absurd and ridiculous. They were just as absurd as the reasons this same Republican candidate gave in 1944 as to why the New Deal could not provide jobs after the war. I wish you would ask him about that now.

Ask him how many jobs there are today. He was going to blame us if there were no jobs. So, if he will give us credit for the 61 million people working today, that will be all right. He won't do that. Sixty-one million!

I said 61 million people. There are more people at work today than ever before in the history of the country. There isn't a man in the United States who, if he wants a job, can't find one—and with good pay. I wish you would ask that Republican candidate sometime how many jobs the Republicans were providing in 1932.

All of this Republican talk about communism in 1944 and again this year is in the same pattern with their appeals to religious prejudice against Al Smith in 1928. They are afraid to go before the American people on the merits of the policies they believe in. So they try to distract the people's attention with false issues.

I want you to get this straight now.

I hate communism. I deplore what it does to the dignity and freedom of the individual. I detest the godless creed it teaches.

I have fought it at home. I have fought it abroad, and I shall continue to fight it with all my strength.

This is one issue on which I shall never surrender.

Now, my friends, the truth of the matter is, the Communists are doing all they can to defeat me and help my Republican opponent.

Just take a look at the facts.

The Communist Party of the United States is today supporting a third-party candidate in an effort to defeat me.

In State after State, the Republicans have worked to get this Communist-supported candidate on the ballot in order to defeat me, and with me, the party of the people who want no share of this unholy alliance.

You can all see the Republican point of view—it is anything to get votes.

But you may wonder why the Communists, with their supposed hatred for capitalism, are working night and day for the victory of the party of big business.

Well, I'll tell you why.

The Communists don't want me to be president, because this country, under a Democratic administration, has rallied the forces of all the democracies of the world to safeguard freedom and to save free people everywhere from Communist slavery.

Our goal is peace—a lasting peace in the world.

It is our conviction that peace in this atomic age is an absolute necessity. But only a peace that is based on human rights and freedom will be a lasting peace.

I propose to keep on doing my level best to win a lasting peace.

That must be done, not only for the people of the United States, but for people everywhere in the world.

In March of last year I announced a fundamental decision of your government, designed to preserve the freedom of the world. In stating that doctrine, I said: "It must be the policy of the United States to support free peoples who are resisting attempted subjugation by armed minorities or by outside pressures."

Our first step under that doctrine was to give economic and military aid to Greece and Turkey, two countries right under the shadow of Communist domination.

The whole world knows of the success of this policy. Now, the Communists will never forgive me for that.

This was only the first step in a broad program to check the spread of communism.

The next step was the European recovery program, known as the Marshall Plan.

You have heard of the heartening results which are now being achieved under this program in 16 European countries. Not only are hungry people being fed, but industries have been reconstructed and farms restored and railways and mines set in order.

As a result of these wise measures the European recovery program is driving back the threat of communism.

And the Communists will never forgive me for that, either.

Let's take three European countries—Italy, France, and Germany—and see why the Communists hate your president so bitterly.

Our aid has given Italy a new lease on freedom. Our aid has helped really decisive popular support for the freely elected government of Italy. It has shown the Italian people that they can solve their economic problems under democracy.

I wonder what would have happened to Italy without our help? I think we all know. The salvation of Italy from Communist tyranny is one of the great achievements of our recovery program.

And for that the Communists will never forgive me.

Our aid has also been a bulwark of free democracy in France. There, as throughout Europe, we are using our economic strength to raise the living standards of the people, and thus to avoid the danger of a Fascist reaction or a Communist tyranny.

And the Communists hold that against me too.

In Germany, we have taken the frank and firm position that communism must not spread its tentacles into the Western Zone.

We shall not retreat from that position.

We shall feed the people of Berlin, and the people of Germany will be given their chance to work out a decent life under a democratic government.

Now, the Communists hate me for that, too.

As an American, as well as your president, I resent the contemptible Republican slur that charges me with being "soft" where Communist tyranny is concerned.

Under your Democratic administration, the people of the United States have thrown themselves wholeheartedly into the support of freedom and democracy against the predatory pressures of communism.

Our sustained, unprecedented worldwide fight against the spread of communism has brought new hope to people everywhere in the world.

Now, on the strength of that record, it is clear why the Communists would like to bring about my defeat, and elect a Republican president.

But I am surprised that the Republican Party should lend assistance to this Communist intrigue.

Let me remind you that the Communist Party in this country reached its maximum strength in 1932, under a Republican president.

Communism thrives on misery. Human suffering nourishes the Communist menace. That menace withers away where there is prosperity, justice, and tolerance.

The real threat of communism in this country lies in the danger of another major depression. The real threat of communism lies in widespread unemployment and arrogant injustice, such as we had in 1932.

The real threat of communism in this country grows out of the Republican policies of the 80th Congress—policies which threaten to put an end to American prosperity.

The real threat of communism in this country grows out of the submission of the Republican Party to the dictates of big business, and its determination to destroy the hard-won rights of American labor.

You can fight communism on November 2nd with a Democratic vote, and you can defeat Republican reaction at the same time.

Reactionary Republican policies invited communism in 1932. We were saved then, but we cannot afford to take that risk again.

If the Republican candidate wants to rid the country of Communists—and I believe he has some of them right in his own State of New York—he ought to begin by shaking off the hand of reaction which now has a stranglehold on the Republican Party.

But somehow, I don't see him doing that.

It all falls into the same old Republican pattern—appeal to the passions of prejudice and intolerance, and hope to get the votes.

All I can say is that I'm proud to be a Democrat. We are engaged in a great crusade—a crusade for freedom, for tolerance, for the rights and welfare of all the people.

This fight is Al Smith's fight.

This fight is Roosevelt's fight.

And now it is my fight.

More than that, it is your fight.

And I'm proud to be making this fight with you for the things in which we believe.

With your help, and your courage, and your enthusiasm, we are going to win this fight on November the second.

— Do you think the problems he faced in his reelection campaign for the Senate convinced him that he could pull out another victory with hard work in 1948?

— I've never looked at it that way, but now that you mention it, there were a lot of similarities. When he ran for reelection to the Senate, nobody though he could possibly win but he said, "If I can go around the state and shake enough hands, that's the key to it and I'll win. Shake hands with people. Get close contact and they'll remember you." And this is true. He drove all over the state in his little Chevrolet and just won by an eyelash, and got re-nominated, and won the election to everybody's amazement. Truman was very popular in the Senate personally. When he went into the Senate Chamber—after being finally reelected— there was a big round of applause. He proved that even though the experts write you off, there's always a chance. And he won reelection to the Senate, the way he won the presidential election of 1948.

Truman cared about the people he met. I could see that. It's one of the things I liked about him. You could see it at a big political dinner, or at campaign rallies. Harry worked the crowd, but he wouldn't look over people's heads. A lot of politicians would, including Adlai Stevenson. He'd be shaking hands with you and looking, "Oh there's somebody over there I must see." But not Truman, he concentrated on you, and then he'd move on to somebody else.

TRUMAN WHITE HOUSE INTERVIEW

I interviewed Truman for a chapter in a book, on how he made his major decisions including the Berlin Airlift. He said, "Well, my mother told me to do what's right, whatever you face." He said, "The military boys came in here, Frank, and stood around the desk, and they weren't too sure about what we should do about the blockade of Berlin."

I said, "The military boys?"

And he said, "You know, the Joint Chiefs of Staff." That's what Truman called them. "They came with all their medals on, the military boys!" I love that. To him they were just the military boys. They weren't going to scare Harry Truman. Isn't that a great line?

— It reminds you of the way he handled General Macarthur during the Korean War, refusing to kowtow to him.

— Yeah, that was his style. You would've enjoyed him so much, because he would sit and talk in that Oval Office the way we're talking now. No pretenses. When we were talking about the atom bomb decision, Charlie Ross, his press secretary, was there, and Truman was telling me all this stuff. And Mr. Ross said, "Mr. President, you just told Frank a whole lot of stuff that's top secret. I don't know what clearance he's got."

And Truman looked at me and said, "Don't worry about it, Charlie. I know Frank's family in Kansas City. They're good people. He's got top clearance." Imagine that! That exchange would've made the current crop of bureaucrats spin on their heads.

When I asked him about his decision to use atom bombs on Japan, he was sitting on the other side of the desk in the Oval Office, and I could see the anguish in his face. People said he didn't feel the pain, but I could tell. He said, "It was a decision made in *hell*, Frank. Remember what old General Sherman said?"

And I said, "What did he say?"

"*War is hell.*" He said, "*We were in hell.* And General LeMay came in here and told me, 'Mr. President, don't use that atom bomb, we can burn up Japan from one end to the other.'"

I said, "What did you say to LeMay?"

He said, "I don't want to do that. I don't want to kill all these people. How many people will we have to kill if we use the atom bomb, maybe two or three hundred thousand? Let's do that, stop the damn war and get out of hell."

He said, "You know you have to take a certain position as president, but you're not always presented with two good alternatives. There was no good decision to make. Either we burn them up or we drop the atom bomb, neither one was good. I knew it was terrible."

Truman said, and he put it very bluntly, which was the way he put everything: "It was a decision made in *hell*, Frank."

I remembered what I'd learned about *hell* in Catholic schools. "What is *hell?* It's a place of everlasting torment that never stops, and war is like that." I went through that hellish suffering with my father. His torment never stopped. He was living because he stuck a bayonet in a German's belly and pulled it out, and the other guy didn't stick it in him. And he lived, but he never forgot that dead man that he had killed. So you don't get over that. That's hell.

My friends who were in the Air Force said they didn't fully realize what they were doing when they dropped bombs on cities. Later on they saw the pictures of the destruction and loss of life and said they'd never forget it.

— It says something about politicians making military decisions who have never experienced war.

— Truman had. Truman was a combat veteran, an artillery officer in World War I. He knew that I'd been in combat zones too. And I was talking to him man to man, not as a reporter to the president, but we were sitting there as two veterans.

— What were the circumstances that led to your getting this exclusive interview with Truman? Did he agree to an extended period of time for the interview?

— The interview came about because he was to be the subject for a chapter I had agreed to write for a book. The Overseas Press Club of New York decided they wanted to put out a book called *Men Who Make Your World*. And they asked Hal Boyle, my friend who was a correspondent for the AP, if he would do a chapter on Truman. And Boyle called

me up and he said, "I don't know anything about Truman. I don't even know how to get an appointment with him. How about you doing this? Would you want to write it?" And I said, "Well, sure. I'd love the opportunity." So I was chosen to write this chapter. The book is composed of a series of articles about people who had really changed our lives in important ways. My chapter on Truman is the first one in the book.

When I called the White House, I said I knew Charlie Ross a little bit. I said "I'm going to write this chapter in a book for the Overseas Press Club, and I am going to come down and I would love to talk to the president." Ross called me back and says, "Sure. The president's going to give you 45 minutes," which is a lot for a personal interview.

I went down to the White House, and Charlie was there with the president. We sat down, and Ross said, "Frank's going to write a story about how you shook the world." And Truman immediately laughed, and we had good footing. So I asked him about everything I could think of and he responded very candidly about his early days in the presidency and he said, "You know Frank, anybody who announces he wants to run for president or be president should be locked up as insane." He says, "This job can't be done by anybody." He said, "But I've got it and I'm doing my best."

— Where in the White House did the interview take place?

— It was in the Oval Office. And he took me over and showed me this globe in the Oval Office that Eisenhower had sent him when Eisenhower was the commander of allied forces in Europe. The globe was on a stand and as he turned this symbol of the earth around, he would touch different parts of it and say, "You know Frank, when my program of technical aid starts to operate. Look at this country here. Their standard of living is horrible. A lot of their people are starving. And we get this program going," he said, "All these countries are going to move upward. They're going to share in the great prosperity of the human race." That was his dream.

— He was a visionary in that way.

— Yeah. Yes he was. Think of all the aid and the programs we gave after the war; we put both Germany and Japan back on their feet. We revived our old enemies.

— It was an unparalleled achievement, do you agree?

— Yeah, I do too. I do.

President Truman presided over the rebuilding of two terrible enemies, and did it with absolute generosity. No fear. You know, after World War I, people wanted to keep Germany crushed. They didn't want it to come back because of the threat. According to Arnold Toynbee, the Marshall Plan was one of the great achievements of human history.

— Did he give you more than 45 minutes?

— He gave me a long time. I didn't keep track of the time. Neither did he. Finally as we were reaching the end, Matt Connelly—the president's appointment secretary—

stuck his head in and said, "Mr. President, you've got senators sitting out here for the last half hour. Are you ever going to get through with the interview?" They knew Truman very well. "Matt, take it easy," he said. "I'll let them come in when I want to. I'm going to finish this conversation with Frank." Once he decided to do the interview and time was set aside, he wasn't going to let anybody interrupt him.

— How'd you prepare for the interview?

— I knew a lot about him because I worked on the '48 Campaign, but my goal was to ask him in his opinion, what were the most important decisions he made and how did he make them. So that was the focus of the interview. I wanted him to be absolutely candid—and he was. He gave me a great gift. He gave me more trust than I had ever expected.

RESPONDING TO CRITICS

And Truman said, "You know, Frank," (this is the thing that several people have noted in that book. I put this quote in my book.) He said, "The Japanese are just as human as you and I are." And I said, "I thought so, Mr. President." Later on I thought, "Why would he say that?" But during the war we regarded them as slanty-eyed monsters. They weren't human!

Not so to Harry Truman. He said, "I thought of those poor Japanese children being burned up by our bombs and I wanted to get that killing over with. I hate killing. I hate war. So for me there was no question. They told me, the atom

bomb would shake the Japanese empire, and conventional bombs would never do it." So I said, "Let's, let's go with it."

— I'd like to ask a question about process here, Frank, were you just taking notes? Or did you just listen and then leave the room and write it up?

— Oh, I, I took notes. I don't know where they are now. Anyway, I took notes. He didn't mind at all.

And then we got on the Berlin airlift; I asked him if he considered the airlift one of his big decisions. "Well," he said, "I think so." He said, "What happened was the military boys came in the office here, Frank. The Russians really had us boxed in." So I said, 'Do we have a right to be in Berlin?' I asked the general in the Air Force. "Oh of course, Mr. President. General Eisenhower made an agreement with Marshall Zukov that we do." "Well," I said, "We're going to stay there. My mother told me, 'Do what's right come hell or high water.'"

Sometimes I wrote by hand but I think this one I typed up and sent it off to the editors in New York. Then this book came out, uh, later on.

— Did Truman make any corrections or any deletions?

— No, he said what I'd written was very accurate. Charlie Ross went over it, of course. Charlie said, "The president's very pleased with it." I had called the chapter, "Man Who Shook the World," but when they got it at the Overseas Press Club they changed it! They put in the headline, "Little Guy Who Shook the World." So I called up Truman and then Charlie and apologized. I said, "That wasn't

my title for it. I don't think the president's a little guy by any means." They put that title on because in those days Harry Truman was regarded as a little guy who just happened to be in power. It shocked me that they did that, because in the chapter I tried to convey the fact that he was no regular person. He had qualities of greatness.

Dropping the atom bomb was not a decision he wanted to make. When the book came out, I got letters from people saying, "how can you absolve this horrible man, who did the worst crime in history?" I really got some hell for it. I watched his face when I asked him, "Mr. President, could you just go over for me how you reached that decision?" And he told me with such painful terms that I knew. You know some people accuse him as being some flip guy, it's just another decision, bring it in, I'll settle it now. I'm a man that makes decisions, "the buck stops here" and all that stuff.

— It wasn't that way?

— Oh no. He was pained. But then when he said he was thinking of the Japanese people too. And other people wrote to me after the book came out, and said that they didn't believe that. They said, "Truman didn't care about the Japanese people. No other book that I read about Truman even mentions that he had any care for the Japanese." I said, "Well, all that I am telling you, unless you think I am lying, and that day in the Oval Office I took notes on it, he said that about the Japanese. He didn't want to kill any more; they were killing too many, so he wanted to use the bomb even though it would cause a lot of casualties, because he also had

been told that the Japanese Emperor would then go on the air and tell his people, "Now is the time to surrender. You fought brilliantly, and in a sense you really won the war militarily but then the Americans have come up with this monstrous new weapon, which is inhuman and so it is acceptable to surrender, because you have been hit by an inhuman, monstrous weapon."

— And it worked.

— It worked.

It is very interesting when you look at that. It says something about history, when people can say that he never did like them (the Japanese), how could you prove that? You can't get into the person's head. Unless you were to go through each one of his speeches and see what he said in reference to it.

— What were your plans after the '48 campaign?

— When Truman won his unexpected victory in 1948, I was working with the White House on speeches for the president. And they asked me, "Would you like to continue with a political job? We don't have any immediate openings on the White House staff, but we think you might be interested in working for the Senate." And I said, "No." I'd never been in a political campaign in my life and I didn't want to stay in politics. They didn't like that very much.

Before I knew it, I'd accepted a job offer from Boston University as a professor of communications. Right after accepting it, I got a call from the White House, asking if I'd be interested in being an administrative assistant to the senior senator from Illinois, Scott W. Lucas, who was in line to become the Democratic Senate Majority Leader, with Alvin Barkley having been elected vice president with Truman.

When Scott called me about the position, I congratulated him on his becoming Majority Leader. And he said, "I've heard some really good things about your writing and your interests, and I'm wondering if you'd be my assistant, and become sub-director of the Senate Policy Committee." I couldn't resist it. I went and talked to everybody who advised me not to do it. The only people who said, "Go ahead," were my wife, who always had the right side of advice, and my literary agent, a woman named Mary Abbott at a firm called Macintosh and Otis in New York.

So, I decided I would accept, but I told Scott that I had to first talk to the president of Boston University. Oh, he was sore. He was mad. He paced up and down his office. "You know how many people we appoint? He said: "We made you an associate professor to start with: that's a lifetime appointment. You said you were willing to write more books. You'll have plenty of time in the summer. And you want to go off and chase a will-o'-the-wisp in Washington?" That's the way he put it.

Boston University is huge, with thirty thousand students. So I said, "Well I'm awfully sorry, but I helped to get Mr. Truman elected. I got so excited at the fact that here was a man that everybody had written off and I want to see what he can do now that he's been elected." The president of Boston University closed the door to his office. And he said, "I can understand; you've got a great opportunity to go to Washington in a top job and you're completely free of any pressures, having previously told them you didn't want the job in the first place." So he said, "I guess you're probably right to take it." But he said, "Don't ever try to come back here on the faculty." I said, "No, sir, I won't."

Senator Scott Lucas was a down home farm boy type of politician, although he wore very expensive suits; he had a top tailor. His friends in Illinois, when I went back there with him, said, "Oh, Scott's gone Washington." I said, "What do you mean by that?" They said, "Well, he's not the man he was when he was out here, pitching hay and stuff." But he was a good senator: answered everybody's phone calls, and responded to his constituents' letters. The *Chicago Tribune* attacked Lucas because they didn't want another downstate farm boy, a Democrat, as the Majority Leader, but he beat them.

UNITED STATES SENATE

— What years were you in Washington?

— 1949 to 1953. When I worked for the Senate, we had air raid drills, especially for senators and staff, and there was a cavern under the Capitol, with shelters for us. But we would go down in there and we really took it seriously that the Russians were going to attack us with rockets. Looking back, it was a form of hysteria. And we went down into the shelter when there was supposedly an attack. We couldn't call our wives or our family and I kept thinking as I went down in there, what if we come up and the city is burned and my family's gone. What are we going to do? We're sheltered and protected because we're associated with a powerful group of senators, who were among the rulers of American society. Why was it that we, we could have this special place to go when the other people just had to take the chance?

— How often did you have these drills?

— Oh, probably not as often as I thought. But they are very vivid in my memory. We took it seriously.

I came to work for the Senate in January of 1949, just a few weeks before President Truman's inauguration. My first discovery was since I was the special assistant to the Senate Majority Leader, I could ride in his limousine whenever I wanted to, which was a lot of fun, all the way to the Capitol, get out of his car, and walk down the corridors to the Senate. I noticed a huge statue, which had the word "Glick" on it. So I asked one of the old men who were sweeping the halls, "Who in the world is that?" He says, "Ah, Glick. He's been standing there for many years, my friend, but nobody knows who he is." So I said, "Just for luck, I'm going to rub his big toe." So I rubbed Glick's big toe every day I worked for the Senate.

— Did you ever find out who Glick was?

— No.

You have the Senate dining room or cafeteria. The private dining room is where senators took their favorite constituents, or important people, leaders in their communities, or for people who came to Washington that had to be given some special dining and respect.

— Was that one of your responsibilities for Lucas? Did you occasionally have to take constituents there?

— I'd often have lunch there with Senator Lucas, and since he was the Majority Leader, the headwaiter bowed and scraped and brought us anything we wanted. That was in the Senate dining room. But then there was this big room called the Senate Cafeteria. It was officially called the Senate Dining Room. The room we were in was called something else. It was a semi-private dining room for senators only and their guests, special guests.

— What about the barbershop?

— I went one time. I got my haircuts usually in the Supreme Court barbershop; that was one of my privileges. One day I was outside waiting for a while, and this black man came along and says, "Come in, Mister, you're working for the Senate Majority Leader helping fight for civil rights. We'll give you priority." And there were two or three senators who were in chairs waiting too. And he turns to them, and says, "You gentlemen can wait a while."

— So you got up and he cut your hair.

— Yes, I got priority because the Senate was fighting over civil rights and I worked for the Majority Leader. And I'd written some of the hottest speeches favoring civil rights. The black barber knew I had done that. So he said, "Those senators can wait a while." So I got my hair cut in the

Supreme Court special barbershop of the United States. Isn't that funny?

SENATOR SCOTT LUCAS

— What were your responsibilities as assistant to the majority leader?

— I wrote his speeches and prepared agendas for the Senate, and he just took them and ran with them. He had a very small staff, with a few people in the Senate office building. Nothing like there is today. There were a lot of parties going on and lots of drinking. My wife and I went to one party given by an Admiral. His daughter was getting married. We went out to his house, and I completely forgot to give Lucas a speech he was scheduled to give that day. And I said, "Oh my God, I've got to meet Senator Lucas at the NBC headquarters downtown. I've got his speech about the program of the Senate for this year." So we drove fast through the traffic and I got there and Senator Lucas was pacing up and down and said, "Where's my speech? Kelly, you're late!" And he grabbed it out of my hand and went in the studio and sat down and began to read it on NBC. "This is what the Senate's going to do this year." He just read it without ever checking it.

He got by with it. And he trusted me, so that when he had to make a statement he would always ask me to write it for him.

— How large was his staff?

— Half a dozen top people. He had lawyers to draft any legislative proposal he wanted to take to the floor, and things like that, but he would go over the bill. They were all dependent on their staff then as they are now. I'd get—I don't remember the exact number, but something like 3,000 letters a day would come into his office: 90,000 a month. And he couldn't read them all.

He'd say to me, "Frank, are you checking the mail?"

And I said, "Yeah." We had a couple of guys who went through the mail and pulled out what seemed to be urgent and then they'd pass them to me. If I thought they were urgent I'd give them to the senator and then we'd try to act on the important letters. For most of the mail, though, we had electric typewriters in the basement of the Capitol, and girls sitting down there; and they would respond: "The senator wants to thank you for sending him your views and you can be sure that he will take them into consideration in voting on this bill or that bill. Thank you very much." Then his signature would go on. The senator never saw most of them.

He couldn't do any better, because we ran from one committee to another, too. The Majority Leader had a big hand in all the legislation. So we'd run from the Foreign Affairs Committee to the Agriculture Committee and the poor man was so harried he couldn't keep up with all that was going on. Nobody could. He was chairman of the Majority Policy Committee. The Majority Leader always had that job; it's the committee where powerful senators, chairmen of other committees, would come in and they would say, "This is what we'd like to get through the Senate." If the Policy Committee majority voted to adopt the proposed bill as part of the program, it usually had a better chance of getting through than any other legislation. It's the top committee in the Senate; they set the agenda for the floor.

— What did you know about Senator Scott Lucas?

— He was from downstate Illinois, from a farming family, a very, very conservative family, and a very cautious family. He was utterly shocked to be called a Communist by Senator Joe McCarthy and attacked by the "Wizard of Ooze", Everett Dirksen, who was in the House at the time and wanted to move over to the Senate. But my job with Lucas was very relaxed, because he was extremely busy with his work over in the Senate office building. Illinois is a big state with millions of voters, and every issue would result in a flood of letters; there were telegrams on both sides. He had the whole staff trying to figure out which way the trends were running. So I had a virtual domain of my own.

As Majority Leader, he had this huge office in the Capitol, with crystal chandeliers that two ladies would come and clean every couple of weeks so they'd be nice and sparkling. He gave that office to me. I had a window that looked out on the Capitol steps. The office was right in the center of the Capitol building, with the Senate and House wings on either side. I could see everybody coming in and out of the Capitol from where I was. It was the Senate Majority

Leader's private office, his public office was over in the Senate Office Building, and that's where he usually stayed.

Very few people got to the office I had. Then there was a little office down the hall where I had an assistant. So it was very cozy, and it was like belonging to some—I hate to use a snobbish word—an exclusive club. But it was.

Lucas was up for election in 1950. And he asked me to go out to Illinois and campaign for him. All my friends in the press said, "Oh, it'll be an easy ride. He's got a big majority with Illinois voters. You'll beat Everett Dirksen very easily." But I didn't like the fact that Scott Lucas had made one major mistake: he voted for the National Health Bill that President Truman had advocated. The American Medical Association went all out against the bill, and there were printed pamphlets in every doctor's office, denouncing Truman and Lucas and others who had voted for that bill. They called it "socialized medicine." And that was a terrible disaster. That was probably the major mistake that Lucas made. But health care was badly needed. He thought the voters would see the truth about it.

To raise money for the campaign, we had these big dinners and invited all the contributors, and we charged $100 or $200, as much as we could. We had a lot of those dinners and Lucas would call up all of his well-to-do friends. He was constantly fundraising. "Now's the time to pitch in for the good of the party, and the good of Scott Lucas." We had a copywriting agency, and an advertising agency. They did all the chores, and we didn't stoop to that. We used some polls, but relied largely on newspaper polls that were already done without any expense for us. Most of them right up to the last week or so had Lucas winning. It was like Truman beating Dewey but in reverse. But the week before elections the *Chicago Tribune* came out with this cartoon—I wish I could find it—in which Senator Lucas is stabbing an American soldier in the back with a bayonet, and blood is running out. The *Tribune* said that he'd betrayed the American soldier by supporting the Korean War. It was a terrible cartoon.

Lucas was defeated by Everett Dirksen and was succeeded in the Senate leadership by Ernest McFarland of Arizona.

SENATOR MCFARLAND

— How long did you work for McFarland?

— Until it became obvious, in the summer of 1952, that he was going to be defeated by Barry Goldwater.

— Did you work on his campaign in Arizona at that time?

— No.

— You didn't? So you stayed on the staff.

— He asked me to come out to Arizona and work there for him but I decided I couldn't.

— What was McFarland like?

— Very nice, very genial, very much like a friendly farmer. I'd go out to his house to work on a speech; he'd put his feet on the dining room table. He'd have on his socks and put his feet up on the table and tell me what his thoughts were. I'd make notes, and then write his speeches.

Personalities of the Senate

In those days I remember how dominant the Southern senators were. The Senate was really controlled by Dick Russell, Lyndon Johnson and some other senators who had seniority. Strom Thurmond was one. I remember Thurmond. What a character he was. He was a sexy guy. He married a young woman and had children by her. It was hard to get these guys to focus on Truman's program, because they thought Truman was an upstart. They had been in office twenty, thirty, forty years. It was like a dynasty, each one of them was like a baron with his own area and it was very hard for a president to get anything done.

There was only one woman senator then, Margaret Chase Smith, of Maine. Helen Gahagan Douglas ran from the House but was defeated by Nixon. Nixon did her in, in a way we won't go into.

— Sam Rayburn was a giant, very much of a giant as Speaker for the House of Representatives. How did you view him?

— A genial, old, bald headed man. I remember how embarrassed he was one night in Washington at a party, when Tallulah Bankhead came over to speak to Rayburn, who didn't have any women that anybody knows, and she says, "Come on, honey, let's go in the next room and fuck."

Speaker Rayburn turned bright red and everybody roared. He said, "No, I can't. Not right now, Tallulah."

— She knew what she was doing to him.

— Tallulah was absolutely uninhibited. But Tallulah had those qualities; she also had an ironic wit.

— Who was at the table?

— Oh, a whole bunch of people. It was a kind of reception, a bunch of people from Congress. I liked Rayburn. I didn't want to see him embarrassed. He was a very staunch defender of civil liberties.

I remember how old everybody seemed to me. I was 34, then, in 1948. I walked into the Senate and there were all these old guys, some of them walking very slowly. One of the first people I was introduced to was a senator in a frock coat—Senator Hoey. He still wore a frock coat! You know, like they wore back in the 1880's.

And I said, "I'm happy to meet you, Senator Hoe-ee." His name was spelled H-O-E-Y. He said, "It's Hoo-ey, son, Hoo-ey." And he clapped me on the back, almost knocked me over. So that's the first time I ever met a senator that admitted that he was involved in hooey. He literally told me that. "It's Hooey, son, Hooey." Senator Hooey. God knows how old he was, I don't remember.

— Who were some of the real characters in the Senate during the years that you were there.

— Oh, Senator Hoey was one. Senator Byrd of West Virginia was a very powerful senator. And when I was introduced to Byrd, I said, "Oh Senator, I hear you produce mighty good apples on your orchards down in Virginia." And he said, "Yes, son, they call me the Prince of Applesauce." And he laughed. He had a good sense of humor. These were men in their late 50s, 60s, some of them 80s, who were relaxed enough not to stand on their dignity, or be pompous.

Another man I liked very much was old Senator Green, Theodore Green of Rhode Island. He was 75 or 80 and he was one of the older members of the Senate. Of course now he doesn't seem so old. I was placed as staff director of the Senate Policy Committee where I met a lot of the older senators. It was only the old boys who sat on the Policy Committee. I remember we always had to have the door opened when Senator McKellar of Tennessee was going to attend a meeting, because when he walked, he walked sort of sideways, with I don't know, arthritis or what. And he'd come wobbling in sideways, and I'd have somebody, who would grab his arm, and pull him, and I'd balance him on the other side. "Come on, Senator." And I'd get him into his chair. That was quite a scene. Senator McKellar.

And then some of the stories they told when they attended the Senate Policy Committee meetings were a little lively at times. And Senator Alben Barkley said one day, "McKellar, I hear you've been down in Tennessee again, and that you've been fucking girls in bathtubs. Now that's not good for you. That'll injure your health." McKellar chuckled and said, "Oh Alben, Oh Alben." Everybody else just laughed. It was rumored that old McKellar would pinch a girl, a pretty girl when she went by; those were the days when senators got away with things.

THE LEGISLATIVE PROCESS

— Looking at the Senate, Republican versus Democrat, was it closely divided?

— It was closely divided, I don't remember the exact numbers, but it was very, very close, only one or two votes between the Republicans and the Democrats.

The relationship between the Republicans and the Democrats was pretty negative on both sides in a way. At one point the Minority Leader, Senator Kenneth Wherry of Nebraska, got so angry with Senator Lucas that he wouldn't speak to him directly. Wherry was a mortician. We called him the merry mortician from Nebraska.

Now, see, the Senate has a wide aisle. Lucas sat on one side and Wherry on the other. I think we were on the left. The majority leader sat there, and right next to him was my seat. And across the aisle was Senator Wherry's seat and his assistant was there. Sometimes they'd get mad at each other, and Senator Lucas would say, "Frank, I think Senator Wherry wants to convey a message to us, and you need to go over and talk to him." So I'd go over there and old Senator Wherry was red in the face. He said: "If you bastards are going with this bill, you better add this amendment." And he'd punch me in the side. "You tell Lucas," punch, punch. I'd have to put up with that. So I'd come back and say, "I can't tell you exactly what Senator Wherry said, but he's very angry and he punched me in the side, and that's a signal that they're really upset over there, and if you can work out some amendment that'll satisfy him we'll get along better." What I remember about that part of the negotiation was getting punched in the side by the Senate Minority Leader; not many people had that privilege, however.

SENATOR LYNDON JOHNSON

— Lyndon Johnson?

— Johnson was a big man, a tall man, a tough man. I don't know if you read the new book out about him, *Master of the Senate*, but in it Lyndon admits he would take any point of view just to get his way. He'd act like a liberal one week, and a conservative the next. Lyndon was an actor. He believed in civil rights but he didn't want to jeopardize it by alienating his following among the Southern Democrats, so when he was with the Southern Democrats, he'd use words like "nigger" and all that, but he wouldn't use that kind of language with the liberals. It was a miracle that a Southern president from Texas got the best civil rights bill through. That was '64, or 1965, right after his landslide election. No one knew exactly how he did it. But this book describes all the maneuvering he did and how he played one group off against another. He was a master of that. Nobody since Lyndon has been able to get a program through the way he could.

He got the War on Poverty through, and all the civil rights bills, and he was just wonderful. But he couldn't quite get a health care plan through, but he got part of it with Medicare.

THE JOHNSON TREATMENT

— What were your impressions of Senator Johnson? You must have had a few encounters with him while you were working for the majority leader?

— Oh Lyndon Johnson was the most impressive man I ever met in the Senate. Terrifying man though. I mean these guys were so incredible. Lyndon never tried to conceal it. He said, "I'll do anything to win boys: I'll lie, I'll twist your arm off your shoulder." He never made bones about it. He didn't pretend to be a gentleman. Of course Truman would never do things like that. He wanted to do the right thing, he never did the kind of stuff Lyndon Johnson did and so he didn't get much through. He got the Marshall Plan through because the Republicans decided to support it. And he did very well in foreign policy, but his domestic record was miserable. He knew it too. He was very frustrated. His friends didn't accomplish very much, because in spite of Truman's victory in '48, the Congress was controlled by this coalition of conservative Southern Democrats and conservative Republicans. We couldn't get any major bills through. That's why I resigned, finally. I couldn't stand it any longer. It was too frustrating.

I wanted leave in '52 and I had an offer of a job from President James Conant of Harvard to be the Washington director for the Committee on the Present Danger. It was an organization he had set up to make people aware of danger in the free world. But I wasn't able to take that job because Lyndon Johnson prevented me from doing so.

I told Senator McFarland of my decision to leave the Senate and accept Conant's offer. I was in McFarland's office when Johnson came in and was told that I was going to leave. Johnson felt that McFarland couldn't function without a good speechwriter and advisor. So he said, "Mac, why don't you call the Pentagon and have Kelly drafted. Give him any rank you want, colonel or whatever, have them cut orders for him to be on duty on your staff." And I said, "Well, do you really mean that, Senator?" McFarland said, "Lyndon, you're kidding." He said, "I'm not kidding." And he went out and slammed the door.

Dick Russell, of the Foreign Relations Committee, was also Chairman of the Armed Services Committee. He said, "Frank, I'd never sanction any such thing as that. Don't worry about being called up for action." And McFarland said, "Well, Frank, you're free to take the job if you want to." But then when I called Tracy Voorhees, who was helping Conant set up the committee, Voorhees said, "You mean Lyndon Johnson was strongly opposed to you doing this?" And I said, "Yes." He said, "Well, we withdraw our offer." They didn't want to get into trouble with Lyndon. That's how much power Lyndon Johnson had, even then. So there it was, I had to go back to work for the Senate, sort of like slave labor, you know. But a few months later I got another offer and they didn't prevent me from taking it.

Senator McFarland's Staff

— When did you join McFarland's Senate staff?

— I didn't go right over after the election in 1950. My phone didn't ring at all for quite a while. And then finally Jack—I can't remember his name now—one of the people in the State Department called me up and said, "We wondered what you're going to do. Of course it's hard for aides of defeated Majority Leaders, but we need some speechwriters in the State Department. Would you like to come down and work on our foreign policy? I felt quite honored by that. They knew I worked on all of Lucas's major speeches about American foreign policy. So I'd about accepted that, and then I went over to talk to them, McFarland had told them I'd had this offer and one of two other offers that I'd got, and then he said, "Well Frank, I won't stand in your way if you got these wonderful offers. You feel free to go and I'll try to find somebody from Arizona to do your job." So I went down to the Senate dining room, and I was sitting having a cup of coffee and feeling kind of shaken up. And in came Bill White, who was a reporter for the *New York Times*, he was a correspondent. And he sat down with me. He and I were good friends. "What's the matter, Frank? You look kind of down." And I said, "Well, I've got a good job lined up." And I told him about the State Department. "I thought it would be interesting, but I sort of got absorbed in the Senate and I want to stay here. McFarland seems willing to let me go to the State Department job." And, uh, I've never forgotten Bill

White got red in the face. "You can't do that!" he said. "Frank, we know you're the man who writes all the speeches. I'm going to talk to Lyndon about this." And I said, "What the hell can Lyndon do about it?" "You'll be surprised," he said. Lyndon was a freshman senator, who still blushed when people called him Landslide Lyndon Johnson. He only won by 78 votes or something like that, some of them supposedly dubious votes.

"Landslide Lyndon." He was only a freshman senator, a new one. Under the rules of the Senate he didn't have any influence. It would have been different had he been in at least eight or ten years. So I said, "Well, uh, Bill, can he have any influence?" "Oh, you wait and see," he said Next thing I knew McFarland had called a meeting. He said, "Frank, I want you to come to a meeting with Lyndon and Dick Russell. They're kind of worked up about your leaving us." I said, "Okay, Senator." So I went there and McFarland said in his Arizona drawl, he said, "Well, now Frank here's got a nice little job with the State Department and I don't want to stand in the way of him and his family, and they pay better salaries down there than we do up here. He wants to take that job, so I told him he was free to go." So Lyndon Johnson spoke up and he said, "Frank Kelly, are you about to take that job and leave the Senate?" And I said, "Well sir, yeah, that's what I was thinking about doing." And I said, "I hope you think it's alright, Senator." And he looked at me, glared at me, "I don't! It damn well worsens my opinion of you. Your job now is like standing on the deck on the battleship next to the leading admiral, because the Majority Leader of the United States Senate is one of the highest ranking men in this country, and you're right at his right hand side. You're going to quit that and go ashore on a goddamn rowboat."

It was all mixed up language, you know? So I said, "Well, sir, I'm sorry you feel that way about it." Lyndon jumped up and he went to the door and he said, "Well, I've told you what I think and I'm getting out of this meeting." And I said, "Senator, I hope you'll always think well of me." He said, "The hell I will!" He slammed the door with a bang and went out. And McFarland said, "Well, Frank, I guess you're stuck working with us for another few years. Lyndon doesn't want you to leave, and I feel that since he feels about it so strongly you should stay. You know Lyndon has influence on a lot of votes." I said, "Yes sir, I'll stay."

So one of the jobs I'd been offered was, I forgot to mention, was working with Tracy Voorhees, Secretary of the Army, who was working with James Bryant Conant of Harvard. They formed a new committee called The Committee on the Present Danger. They wanted a Washington director, and they'd offered me the job. So I called up Voorhees and I told him what had happened. He said, "We withdraw the offer, Frank." I said, "What? What?" "If Lyndon Johnson is opposed to you, we can't have you working on our staff. It wouldn't be feasible in terms of Washington standing. So we'll have to withdraw the offer." And they did.

So there I was, up the creek at the Senate again.

SPEECH WRITING

— Were you writing McFarland's speeches, too?

— Oh yeah. He didn't deliver many. Lucas was more inclined to give speeches on everything under the sun, so I was busier than I was when McFarland came in.

— How was this different, from writing speeches for Truman where you were presenting ideas on notepads?

— For Truman, it wasn't like sitting down and developing a whole speech, usually. We were called the Back Platform Group. Most of the speeches we worked on during the campaign were brief, and put on cards. We made dozens of speeches, at all hours of the morning and night.

— What was it like writing speeches for Lucas?

— His speeches could be any length. I worked on all the major speeches that Lucas made at that time, presenting the agenda of the Senate. He would get up and say, "This is going to be our agenda this term." And I'd worked on that. I don't remember the small ones.

— What was the process like for McFarland?

— I would outline ideas that I had and I thought would make a good speech. If he said, "Okay." I would go back and type it up and give it to him and we'd go over it and then we'd have a final draft. I think in the case of Truman, he called the shots, no doubt about it. Lucas was a stronger senator. McFarland was more concerned with local issues relating to Arizona, where he thought of himself as the authority. He was less confident with national issues, and he'd want me to write the speech. At the time some of my friends said I sounded like a senator. They'd come to see me and I'd say, "We'll give the distinguished senator five more minutes."

— Did you change your style of writing? If I were to take a speech, let's take for an example, from Lucas and then one from McFarland, would the phrases and the way that they would be written be the same? Did you try to capture the voice of each senator?

— I did, to some extent. It was easy for Lucas because he came from the Midwest, he had the same sort of style as I did. McFarland was more the Texas, ranching style, so I kind of made it easy-going, and a ranch style.

Passage of Legislation

— Any major pieces of legislation, when you think of your time in the Senate, that you helped write or get passed that you would like to mention?

— I remember how Lucas tried to block some. I remember the Mundt-Nixon Bill, which was to authorize the setting-up of detention camps in the United States. It passed the Senate over President Truman's veto. In the middle of the night I was there; it was a horrible bill, sponsored by Dick Nixon and Carl Mundt. And Lucas tried to block it, but he was just overwhelmed. Some of the liberal senators voted for the bill, which was aimed at people who were regarded as subversive: Communists, Reds, anyone regarded as dangerous and involved in Communist activities. Most people don't even know it happened, because the Supreme Court knocked it out.

I'll never forget that night and how Lucas tried to stop that destructive bill. I realized then that the Majority Leader didn't have as much power as he thought he did. Truman vetoed the bill, but they still passed it by two thirds. That's one of the worst things I ever remember from the Senate.

— How would you rate Lucas in reference to his ability to get legislation passed? Was he good?

— Yeah. He was good. He was a moderate; he wasn't identified with either the Right or the Left Wing of the Senate. He got along with all of them pretty well.

— Who were the key Republicans, who crossed party lines to help get through as much of Truman's legislative agenda as was possible?

— Well, Arthur Vandenberg was one of the key people who helped us out on many occasions. Wayne Morse of Oregon was good, too.

— What about the passage of legislation?

— The passage of NATO was a big one. I was working for the Senate when the North Atlantic Treaty Organization happened.

— How was it received at that time?

— It was received critically at that time, because it was involving the United States in the affairs of the world and there was still a great reservoir of isolationism. The people of the United States had gotten into two wars, First World War and Second World War, because of our relations with foreign governments and there were still politicians that would get up and quote George Washington: "We should avoid all entangling alliances." NATO was controversial, but it finally went through. Truman was very proud of it.

— What about the integration of the armed forces?

— That was another big thing that Truman pulled off that created a lot of uproar from the Southern senators, and those against desegregation. It was one of Truman's big achievements.

J. EDGAR HOOVER

— Did you have any dealings with J. Edgar Hoover when you were with Lucas?

— I know what Truman called him: "That big fat cop." I was interviewed by countless FBI men in my office in the Capitol. They would come in and ask me about all kinds of people whom I'd been associated with and were being appointed to federal jobs. I remember being interviewed by an agent about Paul G. Hoffman, who was being appointed as the head of the Marshall Plan. This young FBI man said to me, solemnly with his notebook out, "Mr. Kelly, do you regard Mr. Hoffman as a loyal citizen? Has he ever said to you anything that indicated that he had subversive ideas?" I said, "Of course not." I said, "He's more conservative than I am by far." This guy looked, and I said, "Paul Hoffman's a Republican." And I said, "If you guys don't know by now whether Paul Hoffman's subversive or not, after you've been investigating him for 20 years, when are you ever going to make up your minds? When are you ever going to decide?" "Well," he said, "Sir, every time a man is nominated for an important job we have to ask a lot of questions about him and renew our files." I suppose the FBI had files on me, on Hutchins, and everybody.

— Did you ever send away for your file under the Freedom of Information Act?

— No, one of my friends offered to get me my file. I said I didn't want to read it, because they're so full of junk.

My friend Joe Guilfoyle was Assistant to the Attorney General under Bobby Kennedy. And I remember his saying, "Frank, you wouldn't believe the garbage that's in the files here." That was before I worked for the Center.

— Were the senators worried about the files Hoover kept?

— One day, when I worked for the Senate Majority Policy Committee, I was surprised to hear the senators talking about, "What are we going to do when J. Edgar dies? He's got a file on every one of us. Could we get somebody to go down there, a lawyer, and demand the right to read our files before the new director of the FBI is confirmed? Maybe we could get a lot of stuff taken out of the files." Another senator said, "Oh, we shouldn't bother to do that." But they all knew Hoover had files on them.

— Some of the things he did, like against Martin Luther King, should have been grounds for his removal.

— I think against Bobby Kennedy, too. My friend Guilfoyle told me about a meeting in the Justice Department when Hoover came in smiling and said to Bobby Kennedy, when he was then Attorney General, "Mr. Attorney General, we've got some good, new stuff on Martin Luther King. You know, he stayed at a hotel in Cleveland last night with this girl he picked up and we had microphones in the room. And I can give you recordings on what they said to one another. It's really wild and exotic stuff." Bobby Kennedy looked at Hoover and he said, "Edgar, you disgust me. I don't want to hear that damn recording. Throw it away." And Hoover got bright red, and my friend Joe thought that was one of the reasons why Hoover hated Bobby Kennedy from them on. Oh, he really let Edgar have it, and he was so paranoid. Recording a man's adventures with a girl in a hotel room. But Lyndon Johnson usually got along with him. So did Nixon, I think.

Connection with The White House

— How did the senators view your connection to the White House?

— They all used to joke with me about it. The senators would say in the Senate cloak room, which I had entry to, the senators would be talking and I'd come walking in and they'd say, "Be careful around Kelly, don't say anything. It'll go right to the White House." I'd say, "Oh Senator, not more than 80% of what you say will go to the White House." And they laughed, because I was on the phone with George Elsey, Charlie Murphy, David Lloyd and other guys on the White House staff, who were concerned with legislation.

— How would you characterize the Truman administration's dealings with the Senate? How did they operate? How did they get their agendas out?

— George Elsey and Charlie Murphy were the two White House staff members I dealt with the most as assistant to the Majority Leader. Murphy was administrative assistant to the president, as was Elsey. They were constantly looking for votes. They'd call me three or four times a day and I'd call them several times: always counting, counting votes.

WASHINGTON D.C.

— Where were you living?

— I lived in Arlington, Virginia, right across the river, and I drove to the Capitol each day. Washington was all segregated. The blacks kept in the background. I know I tried to get the Senate to pass some civil rights bills of the kind that Lyndon Johnson got through twenty years later. "Oh man, that's crazy. Not going to pass that stuff." It was not going to happen. The treatment of blacks was pretty bad. The Washington I knew was very segregated. And the treatment of women was not good; they were fine for staff members, girls to throw on the couch, but not taken seriously as possible holders of power.

AMBASSADOR AVERELL HARRIMAN

Later on I worked for Averell Harriman, who was the American Ambassador in Moscow. He was there when he could hear the German guns just outside the city. Every night

Stalin would send a car for him to go to the Kremlin. Stalin couldn't sleep, of course. Stalin would be pacing up and down.

— Did he ever talk to you about Stalin's reaction to Germany's invasion of Russia? In the history books it is noted that Stalin couldn't actually believe that Hitler attacked him, particularly after the partition of Poland, and he went into a funk, almost disappeared for a while. Did he ever talk to you about that at all?

— No. Harriman told me by the time he got there Stalin had recovered from his panic. But Harriman said, "He called me in one night and had me come over right away because the Germans were really closing in on Moscow. He was going up and down, up and down, and said, 'Mr. Harriman, I want you to get on the radio phone right away and call the president. Tell him we need so many planes; we need so many of your tanks. Tell the president immediately what we need. Tell him to get right on it.'" And Harriman said, "Well, Marshall Stalin, I'm the ambassador from the United States, I'm not the president. I do not have the power to tell the president to do that." Stalin glared at him and said, "Of course you do. We've looked you up. You're one of the biggest capitalists in the United States, Mr. Harriman. We know how much you're worth. And you get on the phone and tell Mr. Roosevelt what we need right now." He believed his own propaganda. Because Harriman was a big capitalist, Roosevelt had to do what he said!

So Harriman said, "Mr. Stalin, I can't do that." And Stalin said, "Well, you don't want to do it but of course you could. You could tell the president whatever you wanted to and he'd have to do it." So Harriman said he did send a message to Washington about this conversation with Joe Stalin, and I guess Roosevelt got a shock out of it.

— Did Harriman ever talk about his personal views of Stalin as a person?

— Yeah. Harriman was very impressed with Stalin. He said he had had much more of a sense of humor than most people realized.

— Being a Georgian?

— Yeah. And they liked these elaborate jokes. But of course he was so worried about the [the German advance]. He was determined not to give up Moscow and all his advisors were telling him he had to pull back to the Ural Mountains. And of course if he had done that, maybe Germany wouldn't have lost the war. But he didn't do it. "No," he said, "I'm going to stay here; if I'm going to die, it will be here in the Kremlin." So Harriman had all these meetings with him. He said that he was impressed with Stalin's intelligence, his sense of humor and his tirelessness.

PRESIDENTIAL CAMPAIGN

— What was it like to engage Harriman in conversation?

— Harriman?

— Yes.

— Very easy. I had a wonderful conversation with him once because when he offered me the job, which came about very abruptly at the time, I had worked for the Senate and I left the Senate and then did various projects. Then I went with the Fitzgerald Agency in private public relations. And I was very bored with that, (as I have already mentioned). Then, on a rainy day, I remember Jim Lanigan, who was Averell's assistant, came into my office dripping from rain and he said, "C'mon, Frank, get out of this place. Harriman is going to run for president. Truman's giving him an okay. He wants you to be his Washington director. Let's get the hell out of here."

It was crazy. But I called up Fitzgerald and he said, "If you have the chance to work with Harriman, take it. You can come back and work with us anytime you want. We'll give you all the leave you want. He's probably not going to even be nominated, but the contacts you'll make will be so good." So that's how I started. In my first meeting with Harriman, he asked me how much money I wanted for the job. So I named the highest figure I could and he said, "Well, that's all right. That sounds reasonable." I wish I had doubled it.

I asked him, "Where's my office going to be?"

He said, "Well, I'm president of the Franklin D. Roosevelt Foundation. Mrs. Roosevelt wanted me to do that job. We have offices on 16th Street. We'll just take over the Foundation for the campaign space we need."

— How did you find Harriman as a person?

— I liked him very much. I wrote a little booklet about him, which he liked quite well. That's one of the reasons why he wanted me to be the Washington director of his presidential campaign. I read a lot about his work and business, and about what he did in Britain; he was our ambassador there, then he was ambassador to the Soviet Union, so I thought, when he wanted to run for president and asked me to join him, I thought it was a good opportunity. I'd be writing his speeches when we were campaigning. We had our own chartered plane, our own chef, and all that stuff. But Harriman wouldn't let me put on razzmatazz, you know. He'd been a diplomat and a businessman and all that. I painted on the nose of the plane: Harriman Express. And as we were walking out to plane, he said, "Who did that?"

I said, "I did. I authorized it."

And he said, "What? Don't you think that it's flamboyant?"

I said, "Well, you're a railroad man; The Harriman Express. People will like that."

"Oh," he says.

Gradually he got used to it. "You're in a political campaign. This is not like running a business," I reminded him. "You've got to do some dramatic things and make people think of you."

— Was he old school from the standpoint of not wanting to go out and press the flesh?

— Yeah. In fact he was so cool. He said to one woman in Iowa, where we were campaigning, who came up to him and said, "Mr. Harriman, I know that you're a high socialite, millionaire, and businessman, ambassador and all that," she said, "I hope when you get to Washington as president, you won't associate with all those politicians." And Harriman said, "Oh I won't, ma'am. I promise you I won't."

— Did Harriman really think that he was going to be able to do it?

— I think he really thought for a while that he was going to make it. I know that he had conversations with Truman all the time as director of the Mutual Security Agency. But Truman had said to him, "Well, you know I talked to Adlai and he doesn't want it. He's turned it down. So I'll back you all the way." We thought we had a good chance. Our New York director was Franklin D. Roosevelt Jr., FDR Jr. With all his clout we knew we'd get a lot of delegates from New York and we did. And we had a lot of big Democrats for us when Harriman ran for president.

We had a charter plane, a wonderful DC-3, and a stream of publicity. We'd land in different cities, and delegations of citizens would come up to us with Harriman signs. One time in Little Rock, I remember the mayor came up and said, "Mr. Harriman, we're glad to welcome you to the city of Little Rock. I present you with a key."

And Harriman said, "Here, Frank, put this in your pocket."

Later I said, "Now listen, you don't say that to mayors. You say, 'Oh I'm very glad.' Don't turn around and give it to me. Put it in your own pocket."

He said, "Oh, am I supposed to do that?"

I said, "Yeah!"

So in that respect he was somewhat like Rockefeller when he went to a phone booth and tried to make a call with a nickel; he didn't know that the amount had changed.

— Was Harriman out of touch?

— He never ran for any office. He said he felt that was a handicap and it was. But anyway, it was a great experience.

— The planning of the campaign?

— Truman had a lot to do with it, too. He told him a few things about campaigns. We had a good committee in New York and other cities.

So I ended up in the Averell Harriman campaign for president in the summer of 1952. And we went across the country; we had the best campaign organization. Whenever we'd run out of campaign money, I'd say, "Averell, we need money." He'd say, "Well, call up my bank. Call up Ronald." His brother was Ronald Harriman, who ran the Harriman brothers' bank. That was the best way to raise money. Nobody had any influence on us. We had our chartered plane with our own chef on board. The only way to campaign, I'll tell you.

GRACE TULLY, PERSONAL SECRETARY

So, I found myself in the Roosevelt Foundation in 1952, and Harriman said, "Oh, by the way, your secretary will be Grace Tully." I said, "What?" Grace Tully was FDR's secretary for many years. There I was in this huge office with Grace Tully as my secretary! And about the second week she came in and closed the door and said, "Mr. Kelly, you know what year this is?"

And I said, "Of course I do, Grace, 1952."

She said, "Do you remember what year the president died?" Meaning Mr. Roosevelt of course.

I said, "Oh, who would forget that? 1945."

She said, "Mr. Harriman told me I could have this job as long as I wanted it. After I left the White House I've been here but he's never remembered to give me an increase in salary for seven years."

So I said, "Grace, that's terrible. Next time I see Mr. Harriman, I'll tell him that I'm putting it in our campaign budget. We'll double your salary."

She said, "Do you think he would approve that?"

I said, "We'll try." So at the next meeting I had with Harriman we went down a lot of items and I said, "By the way, Grace Tully tells me you've never given her a raise in seven years."

You know he was a multimillionaire; he didn't realize how much the cost of living had changed. He peered at me and said, "I haven't?"

I said, "No."

"Well, are you going to do something about that?"

I said, "Yes. I doubled her salary." I knew he could afford it. He didn't look surprised.

"That's probably the right amount," he said. "She's very valuable."

I said, "She knows everybody in the country."

And Harriman took these things very well but he lived in another world. He was worth four hundred million in those days. That's good pay even right now. He always traveled first class, never had any cash in his hands. When I went with him I had to pay for the taxi. Of course I charged it to him on the expense account but he was just one of those men so rich he never had to think about the cost of living.

— What about Tully? What was she like?

— Oh she was wonderful. She had that Irish spunk you know. And she was a terrific asset to us. I told Harriman, she knows every Democratic politician in the country. So if you want to get hold of governor so-and-so or senator so-and-so to arrange our campaign schedule, all I had to do is tell Grace to get hold of the man. Everyone responded.

— So it was great that way.

— It was perfect. She was so good. She liked her martinis a little bit too much. I liked martinis and other things myself. But she was a tremendous asset and I just can't believe that I had Grace as my secretary. I was so shocked because I admired Franklin Roosevelt. He was a hero. To be in an office in the Franklin D. Roosevelt Foundation with

Grace Tully as my secretary! Wasn't that a dream-like situation?

— It was. How good was she at organizing the office? Did you more or less let her go ahead and handle many things for you?

— Oh yeah. I had a personal secretary who I brought in, a girl named Mary Rita Guilfoyle, who was a sister of a friend of mine in the Justice Department. She traveled with me. Grace didn't travel with me; Grace really ran the office. I just realized I couldn't organize a political campaign by myself in the short time we had.

DEMOCRATIC CONVENTION OF 1952

Of course Harriman did not get the nomination in 1952, but we put up a gallant fight. I tried to get Harriman and Hubert Humphrey together. They wanted to get together; Humphrey was then working for Estes Kefauver and we wanted to put up a ticket of Harriman and Kefauver. And we brought the two guys into a hotel room in Chicago and they just argued for hours about who should be the vice president. They never could agree. When we got to the Convention, Adlai Stevenson decided he wanted to run and Stevenson swept the convention.

After the convention Stevenson offered me a job on his campaign staff, but by then I was again in my periodic revolution against politics. So I said, "No."

So I went to work for the International Press Institute, conducting a study of the treatment of world news by the

American press. So I got into that. That was in '52 and '53. And then I worked for the American Book Publishers Council, helping them fight censorship throughout the United States.

When I told Harriman about my new job, he said, "That's amazing. You had that job all lined up, and so you knew all along that I wasn't going to win?"

"Well," I said, "I hoped that you were going to win. But look at the odds. Stevenson was a governor of Illinois, he had a lot of electoral votes, and you had never run for office. I worked for you because I thought you were the best-qualified person to be president."

I think Harriman would have brought a deeper understanding of international politics than any of the other candidates. So anyway, Harriman and I continued to be good friends, Adlai too, so I went right from the Chicago convention to New York and we had taken a set of offices in the Rockefeller Center just right down the street from where I worked for the AP, years ago, and I started operations.

International Press Institute

— Was the International Press Institute a new organization that was just starting up, Frank?

— The International Press Institute had been going a few years, but this was called the study of International News or the Study of World News—I've forgotten which—and we got, oh what was it—$200,000 I think—from the Ford Foundation. So we opened offices there.

And another little sidelight was that I went over to the Morgan Guarantee Trust Company, right there in Rockefeller center, to open an account for this new study of world news. I took in this check for $200,000 from the Ford Foundation. I handed it to the teller, and she said, "Oh I think our general manager will like to meet you, Mr. Kelly." And so then they invited me to have lunch with the officers of the Morgan Guarantee Trust Company, in this plush dining room, because I had brought in this check for $200,000.

— And you ordered anything on the menu?

— Oh certainly, I was really a class A customer. So I hired a guy by the name of George Palmer as my deputy. He had been with the *Times*, I've forgotten; he was a newspaperman. And we set out to survey…how many papers did we cover…you can find that out somewhere.

— How would you describe the operation itself? Were you reading the news?

— What happened was, I was asked to organize the whole project…

— How did you handle it?

— Well, I finally decided that the only way that we could possibly cover all the major papers of the country (and it seems to me I had a lot of temerity to propose this) was to get to the telegraph editors. Every paper then, virtually all the big ones, had telegraph editors to keep track of the flow of the news. They agreed to take part in our study for one week. We picked out crucial weeks, and they made notes on where the news came from, what they did with the news. If it came

from Latin America, how did it compete with news from
Africa, and how did they decide to play up one country over
another. I think the copies of the reports are in Geneva now.
You might be able to get them there. So it's fascinating to
show how the individual education of the telegraph editors
determined so much of what the American people knew
about what was going on in the world, because most of them
were highly prejudiced. News from Latin America was treated
as way down there somewhere. Of course news from Europe,
as you would expect, had high priority. Asia and Africa were
covered very little, so it was quite a revealing study I think.

— How long did this study go on for, Frank?

— About a year, I think.

— So the $200,000 was to fund the project for that one
year, and to write the report. And then the report went to?

— The report was distributed to all the major
newspapers, and we got a lot of criticism of course. They
didn't like to be told that they were covering some areas of
the world and leaving whole areas of the world just as if they
didn't exist. I sort of dimly felt that this was the case, and I
think we demonstrated it. I think we had an impact on the
subsequent handling of the news by major papers. The
chairman of our advisory committee, a man who drove me
wild, was Lester Markel, then the Sunday editor of the *New
York Times*. He was furious with me for being critical of the
New York Times. He said, "You know we do a wonderful job
of covering international news."

And I said, "Of course you do, Lester."

He said, "I am chairman of your advisory board, and here in this report you've got criticisms of the *New York Times*."

And I said, "Well, my God, you're not the pope. The *Times* is not sacred." He really was angry with me. Lester was a propagandist for the *New York Times* 24 hours a day, and he was very, very bureaucratic and very dictatorial. He wanted to tell me everything that I should do and I couldn't put up with it. Luckily I had some people backing me at the Geneva headquarters of the International Press Institute. Because Lester was just going to raise hell with me; they stood him off. Had to hand it to them.

— Do you remember the other members of the board of directors that you had in the United States?

— I don't remember any except Lester.

— And your staff? How many were there?

— Oh let's see, there was George Palmer and myself, and two secretaries—four people in New York. Then across the country—I've forgotten how many telegraph editors, but it's all in that report.

— So all the telegraph editors were the ones who were feeding it back, then who did the tabulation for you.

— No, we had that done by universities. Journalism departments.

And so they did the tabulation in that way.

— Was the University of Missouri one of then?

— I think so. But anyway that was the outcome in a way of having worked as a Nieman Fellow. The whole impact of a Neiman Fellowship affected me all my life, of course.

— Were you surprised by the amount of criticism the report received?

— Not really. No, I wasn't surprised. I was surprised that my board of advisors in Geneva and the International Press Institute stood behind us; they didn't crumple up under the criticism. McNeil Lowry, the guy who had given me the job, he was the overall international director. I was the United States director, but he backed me up all the way through, whatever criticism we got. And, of course, neither one of us would ever apply for a job on a newspaper again.

FUND FOR THE REPUBLIC.

— How did you manage to land a position with the Fund for the Republic?

— I remember telling Barbara how bored I had become, and how I was hoping that something new and more interesting would come along. She was somewhat psychic, my wife. And she said to me, "Now don't you worry, dear. In a very short time you will get an invitation for a very wonderful job at one of the big foundations in this country." And I said, "Oh Barbara, I don't know anybody with a foundation. Nobody's going to give me a job at one of the foundations. That's way off the beam." Two weeks later Robert Hutchins called and told me he'd like me to be vice president of the Fund for the Republic. The Fund needed a vice president with experience in Washington; just the kind of experience I had. During my years there I had gotten to know every member of the Senate, and many of the leaders in the House. And the Fund for the Republic was having trouble with Joseph McCarthy and his Un-American Activities Committee.

When the Fund was looking for somebody to be vice president and defend them, Hutchins called up Louis Lyons, the curator of the Nieman Foundation. He asked him if he could recommend a Nieman who would be interested in the job. He said, "I desperately need somebody with a lot of Washington experience, who is willing to stand up to Joe McCarthy." And so Louis said, "Sure. Frank Kelly." That's how I got the job. Just like that.

SENATOR JOSEPH MCCARTHY

— Did you ever ask Lyons why he recommended you?

— Well, he just said he thought it would fit me and Louis was a New Englander; he didn't use more than five words if he could help it. It's like he said to me when I was going off to the Army, "Well, you'll come through all right, Frank." He had his pipe going, and he said: "You can come back here, too." He'd look down at his desk and never look at you. "Finish up your fellowship if you want."

— I said, "Oh that's great. Thank you."

"Well, I hope you can make it," Louis Lyons, said. So he never told me why he did recommend me to Hutchins, but he did, and that changed my life greatly. There were other Niemans he could have recommended; he didn't really explain why he had picked me. Like with Harry Truman, I was suddenly into a job I hadn't tried to get.

— Of course, the experience you had both within the government and the military made you an ideal candidate?

— And I wasn't frightened by the possible dangers. I don't know why! At that time, Senator Joe McCarthy and the House Un-American Activities Committee were running wild. The Fund had published a book on blacklisting in television and the movies, showing how many false accusations had been made. Many reputations had been ruined. Fear was rampant in the entertainment industry and among government employees affected by suspicions created by McCarthy's charges of disloyal activities.

When I went to work for the Fund for the Republic, the board was gloomy. Hutchins said, "Well, Frank, of course you were hired to help us with our Washington problems, but don't you think we're going to lose our tax exemption?"

I said, "No, we're not."

He said, "What do you mean by that?"

I said, "We're going to get the press against that committee and we're going to beat them." I knew a lot of people in the press because I worked with the American Book Publishers Council against censorship. I knew dozens of editors all over the country. So I went over to the *New York Times* and asked them to carry an editorial denouncing the Un-American Activities Committee for daring to attack this great Fund for the Republic! The *Times* came out with a blast and the committee didn't know what the hell to do.

And we turned it around. I talked with one of our directors, J. R. Parten of Texas, who was a close friend of Sam Rayburn, Speaker of the House of Representatives. I said, "Could you tell Mr. Rayburn what they're trying to do to us here?"

"Yeah, I'll talk to him."

"They're attacking some of the best people in our country. You know that. We can't let them get away with it" Speaker Rayburn enlisted other leaders in the Congress, and the committee was finally closed down. Joe McCarthy was ridiculed by many newspapers and lost his power. It was a happy time for me, and Hutchins gave me some of the credit for the change in the political atmosphere.

ROBERT MAYNARD HUTCHINS

— Before we discuss the Center for the Study of Democratic Institutions, and your activities there, I thought we could spend some time on Hutchins the person, and what it was like to work with him. Was Hutchins a religious man?

— His father was a Presbyterian Minister. He said, "My father would get us up every morning, the whole family, 5:30 in the morning, kneel down on the bare floor, nothing to eat, and have a prayer meeting that went on for an hour. And then we could have our breakfast." That's how my father was. But one day, Bob said, "You know, Frank, I will never be the man my father was. He absolutely led a life in strict accordance with his principles, but I have gone off in all directions." Of course he had. When he went to the

University of Chicago, he put all that Presbyterianism aside. He led a very social active life; hobnobbed with a lot of radicals. Did a lot of things his father wouldn't have liked.

— Was Hutchins's wit pinned to an individual or an event? How would you describe his wit?

— His wit?

— Could it be stinging?

— Yeah, it could be. It was always…well for an example, the first day I worked there, he asked me to come to his office, and I went in and he closed the door. We just had a board of directors meeting, which I attended. He said, "Well, what do you think of these people you are going to be working with, Frank?" And I looked at him, and I said, "Well, I think in general they are wonderful people, and I am honored to be working with you in particular."

He looked at me and he said, "I wish you really meant that."

I thought, this guy is something. So I stared right back at him, and in sort of a mock anger I said, "I did mean it. I don't tell lies, and you had better remember that!"

He looked at me and he said, "We'll get along." And we did. He was a man who had very, very deep concerns for liberty, and for great ideas that kept our society going.

— Did you see him ever become disappointed with the way his life had unfolded?

— Oh yes. I did an interview with him (it must be in your files at UCSB) for the *Center Magazine* called, "Trees Grow in Brooklyn" about Bob and about his ideas about life

John Courtney Murray, S.J., advisor to the pope,
and Robert Maynard Hutchins, president of the
Fund for the Republic, have a dialog at the
Center for the Study of Democratic Institutions

and how depressed he got. I think one of the questions I asked him was: "Do you ever get depressed?" And he said, "Of course. I often get depressed, and wonder why I got involved in so many things, and I look back at the University of Chicago, where I spent those years trying to reform it; then, when I left, they just dismantled all my programs. I felt like I was just the stopper in the bathtub; when I left, the water ran out."

And I remember talking to him about autobiographies one day. And he said, "I have a good title for mine."

I said, "What would it be, Bob?"

And he said, "*Skunk at the Garden Party.*"

Isn't that some title? For a brilliant man who had twenty-seven honorary degrees and was regarded as one of the great American educators? I said, "Oh, Bob, you wouldn't use that, would you?"

He said, "Well, all right. How do you like this one: *Sink to My Level*; that would be the title of my autobiography."

Can you imagine that? I think I put this in that interview. I was so stunned, you know, at the depth of feeling in this brilliant man. Well, at another time he said, "I look back on my life as an avenue of ruined monuments. Just like a sculpture, I was going to create a university with great ideas all around and with great professors. But the faculty and trustees would take my programs and tear them apart, and put two heads on whatever I was sculpting, and say, "There's what Hutchins' program was." He said, "By then I was disgusted with it." Isn't that sad?

— Do you feel that in some respects he died thinking he was a failure?

— Oh, he was feeling very sad when he died. I saw him just a day before he died over at Cottage hospital. I told him I was working on my book about the Center. And he said, "Good. Don't rely on what anyone tells you. Go into the files and see if you can find letters and documentation. Don't rely on what people will say."

When reporters would ask Hutchins, "What good is the Center?" he would say, "Well I'll refer you to Thomas Edison who was asked, 'What good is the light bulb?'" You know. And then he said, "Edison said, 'Well, what good is a baby?'" So all that stuff about "What good is it?" just offended Hutchins. He was dealing with ideas that were beyond judgment.

FINANCIAL STRUGGLES

— How difficult was it to raise funds for the Center?

— Well, when we first accepted jobs with the Center, we were all told that they wouldn't be permanent because the Center had a limited grant of 15 million dollars from the Ford Foundation and it spent most of its first years giving away money to civil rights groups in the South, to uphold civil liberties down there and to finance various studies of the impact of McCarthyism and blacklisting in Hollywood, and in radio and television. These were very, very important studies, but they took a lot of money. So the time the idea of starting a Center came, as you'll find in my book, the Center had used up almost half of the 15 million. So Hutchins told every one of us that we'd move to Santa Barbara, we would put out reports, and we'd show the world what an absolutely free dialogue center could do, and then see if we could get the support to keep it going. So we got out here in 1959, and we tried eventually a few years later to apply again to the Ford Foundation for funding as well as to five or ten other places. But they said, "No, absolutely not." We were too controversial.

So then Hutchins called us together—Ping Ferry, Harry Ashmore, and myself. We were the officers with Hutchins and he said, "What shall we do? Shall we put out a lot of very drastic comments on American society and close our doors, being happy that we had had a great impact with these reports, or shall we try to keep going about raising money?"

Ping Ferry, who was the firebrand among us said, "Bob, that's the way to go. Let's put out some of the most smashing reports that ever existed on the corruption that is in our society and all the terrible problems and how people have failed to solve them and close our doors in a great, smashing finish."

Then Hutchins turned to me and he said, "Well Frank, what do you think?"

And I said, "Well, if we're doing good work, why should we give up? Why should we say, 'We're going to do it for a few years and go out in a blaze of glory?' Why don't we see if our good work is valued?"

225

So Hutchins said, "I agree with Kelly. We're going to try to raise money."

ELEANOR ROOSEVELT: ROBERT E. SHERWOOD AWARDS

I always admired Eleanor Roosevelt. She was to me the forerunner of what women of the future are going to be like.

— Did you spend much time with her?

— Oh, I knew her but I didn't spend a lot of time with her. She came to the offices of the Fund for the Republic in New York fairly often because we had a contest for the best television plays, honoring a writer who worked for FDR, Robert E. Sherwood. So when we got some entrees, we'd get in touch with Mrs. Roosevelt and the other judges and they would come to my office in the Lincoln Building, and we would view these shows that were submitted for Robert Sherwood awards. And it was a great delight to know her. She was such a charming person, could light up a room with her smile. When I first met her I thought, "Oh! This is the homeliest woman I ever saw in my life." Then she smiled, and I tell you it was like a thousand candelabra going on. She was transfigured!

— What was it like to enter into a conversation with her?

— Oh it was very, very open. She wanted to know what you thought. She didn't pour out her views and say "This is the way I am," you know, "I'm a world famous woman and you must listen to me." She was ready to listen to everybody and absorb ideas from anybody.

I had a secretary, named Penny, who worked for me at that time. She was from Mississippi. Her real name was Comeeta. And I asked her, "Where did you get the name Comeeta?" She said "My father named me for Haley's comet. It's really comet-a." And she said, "I hated the idea of being named for a comet, so I got the nickname of Penny." And one day she comes into my office; her eyes are shining and she said, "Mr. Kelly, Mr. Kelly, I think I saw Mrs. Roosevelt in the ladies' room here."

And I said, "Well, that's quite possible. She has to go to the ladies' room like everybody else."

"But she's here," she says, "in the offices of this place!"

I said, "Sure. She comes here regularly, as one of our judges."

She said, "Oh my. She's such a great person. Can I call my father in Mississippi and tell him I met Mrs. Roosevelt in the ladies' room?"

I said, "Sure. Call him up." Eleanor Roosevelt was a legendary figure in her own time.

I remember watching her at the 1952 Democratic Convention. She was for Stevenson. She pushed him. She pushed a lot of people. If she saw a talented person, she'd help that person find more and more opportunities.

One of the greatest things that Harry Truman did as president, in my point of view, was to appoint Mrs. Roosevelt as the Chair of the Human Rights Commission that wrote the Universal Declaration of Human Rights that the UN then adopted. She wrote it, and she got it through. It was a struggle for her, too. A lot of people just gave Truman hell. "Why are you appointing a woman to that job? A woman as Chair of the Commission on Human Rights." And Truman stood by his guns. Senators told him to withdraw her appointment. He wouldn't do it. He was strong that way. He liked her better than he did FDR.

CENTER MAGAZINE

— Who started the Center magazine?

— The magazine was started by John Cogley, who had a good background as an editor for *The Commonweal*—a Liberal Catholic publication. Cogley also served for a while as religion editor of the *New York Times*. Hutchins wanted our ideas to get out as widely as possible. So we started out by publishing these booklets. And then Cogley said, "Why don't we try a magazine?" So he was largely responsible for it. He and Don McDonald, but all of us were sort of informally editors of the *Center Magazine*.

JOHN BIRCH SOCIETY

— The Birch Society really thrived while the Center was flourishing in Santa Barbara. Were there any attempts at dialogue with them on anything?

— Oh yeah, I invited them time and again. I'd call up and say, "We're having a dialogue, would anybody like to come?" In fact, I went down to their Santa Barbara office once and picked up a Birch member and brought him up to the dialogue. And I brought him back downtown. He didn't say a word. On the way back I said, "What did you make of that?" He said, "Well, I don't know what you were really talking about there. On the surface it sounded like nice, reasonable conversation, but we know you have another purpose beyond that." I couldn't convince him. I wasn't surprised; their little "Blue Book" refers to dedicated Communist conspirators such as Dwight D. Eisenhower, Robert Hutchins, Frank Kelly, and a number of others. We're all named in it.

The Encyclopedia Britannica Project

— What do you remember about the Britannica project—when it was initiated and how it played out over time, and how the individual articles were received?

— I think that Hutchins relied a great deal on Stringfellow Barr and the other scholars for their participation. Another man involved in the Great Books Program was Scott Buchanan of St. John's College. They had a big part in the Britannica articles. It was the first time that Britannica had ever tried to bring together a lot of subjects under general headings and relate them to one another. You can see the effects in that collection of that edition of the Britannica which Hutchins gave me.

— This one here with the blue bindings?

— Yes.

— Bob gave me that set when it came out. A lot of the articles in there were affected by the meetings we had at the Center, and many writers who were involved in it.

— Was the project an offshoot from the Syntopican and the Great Books curriculum?

— No, it was different entirely. But it was also, for Hutchins, a way of getting some money for the Center, because the money we received from Britannica helped us to keep going while we tried to raise money from other projects.

— How were the root articles vetted? I know Wheeler wrote one. Did Ashmore have one? I don't remember. I don't think he did.

— No, he didn't.

— Did the various people who were selected to write the articles bring them back to the Center and did you have a series of meetings?

— Yes.

— How did Hutchins view the project?

— He always felt that the old Britannica was just thrown together from various topics. He wanted it to have much more of a comprehensive organization. Bob always wanted to bring together things in a comprehensive way so that you could understand the overall picture, and that's what these articles were intended to do. I think he made a lot of the arrangements himself with various scholars on that project.

— Did Britannica initiate the project?

— No, I think Bob really initiated it, and he sold it to Bill Benton, who was the publisher of the Britannica. And since they were old friends going back to Yale, it wasn't too hard for him to sell it. Benton knew the Center needed a big project that could be well financed, so I think their interests worked together.

— Was Hutchins satisfied with the project once it came to fruition?

— Well, Hutchins was never satisfied with anything, which you can see in the quote about what he said about the Center. "The Center's not a very good center, but it's the only one there is." He always thought that you should take chances intellectually as well as in every other field. That you should launch projects with noble ideas and if they didn't work out completely, at least you would stimulate other people to think outside of the box.

So he said, let's do what we can, in the areas that we have some influence. The Britannica is still used as a reference book, a quick study on many topics. Who knows how many students we'll reach? That was the Hutchins approach.

PACEM IN TERRIS CONVOCATION—*Henry Luce*

— When did you meet Henry Luce? And what were the circumstances that led to the International Convocation on *Pacem in Terris*?

— I got to know Henry Luce pretty well later because he was the one who helped us sponsor this International Convocation on Pope John's encyclical, *Pacem in Terris,* that I persuaded Hutchins to do in the 1960's. When the encyclical *Pacem in Terris* came out, like many other Catholics I read it. I was impressed with it; I admired Pope John. I was sitting at my office in the Center for the Study of Democratic

Institutions a few weeks later, when my friend, Professor Fred Warner Neal, a former Nieman who had been one of my classmates at Harvard, came by. (See how the Nieman Fellowship got interwoven in my life.) Fred had been in the class of '46, my second class, and he called me on the phone and he said, "Frank, have you read this great statement from Pope John?"

I said, "Oh yeah, I read it, Fred. What about it?"

He said, "Well, aren't you going to do anything about it"

I said, "What do you mean?"

He said, "Isn't the church going to sponsor worldwide discussions? This is a great document. This could end the Cold War."

I said, "Well, I don't know Fred. I'll check with some of the local leaders of the church here."

So I called up the people at the Old Mission, I think it was Father Virgil Cordero, who I talked to, and said, "What about the encyclical? Are you planning on having some discussions about it? It's a very great document."

"I'm sure it is," Father Virgil said. "But any plans for international discussions would have to come from the Vatican. We couldn't do it from here."

I called my friends at the Jesuit church here in Santa Barbara, and they agreed with Father Virgil. I reported the responses to Fred Neal.

And Fred said, "Look, Frank, this document has got to be brought to the attention of the world. If the Catholic church won't do it, see if you could get the Center for the Study of Democratic Institutions to do it."

So I thought about it for a while. I said, "Okay, I'll give it a try." And I went into Hutchins' office, which was next to mine, and I told him about Fred's call. He knew Fred Neal. And then Bob Hutchins looked at me with mock horror. He said, "You want me, a descendant of a long line of Presbyterian ministers, to put on a worldwide meeting based on a pope's encyclical? Get out of here, Kelly!"

I said, "That's exactly what I want you to do."

And he stared at me for a while and he said, "It's an outrageous idea, but I like it. We might try it, Frank, but you know we're running out of money. We're six months from closing. If you can find the money for it, we'll do this thing. But I don't know where you're going to get the money."

I said, "Well, Bob, will you let me try it out on some of the directors of the Center, who have a lot of money? Maybe one of them will like the idea."

"Sure," he said, "give it a try."

So I sat down in my office and pondered who would be most interested. The first name in my mind was a Jewish director named Seniel Ostrow. He had a wide range of interests. I sent it to Ostrow, and he called up two days later. He was all on fire with it. Ostrow told Hutchins: "Bob, I'm coming up there to meet with you and Frank and anybody else on the Center staff. And we will raise the money. Let's go ahead with this thing. Put it on." And that started the ball rolling. We eventually got a big grant from Henry Luce, and

TIME and *LIFE* gave us tremendous coverage. We even had a hand in inviting the pope to come to the United States. He didn't come to our meeting but he came a few months later. The *New York Times* said that we had played a part in getting a pope to visit the United States. He spoke at the U.N. General Assembly, calling for an end to war.

All that came out of a phone call from a guy down at Claremont, California, who was a Protestant in the first place. I guess I was moved too. I read the encyclical, and it occurred to me to launch public discussions of what the pope had said. The church leaders didn't encourage the discussion of Catholic pronouncements. Even during Vatican II and afterwards, you didn't expect the pope to urge the people to examine his proposals.

Later on, in a publication put out by the U.S. Institute of Peace, they cited our work in promoting the pope's encyclical as an utterly amazing development: that a secular institution in the United States, the Center for the Study of Democratic Institutions, had sponsored these international meetings based on that papal document. They didn't know anything like it!

— I'd like to take a step back, and spend a few minutes examining the actual workings of the Center. Using this program as an example, what was the process at the Center for a program like this?

— Well, in this case, Hutchins called me and the other officers, Harry Ashmore and Hallock Hoffman, into a meeting. And we said, "Well, how can we get this thing promoted? And who will sponsor it?" And there was a foundation in Wisconsin, and somebody knew somebody there who put in some money, for a preliminary conference at the Frank Lloyd Wright's Conference Center in Wisconsin to talk about how this could be organized. We invited a lot of professors; we invited people who had written articles on the Cold War and all that. So we got good response from them and then I don't know whether it was I who suggested it or somebody else said, but I knew Hutchins was a close friend of Henry Luce. They went to Yale together. And I said, "I hope we can get *TIME* and *LIFE* to get in on this."

"Oh, Frank, this is pretty far out for them," Hutchins said.

"I'll call Luce," I volunteered.

Luce got excited. We were featured in *LIFE* in four or five pages. And *TIME* magazine covered it. And they put up money to sponsor. We had our open session, our first public session in the General Assembly Hall at the United Nations; we had two thousand people there from all over the world, and speakers from both sides of the Iron Curtain. We wanted to get President Kennedy to speak but he said he couldn't but he almost did. Wait. Was Kennedy in power at that time? Well he was at first in '63. He was going to consider it but he got killed. And Lyndon Johnson became president. Johnson said he might do it and then he decided he wouldn't. He passed it on to Hubert Humphrey. So Humphrey spoke as the American representative at our conference at the U.N.

— Did Supreme Court Justice Douglas get involved too?

— Oh yeah. Bill Douglas was very enthusiastic. And that wasn't the only meeting we had. We had one in New York with two thousand people, and another meeting at the Center of all of us who participated at the organization, and we said, "Well, maybe we should have another meeting in Geneva or someplace like that to follow up on all the ideas that had come forward." So we got the funds for that and the next thing we knew, we were having a big meeting in Geneva in 1967. Martin Luther King was at the Geneva meeting.

He gave one of his speeches denouncing the Vietnam War. I'll never forget that. There were State Department guys there at our conference too, and they were very angry with Dr. King. "What business does he have criticizing the United States at a meeting on foreign soil?" It's alright in the U.S. but to criticize America in a conference overseas, they thought it was terrible. Of course, we didn't. We thought it was a great speech.

And I had one brief conversation with Dr. King during an intermission at the conference. He was just sitting over there by himself, and he looked so sad and brooding, so I just went over and talked to him for a while. I always admired him and was impressed by him. He gave such a fiery speech at that conference, one of the best, about why the United States was wrong to be in Vietnam. He delivered it from the heart, and that struck all of us and impressed all of us. It was one of the best talks given at our conference.

— Were there others just as impressive?

— Abba Eban impressed me a lot. He was the foreign minister of Israel. Great man. And later on he came to Santa Barbara one time and Hutchins asked me to take him out to dinner and so he and I went down to the Harbor. We spent a whole evening together. I was impressed with him. I think he should've been prime minister. But he was there in Geneva and he made a great speech. There were so many people.

— How did Hutchins react to this great success?

— Bob Hutchins told an historian, I don't know from where, but somebody told me that Hutchins told the historian that, "Kelly persuaded me to get into the *Pacem in Terris* Conference, and it was the biggest thing the Center did in many ways."

— Did Hutchins participate in it too?

— Oh yeah. He also made some wonderful talks in our conferences.

Anyway, while John Cogley and I were in Rome, I was talking with John about our plan for an international conference on the pope's encyclical *Pacem in Terris*. John said, "Well, you ought to talk to the man who helped the pope to write it."

I said, "Well, who is he?"

"He's a monsignor—Pietro Pavan," he said. "This is the man who was Pope John's ghost writer; he did most of the work on *Pacem in Terris*. Would you like to meet him?"

And I said, "Certainly." He was out at Castel Gandolfo, the pope's summer residence out on the edge of Rome. So I went out there to meet him. And I said I wanted to talk to him about the plans for holding this meeting. He wanted to find out all about us. Who were we—the Center of the Study of Democratic Institutions? So he said to me, "Do you mind if we go out here in the garden and walk up and down together?"

And I said, "No, Your Eminence" or whatever I called him.

He kept looking at my face and he said, "Stand over here where it's a little more light." And he was studying my face, I tell you, with piercing eyes. Finally at the end of this long walk and conversation, he said, "I believe that this is a real idea. It has real substance."

I said, "Of course it has."

He said, "You know, we get so many people in Rome coming in with wild ideas. I've got to protect the pope from getting involved in something that might not have any substance. But I see that you are on fire with this idea. I'll recommend it to the pope."

So I said, "Well how about you coming to the Center in Santa Barbara, spending a week with us, and talking about *Pacem in Terris* so we can prepare for the conference?"

"I'll think about it." And he did. He came. He stayed right in our house. He slept upstairs. He looked out on our garden and he said, "Bella vista, bella vista." He loved this house. He stayed with us for a week and we had all these meetings at the Center discussing the encyclical and who should be invited to talk about it.

— Did he talk about writing the encyclical?

— Oh he did, oh yeah. Wonderful story, he told me. He said they were working away on it and it got to be pretty late at night and the pope got tired and he pushed away from his desk, and he said, "Pietro, let's have a glass of wine or maybe even a small bottle of wine. Go around this big barn of a place (referring to the Vatican) and see if you can get us some good wine."

And Pietro said, "I started to the door and said, 'Yes, Your Holiness, I will.'"

And the pope said, "Get us some good French wine. I'm tired of this Italian kind."

"As soon as I found a bottle of good French wine," Pietro said, "The pope and I celebrated the ending of *Pacem in Terris*." That's a good little story.

— Did he write it himself or was it based on a dialogue that he had with the pope?

— I think Pietro wrote the draft, but he clearly had a dialogue with the pope. Pope John claimed that he was walking in the Vatican garden and the Holy Spirit spoke to him and said, "You've got to open the doors and let some air in. The church is stifling." It had been frozen for centuries in these medieval patterns; Pietro said the first time Pope John opened the church up to the cardinals, they were terribly upset. Naturally they would be, with the internal fighting that followed his opening the windows and having bishops coming from all over the world. I think Pope John was the biggest revolutionary since Jesus, probably. He surely shook up the church, and they'll never close those doors again. They'd like to. But anyway that was a great experience.

— So he stayed here in Santa Barbara for a week.

— He and Barbara and I had good conversations. He was wonderful.

— Was he open to American society and what he saw?

— Oh yeah. He was very interested in the Center and what we were doing: the dialogues. We took him around town. We had dinner parties. You know Italians are very familial. And he was.

— Was this his first trip to America?

— I don't know whether it was or not. Later on he was made cardinal. I think it was his first but I'm not sure.

— Did Fred Neal participate in any of the programs?

— Oh sure. Fred Neal was a participant. He got invited to write papers for the *Pacem in Terris* Conference. He's dead now, but we shared a lot of reminiscences. If he hadn't made that phone call it might not have happened. I don't think as a good Roman Catholic boy I would have thought of it. All these wonderful things, in which I'm involved, I never sought them, I never thought I was going to be involved in such things. Why did all these things happen the way they did? I don't know.

— Serendipity.

— It was fun. Fred Neal had quite an impact on my life. So did other people who persuaded me to engage in wild ideas.

INSTALLATION OF POPE PAUL VI

About the time that we were discussing the *Pacem in Terris* convocation, my friend John Cogley called me and he said, "Frank, you know Pope John died and they're going to install a new pope. Would you like to go to Rome and watch that with me? I'm with the *New York Times*, we'll get into everything."

I said, "Gosh, that would be great." So I went with John Cogley in '63 to this tremendous event, the installation of Paul VI. Our seats looked down at St. Peter's Square and we watched these thousands of people coming from all over the world, and we heard Paul give this marvelous speech in eight or nine languages. It was a thrilling occasion.

And then the next day Pope Paul decided that he was going to hold a press conference. I don't know of any other pope who had ever done this, but his father had been an editor in Milan. So Cogley and I went. I had been feeling pretty groggy. It was a terribly hot summer in Rome. And so Cogley spoke to one of the Swiss Guards: "My friend isn't feeling well. Can we go in now, before the rest of the journalists arrive?"

"Oh, yes sir."

So we went in and we had front row seats. The place filled up. I tell you it was so jammed, the last people to come in were two little nuns. I remember thinking: how are they ever going to get in there? And they just pressed by these little Swiss guards, pushed their way into the chapel. And then the pope came. He sat on a chair that was about three levels up from where we were and gave a wonderful talk. And then he made a mistake. Of course somebody later said he wasn't quite infallible, he'd just taken office. Maybe I said that, I don't know. But he said, "Gentlemen, ladies and gentlemen, my father was a journalist, an editor in Milan, and I want this conference to be a gathering of friendly journalists. I'll shake hands with you folks." He started down the steps to shake hands with this crowd of journalists and that was a terrible mistake. The crowd behind us just pushed us up in a strong wave, and I came face-to-face with the pope. He put out this pale, Italian hand. I remember he had the big ring, the holy of St. Peter, so I shook his hand but I couldn't let go. It was like a dream! Here was a kid, a Catholic kid from Kansas City in Rome, face-to-face with the pope! Cogley jabbed me, and said, "For God's sake, let go of the pope's hand!" They had to separate me.

Meanwhile the Swiss guards were being knocked down right and left by the crowd of journalists. They finally got the pope out of there but that was a very memorable experience.

— What did he say? Did he say anything to you?

— No, he just gave me his hand and smiled, you know. And I kissed his ring. I was in a daze. I couldn't believe it for days that this really happened. No, how could you? These things keep happening to me all the time. I get into these amazing experiences. How many people are ever going to have an experience like that? I think Paul was a good pope too. I wish I could've met Pope John, though. He must've been a great guy.

BOOK ON CELESTIAL BEINGS

— Frank, I thought we could continue on with our discussion of major figures who have been in your life, and you'd like to include in your next book. You mentioned Aldous Huxley.

ALDOUS HUXLEY

I've known many people in terms not of their fame or extraordinary life, or their special achievements as writers, or editors, or politicians, and in this book I want to include people in terms of their qualities as spiritual beings. And I was thinking of one of them who struck me very deeply—Aldous Huxley. Of course, he was a well-known writer. He used to come to the Center for the Study of Democratic Institutions. And we talked about life and future possibilities for another life, and how he coped with his blindness. (He was almost blind, you know.) I remember one thing that he said to me that I want to get into this book; he had been away from our meetings for quite a while, and we decided to have one, and it seemed important to have Huxley there, so Bob Hutchins said, "You know Aldous pretty well, why don't you call him up and invite him to this meeting. So I called him and said, "We have been missing you a lot, where have you been?"

He said, "Well for one thing, I have been in Rome, at a meeting of the Food and Agricultural Organization. I am on their board. And Frank, we had a private audience with Pope John the twenty-third. I thought of you because you and I have talked so much about what is there beyond this life, if anything." And he said, "I want to tell you that when the pope came into this room there were six of us waiting for him. At least I for one could see a heavy darkness surrounding him, almost as if he were in a coffin. But then out of this darkness there was a beautiful brilliant light coming forth. And I wanted to tell you about this Frank." (This was shortly before Pope John died.) So then Huxley said, "I would like to get to your meeting, Frank, but I am not feeling very well. Call me back in a couple of weeks, and we'll see what we can work out."

Well, it turned out he had a fatal illness and I didn't know it; and he was virtually at the point of death at the time I talked to him. Never gave the slightest impression he was ill or anything. He died, and didn't get to our meeting. His wife, Laura Huxley, came to one of our meetings at the Center, and sat next to me at lunch. And I said, "You know, I think I talked to Aldous one of the last times before he departed." And she said, "Oh yeah, I was there; I heard what he said." And I said, "Was it a peaceful death?"

She said, "Well, except for one thing: when Aldous looked at me he said, "You know, Laura, I am so tired; I have done so many things in this life, and I go to one meeting after another. I've written a lot of books, spoken on television programs; I just want to have some peace and rest, but you know I am not going to get it." I said, "Why, dear, what are you going to be doing?" He said, "I am going to help people go across from this life to the next." And she said, "Really, dear." "Oh yes, I am going to do it," he repeated.

So I said to her, "Laura, have you had any reports about this since he died?"

She said, "Oh yes, I have had dozens of letters and phone calls from people, whose friends or relatives were dying and they claimed that Aldous appeared and was very reassuring, and in a warm way, escorted the dying person across the boundaries of this life to the next.

And so I said, "You know that's interesting. A young man here at the Center for the Study of Democratic Institutions told me about his father's death. This young friend went to visit his dad, and when he came back he walked into my office and told me, "I want to tell you what happened to my dad, because you are probably the only person who would want to hear about this, because you are interested in spiritual experiences."

The young man said, "I was with my father, and all of a sudden he sits up in bed and he says, 'Gene. (This young man was named Eugene Bailey). What's Aldous Huxley doing here?' And I said, 'Where, dad? Where?' He said, 'Standing right there next to you.' And I said, 'I can't see him, dad.' My father died twenty minutes later. And you know what puzzled me was that my father liked Huxley, read all of his books, admired him as a writer. But he wasn't a close personal friend. So why in the world would he apparently have a vision of Aldous Huxley when he was dying?"

Laura Huxley said, "That's it. It's happening all over the place."

— Isn't that amazing?

— I thought I would like to get that down, I don't know if anyone else has recorded that.

— I have never heard of that before. What programs was Huxley active with at the Center?

— He was especially active with our program on ecology. This was back in the late '50s or early '60s. The Center was started in '59, so it could have been right after the Center began. We decided at one of the first meetings that we wanted to do some studies on the environment or, as we called it then, ecology. We asked Huxley if he would be a director of the study and he said he would. One of our first publications was called the *Politics of Ecology* by Aldous Huxley. It was based on our discussions at the Center. And we got a lot of negative letters from people. Why are you people up there in that ivory tower wasting your time talking about the environment, global warming and all that stuff? This was in 1962, when we published the pamphlet. I said Aldous Huxley was always in the forefront. That's what he was interested in and why he would come to a lot of our meetings.

— When he came to the Center, how active was he?

— Well, he sat at the table in the dialogue, and he often led discussions. He would have a paper he had written or something he wanted us to take up.

— Did he come and actually work as a Senior Fellow for a while?

— No. He didn't have an office. He was like other visiting scholars that we had. Quite a few of them came in and out of the Center.

— From the standpoint of being someone who had met Huxley, and observed him, and entered into the public dialogue with him, in private, as a conversationalist, how would describe him?

— Very delightful, very easy-going and very perceptive, even though he couldn't see very well. I knew that. But I just loved to be in his presence, because he was a very benign presence. He was very confident that human beings had one of the potentialities of immortality. And, of course, he and I believed that too, so we were more simpatico than some of the other Center scholars who were pretty skeptical and were not interested in that at all. I remember he wrote a book, what was it called, something to do about ongoing life or something like that.

— He also dabbled in Buddhism, from the standpoint of there being life after death.

— Yes, he did. He was very interested in Buddhism and Hinduism and all the major religions.

— Did he have a connection with Timothy Leary at Harvard, and LSD?

— I knew he had taken the LSD drug with Leary.

— Did he talk at all about that to you?

— A little bit. He said it was a wonderful experience. He had no negative effects. He said, "Some people, Frank, when they take LSD they get terrible nightmares with the feeling of threat, but all that I got was this ecstatic feeling of being connected with the whole universe. I could look at a flower and stare at the center and see that flower connected to the earth and the sky and the whole universe. It was a wonderful experience." He was just fascinated. I never took LSD though. Of course he was a member of an experimental group, he and Steve Allen and other prominent people. John Courtney Murray, one of our theological consultants, told me about his experiences too.

Huxley was eclectic, but it was interesting to see what he did with the various subjects he tackled.

President Jimmy Carter—Dialogue with a World Citizen

— When did you meet Jimmy Carter?

— I had a telephone call in 1975 from a friend of mine in Santa Barbara who had been a financial supporter of the Center for the Study of Democratic Institutions, a very active, very outspoken woman, named Betty Stevens; I knew Betty and her husband. I think he had died at that time. But anyway, she said, "Frank, we've this little governor of Georgia coming to visit us. We have given him some money, for his campaign to become president. He is dying to come to your Center, and have a dialogue with your Fellows. Can you arrange that?"

I said, "Oh, I think it will be a go. I'll call you back." To my surprise, when I went around the Center, the first person I talked to, of course, was Rexford G. Tugwell, who had been a "Brain Truster" for President Roosevelt. And Rex said to me, "Frank, why should we have a dialogue with this little man from Georgia? How many electoral votes does Georgia have? You know he is not going anywhere; he is not a serious candidate." So I don't know why I said it, but I said, "Well, Rex, just imagine that this long shot, this guy who is unthinkable now, picks up steam, and he gets nominated. Wouldn't you want to help him to have some advice that he could only get by visiting here, and hearing you?" I knew Rex had quite an ego. He said, "Oh, all right, I'll come to the meeting." I had to talk everyone into coming.

So I finally got a good quorum, and I called Betty back, and said, "Sure." We set up a time, and she said he is going to be speaking here, and he is going to a prayer breakfast." She added: "You have never been to a prayer breakfast, probably." I answered: "No, but I am finally going back to my faith." I said, "I would be interested. Where will it be?" She said, "Down at the Hotel Miramar. I am sure you would be welcomed."

So I went to the prayer breakfast that morning. And I was amazed by this man Jimmy Carter, who didn't talk like other politicians. He reminded me of Harry Truman to some extent, because Truman didn't follow the ordinary political way either. When Carter came out to speak in the hotel, he knelt down on the floor, in front of the speaker's table, and

Tom Storcke, a newsman in Santa Barbara,
and Frank Kelly

prayed: "The Lord guide me, in every word I say today." Then he got up and went over to the speaker's microphone, where he gave his speech. I told Betty later, "This guy is amazing." I've never covered a politician who acted like that. And it was real. He wasn't putting on a show. In all his books he mentions how he prays every day, and the power of prayer. I have a number of his books. He inscribed some of them for me.

A few hours later he came to the Center, with Jody Powell, who was one of his Georgia companions. So we sat down, we had a very lively dialogue; I could tell that Tugwell and the others were amazed at how much this "little governor" knew. He raised some good points.

— He was a disciple of Admiral Rickover, who started the nuclear Navy.

— Oh, he admired Admiral Rickover tremendously.

— How would you describe the tone of the meeting at the Center? Was this an impromptu discussion?

— Yeah.

— Did he bring an agenda with him?

— He just came in and delivered. He said, "I am going to talk very informally, and I know your dialogues are freewheeling. I am going to tell you my opinions right now, about what is going on in the presidential race, and about my philosophy. And then I want you to ask me any question that comes to your mind. I want to have a real far ranging discussion or dialogue as you call it." So we said fine, and we did. And he didn't bar anything. So at the end of the session he leaned back in his chair. And he said, "Now, I think some of you people here today are very doubtful about my political candidacy. I want to tell you: go back to your office today, you have a note pad, write on there March 15, 1975, a Governor of Georgia, Jimmy Carter, was here and told you that he was going to be the Democratic candidate and get elected as your next president." We all sat there; nobody knew what to say. So I said, "Thank you, Governor," and all the scholars went back to their offices.

I walked out with Carter, and I said, "By the way Governor, there is a lady here from Georgia, our cook—who cooks for our staff lunches. She is dying to say hello to you. "Sure," he said. So we walk back into the kitchen. Carter leans against the stove, and our cook was a wonderful black lady named Queen Jones. I always wanted to introduce her to a man named king, so they could get married. But Queenie was unabashed; you know she asked the governor this and that, and he fired right back.

We then went into my office. "I want to give you my private phone number," he said, "if you are interested in getting in our campaign, just call this number and we'll send you some material. And ask you to join us whenever you can." So I said, "Thank you." And I took the card, but I never did call. I was so fed up with losing candidates. But I have never forgotten that day. I kept in touch with him, and when my wife died he wrote me a beautiful note. I have several of his books, inscribed by him. Imagine telling us, in March of 1975, when he was about four percent in the polls, that he was going to be our next president! Have you ever read the book called *Marathon*, about the Carter campaign?

— I haven't. But I have read some of his poetry.

— Yeah, good poet.

— And I followed him from the standpoint of listening to some of his talks on Africa and what he wants to do there. And how he has been an observer for elections around the world.

— He is a global man: A glorious Being.

NUCLEAR AGE PEACE FOUNDATION

— How was the Nuclear Age Peace Foundation started?

— David Krieger came here to my home, twenty-some years ago, and presented his idea for a foundation to help rid the world of nuclear weapons and stop the arms race. David and I had worked together for the Center for the Study of Democratic Institutions. He had read my book about Truman, in which the president told me that humanity must put an end to war or face annihilation by weapons of mass destruction.

— Was this after your trip to the Soviet Union?

— Yes. And I said, "David, it's a wonderful idea and I think it's probably worth trying because something like this should exist in the world. But I think the chances of our getting very far are very slight." I told him very frankly, "But if you want me to, I'll work with you on it and see how far it will get. But I just think," and I told him about my experience in Russia, "how tough it's going to be." And that's why I admire David so much. He went right ahead no matter how tough it was and he's really got the Foundation to the point where it's well recognized after twenty years.

— When we look at institutional change, and the problems associated with achieving it, how do you view the prospects of producing change through the efforts of foundations like NAPF and the Center for the Study of Democratic Institutions?

— Well, Hutchins used to say, "You never know whether you're accomplishing something or not." He used to say, "People say to me: 'What good is your Center? All you do is talk and put out publications.' And I'd say: What good is Harvard University? How do you know it's a good University? You don't. You put out the best ideas you can and work as hard as you can." Gandhi said, "Never worry about results. Just do what you think is right." And that's what you have to do.

— One step at a time. So David came to you with this idea. Were there others involved in establishing the Nuclear Age Peace Foundation?

— Yes. Besides David and myself, there was Chuck Jamison, a lawyer here in Santa Barbara, and Wally Drew, a stock broker, and a teacher. Anyway for a year, we met in Chuck Jamison's law office downtown.

— Were these meetings every week?

— Just the four or five of us once a week. We talked about all the possibilities; and finally one day, Chuck Jamison said, "Well, I think we ought to create a nonprofit

corporation. I'll draft the papers. I know how to do it legally."
We had to have some officers and he turned to me and said,
"Frank, you should be president and David should be vice
president."

"Wait a minute." I said, "This is David's idea. David
should be president. If you want me as vice president, fine."

Chuck Jamison said, "But David isn't as well known as
you are." I insisted, and David was elected president. I think
it was only right to make him president. And he's done a
tremendous job. That's how the Nuclear Age Foundation got
started.

— How would you characterize those early years? Was
there a feeling of optimism?

— David felt we could promote change. That a lot more
people would respond than we might think. I was sort of
influenced in favor of doing it because I'd been involved with
the National Peace Academy campaign, which led to the
creation of the U.S. Institute of Peace. That idea was first
talked about at the time of the American Bicentennial, when
two senators came forward with the idea that we should
revive the idea for a Peace Academy; it got under way again. I
was asked to join the board. And the idea was that we'd see
how many people would be interested in such an institute. So
we went to a direct mail house; I don't know if you know the
Anacapa Fund here in Santa Barbara.

So I said, "Will you make a test mailing for us?"

"Sure, I'll do a test mailing." He was astounded! He came back and said, "My God, I think this thing might go. I've never seen such a response to a test mailing."

We sent out a couple of thousand letters. We got a fifteen percent response, instead of the usual one or two percent that such surveys receive from such a mailing. So we started. We mailed out two or three million letters, and we got forty-five thousand members. We had members in every state, in every congressional district, pushing the idea of a Peace Academy.

Ronald Reagan came out and said it was a terrible idea and he would veto it. We still got it through both houses of Congress, and Senator Mark Hatfield actually attached an amendment to a Defense Department bill at 2 o'clock in the morning, a bill giving the Pentagon another couple of hundred billion that included ten million dollars for a Peace Institute to get it started.

— So that experience must have given you some assurance that it was possible to establish the Nuclear Age Peace Foundation?

— Yes.

We organized in every congressional district to bring pressure on Congress to authorize the creation of the Peace Institute. We had a specific goal there. Whereas in the Foundation we didn't have the same type of goal; we had a wide goal, the ratification of the Nuclear Nonproliferation Treaty by all nations and the eventual destruction of all nuclear weapons. The first step was to get the treaty ratified and enforced by the International Court for Justice, now the International Criminal Court. That's something we put forward, which the Bush administration opposed.

— When I interviewed David, he talked about going to Hiroshima and seeing the museum there and being very much affected by what he saw. Had you talked to him before about Nuclear War?

— No. David and I knew each other only slightly when he was at the Center. I didn't see much of him after the Center closed, but I always liked him. I vividly remember the day he visited me here, and he said, "I think it's time to create a foundation to study and to develop ways of dealing with the nuclear danger." He said, "Do you remember Einstein said the release of nuclear energy has changed everything, except our thinking? Because we have not changed our thinking we are drifting toward an unimaginable catastrophe."

— And he was right!

— Thank God for the luck we have had so far, that no one has pulled the trigger again.

The thought of establishing a foundation dedicated to ending the threat of nuclear weapons interested me, because I remember talking with President Truman when he told me about the agony he went through before he decided to take us into the nuclear age.

That was more than twenty years ago. David's idea for a foundation came at the height of the Cold War: it was before the fall of the Berlin Wall, and the prospect of war with Russia was very much a reality. The United States and Russia had missiles pointing at each other. Concerned scientists like Carl Sagan were calling for an end to the madness. His book *Nuclear Winter* portrays in graphic detail the consequences of a nuclear attack:

> ... Except for fools and madmen, everyone knows that nuclear war would be an unprecedented human catastrophe. A more or less typical strategic warhead has a yield of 2 megatons, the explosive equivalent of 2 million tons of TNT. But 2 million tons of TNT is about the same as all the bombs exploded in World War II—a single bomb with the explosive power of the entire Second World War but compressed into a few seconds of time and an area 30 or 40 miles across...
>
> In a 2-megaton explosion over a fairly large city, buildings would be vaporized, people reduced to atoms and shadows, outlying structures blown down like matchsticks and raging fires ignited. And if the bomb were exploded on the ground, an enormous crater, like those that can be seen through a telescope on the surface of the Moon, would be all that remained where midtown once had been. There are now more than 50,000 nuclear weapons, more than 13,000 megatons of yield, deployed in the arsenals of the United States and the Soviet Union— enough to obliterate a million Hiroshimas.
>
> But there are fewer than 3,000 cities on the Earth with populations of 100,000 or more. You cannot find anything like a million Hiroshimas to obliterate. Prime military and industrial targets that are far from cities are comparatively rare. Thus, there are vastly more nuclear weapons than are needed for any plausible deterrence of a potential adversary.
>
> Nobody knows, of course, how many megatons would be exploded in a real nuclear war. There are some who think that a nuclear war can be "contained," bottled up before it runs away to involve much of the world's arsenals. But a number of

detailed analyses, war games run by the U.S. Department of Defense, and official Soviet pronouncements, all indicate that this containment may be too much to hope for: once the bombs begin exploding, communications failures, disorganization, fear, the necessity of making in minutes decisions affecting the fates of millions, and the immense psychological burden of knowing that your own loved ones may already have been destroyed are likely to result in a nuclear paroxysm. Many investigations, including a number of studies for the U.S. government, envision the explosion of 5,000 to 10,000 megatons—the detonation of tens of thousands of nuclear weapons that now sit quietly, inconspicuously, in missile silos, submarines and long-range bombers, faithful servants awaiting orders.

The World Health Organization, in a recent detailed study chaired by Sune K. Bergström (the 1982 Nobel laureate in physiology and medicine), concludes that 1.1 billion people would be killed outright in such a nuclear war, mainly in the United States, the Soviet Union, Europe, China and Japan. An additional 1.1 billion people would suffer serious injuries and radiation sickness, for which medical help would be unavailable. It thus seems possible that more than 2 billion people—almost half of all the humans on Earth—would be destroyed in the immediate aftermath of a global thermonuclear war. This would represent by far the greatest disaster in the history of the human species and, with no other adverse effects, would probably be enough to reduce at least the Northern Hemisphere to a state of prolonged agony and barbarism...

As I listened to David that afternoon, I kept thinking about the days when I worked for the Senate. And we had air raid drills, where the senators and their staff would go down to this secret hiding place beneath the Capitol. The ceiling was braced and we were sure we could survive, but I always felt guilty when we went through these drills. We were not allowed to call our wives and take anybody with us. The shelters were there to save the Senate and the Senate staff… It was a terrible feeling.

So I was working on that when David came around, and I told him so. I said, "Well, I am very interested in this because I know President Truman said to me and others that this is the greatest danger we face." And you remember Truman wanted all nuclear weapons put under international control, and almost got a peace for that, and everybody jumped on him. So David and I met with Wally Drew, Charles Jamison, and a schoolteacher from the Crane School. We met in Jamison's office. After the teacher dropped out, it was just the four of us: Drew, Krieger, Kelly and Jamison.

Initially, I was quite skeptical to tell you the truth. I've admitted this to David. But I thought it was worth a try because the danger was so great. Then I had the example of experts saying, "Nobody is interested in a Peace Academy," and then they found out they were wrong. The people out there were more than willing to get involved in something to counteract the war fever that was in this country and elsewhere. So that is why I decided to go with David because of the response I got with the National Peace Academy campaign.

— Did you start the same way with the Nuclear Age Peace Foundation, with a mailing to get support?

— No, we talked about that but we didn't start out that way; we just decided that we would hold conferences, and give awards, and start educating people about nuclear danger. We thought if we tried to start a membership campaign, we didn't know exactly what mission we would give our members. In the case of establishing a Peace Institute, it was easy to define goals and objectives. But the problem of nuclear weapons is gigantic and so vague in a way that we decided we wouldn't go that road, although maybe we should have.

IMPACT AND RESPONSE

My whole life I've dealt with people saying to me, "How do you know that you've had an impact? How can you tell?" And my answer has always been, "I don't know." So I say that I have lots of letters from people, since we started the Nuclear Age Peace Foundation more than twenty years ago, saying, "You're having an impact."

I think we've been imaginative. We've had wonderful dinners, we've given awards to a lot of people, and the number of people who take part in our activities continues to grow. Our membership is growing; our website has had thousands of hits. So by those objective terms, we are growing and expanding. As to whether we have changed the atmosphere of the world, I don't know—but I think we are making an impact. Well, we started out with a quote from Einstein; one of my favorite quotes: "The release of nuclear energy changed everything except our thinking. And so we drift toward unimaginable catastrophes." That was the original motto we started working with to change people's thinking, and I think it's happened to some degree. Now whether it's happening fast enough to avert the catastrophe, I don't know.

I think some of the recent findings, and discoveries brought out on television about North Korea and Iran, helped make people more aware of the danger. Through the web site we have gotten about twenty thousand members around the world. So I think the fact that certain events happened have made people conscious of this danger, helped us in getting some support for our programs. David Krieger is a wonderful fund-raiser. Wally Drew had a friend named Ethel Wells; and Ethel became interested in the foundation, and has remained a major donor. She has been a very important figure, and very unassuming who wishes to remain in the background.

FUTILITY OF NUCLEAR WAR

Just the other day there was a group that had a meeting that said that if one nuclear weapon was dropped in the western part of the United States, our hospitals couldn't cope with it; our whole system would break down! There's no way of coping with a disaster like that. And we can't. We say we can make emergency plans. We can't. There's no way that our whole total society can cope with a monstrous thing like that.

— I've read reports about bureaucrats trying to devise plans for mail delivery after an attack?

— It's absurd! You know, Ronald Reagan said a great thing, when he said, "A nuclear war cannot be won and must never be fought." That puts it up pretty well don't you think?

— I agree.

— Ronald Reagan understood the futility of nuclear war. He wanted to get rid of all the warheads; but his advisors wouldn't let him. When he had that meeting with Gorbachev in Iceland, Secretary of State George Schultz reported that Reagan said, "Why don't we just agree to get rid of all these nuclear weapons?"

And he said, "Oh now Mr. President, we're not prepared to make that proposal official." So it died away. But that's what we've got to have. We've got to have people waking up; whether they'll wake up in time, I don't know. But I think that the Foundation has been very useful to wake more and more people up.

It's as if the public is in denial. The press continues to report on problems; for example, the other night *Front Line* aired an excellent program on how close India and Pakistan came in '98 to actually using atomic weapons. It was scary!

Look at the Cuban Missile Crisis. If you read the Kennedy tapes, you'll see that some officials were contemplating the use of nuclear weapons. Thank God we had a president then who didn't want to go to war. *Thirteen Days: A Memoir of the Cuban Missile Crisis,* by Robert Kennedy is an excellent book on how the Kennedy administration avoided war; it should be required reading for students.

Thank God, we didn't to go war. If that would happen now, I think Bush might sanction it. Don't you?

— If they told him to do it.

— That sounds terrifying. It's why I think the Nuclear Age Peace Foundation is more valuable than ever right now. I wish that more and more people could wake up. People are in a dream state; they are worrying about this, that and the other. And here are these thousands of nuclear weapons that still exist in the world. I'd like to see our membership grow to 50,000 or something like that. Then, maybe we could have some concrete successes in getting the number of weapons cut down and steps being taken toward the abolition of those weapons. That is what we need. Get rid of them.

But even when the United States had an opportunity to work with the new leadership in Russia to get rid of the stockpiles of nuclear materials, Congress seemed paralyzed. It refused to fund the programs, and the last two administrations failed to make it a top priority, even when it became apparent that the scientists in charge of stockpiles of material had not been paid. It's very difficult to understand.

FOUNDING MEMBERS

— What role did Wally Drew play in establishing the Foundation?

— Wally Drew was involved in a number of the civic organizations in Santa Barbara. He was a widely respected officer of Smith Barney. He had a certain, I don't say Republican, but a certain conservative background that we needed. David and I were associated with liberal causes and organizations, so Wally was very important in getting the Foundation going. Especially in getting the big gifts from Ethel Wells and others.

— How important is it for a foundation like the Nuclear Age Peace Foundation to attract bipartisan support?

— It's important. With Wally's support, the Foundation received funds from individuals who would never have helped out had it not been for him. You never saw him when he was in his prime. He was so appealing to people and to many clients with all kinds of backgrounds. If Wally was connected to the Foundation, they would at least go along with it, or at least give a little support.

— What do you know about Wally's background?

— Wally? I think he was born in Wisconsin. After college he went into journalism, and was a newspaperman for a while, before he got into the stockbrokers business. We must have some kind of biographical material on Wally at the office. I don't know what he studied. He graduated from the University of Wisconsin, and then he went to work as a young reporter. I don't know how he got into the brokerage business.

— Charles Jamison. What do you remember about him?

— Charles Jamison was a well respected attorney here in Santa Barbara, and he had been a veteran of World War II; I think he was in the Pacific—Guadalcanal, and all those places. So he had enough of war to realize that we had to stop it, and read enough about nuclear weapons to be easily convinced that they were a great danger. We went for about a year, just discussing in his office various way of getting the Foundation launched. I have forgotten how finally we did do it. I think it was with our awards system.

PEACE LEADERSHIP AND WORLD CITIZENSHIP AWARDS

The Peace Leadership Award dinner is an important event, and I have forgotten how many years ago we also started giving a World Citizenship Award, so we give two. And that helps because we can get two people of international standing. It helps us in building up the attendance at our dinners.

— Are both awards given the same evening?

— Yeah. A few years ago we gave the Peace Leadership Award to Arthur N.R. Robinson, the former President and Prime Minister of Trinidad and Tobago, and the World Citizenship Award to my close friend Robert Mueller. But it's just not political figures; we have also given the World Citizenship Award to entertainers like Harry Belafonte, and others who have worked for humanitarian causes.

— An excellent choice. Belafonte has taken a strong stand on a number of issues relating to peace.

— He is a good man. He doesn't shy away from controversy either. You may want to look at his speech he gave, and select a passage or two. It was a moving address.

...Most people in this country only know what is on the front pages of the newspapers, what they see on CNN, or what Peter Jennings says on ABC. We talk very little about the over 3 million people who have already been murdered in the Sudan—the war that's been going on longer than any other war on the planet. You don't hear too much about them. After all, they're just happy natives and that's the way they are. They're very primitive. They have that Neanderthal kind of behavior. We Europeans, we Americans, we are the fortunate ones, we will just wait for the inferior countries to catch up, and when they're ready and they have earned our preoccupation we will go help them in some way.

And, of course, there is Columbia and all that we've done to crucify that nation, turning it from a rich, agricultural, productive state into a beggar nation forcing tens of thousands of children to come into the world deformed and plagued by malnutrition. There are so many things that go on in so many places in the world that we hear very little about. The world is engulfed in war.

The struggle in the United Nations over borders seems endless. How many more borders are now being created? Israel, a new promising nation, was seen as a wonderful experiment in democracy. I sent my brother there to live, to look at this new experiment, to be touched by what he would learn, and to come back here and give instruction. It was so wonderful that in our daily exchanges, Dr. King should have seen so much in the future of Israel and the future of so many other nations that were in formation. How sad it is that he was taken away from us in the way in which he was.

Three days before he was murdered, Dr. King was in New York, in my home. My home was where he did a lot of his writing and where he framed many of his speeches. We had an intimacy and we shared many moments of thought and reflection together. On this particular night, just a few days before he went to Memphis, he seemed very troubled. He was troubled quite often, but this time he had a peculiar look. I said to him, "What's troubling you, Martin?" And he said, "You know, Harry, we worked hard and long for our cause, to fix segregation, and now we're moving full force into the future of integration, and hopefully we will be able to shift from what we're doing to the new campaign for economic rights and economic freedom and to get rid of economic oppression. But I'm troubled." I asked, "What troubles you?" He said, "I've come to believe that in our movement, looking for integration, we are integrating into a burning house." When I heard him say this, I realized that it wasn't that we had not thought about how you shape America as a country, but we had not thought about how you shape America's citizens in the wake of all that had gone before us and during our day. After some exchange on the matter, he said he had to go to Atlanta first, before Memphis. I said, "Listen, in this view that you have of us integrating into a burning house, how do you suggest we fix it?" He said, "It's very simple. We're all going to have to become firemen."

— Who was the first recipient of the Peace Leadership Award?

— My friend Claiborne Pell, who was then Chairman of the Senate Foreign Relations Committee. I suggested to David that we have a dinner here and give him a Peace Leadership Award. And Claiborne Pell agreed to come. He was the first to receive the award, and each year since we have nominated another outstanding person.

The list of recipients is truly outstanding, and includes the following:

Judge C. G. Weeramantry, 2008

Peter Yarrow, Noel Stookey, and
    Mary Travers, 2007

Blasé Bonpane, 2006

Daniel Ellsberg, 2005

Walter Cronkite, 2004

Jonathan Schell, 2003

President Arthur N. R. Robinson and
    Dr. Robert Woetzel, 2002

Craig Kielburger and Hafsat Abiola, 2001

King Hussein bin Talal of Jordan, 2000

General Lee Butler, 1999

Jody Williams, 1998

Lord Yehudi Menuhin, 1997

Anne and Paul Ehrlich, 1996

Rev. Theodore M. Hesburgh, 1995

Helen Caldicott, 1994

Dr. Carl Sagan, 1993

Mairead Corrigan Maguire, 1992

His Holiness the XIVth Dalai Lama,
    Tenzin Gyats, 1991

Archbishop Desmond Tutu, 1990

Captain Jacques-Yves Cousteau, 1989

Right Honorable David Russell Lange, 1988

R. E. "Ted" Turner, 1987

Honoree Dr. Rodrigo Carazo, 1986

Admiral Gene R. LaRocque, 1985

BOARD OF DIRECTORS

— In reference to its growth of the Foundation, and the make-up of the Board of Directors, you have Richard Falk, David Krieger, yourself. Then you have Sue Hawes, Lessie

Frank King Kelly with Walter Cronkite at the
Peace Leadership Award Dinner, 2004

Nixon Schontzler, and Anna Grotenhuis, among others; and the gender mix is about equal, which I am sure was something you favored considering your desire to see more women represented at the Center.

— I was very insistent with David that we try to get at least equal representation of women on our board and as consultants. I said, "I wouldn't even mind a majority because I was so keenly aware of how damaged the Center for the Study of Democratic Institutions was, with only one woman. So, we have a pretty good representation.

— What role does the Board of Directors play in the organization?

— David is pretty careful about bringing items before the board. Most of the ideas come from David and myself, and occasionally in the old days from Chuck Jamison, but the board is pretty active. They are very supportive.

ADVISORY COUNCIL

— And the Advisory Council?

— That is something we had at the Center for the Study of Democratic Institutions. I told David I thought it was important to get as many big names in different parts of the world as possible. You wouldn't have to have them on our Board of Directors; and they probably wouldn't have to come to Santa Barbara for meetings. But their support would prove crucial in achieving our goals, and advancing new initiatives the board may adopt. The membership includes such noted world citizens as: Hon. Rodrigo Carazo, the former President of Costa Rica; the Dalai Lama; Queen Noor of Jordan; Hon. Arthur N.R. Robinson, the former President and Prime Minister of Trinidad and Tobago; Archbishop Desmond M. Tutu; and Judge C.G. Weeramantry, the former vice president of the International Court of Justice. The entire membership can be found on the website for the Foundation. Their advice and counsel has proved invaluable to David and the Board of Directors.

— I noticed that Ted Turner is also a member. His work with the United Nations and as founder of the Nuclear Threat Initiative set an example for others to follow, which was followed by Bill Gates and other philanthropists. How did he become involved with the Foundation?

— We gave him an award. I was reading the *Los Angeles Times* one day, and I saw there an article, which said something like this: "An eccentric millionaire, Ted Turner, has decided to set up the Goodwill Games in Moscow." President Jimmy Carter had withdrawn the United States from the 1976 Olympic Games in Moscow in retaliation for the Soviet invasion of Afghanistan. After reading the article, I called David and suggested that we give Ted Turner an award. David said, "Well, I guess we could. How do we get in touch with him?" I said, "I don't know. Let's write him a letter." So we did. And he accepted. He was getting many awards in those days.

When he came out here, David and I went out to meet him at the airport. He landed in a private plane and we pulled up alongside the plane. He gets out of the plane with the most beautiful blonde you have ever seen, like Marilyn Monroe, a gorgeous woman. And he gets out, and I said, "Welcome to Santa Barbara, Mr. Turner." He whacked me on the back and said, "Don't call me Mr. Turner; call me Ted."

— Was it Jane Fonda?

— No it wasn't Jane Fonda. This was before Jane Fonda. He introduced her: "This is Jacky. She drives racing cars for fun." So we all get in the car. One of our board members had a big limousine, and so we all got into that. I am sitting next to this beautiful blonde. I said, "Have you read any of the material we sent to Mr. Turner, the booklets about the Foundation."

"Oh yes," she said. "I've read them all." And Turner spoke up, he said, "Yeah, I depend on her to tell me whether they are good or bad, and she's given you a good recommendation." That's why he decided to accept our award. This blonde told him it was a good idea. So we took him over to the Red Lion, and he gave a wonderful speech that night.

I heard him give one at Harvard that was quite interesting. One of the students stood up, who was from the Kennedy school, and apparently the Kennedy School was thinking of starting another program. The student made a pitch for some money, by suggesting that Turner might want to support the program. There was a long pause, then Turner said, "I applied to go to Harvard, and you turned me down. So what I am thinking," he said, "Why don't we let the

Harvard boys take care of that one; if you wanted my money, you should have given me what I wanted then."

— That's funny.

— He is a character.

— He sure is. But there's a serious side to him. I watched Charlie Rose interview him this April, and when Rose asked him to identify the most serious challenge facing the world, Turner said nuclear weapons, and called for total nuclear disarmament.

PUBLICATION PROGRAM

— What about the publications program?

— The Foundation has published a number of books, and a series of pamphlets, highlighting the activities of the Foundation, and more recently the Internet has come to play a greater role. Have you seen the Foundation's book *Hope in a Dark Time*?

— Yes.

— You know, the first edition sold out immediately and we're on the second edition already. I think that's a good sign. The Foundation has published a series of pamphlets and a few books; but the Internet has played a major role. The monthly newsletter, *The Sunflower*, which David oversees, has proved invaluable for informing the members, and as a means to reach out to government officials and the general public.

SWACKHAMER PEACE ESSAY CONTEST

— What's the history behind the Swackhamer Peace Essay Contest?

— Gladys Swackhamer was a dear old lady in a wheelchair, who started coming to my series of downtown dialogues, called the Hungry Club Forum, which I hosted for about ten or twelve years, back in the 60's or 70's. You were supposed to bring your own sandwich. We didn't supply any refreshments. Trinity Episcopal Church gave us the use of their guild hall. We met there, I forget whether it was Wednesdays or Thursdays, for about ten or twelve years. And this one little old lady came in a wheelchair, and I would look out, introducing the speakers, and she had already nodded off. But she was so sweet and I talked to her quite a bit.

Then one time she didn't show up and I found out she was ill out at Val Verde; she was in the infirmary out there. So I went out to see her several times, and she invited me to come out and meet some of her friends. And lo and behold when she died, she left I think a third or a fifth of her assets, which amounted to about three hundred thousand dollars, to the Foundation. She said, specifically because I had paid attention to her when she was ill, one of the few people who came to see her. I didn't realize I was fundraising. But she was so impressed by that. Oh, you know, when you are aging like I am now you appreciate it when people still want to keep in touch with you. The infirmary out there is a very beautiful place, so empty and lonely. I sat by her bed and talked to her.

She wanted us to start a series of essay prizes, for young people, on what they would do to for peace. This year we have—David could tell you the exact number—but I think it is seven or eight hundred. And every year now it has been growing. The essays are from college students and others on what they can do about working for peace, particularly nuclear peace. So that has worked out well.

— What do the winners receive?

— Well, every year we give out several prizes. I think we give them enough for a year in college or something like that.

— That's great.

— Yeah. I really cared about the old lady. I could have brushed her off, I guess, when I saw her falling asleep and never made contact with her. I am not breaking my arm patting myself on the back, but you never can tell, can you. She was sitting there. I had no idea in my mind that she had a fortune. Or that she would leave a large part of it to the Nuclear Age Peace Foundation.

— It also demonstrates that people who have money can really do something worthwhile with it, by passing on the torch so to speak, and keep the light burning.

— That's good.

Frank Kelly Lecture on Humanity's Future

— What do you remember about the origins of the Frank King Kelly lecture series?

— It came about because David Krieger said to me one night that he wanted to establish something to carry on my memory because I was one of the founders in the Nuclear Age Peace Foundation, and helped to create the United States Institute of Peace and all these other things I'd been involved in over the years. And he said, "I want the Foundation to create a series called 'The Frank Kelly Lectures on Humanity's Future' and I want you to give the first lecture." That's how it came about.

— What was the title of the lecture?

— It's called "Glorious Beings." In it I focus on the idea of the future. How the future affects humanity. We're always thinking of the future. And now more and more in this age everybody is concerned about the future. Everybody's predicting economic trends, population trends, and moral trends, you know. And our lives are very largely now focused on the future. The thing about the future is that you can't control it. And that makes it wonderful, in my view, because there's always more over the horizon than humanity will ever grasp.

— A humbling effect on the human psyche, and one that should make us a little cautious as to how we should proceed.

— Yes, a humbling effect, but also an exalting effect, because in "Glorious Beings" I point out that we *are* connected with a glorious universe. We come out of this glorious universe and we have these capacities that are far beyond our own recognition. We do not consciously understand what marvelous beings we are.

Professor Richard Falk, from Princeton, gave the next lecture. In it Falk dealt with the threats to civil liberties caused by the terrorist attack on the Twin Towers. He depicted the great dangers looming over free human beings who were determined, apparently, to create a Department of Homeland Security, where everybody's focused on security, security, security. In his view, that is the wrong focus; instead the focus should be on courage and ingenuity, and faith in humanity's capacity to get beyond any problem, any crisis. Richard Falk did a beautiful job.

The plan is to eventually publish an anthology of all the lectures when we get a few more.

— Are you involved in the selection of the speaker?

— I was this time because David Krieger wanted me to be. I said, "Maybe I shouldn't be." He said, "Why not? You've got people in mind, who you think would do a great job, so let me know who they are." We both agreed that Richard Falk would be great for the second speaker. And he did a very good job.

— Looking back, how do you view the Foundation in respect to where we are today in the ongoing struggle to rid the world of nuclear weapons?

— In the years since then, the nonprofit, nonpartisan, instructional education and advocacy organization we launched together has provided leadership toward a nuclear weapons-free world under international law. It has been a voice of conscience for our nation and the world.

Our message is that nuclear weapons threaten the future of all life on our planet and it is the responsibility of all of us, working together, to end this threat forever. We believe that peace in a world free of nuclear weapons is everyone's birthright. It is the greatest challenge of our time to restore that birthright to our children and all future generations.

In our 2008 report to our members, Dr. Krieger describes the new DVD on "Nuclear Weapons and the Future" which is designed to educate people everywhere and to show how they can make a difference in ending these dangers. The DVD has had showings in more than 100 countries and all 50 states in the U.S.

We have also created an *Appeal to the Next President of the United States* for U.S. leadership in taking seven steps to secure a world free of nuclear weapons.

BARBARA'S ILLNESS AND DEATH

— One of the subjects we have yet to talk about is Barbara's death. I realize it's hard to talk about but I would be remiss if I didn't at least ask if you wanted to say something about your wife's illness and death, since she played such a pivotal role in the unfolding of your life, the person you spent 54 years with. Do you remember when she came down with cancer?

— Let's see, she died in 1995. And she had it for about two years. She was having abdominal pain. She was a very intuitive person, and she begged the doctor to do an exploratory operation in the region of the colon. She said, "I am afraid something is in there." And he had all these diplomas on his wall, and he said, "Oh, no, no Mrs. Kelly. You just have diverticulitis. Take these pills." So finally she was in such terrible pain we had to rush her into the hospital; when they opened her up, they found a cancer as big as a grapefruit, which had been growing in there, and she knew it.

Barbara was the kind of person who intuitively knew things that most people don't. She had an awareness of what was happening to her and other people. I feel sort of guilty for the fact that I didn't press and take her to another doctor. But we had been going out to the clinic, I won't name the clinic, all these years and we had confidence in these people. And after she died one of my sons, my older son, wanted me to sue the clinic. I knew that Barbara didn't want to file lawsuits against doctors. She said, "Sure, they make mistakes; they have the power of life and death in a way over us. But to make it into a legal fight, it is just not something that I want to do." I knew she didn't want to do it. So I didn't do that. I just let it go. Maybe I made the wrong decision.

So anyway, when she died, she had been so close to me for so many years I felt like a big wall had fallen down and beyond that wall there was chaos and I didn't know how I was going to function or whether I should function. I thought maybe it is time to let go. You know, how long does a man live? I was 81 years old. Before she died she anticipated this. She told me, "I know you are going to be lonely. We were very, very close, and I know how I would feel if you died, and when I go it is going to be a disastrous feeling for you. And I want you to keep going as much as you can, because I have this feeling that you still have some things to say, and that you can be an example for many people on how to deal with life hopefully and creatively. So I don't want you to let go or give up."

And in the meanwhile she had brought in this friend of hers, this beautiful woman named Christine Boesch, who she called her soul sister. She asked Christine to be with her when I was there, and as the last moment approached she said to Christine, "You know, Frank is going to be very lonely after I am gone, and I hope that you will look after him."

So Christine took that very consciously, as she does everything. And she became my closest friend, and encouraged me to do a lot of things; to write some more things, and to finish my book about Truman, which came out in 1998, three years after Barbara died. So I could feel that my wife was advising me, as she did in life, even beyond in the next stage. A lot of people have told me about things like that. Dr. Robert Mueller told me, after his wife died in Costa Rica, he had her buried near this little house down there and he'd go out there almost every day and sit by the grave and ask her what he should do, and to give him advice, and she would always come through. There would always be an inner response. So I think it is beautiful.

— It is.

FRIDAY NIGHT DISCUSSION GROUP

— Although not associated with the Foundation, your Friday night discussion group is representative of a theme that runs through your entire public life. Would you agree?

— Yes. It's a basic belief of mine that one of the most significant things in a democracy is to have meetings in your home, and not in halls or at the universities. And that's what I've tried to do with these Friday night meetings I started two or three years ago here in my own home in Santa Barbara.

I've periodically asked the members who come here regularly, "What do you get out of this? What benefits do you think you get from coming?" We range over everything. And I went around the circle and they all said, "It's a unique experience that we don't find anywhere else."

The average person associates public discourse with what they see on television: debates where people shout at each other, or big meetings where speakers get up and harangue the crowds. There's very little quiet, informal, wide-ranging human discussion by ordinary citizens. But I have such discussions in my home.

Actually it was Christine Boesch who suggested the value of having such a group on Friday nights.

I begged Christine to marry me, because I felt that Barbara wanted us to be together. She decided that she couldn't try to fill the role that Barbara had in my life, but I continue to consider her the beloved woman in my last years. I will always love her, just as I loved Barbara.

I will love them both forever.

CONCLUDING COMMENTS

— I'd like to end with the article you published in the *Saturday Review* in 1970 at the invitation of Norman Cousins. For me it captures your sprit, and the drive you continue to exhibit in search of a better world.

Thank you, Frank.

A Report on the State of Mankind: 1970

By Frank K. Kelly

At the very moment of lift-off there is no sense of movement, an astronaut said. Man may have passed his own moment of lift-off into ultimate change. Now we have a sense of voyaging in ways that are stranger than our dreams.

The word has passed through cities and towns of Europe and the Americas, through the ancient streets and paths of Asia and Africa, to the nomads carrying transistor radios in the Himalayas and the Andes and along the Amazon and the Nile: Man lives on a beautiful colored ball, traveling at high speed through enormous darkness toward the fires of countless suns. The landing on the moon confirmed the solidity of other worlds. Many of us expected to see what we saw; many accepted it with a shrug or a smile. To young people already aware of science fiction, it was a happening that had happened long before. But the sight of our little globe shining in space made us realize that we can be inside and outside at the same time.

In each of us, now that we know so much and know how little that is, there are two states of being, embracing and struggling: Mankind I and Mankind II. We are still attached to the earth, but our minds move in and out in a dizzying rhythm.

We are changing so swiftly that we do not know what we are or what we may become.

Since Hiroshima, we have known that the old man must die. The man of devouring ambition, the consuming man, must give way to the new man, the learning man, the man of understanding, the servant of life. The future depends upon our opening of ourselves to the emergence of the servant. The great transformation now is the realization that everything can be transformed. Men and nations still fight for land and resources, for principles and pride, but the skies are full of satellites riding high above the drawn lines. No one is dominant over his own destiny; no one can really control any territory anymore.

As we awaken to the knowledge that we have been lifted into ultimate changes beyond our dreams, some of us are fearful, others feel a terrible joy. Many believe that scientists will develop fairly clear explanations of where we are going or build a Great Computer that will bring together all the factors necessary to make a new web of life. There may be thousands, perhaps millions, of unknown factors—but they will be found, the worshipers of New Science believe.

Many have refused to think any longer about immortality of the soul; they contend that man is on the verge of discovering ways of everlasting physical survival. A temporary embodiment of invisible forces, he is learning how to remold the body in which he finds himself. With fabricated parts, man may go on and on from world to world. Death will be confined to lesser forms of life.

Many others believe they are participating in a revolution of the spirit. Institutional churches may be growing in some ways, disintegrating in others, but there are religious torrents running among the young and the old, among people of all ages and places. Mankind II may combine this spiritual revolution with an enormous effort to preserve or reconstruct the web of physical life. The blood sacrifices of Jesus and Gandhi, of Martin Luther King, of John and Robert Kennedy, of all those torn by violence, may be truly honored by those who make the future.

We now have a growing awareness of the importance of the person. Each man is a universe penetrated by other universes. A world begins with each of us, and no one knows its end. What spirals on toward an unknown destination cannot be contained in a vehicle of culture and civilization or described as a collection of invisible atoms linked together into a visible whole. The urgency that shook atoms together into a brain, that began to look through eyes and speak with tongues, is transforming man as man transforms all.

In this transformation we naturally want the strength and goodness of the old man to survive in the new. But the kind of valor and toughness in the old man may now have to yield to a new valor—the courage to surrender joyfully, to accept the fact that we are all closely related to one another, breathing upon one another, touching one another whether we want to touch or not.

The signals that will guide us in the continuing voyage into the future will be the signals of persons in contact—mysterious persons with universal human rights, men like women and women like men, aware that the whole wonder of mankind can be deciphered in every human face, aware that we are all going together and we won't know where we're going until we get there—and then we'll go beyond.

The spread of compassion in the midst of killing the world over indicates that the old man is being replaced. He may refuse to acknowledge that there is any grace in surrendering to peaceful change. He sinks slowly down within us, with roars and rages, retreating into darkness with his scarred shield firmly held, dying with a warning that he may return. Cool eyes of cameras in the skies record the monstrous miseries, the self-inflicted wounds, the crucifixions that men put upon others and upon themselves. But such things are not regarded as inevitable anymore. Even those who say that fighting cannot be quickly stopped —and a bitter truth is on their side—do not want war anymore.

In the United States, Japan, Germany, and other nations where radical groups have been controlled by force, leaders seek better solutions to the problems that provoked the violence. Many are calling for drastic changes in the technological society that has crippled or alienated so many people. Wars are no longer considered profitable; industrialists and students alike have recognized that settlement of disputes by armed conflicts must be abandoned.

The gloomiest predictions made during the years since the establishment of the United Nations have not yet come true. The U.N. has been relatively feeble from the beginning—largely dependent upon the major nations, which have often failed to give that support. Yet the U.N. and related agencies—the World Health Organization, the Food and Agriculture Organization, the International Labor Office, the International Bank, UNICEF, the U.N. Development Fund, and many others—have helped to build the foundations for a community of humanity. U Thant has cited the process of decolonization that has "liberated nearly a billion people in less than a quarter of a century—a development on a scale that was inconceivable in 1945 and in which the U.N. has played a central role...The obligation of the rich nations to assist the poor ones is now widely regarded as a normal feature of life and a new moral precept in the international community. And I think of the Universal Declaration of Human Rights, the effort to make it increasingly applicable, and the endless struggle against racism and discrimination in all their different forms that has been and is being waged at the United Nations."

The Secretary General also has stressed the increasing internationalism of young people. "Nothing could do more," he commented, "to increase the effectiveness of the United Nations than a modification of the concept of national sovereignty in harmony with the intellectual and technological realities of our time. There I believe that artists, scientists, businessmen, those who deal with communications of all kinds, and the young people can help us in a decisive way."

The young sing of answers "blowin' in the wind." All people now realize that the world's winds blow from one continent to another. We breathe our neighbors' air, and they breathe ours. Without clean air, we will choke and die together.

In matters of environment, the implication is clear. Mankind will have to choose between material progress and the continuation of life on earth.

Sverker Astrom, the Swedish Ambassador to the United Nations, recently proposed a resolution calling for a world conference on what man is doing to his environment. Representatives of fifty-three nations endorsed the proposal, and it was adopted unanimously by the General Assembly. The conference will be held in Stockholm in 1972, but all governments concerned by the swelling tide of pollution obviously have been confronted by demands for more immediate action.

Ambassador Astrom told the Assembly: "Even if we avoid the risk of blowing up the planet, we may, by changing its face, unwittingly be parties to a process with the same fatal outcome. Indiscriminate and uncontrolled use of modern technology, indispensable as such technology is for economic and social progress, may set trends in motion which lead to unforeseen harmful effects in unexpected places."

Ambassador Astrom suggests that the conference might prepare a "Universal Declaration on the Protection and

Betterment of the Human Environment." He said he did not know whether many of the damaging effects of runaway technology are irreversible, but he felt that steps to halt pollution have to be taken as swiftly as possible.

In Sweden, a national Consultative Board for Environmental Problems has been created to check the contamination of air and water. Swedish experts found that many pollutants were coming from the high chimneys of Britain and West Germany. Builders of such chimneys in Britain had claimed that their acrid fumes would be carried far from the United Kingdom—perhaps as far as Moscow. The Russians, becoming alarmed, have begun to show more interest in international efforts to control pollution.

Man may have to consider the effects of weather-changing experiments. Should the weather-modifying projects conducted by the United States, Israel, and other countries be monitored by an international commission? Israel has produced rain vital to a parched land in the Middle East, but what will be the long-range consequences? Can computers take into account all the filth spewed by factory chimneys, fallout from hydrogen bombs tested in the atmosphere by Communist China and perhaps others, effects on the earth's crust of underground explosions set off by the Soviet Union and the United States, and all the other repercussions of technological devices?

The crisis of environment will certainly be one of the great issues of the seventies. President Nixon has established a council to consider all environmental problems, and the governors of many states are studying what needs to be done. Representative Richard L. Ottinger and other members of Congress have proposed a constitutional amendment that provides for an "Environmental Bill of Rights." Senator Gaylord Nelson of Wisconsin has called for a "national land and ocean use policy that will set environmental standards with immediate sanctions for violators."

Political scientist Harvey Wheeler has predicted a "new politics of ecology." This issue, Wheeler said, "produces conflicts in the realm of knowledge and thought, in Teihard de Chardin's 'noöphere.' Here we need new policy-forming institutions, based on a different kind of representation, eventually producing new parties devoted to the policies of ecology."

The question of saving life on earth has become most pressing in the United States; the effects of pollution have become most noticeable here. In California and New York protesters with a wide range of political views have become almost as concerned about the preservation of environment as they are about the Vietnam War.

Divisions between reactionaries and radicals, conservatives and liberals, have become blurred in the struggle to save the air, water, and fertile earth necessary for human survival. Activist students participated in a conference convened by Governor Ronald Reagan of California and heard Mr. Reagan admit that California had been severely damaged. "We messed it up to begin with," Reagan said. "And we can clean it up. The opportunity is ours. The responsibility is ours."

Two powerfully phrased resolutions offered by California students were adopted at conferences on "People and Air" and "People and Water." A twenty-year-old girl from the University of California at Davis asked the state government to ban internal combustion engines in California by 1975. Another resolution, offered by a student from Berkeley, demanded reconsideration of a gigantic water project on which the California state government has already spent many millions of dollars. The resolution said: "Recycling of waste water and desalinization must be given a higher priority than long-distance water transport." It added that "the California water plan must not undergo any further development without further study of the degradation of the ecology of California." Meeting at Stanford University, 200 student leaders formed a confederation to create "more public awareness of our environment crisis through widespread education, the electoral process, lobbying, economic boycotts, and public demonstrations of concern."

People in other states have prodded legislators and governors, judges and city managers, industrialists and union leaders to join the struggle while time remains.

The sign of unity is a sign of hope. This spring there will be a gathering in San Francisco to celebrate the first twenty-five years of the United Nations, to look at the dangers through which mankind has passed, and to renew mankind's confidence in the future. In my view, this would be the right time to present a report on mankind and life on earth. California would be the right place to assemble those who might produce the ideas and the fiery determination needed to save earth as a home for man.

Two other major issues to be faced by mankind are population control and the expansion of food production to feed the hungry millions now on the planet.

The prospects for many countries have improved enormously in the last few years, with the doubling of wheat, rice, and corn crops in Asia, Africa, and Latin America through the use of new types of grains, spoilage control, availability of fertilizers, better irrigation methods, and more use of machines. Barring unforeseen disasters, India expects to produce enough food for her 550 million people in 1970-71. Mexico now produces enough wheat for her population and ships a half-million tons of grain to other countries. Indications are that Pakistan and Turkey will also be exporting grain in the next few years. A study recently released by the U.N. Food and Agriculture Organization indicates that by 1985 the demand for food in the poorer countries will be about two-and-a-half times the 1962 level. New types of wheat, rice, and other cereals are expected to meet this demand, using only one-third of the area now under cultivation. Land not used for cereals will be released for other crops.

These trends may give us enough time to bring the world's population under control before mass starvation occurs. Two distinguished groups recently have issued reports strongly recommending the establishment of a U.N. Commissioner for Population. The United Nations Association Policy Panel—headed by John D. Rockefeller, III—said that such a commissioner should be added to the U.N. Development Program and should administer a fund of $100-million annually for family planning activities. The Commission on International Development, supported by the World Bank and headed by Lester Pearson, former Prime Minister of Canada, recommended "the United Nations should appoint a Commissioner for Population. An international program should be launched through the World Bank in consultation with the World Health Organization for the mobilization of research in the field of fertility control."

There has been a most hopeful change in attitude toward population control in India, Japan, Pakistan, and other countries, where thousands of men have submitted voluntarily to sterilization. If the new man—the man of compassion, cooperation, understanding—is to dominate the development of mankind in the future, every human being must cooperate. It is clear that people in all parts of the world are awakening to this necessity.

The material resources of the earth are limited and must be conserved. But limitations on the resources of the spirit—the functioning of the mind, the outreach of human sympathy, the awareness that many men still have of an awesome presence given the name of God—have not yet been discovered.

U Thant pointed out the bitter paradoxes of the last twenty years: "On the one hand, there is the remarkable effort of the international community to define common aspirations on a world-wide and regional basis. On the other hand, it is clear that, in spite of the greater awareness and demand for the respect of the individual, serious violations of human rights, including resort to violence and terror, continue to occur."

In 1970 the struggle for human rights will be given more attention than ever before. Many people, young and old, black and white, rich and poor, socialists and businessmen, intellectuals and activists, are now seeking ways of coming together. Huge gaps in understanding and communication have always existed. But this is an age in which these gaps are being recognized and fully explored.

As Mankind II develops, a global dialogue on the rights and duties of man must be initiated and supported by people with many varying views. As we travel outward and inward on the immense journey into an ultimate transformation, we must speak of what we owe to one another as well as what we expect of one another. Our duties to one another in the crisis of our age are very great.

Many eyes have been opened. Many governments have begun to see the folly of what is being done to the earth. The Strategic Arms Limitation Talks indicate that the United States and the Soviet Union want to turn away from the monstrous arms race that has been devouring our substance and shadowing our lives. The emergence of man as the servant of life must be encouraged. The reasons for hope must be shown as clearly as the reasons for alarm.

All education institutions and nongovernmental organizations concerned with the building of a "social and international order" for the attainment of universal human rights should unite to sponsor a continuing report on the state of mankind.

The Center for the Study of Democratic Institutions, the World Man Fund, the Fund for Peace, the World Academy of Arts and Sciences, the John XXIII International Institute, the World Law Fund, the Center for the Study of the Future of Man, the United Nations Associations, the World Federalists, the Cooperators (a newly founded society), and others should devote part of their resources to the formation of a Council for Humanity. The council would present a series of statements by spokesmen for mankind: men and women from a wide variety of countries and cultures.

The council might be composed of leaders from the sponsoring organizations. Half the members would be chosen by youth organizations, and none could serve more than a year. The council would have a very small staff, so that no opportunity for the formation of a bureaucracy would arise.

The first council would simply be charged with beginning a discussion on the state of mankind. Council members would examine the vital issues and make recommendations for national and regional action. Every country would be asked to provide at least four hours of free broadcasting time each month for statements by council speakers. Additional time would be provided for commentaries and criticisms and suggestions for statements from other viewpoints. Newspapers and leading magazines in all nations would be asked to carry the texts of these statements or extensive summaries.

At the end of each year, a day for mankind might be celebrated. The statements of the spokesmen would be published in many languages, in an annual report, and distributed to schools and libraries all over the world. The people of the earth would be urged to write to the council, giving their views and their ideas for speeding the development of a world civilization.

The vast resources of information available through the U.N. and other organizations could be used by members in preparing their statements—but they would speak as persons, communicating with other persons, not as officials speaking for governments or to governments.

There is a turn against war. There is a turn toward the unity of man, stronger than all strife and divisions. There is a turn toward hope. There is a growing realization that we have lifted off into a new age. There is pain ahead. There is suffering. There is stretching of the very being of man, and the fear that the transformation of this time will change us more than we ever want to change. But while there are voices that we can hear, let us listen to them. Beyond the darkness, there may be light.

POSTSCRIPT

My father is now 94 years old. He still hosts "dialogs" at his house every Friday night, lectures in Santa Barbara, is an active board member of the Nuclear Age Peace Foundation, and traveled to Kansas City recently to be the keynote speaker at the opening of the new Truman Library.

Several times a week, he also walks, in a park above the beach, with his walker and with the help of his long-time friend and companion, Fabio Duran. He still has a "hello" and a smile for every pretty girl he passes.

Above all, Dad is still focused on the transcendent goodness of the human spirit—the essential nature of which is expressed as respect, appreciation, and love for others, and the unlimited potential we, together, share.

His positive determination and conviction about humanity still shines, undiminished. As proof, here is a letter he has just drafted to President-elect Barack Obama.

Mary and I, and our sons Chris, Matt and Michael, salute Frank King Kelly for a lifetime of achievement.

We love you, Dad!

— Terry Kelly

President-elect Barack Obama
Washington, D.C. 20510

Dear President-elect Obama:

In your fine book, *The Audacity of Hope*, you emphasize the necessity of recognizing the constructive and creative powers of humanity.

In my 94 years on this planet, I have witnessed one great transformation after another, supporting the enormous value of hope and creativity through humanity's tremendous achievements in the 20th and 21st centuries. I saw the world recover from the terrible economic depression of the 1930s. I saw the League of Nations rise and fall – and the emergence of the United Nations. I saw Europe, torn by centuries of national antagonisms, evolve into a European Union. I saw totalitarian regimes in Spain, Italy, Germany, Russia, Africa, Asia, and South America give way to governments more responsive to the needs of the people. I saw women attaining their rightful positions in many cultures. I saw the leaders of many religious organizations finally working together. I saw the development of a new world communications system through the Internet.

Now, to serve the interlinked global community of the Human Family now evident all over the world, I advocate the creation of a Center for Humanity's Future, focused on hope and creativity. Such a Center should be a place of light and listening, a place of friendly exploration and encouragement for people to become even greater than they are now, a launching pad for good ideas from everywhere. It would enable us to travel into new dimensions; to open new paths before us – to dance forward into the future with high expectations, celebrating life with everlasting expansions, rising and traveling far and fast.

This would be a revival of my proposal, endorsed by former President Dwight D. Eisenhower in 1962, for an Annual Celebration of the Creative Powers of Humanity. That proposal was made in an article published by the *Saturday Review*, an American magazine edited by the late Norman Cousins.

I originally offered that proposal, based on my experiences as a founding officer of the Center for the Study of Democratic Institutions, led by Dr. Robert M. Hutchins. The Center was created in 1959 by the Fund for the Republic, an educational foundation established by the Ford Foundation to help uphold the American Constitution and the Bill of Rights. It had a major impact on the world's horizons for 22 years. The Center helped to prevent a war between the United States and the Soviet Union. It fostered efforts to end the tragic conflict in Vietnam. It was a pioneer in the environmental movement. It shed light on the political and economic activities of corporations and labor unions. It sponsored discussions of the significant roles of religion in a free society. It called attention to the strengths and weaknesses of the mass media. It published a model for a New American Constitution, designed to protect civil liberties, wipe out racism, and establish human responsibilities for a constructive future. It brought together thousands of people in dialogues and conferences in Santa Barbara, San Francisco, Chicago, New York, Washington, Malta, and Geneva. It became an "early working framework" for humanity's future.

In my 16 years of participation in the Center's work, I gained a full appreciation of the value of long-range thinking. I heard the ideas of brilliant people from every field – atomic scientists, astronomers, biologists, philosophers, anthropologists, diplomats, military leaders, bishops, theologists, psychologists, novelists, poets, painters, peace activists, Supreme Court judges, senators, governors, presidential candidates, playwrights, labor leaders, state and local legislators, economists, and others. I argued with Nobel Prize winners and questioned scholars who were employed by the Center to make major revisions to the Encyclopedia Britannica. Groups of these scholars regularly examined the future of law, economics, philosophy, religion, and politics.

On the Center staff, we planned and held meetings on science and world affairs, on the systematic study of technology, on the prospects for democracy in the new nations that arose after the collapse of colonial empires, on the possible changes in the American character in our affluent society, and the inseparable connection between American problems and world problems. We had an insatiable thirst for knowledge about everything that was going on in every area of human society – and we were intensely concerned about the effects of current events on the old and the young. Tongue in cheek, we were accused of inventing a new sin – "intellectual gluttony". I was among those guilty of that sin. I wanted to know all there was to know about everything.

At the invitation of Norman Cousins, I wrote the article in the *Saturday Review* advocating an Annual Report on the State of Humanity, to be presented with a global Celebration of Creativity. It attracted the attention and support of former President Eisenhower and other leaders.

Every year, an American president gives a State of the Union Address. I hope that as our next president you will go beyond that. I hope that you and future presidents will give their views on the State of Humanity – recognizing that Harry Truman was right when he said that all human beings are members of "one great Family".

After The President's Report on the State of Humanity, I suggest you host a Global Celebration of Creativity. Artists of all kinds – painters, singers, actors, dancers, poets, musicians, mystics, healers, prophets, mediators, meditators – could lead Community Celebrations around the world. Those Celebrations could make us fully aware that we are the interlinked, and we all have godlike qualities. We are linked inexorably to the "cosmic generosity" pouring through the universe.

The Celebrations could spread the light of "Eternity's Sunrise" over our beautiful earth. They would honor all the wonderful works of compassion going on in many places, encouraging everyone to feel loved and respected, drawing everyone to welcome the future in good order.

Senator William Proxmire of Wisconsin and several other senators tried to get the Congress to pass a resolution endorsing such a Celebration of Humanity forty-five years ago. The Congress did not act on the idea then – but it might do so if as our new president you and other leaders adopt the idea. I commend it to your consideration.

Good luck and Godspeed as our new president!

Sincerely,

Frank K. Kelly
Senior Executive Vice President
Nuclear Age Peace Foundation

PART II

SELECTED WORKS OF

FRANK KING KELLY

CONTENTS

Frank Kelly in his college years —
University of Kansas City, c. 1935

CRATER 17, NEAR TYCHO

*A tale of the space-ways,
and an outlawed ship fighting
against the deadly problem of weight.*

I.

City of New York, 2021 A.D. Riot in Gotham Square.

Up past the swinging sweep of the city's great roof a rocket roared, hung poised in mid-flight, and expanded in a murderous mushroom of spitting green fire. Then followed the thin whine of an alarm siren, rising to a grating scream, dying away again in soundless crescendo as the range of its vicious vibration passed beyond the ken of human hearing. Then against the murky back drop of the night sky, blue fan lights began to prick, circling low, just skimming the rounded shoulder of the mighty roof.

Blue glare and white beam criss-crossed; the white beam rebounded searingly across the torn blackness and vanished, closely followed by an explosive echo, as of thudding thunder. The blue fingers of the giant's hands that seemed to claw the heavens thickened in answer, pushed upward more ascending columns of deadly azure brilliance in whirling clusters of light. The motors of distant patrol planes thrummed in sudden swift surge, like the beating of ten thousand drums, like the hammering roar of sea surf rolling against rock cliffs.

Loud-speakers blared, catching up the heavy overtones of an old man's spoken voice, tossing the sound out in great waves of concentric violence that spread in widened rings of noise over the city. The voice almost reached through the miles of space that stretched between the confusion and the banked slip-cradles of the interplanetary freight docks, perched high on the edge of the huge roof.

Almost, but not quite. It faded to a dim mutter here, like a behemoth growling hoarsely to rebellious midgets, with the last words swallowed in a backwash of innumerable tiny sounds, which grew swiftly to the roaring of a rising mob—

The small man sitting beside Rafe Brand jerked around nervously on a pivoted seat, and shot a disturbed glance out through the narrow slit of transparent glassite before him. From here, in the check tower of the great freight dock, the broken surface of the roof swept away into dimness. Flood lights hammered down in steady glare, etching the gleaming tracks of monorail trucks against a white background of thick glassite. Freight ships, dark and deserted, hugged the snug embrace of slip-cradles all along the dock.

Only one vessel, and the closest to the ungainly tripod of the check tower, was agleam with light. The scarred sides of the black hull still glowed with red heat, still crackling to the friction-stress of atmospheric passage. The name glittered in luminous green letters: "*Isis*, Stellar Ship 946 RV, Cargo. Mars-Earth Cleared."

The check man shrugged and turned back to the clicking board in front of him. His swift hands played over the punch panel, keyed to the rising drone of his thin voice:

"176 tons, Earth Weight, beryllium. Mars checked, 943 kinolotts. Gravity loss, 1.43. Checked. Next way line—"

Brand leaned forward, bright eyes hiding the surge of feeling deep within him, head tensed to the sound and stir in the dim distance. He spoke in a husky voice: "What's breaking over there? Got the look of a first-class war."

"Maybe it is a war."

"I don't sniff the idea."

The other swung in his pivoted seat again. His eyes looked Brand over in swift appraisal; he saw a tall, solid space man, deeply colored by glare of sun and heat of stars, body corded with responsive muscles, dark fierce face topped by graying thatch of black hair. Stenciled across the tunic front of a shabby uniform were the words: "Freight Commander, Interstellar Corporation. License registered. Tape Spool 3876. Earth recorded."

After a minute the check man said: "You been away some place for a while, haven't you?"

Brand made a little motion with one thick hand. "A while, yes. You could say that. A long time. I've been cargoing stuff for Interstellar the last eight years. Since I got my license."

"What channel you been workin'?"

"Mars-Jupiter."

"Long jump."

"Yes."

"Just switch channels this trip?"

"Yes."

"Mind tellin' me your name?"

"The name's Brand—Rafe Brand."

The flat face of the check man relaxed. He nodded. "I got you. Mine's Garnet."

They touched hands.

"You asked me what was goin' on over there."

"I'd kind of like to know," Brand said.

"It's nothin' you could call new," the check man said. "Riot in Gotham Square."

Brand hesitated an instant, purposely not quite hiding the puzzled uncertainty he wanted to show in his eyes. The other leaned close, glanced once again around the narrow outlines of the check room, in a swift leaping jerk that took in everything.

"You look right to me, so I'll tell you something."

"Thanks," Brand said, allowing himself the edge of a smile.

"There's been a riot in Gotham Square every week for months. You oughta get the idea. It's the custom to give the Bottom Levels a chance to tell what they think about things, in a mass meeting called every seven days. Not that it means anything, of course. They talk, they do a lot of silly gassing—and the Controls shove the records of the meetin' away under a mountain of red tape. Nothing ever comes of it, see? The Controls just go ahead and do what they want."

Brand's face was very smooth and quiet, perfectly impassive. No muscle quivered to show that the man was telling him things he already knew. His head moved slowly.

"I believe I get you. A kind of safety valve. No meaning to the thing, the meeting, I mean—except to let off steam that might burst if they sat on it too hard. Smart scheme."

"Just that," the check man said, and grinned; but the grin twisted his thin features in a bitter outline.

He watched Brand narrowly, almost with suspicion. He was sorry he had talked. Better not go too far, with this silent man from space. Didn't know who he was. Might be a Control. Couldn't tell him you had a son who'd got too much in the open during a riot in Gotham Square—and died, with the sour smell of an ion beam burning through his lungs. Better keep a tight mouth, keep it buttoned.

"Just that, smart scheme," the check man said again. "Only it hasn't worked out just as they figured it. The Levels have raised merry hell. They've forced the Controls to give them representation of one man in the upper council. Tonight they say they've discovered their representative, Gagin, has sold them out."

"You mean—" Brand began, and paused. His lips laced tight, and he nodded. His mouth moved soundlessly, but the other caught the thin echo of muttered words: "The dirty piece of static space!"

"I call him the same thing," the cargo checker said, grinning.

Brand said: "Call him what?"

"Didn't you say something?"

"No."

"All right," the checker said, still grinning.

Brand stared as if he hadn't heard; his face blank and smooth again. The small man turned around, and began to work at the controls of the infra-penetrator. Brand watched, one half of his brain tuned to the meaning of the other's words with their undercurrent of quivering bitterness, the remaining half taut and strained, concentrated on the dial readings of the infra's mechanism.

He jerked his body closer to the shut circuit of the control switch; if this check man was on his job, drove the searching infra-beam in through the thick stellite hull of the *Isis* to the aft hold, brought out in clear outline what lay there, that would then automatically be recorded in cargo files with photographic clearness.

It was Brand's unswerving resolve that the check beam would not sweep through the *Isis* again. Already it had gone once, half power, preliminary check—and come dangerously near to the secret of the cargo ship, deflected off the aft hold only by the smooth flow of the interference stream that had been set up there. But the dials had jumped and jerked, registering an obstruction, and only the sound and confusion in the distance had kept the checker's suspicion from speedily rousing. Hard thing, this was what he had to do. Hard to turn on this unsuspecting friendly man, drive the butt of his electronic pistol into the base of the thin neck, snap out the other's little life—but he could take no chances. There was more lying in the balance now than one little man's life.

The checker was speaking again nervously, eyes on the distant flurry of lights, his narrow body tensed to the flare and burst of police rockets, his thin ears tuned to the wail of screaming sirens.

Brand stiffened a little, leaning forward. "Think the Bottoms have any chance of winning?" he asked. The resolution was half formed in his mind to give the other a chance at a longer life. If he spoke now against the Controls—

The small man hesitated, looking at Brand queerly. "Not a chance in hell. No more chance than a space man with a smashed oxygen tank, two thousand miles off side his ship. The Control police will wipe them out."

"I think so myself," Brand agreed gravely and hid the tightening purpose in his eyes. The check man would have to die.

So the little man thought the Control police would wipe the Bottom Levels out with ion beams and paralytic gas, and fire shells smashing downward! Well, his mind might change if the penetrator drove through to the stacked cargo in the aft hold. Row on row of small stellite containers lay there. And inside them—odd-shaped things, harmless enough in look, deadly in sting: the coiled deadliness of the Martian sound oscillators. Hundreds of them, charged and ready.

Even the Controls wouldn't have a weapon that could stand against the Martian whirling death. Sound fields that dropped down in singing streams and ripped the atoms of matter apart, swung them wide in racking confusion. Oscillators tuned to the vibration level of human bodies, that could maim or kill at will.

Brand's eyes jumped to the smooth dial of the chronometer on the wall above the penetrator control board. One fifty-eight, Eastern terrestrial standard time. And Gar had said they would meet here at two.

Gar would have men, trusted and sworn to the cause of the Bottoms, to muster up the sparse ranks of his own space handlers, now waiting quietly in the central cabin of the *Isis*. Swift transfer of small heavy containers to purring monotrucks, an interchange of instructions, and Gar would be gone with his cargo of death. And the *Isis* would be swinging up again through silent space, roaring out past the city's roof to meet the curbed arch of the black sky. There were men in the crater stations of the Moon, sickened of the tyranny of the Controls, eager for battle. The *Isis* would come back crowded.

Brand sent his glance past the shoulder of the cargo checker, through the glassite slit in the wall of the narrow room. He saw the gleaming ribbon of stellite that marked the path of a mono-car. One track was humming, swaying to the furious passage of a heavy body. He saw the coming car, glittering under the flood lights—a small, blunt-shaped object, shifting rapidly through the distance.

The check man was intent on his work and did not see. He was reaching out a thin hand for the control switch of the penetrator, his high voice beginning to drone: "All right, Brand. Preliminary check complete—"

His voice died, cut off in a sudden choking silence. Brand's hand rose once, fell hard, bronzed fingers wrapped about the thick hilt of his electronic pistol.

The little man stiffened, head lolling, the glaze of quick death creeping in behind his blank eyes. He dropped forward, limply crashing against the dull metal of his control panel.

Brand shoved the gun back inside his uniform in a quick flick of the wrist, then turned, stood just at the edge of the low doorway, shivering a little. Not easy to kill a man like that—take him from behind, without warning, without a chance to fight back. And yet any other way might have meant failure.

Failure for the millions under his feet, the Bottom Levels of a top-heavy civilization, the base of the human pyramid. The millions deeply buried under tons of stellite and glassite, living and dying out of sight of the Sun and Moon, oblivious to the slow march of white stars in the purple pageantry of the night sky. Not to breathe clean air, nor see the Sun, the glory of it. Not to smell the warm odor of the Earth in spring, nor stiffen to the whining whiplash of winter winds. Not to be a part of the world's ancient heritage. All that was denied men, unless they were born in the circles of the upper councils, unless they were of the Controls—Well, all of that was going to be changed.

The distant mono-car was coming fast, the rail shivering to the smash and flash of the speeding projectile. Suddenly Brand stiffened, stared with dark, incredulous eyes, his fists clenched at his sides. A sharp foreboding of disaster struck him—the car was too small to hold the men Gar had promised to bring. Then something had gone wrong.

II.

It was close enough now for Brand to see the insignia stamped on one round gleaming side of the car: "One Man. For Freight Only." Something wrong! This must be Gar coming to tell him—

It was. He knew that at first glimpse of the slight figure of the man below, that tumbled in wild haste out through the snapped-open door of the mono-car, and came panting up the narrow ladder of the check tower.

Terror was riding the man under him—beating a tattoo in the quick *spat-spat* of the running feet, the harsh, ragged murmur of the other's gasped breath. The dark head turned and looked up, caught the outline of Brand's body in the doorway.

"Rafe! You're here!"

"I'm here," Brand said slowly. "But your men—the men you promised you'd bring—"

"Gone, all gone! The fight I've had, making it out this far—"

Then Gar was there beside him, swaying a little, his grim face green and white under the cold impersonal glare of the roof flood lights. A red stream dribbled in a zigzag flow along the drawn skin of his jaw, cascaded down across the split lips. One arm of the dark man was hanging queerly at his side, swinging limp and useless.

"Steady!" Brand said quietly.

He caught the thin shoulders, held the other braced for an instant, let him catch lost breath. Then Gar straightened and nodded, and jerked away. The tight lips moved, formed into what was the shadow of a smile.

He said: "All right now. I can take it."

"Sure!" Brand said. "Sure, you can!"

He waited.

After a minute Gar said: "We've got to get away from this place. Got to go now. Before they finish us both. The *Isis* can take off again, any time?"

"Yes," Brand said.

Gar passed a trembling hand across a white face. "The riot started tonight in Gotham Square when—"

A picture leaped in Brand's mind at those few words. Gotham Square. Not a square at all, but a huge cavern in the depths of the Bottom Levels. Seats, ring on ring, tiered mountain-high. Packed with the thousands that were lucky enough to fight, steal, or beg a way in. Surrounded outside, in dimly lighted corridor, by the millions of the city canyons. A raised stage, with microphones and amplifiers for the speakers. A jutting dais, the place of honor, for Gagin, honorable representative of the lower people in the Control councils.

Gar muttered: "It was awful! Massacre!"

And Brand said, quietly: "Better tell me what happened."

But some deep instinct in him told him that he already knew. Gar was talking again, in a high-pitched voice, words and sentences tumbling out through a nervous mouth in rapid flight, incoherent, breathless, yet somehow shaping a vision of chaotic pandemonium that had been.

The news had seeped through, down to the lowest levels of the city, to the half men who lived in almost complete blackness, that Gagin had sold his vote to the Controls. And this night Gagin was there to speak to his people.

Gagin was there. Pale-lipped and jerky-eyed, and with fear quivering in every line of his body—but there, under the fierce eyes of the crowd, which sat in thunderous silence, harshly staring. Others were on the platform, a few score of them, including Gar, a handful brave enough to mock the wrath of the Controls by setting themselves up as an advisory group to the Lower Levels.

Gagin made a speech. Not, Gar said, a speech really at all, but a muttered gibber, hideously distorted by the man's terror. The crowd had remained quietly through it all, until the finish; at the end there was a little silence—a terrible stillness in which no one moved or spoke.

Then the crowd went berserk. And Gar had gone along with them. Quick, light, swift-fingered, his hand had gone to the needle pistol at his belt, come up, flashed in a sputtering arc of flame, tearing into Gagin's shuddering body. Behind Gagin a rocket flared, rising up past the mob in a flaring burst of scarlet glow: in the crowd there had been someone sent by the Controls. Sirens whined, wailing through the packed corridors of the canyons. Helicopters dropped from above, plummeting down through a widened opening in the city's roof, fire shells and ion arcs slamming in hot flight before them.

"I got away," Gar said softly, and shuddered under Brand's hard grip. "I got away. Came here. How—I've forgotten. I stole a mono-car, broke through that mob, got up on the roof—"

His voice died, came again in a great burst: "I killed Gagin. They'll get me, some way."

Brand sought Gar's one good hand, crushed it in a long, slow pressure that spoke more than all the words he knew and gave evidence of all that came crowding to his tongue.

He spoke slowly: "You're sure no one saw you come across the roof—followed you?"

"I told you. I can't remember."

"I know," Brand said. "But you think—what?"

"I think they did," the other muttered, the words flat and dead.

His eyes were on a spot beyond Brand's shoulders; his glance swept out to the dark sky. Lights stirred and whirled in that sky, shifted with the purring hum of helicopter motors; white beams stabbed down across the roof.

"They're coming now."

Brand stood up straight and faced the scarred hull of the *Isis*. "Then we'll fight with what we've got, old son—and go down battling."

The other's bloody hands went up to his face. "No. Rafe, don't you understand? That's why—I killed Gagin."

"What do you mean?" Brand demanded.

"I believed in him, told him what we were going to do. I told him about the oscillators, about you. And he carried it all to the Controls, let you walk into this. This is the trap they set for you."

Brand struck his fists together. "They don't know what they're walking into. We'll do what we can—with the oscillators. We'll take some of them with us when we go out."

"Even that," Gar said numbly, "we can't do. The alloy. The X stellanium isotope in the coils isn't—"

"You mean—its not there?" Brand said. He stood stunned.

Gar muttered: "I mean that. It's not there."

Brand fought the rising surge of despair that swept up in his throat, choking him. He stirred, whirling on the other. "For all that, Gar, we've still a way left clear. The *Isis* is space-ready. If they try a blockade, we'll break through."

Hope wakened in the slight man's dark eyes. He hesitated an instant, as if considering. Then:

"You're right! We'll take the *Isis* and hit out for the Moon. The Controls haven't taken over the crater stations yet. I didn't have time to spill that to Gagin. Rafe, if we could do it—"

"No time to talk now," Brand said swiftly. He was standing on the first rung of the check-tower ladder. "Down with you. Varney's standing by. He expects to pick us up—but not for the reason we've got now. We were waiting here to unload the oscillators."

"I know."

Gar nodded, and followed him down the ladder, swung across the smooth floor of the great roof, moved up the rising ramp that led to the cargo ship's cradle. Brand flashed the signal. The huge gimbaled door of the airlock began to swing on balanced pivots, turn inward, gave a glimpse of the lighted interior of the freight vessel.

The lock stood open. Dan Varney, Brand's tall second in command, halted in the doorway, staring. Brand swung an arm behind Gar's shoulders, helped the other up across the lock, into the control room of the *Isis.*

He jerked round on Varney. "We've got to get action, Dan. Bad break. Gagin sold out to the Controls. Gar, here, came to warn us. Police fleet overhead. Get the lock closed and take us upstairs."

"Blockaded above?" Varney asked slowly.

"Don't think so, but might be."

"If we are?"

"Break through. Use forward ram."

"We're going out of the atmosphere?" Varney asked quietly, his hard brown face unchanged and impassive. If he felt any amazement at this sudden turn of things, he didn't show it.

Brand hesitated an instant, not looking at Gar. "How are we on space supplies?"

Varney shrugged, drawled: "Fair. Might make it."

Brand flung his voice out in a sudden burst: "Then hit for the Moon."

"We'll base at crater 17, at the edge of Tycho."

Varney gave a flicking gesture that was as much of a salute as Brand ever received from him, and turned, swung across the close, metal-walled room to the handling set-up of the freight ship. Giant Donlin sun engines began to turn over, build up pressure for the huge backlash of energy that would stream out behind and send the *Isis* hell-driving up through open space. Light glowed on the small face screens of the ship's individual visa plates and died again as Varney finished giving orders to each member of the ship's crew.

Brand walked straight to the big television panel at the side of the airlock, dropped into the comfortable bucket seat before it, shifted directive dials. The scene above and outside the freighter showed in sharp, clear outline—the silent check tower, with the crumpled body of the check man dimly visible, dangling limply over the top rung of the descending ladder; the pale ribbon of the mono-track, stretching away to nowhere; the flood lights hurling down showers of cold glare.

And above in the distance, contrasts in the black mirror of the sky, heliships were drumming on in massed flight, white beams flashing nervous fingers out before them. They were close now, closer than they had been when Gar and Brand had fled down the check-tower ladder. Even through the thick sound-insulated hull of the ship the roar of packed motors came rumbling. The crackling crash of ion beams searing through shuddering air smashed against Brand's eardrums.

He swung on Varney. "Got any pressure?"

"Pressure building," Varney snapped laconically.

Brand looked at Gar, still standing dazedly by the closed panel of the lock. "Strap yourself in there," Brand ordered, pointing to the curved outline of a chair equipped with acceleration compensators.

The other obeyed quietly.

Brand gave the "General Attention" buzz on the ship's communicating web, spoke crisply to unseen men standing by in compressor rooms and firing chambers:

"Give me pressure. And remember we're not taking off easy. That's all. Emergency stations."

"Pressure, sir!" Varney roared from across the room.

Brand tersely nodded. "Shoot it through, all channels!"

"Everything we've got?"

"Everything we've got!"

Varney's heavy fingers danced over the gleaming studs of the control board. A split second of no response—then roaring speed, coming into action. Plumes of repulsion streams stood out in long peacock fantails behind the exhaust nozzles of the thundering ship. Brand watched sky and roof and distant stars go whirling by in glittering confusion. Then it was over. The *Isis* zoomed through the Earth's atmosphere, crashing through screaming air, scarred sides red-hot with friction stress.

"Below!" Brand yelled in triumph. "Look below!"

Gar followed his eyes. Below and behind massed helicopters fluttered in baffled rage, stabbing out hot fingers in blue beams of swift force that almost touched and scorched the speeding freighter—almost, but not quite. The *Isis* was gone before the beams crossed in liquid fire.

Gar lay limp in his seat, crumpled under the crushing shock of sudden acceleration piled on top of his already weakened body. Brand got up, went to him across a firm floor held steady by gravity grids under stellite plates, made a swift examination.

Gar was knocked out. Brand picked him up gently, carried him past the visa screen and through a narrow door, into the officers' sleeping cabins. Then Gar was taken into Brand's own room, after the freight captain had finished some rough, quick surgery. A broken arm and a sore jaw—nothing too deeply hurt for repair.

Varney was waiting for Brand when he came out and closed the door.

The other faced him with grave thin eyes. "What happened, back there?"

The captain told him, in brief, sharp strokes that drove it home. When he was finished Varney said in a soft voice:

"This doesn't mean anything—after what he did on Earth—but it's something we've got to figure on, Brand. We weren't counting on an extra man for this trip."

"No," Brand said slowly; "you're right, there. We weren't. And we were expecting to pick up some stuff to carry us back over from Gar's end of the line."

He was silent an instant, meeting Varney's eloquent eyes. "We'll go easy, understand? We'll stretch what we've got, both ways from the middle. We can make it go a long way."

"Sure!" the other said, very low. "Well, it might last—but if it doesn't?"

"If it doesn't," Brand answered, looking straight at him, "one of us will have to—drop out."

III.

They both knew what that meant. Varney jerked a little, then straightened, his face falling into set lines. It took—nerve. Yes; you needed nerve to take your last look on the bright face of life and say goodbye deliberately to all life meant. You stripped, made the slow walk to the emergency lock—and then were shot spinning out into the frozen blankness of interstellar vacuity. There were a few men brave enough to do that—if it meant a chance for a better life to millions; if it meant that there would be some left to—well, carry on, to fight again.

"Right," Varney said gently; "I see what you mean."

They fell silent after that. There wasn't much more to say. Hours swung past, measured out by the ceaseless click of the little chronometer in the wall; hours, counting by Earth time—nothing at all, here in space.

The Earth, that had been concave, now changed, melted first to an indistinct outline obscured by clouds, then assumed the round convex bulge of a great ball slightly flattened at the ends and bulging in the middle. Varney kept sending the pick-up beam of the televisor back through infinity to the bright Earth, fingering out to contact the first distant shimmer of movement in the void space behind them—movement that might indicate the coming of the Controls' ships in dogged pursuit of the freighter. Nothing stirred. All quiet. The freighter drove on through nothingness, engines thrumming, compressors sobbing and groaning under the hard load of top speed.

Figures changed and multiplied in Varney's cold brain. Calculations, integrations, all the abstruse formulae of space-time navigation. The *Isis* could do one thousand Earth miles per hour, with maximum freight load. One thousand! And the light ships of the Controls could make three with ease.

They had no chance—unless there was a long delay and the freighter took too big a lead. Even then, if they were carrying an overload of one man—

They took alternate watches. First Varney for eight hours, Earth-recorded; then Brand; then Gar, sore from his bruises, his battered head still topped by a white crown of bandage. Eight hours each they spent strapped into the control seat, eyes taut on the winking panels of the great directing board, fingers and hands busy at switches and studs. Eight hours free they had, to study the televisor screen, to talk, to drop down the engine-room ladder to the compression chambers and firing compartments, to think. That was the worst—thinking. But they had eight hours' sleep; and, sleeping, sometimes they forgot—

Brand touched Varney lightly on the shoulder in the middle of the third day, nodded, and took over. The tall man stood up lithely, muscles stretched, grave face relaxing in a long yawn.

Brand sat down, swung the revolving dials, tensed his eyes for a first glimpse of the white Moon on the lookout plate just above the control board. Crater 17, near Tycho. That was refuge. If they got there, they were through untouched. The Controls might know they were on the Moon, might make an effort at finding them, might savagely search; but the Moon wasn't mapped and zoned and guarded as the Earth; there were wild places untapped by the visa beams of the Council patrols. Crater 17, near Tycho—

Varney spoke in a low voice from behind Brand, startling him. The tall man was staring at the complacent face of the chronometer. "More than two days, Brand. And no sign of their coming after us. I actually think—I actually believe we're going to make it."

Brand nodded slowly. "Yes. We've held even at about one thousand per, all the way from atmosphere. Thirty-six thousand miles—gone. And still we're not yet close to the Moon—if the patrols come out here, hunting us—"

Varney rubbed a hand slowly across his lips. "I know. But we've been lucky. Maybe the luck will stay with us. Air's holding out. Food's lasting. The men aren't grumbling any more than usual. We've even a little water to spare, now that I changed the set-up in those condenser coils."

"Yes," Brand said again.

Varney noticed how drawn the other's face looked in the faint light of the control room. They had cut down on the juice that fed the cold globes, even though that was so little, to save power for the recoil streams.

Brand took his eyes from the unchanging glimmer of the directing board; he shot a glance across at the closed door leading to the sleeping cabins. Gar was off watch and asleep.

"Varney, get this. And tell me what you think. But quietly. We don't want to let Gar know until we have to, if what I've noticed is true. And it is true. The air's not holding. It's going bad. You've sensed that?"

Varney exclaimed sharply. His face whitened; he shuddered a little. Then he caught a grip on himself. He could be as big as Brand. Yes.

He took a heavy breath, drew a long draft of the ship's air into his lungs, and it made him sick. It was acrid, sour, with a rank staleness that spoke of its being used over and over again—passing through many men's bodies, expelling itself in a burst of lung effort, emerging charged with carbonic gas. Building up its percentage of that stifling gas, until it could be used no longer. Slow death would follow then, death by smothering, by suffocation—unless the air was changed, cleansed, made fresh again by the oxygen compensators.

Varney came to a sudden full realization of what a delicately balanced mechanism this ship was. Like most space handlers, he had taken it all for granted; it worked, because it was made to work. Well, maybe in a few more years men would be laughing at the crudities and inefficiencies of these hard-shelled monsters of thick stellite; maybe! He knew they would be, some day in the future. But not now. It was still new, this going out into space in a precarious bubble of welded metal, pushed forward through a void by forces little understood even by those who used them. Men had many things yet to learn about the space between the worlds.

Ships had conquered it, driven out across nothingness even from planet to planet, carrying men in numbers, loaded with what man called useful machines and weapons and supplies, complex mechanisms that made life livable in the roofed craters of the Moon, even on Mars.

But there were ships always being lost. Ships that got out of touch with beam-communication stations and drifted from known channels into some unknown limbo of forgotten space—and never came back to tell what they found there. Ships that broke down in mid-voyage and hung helpless between the pale planets, circling like small new worlds, starved satellites, until the men within them went mad and destroyed themselves—or fell back in a long dive against the hard face of a mocking Earth.

There was a balance that must be held in every ship, no matter the cost. Varney remembered reading of the first primitive submarines that cruised Earth's waters. It had been like this, underseas. So much air; so much space to move around in; so much food; so much to drink. It was that way here, in the void—a balance of interdependent factors; a balance nicely calculated between the crew number and the air used and the food consumed and the water absorbed. That was on one side of the equation; and on the other, the storage supplies and the power build-up to carry the ship from world to world.

Something clicked in his mind, like the separate pieces of a picture puzzle falling together into one whole. There were eight in the crew. Counting himself and Brand, the ship carried ten. It was built to carry ten. No more. But they had Gar now. One man always left over. One too many. That left the equation uneven. It destroyed the balance—

He faced Brand, eyes smoothed out, hiding what he felt. He said slowly: "I'll have a look at the compensators. If we can pull a little more oxygen out of them—"

Brand nodded, a little more briskly, displaying a faint hope. "Even if we've got to cut down on what goes into the recoils, we'll have to do that. We can't live out here with no air."

Varney jerked a brief salute and was gone down the ladder to the machine room. He picked his way carefully along the metal plate of the catwalk, cautious not to put his feet down outside the laced grids of the protective flooring. Gravity compensation had been blocked off outside those grids—saving power.

He stopped slowly, stood facing the compact mechanism of the oxygen compensators, a quick glance jerking up along a narrow row of dials to a curving cylinder of transparent glassite. A warm opalescent fluid gently stirred against the bottom of the gleaming cylinder.

Varney's lips tightened; he bent down, touched the controls of the indicators. Looked up again. Waited for the response. None came. The compensator was dead.

A long time he stood there staring, his lungs struggling in the thick atmosphere of the aft section of the ship, his eyes beginning to smart from the effects of the rancid air. His vision was not as good as it had been; objects a little distance away he saw as through a slowly descending curtain of fog.

He raised his hands and looked at them. They were cold. His blood circulated sluggishly. He felt an uncomfortable weariness in his legs and arms.

Something stirred in hesitant movement behind him. He turned indifferently; the action roused him a little. His mouth went angrily taut. It was one of the firing crew; a thin, small man with a huge head and slitted flickering eyes.

Varney said: "What's this? What're you doing this far forward?"

As he spoke he shifted his body slowly, to hide the indicators of the air restorer, but the quick glance of the little man was there before him.

The other said in a thick voice: "I come to find out about the air. We're finding it hard, back aft. You got to shift a little power from the compressors. If you don't—"

Varney's frown tightened as he recognized the man. "Jorgenson! You don't mean—mutiny?"

Jorgensen shrugged. The pointed little eyes met Varney's confused glance. "I ain't said that, sir. But we're all a-havin' trouble with the breathin', and we can't think none too good. We got to have better air, or we ain't gonna be able to hold pressure."

Varney relaxed and nodded. He moved aside, giving the other a clear view of the needle readings on the compensator dials. "Then take a look at this thing, and you'll see the reason we've all been having trouble."

The little man barely glanced at the squat mechanism. Dropping his eyes, Jorgensen said: "Beginnin' with what you spoke last sir, I think that ain't the reason for our trouble."

"No?" Varney asked harshly. "Then what is?"

"We've got one man too many aboard here."

The chief officer looked at the other in a sudden burst of scorn. "You mean you're not willing to take a little bad medicine with the rest of us—you're looking around for a Jonah already?"

The smaller man said in a low voice: "Puttin' it to you plain, sir, one of us has got to drop out through the E lock of this ship. When that's done, we'll be right again, and we won't have no more trouble."

"I see," Varney said softly. "So it's that simple?"

"Yes, sir."

"Who would you like to be the hero?"

The little man looked up, his eyes hitting Varney in the face. "We're every one of us aft ready to take our chances with the rest of your forward group, sir. If the captain asked for volunteers, I'd offer to go myself."

"I really think you would," Varney muttered.

"Yes sir."

Varney saw that he meant it. His face was steady and still, and the sharp little eyes glinted in it like points of unchanging stellite.

Varney straightened back his own shoulders. "I'll speak to the captain."

"Yes, sir."

"Now about the compensator. Think you can fix it?"

"No, sir."

Varney stared at the set face. "Sure of that?" he asked quietly.

"If you want it straight, sir—there's nothing to be done about the compensator."

"Hopeless," Varney muttered, as if to himself.

"Yes, sir. The bottom coils are burned out."

"I understand," Varney said softly. "Return aft. I'll send for you, all of you back there, when the captain is ready to make his decision."

"Right, sir," the other said.

He had vanished before Varney could speak again, his slim body jerking in between the clicking mechanisms that filled the long room. At the far end of the catwalk a door opened for an instant; the lurid light from a compressor chamber flared out in a circular spot of flickering glare, then was gone.

Varney swung, on legs a little bit unsteady, and returned along the narrow metal path, following its windings back to the base of the flat, straight ladder leading up into the control cabin. He climbed the ladder very slowly.

IV.

Brand was doing something at the control board, shoulders bent, face and head hidden and savagely absorbed, fingers pulsating over shifted studs. Varney walked up quietly behind him, touched his arm.

Brand jerked round like a cat, his eyes flaming. "What the hell!"

For an instant he didn't seem to know where he was. Then he said: "You didn't change the set-up on those compensators this quick?"

"No," Varney said.

Brand flared: "Then what are you doing back here?"

Varney waited a little and then answered: "There wasn't any use changing the set-up, chief."

"Why?" Brand demanded.

"It wouldn't do any good. The lower-coil system is gone, burned out, trying to carry a constant overload. Oxygen's not getting through now, at all. No good trying to do anything with a break like that."

There was a change then in the way Brand looked, so deep and indefinable that it was only partly reflected on the surface of his eyes. He just looked a little more tired, his eyes went back a little deeper in his head, and his lips closed tight—that was all, but when it all was added up it made a big change.

"I thought we were due for something nice about now," Varney said; he grinned. The grin was unpleasant to look at.

"I've got a cute surprise, too," Brand said. "A swell thing I'm going to spring on you. But I think I'll wait till I hear what else you've got to say. You've got something else, haven't you?"

Varney nodded. "Yes. Yes; I have."

He stopped as if something held his voice. Then words came to him again, flat and strained: "I met Jorgensen, looking over the compensator. The men know about the air. They're having a bad time of it aft. They're asking you to—"

"Of course," Brand said, holding his face still. "They're crying because we're carrying just one man too many. And they want me to ask somebody to walk out and leave the party, so there'll be more fun for those of us who are left. Am I right?"

"You're right," Varney answered.

Brand knew there wasn't much to talk about. Now it was in the open, and they all had to stand up and face it. Face it—face what? To go out alone into space. To be stripped, fitted into the emergency lock, and shot projectile-like into indifferent infinity. That took a little bit of nerve.

Brand raised his head. "Now let me show you what I've got for you," he said. "In some ways, it's a better joke than what you brought me. Look there."

Varney stared at the scintillant screen. He saw what was shown on that glimmering bright surface, but his mind didn't really take it in. He knew it was there, the screen didn't lie, it was just a clever mirror to show whatever came within range of its activating beam—yet he didn't believe the message of his own eyes.

But it was true, all right. On the screen lay the clustered glitter of a Control space fleet, driving out from the spurned Earth directly in the path of the fleeing *Isis*. Speed and power and grace and gray, gleaming bodes, swiftly overhauling the slow freighter. And the air in this ship fast going! No; not going, either; the joke was bigger than that—the air was being poisoned by the workings of their own lungs.

Varney laughed.

"Don't do that," Brand said, shuddering.

"Sorry!" Varney jerked. He glanced down at his hands. "You were right. This is a better joke than any I know. Let me go first. I'll do it gladly."

Brand sat a while in silence, looking at Varney. Then he unstrapped himself quietly, locked home the automatic controls of the freighter and came over to where Varney stood. He held out one hand slowly. "I've believed in you, friend, and I haven't been wrong. But you're not going. Shake hands with me once, will you?"

Their fingers locked, broke, and parted.

Varney said: "I'm the one to do this dance, chief. Who's better fitted for the job?"

"I am," Brand said heavily.

Varney shook his head. "You? Not you! You'll be needed, to break the Controls, as some day they're going to be broken. When we finish what we started out to do this time. Gar? He's needed, on Earth. Sometime soon he'll be able to go back, and he'll lead his people. He's got the brain and the force and the power to lead them, and when the hour comes they must be led. Now for me, I'm ready to take on anything. I've got nothing behind me that I'd care to cling to; and nothing I can see just ahead that would be worth more than my chance to do this. You know— I've wondered, now and then, how it would really feel to step out there in the great open places—alone."

Brand said, savagely: "Very pretty, but all wrong."

"Why all wrong?"

"Dead wrong," Brand said. "You're our navigator. Forgotten that?"

"You can navigate," Varney said, and he laughed a little. "Forgotten that?"

"I can navigate," Brand said, "but not the way you can. With you, the ship has a double chance to pull through. To get to Tycho with Gar and the men and keep the fight going. That's all any of us can ask."

"Yes; you're right," a slow voice spoke close to Brand's ear.

Brand looked startled, glanced at Varney, but Varney had not spoken. The door of the sleeping cabin was standing open, and Gar had come into the control room. He stopped, his head upright between his straight shoulders, his eyes watching them with faint irony. "This thing seems to be up to me," he said quietly.

"No!" Brand cried, his voice coming out of him in a protesting explosion.

Varney muttered something.

"Look, all the pieces fall in," Gar said, as if he hadn't heard either of them. "We'd have got away, clean, if you hadn't picked me up back at New York, Rafe. If I'd just warned you, and then ducked back underground, the ship would have gone straight through to Tycho, and no trouble. Now—well, we're pretty close to being finished—unless something changes. If we tried to fight it out, with the air getting bad and one man extra aboard, we'd get wiped from space. No heroics in this at all. There shouldn't be, if we all think straight. I'd like to go right now. No use in standing around and waiting until it's too late to do any good."

Varney and Brand stood silently looking at each other. When it had been thrown down in front of them like that, they both knew that Gar was right, that was the truth. There was no finding any way around it.

But Varney jerked his hand out in a little gesture and talked: "You've both left out something. The crew's in this. They're all Bottom Level men. It's their cause as much as ours. We've no right to deny them a chance to say what they think about it. And Jorgensen had the right idea. We'll use it, with variations. We'll call for volunteers—and vote on the men who want to step out for the good of the rest of us. The man who's found least valuable to the ship—he goes."

Gar hesitated. Then he nodded, looked at Brand. "It sounds fair enough to me."

"Yes; it's fair enough," Brand muttered. "All right; we'll do it that way. Call them forward, Varney."

The tall man stepped to the ship's communicating tube and gave the "General Attention" signal. Response came back swiftly in quick bursts of words from rapid voices.

The men trickled forward slowly in ones and twos. They lined up opposite Brand and Varney. "Big Lan" Margot, the chief compressor technician, boss of the bunch, with his shambling walk and hesitant grin, flashing like a gleam of light over his heavy dark face. De Celle, the French Earthman, thin and quick and sharp, like a polished rapier bending and straightening and casting off sparks of direct glow. Su Gan, the small Moon native, half terrestrial in his parentage, and showing the best alchemy of mixed blood—a little man, fast on curved feet, eager to please, glad to work, with a birdlike glitter in round eyes. Eight of them, filing in, crowding the small room, standing uneasily against the wall, wedged in between the control board and the televisor panel, staring with grimy, uncertain faces at the glimmering cluster of reflected glow shown on the screen.

Jorgensen came in last, moving up the machine-room ladder with slow deliberation. He took his place near the televisor, his thin-eyed glance tightly focusing on Brand's body.

Brand faced them. "Jorgensen's told you by now what we're stacked against. I'm not wasting words with you. You're men, not children. You've got nerve or you wouldn't be here. You knew you'd have to fight when you came on this voyage. What I've got to offer is fair to all of us, from myself to Jorgensen."

Jorgensen nodded, suddenly spoke: "You're going to ask for a man with nerve enough to go out through the E lock, aren't you sir?"

Brand hit him with direct eyes. "That's what I was trying to say. I'd like any of you who, of your own will, are ready to go out through the emergency port—to take one step toward me."

Margot shuffled forward. De Celle was a unit with him, in a quick skipping jump. Su Gan sidled across the smooth floor on lithe feet. Jorgensen walked even with them, still using that slow deliberation in the way he carried his body, as if he held a sense of successful purpose exulting within him.

Brand looked them all over again. Every man of the crew stood in an even line stretching across the silent room. Brand felt his eyes smart with moisture, and it was not all due to the bad air.

His voice snapped hoarsely: "I'd counted on this. That makes all of us, myself and Varney and Gar having already decided, who are willing to step out—for the good of the ship. We've hit upon this idea to settle it: we'll take a vote, and the man voted least valuable to the cause as a man and as a leader—will go. You agree?"

"There's no need for that," Jorgensen said softly. He took another step toward Brand; and then, turning, he swung on the men who remained in line.

"We don't have too much time," Jorgensen said with composure, "No good wastin' part of it takin' a vote. It's me that's dropping out through the lock."

There was a period of silence. None of the men objected. A slow smile twisted the little man's lips, as if he was watching himself from a point of observance in the far distance; listening to the faint irony of his words, and laughing without bitterness at his fine play acting. Only it was not play acting. It was real. Little Jorgensen was going out through the side port—for the good of the ship.

Varney put his eyes on the small man's silent face. "You want to do it that badly?"

"I've read stories from the recording spools on Earth," Jorgensen said, "and I'm trying to prove you don't have to be big to be a hero. I want to know what the taste of glory is like to have in your mouth."

Gar moved as if in protest, and Brand's eyes tightened in narrow lines, but Varney went to Jorgensen and they began working together coolly. With quick leaping jerks of his long hands over his body the small man was stripping himself, sliding into the cool embrace of a metal-armored space suit, then motioning to Varney to get at the mechanism of the emergency lock.

Finally he stood at the edge of the inner panel of the port, the face plate of the suit opened for the entrance of death. He turned his eyes once around the room, stopping his glance on Brand and Gar. He laughed a little, the sound echoing hollowly from within his clumsy suit.

He called over to them: "This is a great thing I'm doing, isn't it"

Brand didn't answer.

But Varney grinned. "Yes; you'll be a hero of the cause."

"After I'm dead," Jorgensen agreed and laughed.

"After you're dead."

None of them heard what Jorgensen said next, except Varney. Varney wasn't sure he heard it, either. But he thought Jorgensen whispered:

"I'm glad to do this thing. You know, it's only right I should be doing it—I'm really a Bottom Level man—"

Then Jorgensen took a big breath and said quickly: "Never think it wasn't worth it, will you? All right, I'm ready."

Varney spun the dials feverishly, his damp hands slipping on the knobs of the smooth metal.

Brand came out of his daze, ran across the room, shouting in protest: "Can't let him do this! No, stop—"

He was at the lock, pushed Varney away, Gar following close behind. Varney stood staring at both of them, something sardonic in the twist of his thin mouth.

"You're a little bit late to stop the party," Varney said. "He just passed out."

V.

Above the sound of Varney's cold laughter, they heard the swift puff and burst of outward leaping air, as the outer lock panel opened to Jorgensen's body. And after that—well, after that, no sound got through from the void into the control room.

"He had what you might call—insides," Varney said heavily. "He stepped right into it."

Gar was staring at the small look-out plate over the control board. His hand jerked around in a queer circling gesture.

"Come here, Rafe. You can see—what's left of him."

Brand came and stood beside Gar, and they strained their eyes together. Closely watching, they both saw it—the small armored body, still spinning behind the ship, turning over and over with the force of the outrushing air not yet spent. Some vagrant gleam of light, traveling aimlessly from Moon or stars or Sun, struck the metal suit, glittered brightly for an instant, showed them a vision of Jorgensen's face, tucked inside the helmet.

He had left the face plate open, as they remembered. His eyes, bigger than they had been in life, as if death had been astounding, were shut, tightly closed by covering lids, as if at the final instant he had been unwilling to look out at the void into which he was mercilessly driven— but there was no fear frozen into the calm lineaments of the fading face.

There was something scarlet around his lips and eyes, like the red fringe around a Spanish shawl—blood it must have been, from burst vessels and ruptured veins, wrenched by the sudden removal of air pressure normal to an Earth-woven body; but still again there was no great change, not as much as Brand had believed there would be. He seemed simply to writhe in disturbed sleep.

The indifferent sliver of light, having been reflected from the little armored body to the eyes of the watchers, dwindled as Jorgensen dwindled, until finally they both vanished, leaving the steady lanterns in the sky which had always been there—the unchanging stars. Jorgensen, little Jorgensen of the Bottom Levels of Earth was buried in the black shroud of space.

Brand spoke harshly, breath pounding his throat: "The most horrible death any man could have. And we sent him to it—"

"You really think it is so horrible?" Gar said quietly, still staring, oddly fascinated. "I don't agree. He looked pretty peaceful."

"I thought that, too," Varney said. "Oh, I don't suppose it was so bad."

Brand looked sharply at them both and swung away. He passed a hand across his face, rubbed his eyes hard, shook himself, and slid down into the seat in front of the control panel.

"Send the men aft," Brand muttered. "We've got to get moving faster. Varney, how much air reserve have we? I mean the stored oxygen we put aboard in emergency supplies—for use in case the compensator failed? The compensators are gone now; you'd better get to using that reserve."

"Right," Varney agreed and nodded. "I think we've got enough to carry us to Tycho—with one less man. And if we can pull away from the Controls—"

"I'm trying that last now," Brand said grimly, hands working at the great board. He sent out an attention call to the aft-compressor room.

Margot, the chief technician, rumbled an answer.

"You giving us all you've got back there?" Brand demanded.

Silence.

Then Margot said hesitantly: "I might do a little better, chief, if we cut down on lights and gravity in the grids—and if you're willing to take the chance on blowing the fire coils."

"We'll take that chance," Brand said. "Jorgensen took a bigger one."

Margot stiffened. "Yes, sir."

For a little while after the other had cut off, there was no change.

Then speed came into the dials before Brand. Black needles trembled on pressure gauges, shifted far over toward the limit of the dial, edging past the red tracery of the danger point; the dark fingers of the acceleration indicators began to feel the purring flow of power, climb upward. Still the fleet of the Controls came on, kept creeping closer. Gar and Varney watched the clustered ships behind grow larger on the televisor screen, take shape and solid outline, strengthen into entities separate and distinct, in place of blurred blobs of distant light. Brand muttered softly, stabbed his hands against the green handles of the master switches in a sudden frenzy.

Varney asked: "Still gaining?"

Brand answered in one clipped breath: "Still gaining. Oh, if I could have a little more power!"

Gar's voice came: "We could cut off this big screen you and I are using Varney, and keep track of the Controls from Brand's lookout plate. Would that help?"

"Yes," Varney muttered.

"Help?" Brand echoed. "It'll help plenty. Got any more ideas like that, Gar?"

"One more, and then I'm afraid I'm through."

"Well, let's hear the one you've got."

"Right!" Gar said. "Cut off all gravity from the grids. Under this acceleration, we'll scarcely miss it, and the grids eat a little power, don't they?"

Brand nodded. "Sure, they do. While I'm connecting with Margot to tell him that, Varney can block out that screen. O.K.?"

"Yes," Varney said.

He leaned forward, changed the set-up of tubes and condensers, snapped a switch, disconnected circuited wiring. The huge screen dimmed, faded, grew dark. Gar nodded, moved across the room to Brand's position, stood behind the other, watching. Varney followed silently. Standing side by side, they were both suddenly very still.

Brand muttered: "Close!"

"But it's not enough?" Varney asked heavily.

Brand's eyes flickered. "No. It's not enough."

Gar spoke, not looking at Varney: "How much more will it take to put us over?"

"Don't know exactly," Brand said. "But only a little more, and we'd be clear—with the lead we've piled up in three days."

"Then they've stopped gaining?" Gar asked eagerly.

Brand snarled at him without patience. "No! They're still coming up on us, but we've shaved down the difference in speed. Their lead ship is making three thousand even; and the *Isis* is sticking just above twenty-eight hundred—"

"How much of a lead have we got?" Varney demanded.

Brand hesitated an instant, glancing at dials, calculating fast. "Around twenty-five thousand miles. And we're losing that."

Decision came in his eyes. He snapped the attention call again; got the chief technician growling at the other end of the connection. Then he said: "You've taken out all the stuff you were using for gravity?"

"Yes, sir."

"Then tone down on heat and air circulation. And anything else you can think of. We've got to have every atom of power you can scrape together. Understand that?"

"Yes, sir."

"Break."

Margot broke communication.

Brand looked at the two standing behind him. "Listen," he said. "We're in for a taste of cold for a while—and some other things. We're none of us going to be very comfortable, but we'll do the best we can. Get in those seats and strap yourselves—tight."

Varney obeyed in slow silence; but Gar clung to the back of Brand's place in a tightened grip, waved the other away.

"I'll stick here a little longer," he said. "As long as I can hold out. I might help, some way."

Brand shrugged. "All right. But watch yourself." Gar caught at that thought. Help the ship, some way. If there was only something he could do. There *was* something he could do, something he had to do. He had known it for a long time. Might as well admit it now, no use hiding it from himself—he'd been afraid, he had let Jorgensen—

He loosened his hold on the rounded edge of the control chair, took careful steps across the room to where Varney sat strapped in, each movement lifting his thin body high off the floor grids, to come drifting down again in a slow float. Queer sensation, that was. No gravity in the grids, nothing to hold you back, pull you down; a feeling of exultance went through you, walking like this—smooth power flowed through your muscles, you glided with light easiness.

He touched Varney on the shoulder.

Varney said, not moving his mouth: "What are you trying to do?"

"Don't you know?" Gar said, staring straight into his face.

Varney dropped his eyes. "No."

"It's just my job," Gar said simply. "I tried to shift it off on Jorgensen's shoulders, but I didn't get by. I'm glad I've got the chance to make up for that in the only way I can."

"Sit down here," Varney said, not answering him. "I'll strap you to this seat next to me."

"You're listening," Gar said, "and I know it. I let Jorgensen go, because I was afraid. And because I didn't believe in this thing as much as he did. I thought what Brand thought and you thought—for centuries some men have been trying to do something for the bottom of the pyramid. None of them, so far, have succeeded very greatly. And I thought it wasn't worth dying for. But it was—little Jorgensen showed me that it was."

Varney said: "Maybe you're right. But what can you do, now? He's gone. He dropped out, and it didn't do us any good. What are you going to do now?"

"I'm using power," Gar said softly. "Every time I breathe, I use a little power, I'm holding the ship back a little. I haven't got weight, with the gravity gone, but I've got mass. I'm a drag pulling the ship down. So I'm going to stop breathing. I'm going to leave the ship."

"You're out of your head," Varney said. "Jorgensen went that way; one is enough. We'll get clear without any more of that."

Gar stood there, swaying a little on his uncertain feet. "No use lying, Varney. We both know the truth. You were thinking of dropping off yourself."

The other's eyes changed. "No. I wasn't. That's what bites into me. I wouldn't have the nerve. I'm scared."

"So am I," Gar said softly. "But you'll help me, won't you?"

A curtain of silence stretched between them. Brand was muttering again at the controls, his voice disjointed and incoherent, a heavy murmur creeping out across the room. Gar waited.

Varney made a harsh sound in his throat and looked once at Brand's curved back. Then he nodded and began to fumble with numb fingers at the straps binding him in.

"If you want to go," Varney muttered. "I guess I can't stop you." He jerked upward out of his seat, rose high, touched the room's ceiling with his shoulders, dropped at a long sloping angle to the floor. Brand heard the thud of that light fall and swiftly turned.

"What're you two doing?" Brand asked.

His glance shifted to the space suit, sprawling in an ungainly awkwardness on the floor near the E lock. Then he knew.

Gar stood silent a while. Then he said: "I'm doing what I should have done, before Jorgensen dropped out. He gave me back my nerve. It's my job. He tried, but he couldn't do it for me. Maybe what I'm going to do will give the chance to you and Varney to get through. You've got the ship to work clear, and the two of you can do it. That's your job."

Brand didn't speak for a long space. He sat still, meeting Gar's steady eyes, listening to the other's words. Then he moved. "Varney," he said. "Take over here. I'll handle Gar. If anybody else goes—"

"It won't be you," Gar said flatly.

Varney stood hesitant.

Brand roared: "You got what I said! Take over."

Varney took over.

Brand glanced at him once, and stood beside Gar. "I'm not letting you do this," he said quietly. "Understand that?"

Gar took a slow shuffling step toward the E lock. Bending down, he lifted the heavy metal-fabric suit with both hands, held it out.

"Hold the suit while I strip," Gar said. He grinned. "Funny—I'm going out the same way I came in, wearing skin over bones."

Brand's legs shook. He turned his head, hands still at his sides. "Gar, you've got nerve."

"Nerve?" the other muttered. "Maybe. Maybe I have. Hold this suit."

"All right!" Brand said, the trembling burned out of his voice.

He stood the suit up on the stiff metal legs, then held it with steady fingers, even helped the other slide slowly down into its metal embrace. There came to him the power to fit the helmet close in the neck groove, lock mesh slips fast, give Gar one last steady look through the open face plate.

"All set?" he asked.

"All set!" Gar said.

Brand found it possible to be proud. His fingers plunged at the mechanism of the inner lock. The smooth panel moved back, merged into a narrow opening. Opening into space—Gar came close, brushed across Brand's body, felt the other touch against him, and stood head down inside the lock.

The trembling shook Brand's legs again for a long instant. He stumbled, swayed against the closing switch, flung it over in a quick convulsive jerk. The inside panel snapped shut.

"Now," he muttered softly.

His fingers flashed up again, spun the gimbaled control that released the outer plate, sent air and man spinning in headlong flight from the lock. He heard the gushing whine of gas expanding into free space, caught the scrape of a metal body against the ship's side. He straightened, eyes dim. Gar was gone.

VI.

Brand went across slowly to where Varney worked with feverish fingers, body crouched, face bent over the lighted mechanism of the power board, head twisted away. He touched Varney. Varney looked up, eyes squeezed in a painful pin points.

"He dropped out?"

"Yes," Brand said. "All through—all through!"

Varney hesitated, respecting the meaning of his sudden silence. Brand remained staring at the vision plate inset above the controls, his eyes fixed on a glinting point of light—light reflected brightly for a time from the spinning metal body drifting back through the space behind the ship. Brand shook himself, rubbed a harsh hand across his face. He looked at his fingers in the dim light. Moisture there. Shouldn't be. Sweat. No. Not sweat—but his face was for some reason a little damp.

He glanced up again, and saw the clustered glow that held the center of the visa plate. The antagonism within him was intensified into flame; he felt a terrible hate for the ships behind.

"Varney, how much lead—now?"

Varney calculated swiftly, fingers flying. "Twenty thousand."

Brand caught his breath. "Twenty thousand! Speed?"

Varney stared, his eyes frozen on the steady dials of the banked board before him. Then he swung around, exultance throbbing in swift words: "Speed approaching three thousand!"

Brand cried out hoarsely: "Then soon they'll stop gaining! And we've a lead of twenty thousand!"

He sucked wind into his lungs. "Say, we're pulling clear!"

"It looks like it," Varney said, grinning. Then his smile was wiped off his face.

Brand looked at him. They both held the same thought and knew it.

Brand asked softly: "Varney, when did we cross twenty-nine hundred?"

Varney's glance shifted.

"Tell me," Brand said in a fierce voice. "You've got to tell me. And don't try to lie."

Varney knew what the other meant. He said: "Just before Gar went out."

"Before!" Brand groaned.

He stiffened and stood up straighter, hands gripping the edge of the control seat. "Before Gar went out—Then what he did wasn't necessary. We could have gone through without having him—you've checked on that?"

Varney steadily faced him. "I've got it down here, tabulated. But you've forgotten something. Twenty-nine hundred wouldn't be enough. We needed three thousand. And we've got it. Gar put us over. We'll cut across just in front of that meteorite cluster, holding three thousand even, and the patrol ships will hit the thick of it. When that happens, they've lost us, and they'll know it. They'll turn back."

Brand nodded dimly, as if no more than half comprehending. He moved his head, then his eyes took on a bitter keenness again. "All right; I'll take over. Are we close enough to start calling 17, Tycho?"

Varney nodded. "Think so. You mean, then—we're going to keep on fighting?"

Brand said: "Why ask a damn fool question like that? Didn't— wasn't that what Gar wanted?"

Life was in Varney's face again, a spark lighted his bleak eyes. "Yes. Gar—and Jorgensen."

"And Jorgensen," Brand said softly.

He was watching the glimmering square of the televisor reception plate. It was beginning to pulse and flicker, as if jerking to the impact of a tight short-wave beam, reaching out across blank space to the speeding ship.

Brand expelled a sudden swift cry of triumph. He moved his fingers in a rapid, intricate tracery. The screen shifted, gave a short vision of the looming face of the giant Moon, showed a stabbing flash of light leap up and die in a lunar crater, faded and came again. Then the beam plunged deeper through infinity, changed to detail, caught the outline of a bleak sending transmission room, with a tall man working at the controls of a high-power televisor. The man nodded and grinned, feeling the contact and gave a swift salute.

"Crater 17, calling the *Isis!*"

"Contact made!" Brand cried.

"Contact made!"

Varney made a strangled sound of joy, gripped Brand hard. Brand half turned, then swung back, built up closer connection with the distant sender.

The snap faded from the captain's voice; abruptly he looked over his shoulder at Varney, muttered: "Take over again."

Varney nodded, helped Brand up from the narrow seat, then buckled himself in, and sent a call to the machine room for gravity to be poured again into the grids. Margot stolidly took the order and agreed.

Varney, on impulse, swung the light beam away from the crater near Tycho, sent it back along the ship's arc to the dimming blur of confused light that was the Controls' fleet; dark objects, great jagged groups of iron and stone, swept in between the *Isis* and the pursuing fleet, blotted out the savage ships. Varney's lip curled in a vindictive grin at the sight of the sudden scurry of movement in the patrol.

"I hope they break their damned necks!" he muttered then jerked at the dials before him, fingered out again for contact with the crater transmitter—Got it!"

"Crater 17, calling the *Isis!* Why don't you answer? Why don't you answer? Contact broken."

"Contact made," Varney said, grinning. "Got you the first time."

"Is this the *Isis* again?"

"Right!"

The other flashed: "Did you have trouble coming over?"

Varney's lips laced. "Yes. Bad trouble. Everything wrong on Earth. Gagin sold out."

The answer came: "We know. Controls have had patrol ships sweeping Tycho for three days back. But we didn't get the whole set-up here. We are waiting for orders."

Varney swung. "Brand, you heard that? What'll I give them?"

Brand was looking back through spurned space, eyes straining for a last glimpse of a spinning metal body. He straightened, came over.

"Brand talking. Give you plenty of orders when we berth there. Have the A-cradle ready, and we'll use it shortly. I'm bringing the *Isis* straight in."

The distant operator nodded. "Right, chief! We'll be ready."

"And we're coming," Brand said harshly. "Break!"

The connection faded. Varney sat staring, face blank, fingers relaxed and numb, touching the cool metal of the huge directing panel.

He glanced away, followed Brand's eyes out through space: "They've beaten us."

"This time," Brand said savagely. "But we're going to fight again."

Far behind them indifferent splinters of light struck for an instant on the shapeless blob of a metal-fabric space suit—and went on to blaze in blurred brightness against the sides of the shining ships, the patrol fleet, turning back toward Earth.

STAR SHIP INVINCIBLE

*A novelette of courage and fear, beauty and horror and pathos–evoked by
the dread, unfathomable menace of the "sink hole of space."*

I.

He had been sitting hunched on the high stool of the operator's chair, elbows on the smooth ledge of metal that encircled him, when the receptor tube spat a harsh wound in his ears, a sibilant warning note. He thought, "What now!" but straightened with alacrity, his stiff back shaping a tense angle.

He jerked his head upward in an arc, nostrils widened, his thin nose slightly trembling, as if he could smell what was vibrating through the receptor channel. He forgot how cold he was, and how his stomach ached faintly from many days on a diet of compressed-food tablets, and how he wished his relief would come, because he was lonely, the universe seeming strange and hostile all around him.

He could see too many stars from this round room that bulged in a curve outward from the top of the Jupiter Dome. It was not good for a man to see too many stars too long.

The snapping sound cracked like a whip in his ears again, and a voice roared: "G-16, the Dome!"

"Jupiter Station," he said quietly. "G-16 responding. Graham at the key. Ready."

The hard voice rumbled: "Build for visual projection. S 1. Jan Garth will speak to you."

"Standing by," Graham said. "R tube clear. Projection coming—what channel?"

"A-channel," the voice boomed. "Beam Central, Earth, sending. Set up cross waves for head and shoulders. Use tight beam on a reverse arc."

"Power?" he asked faintly. "We're low here. The supply ship you were going to send—"

"All the power you've got," the voice cut in, brusque and commanding.

"Right," Graham muttered.

His hands, supple in metal-fabric gloves, caressed the complex panels in front of him as if he were playing a delicate musical instrument. He kicked a lever attached to one leg of his stool and the tripod chair began to revolve, slowly and smoothly.

As he turned he touched studs. The power tubes that ringed him in concentric rows hummed and howled, then went achingly silent, as the pulsating tight beam passed the wave band of audible reception.

His eardrums hurt: there had been a soundless concussion, and a golden sphere, slightly flattened at the ends, had come into being directly over his head. It hung suspended between the four great mirrors over him, spraying his face with lances of swirling light. He worked his lithe hands, fast.

A blue luminosity grew from his keyboard, spurted upward from the power tubes, forming like sapphire frost on levers and studs. Azure spears pushed at the glowing globe. His fingers danced over the power panels. The globe was held in balanced suspension in a basket network of crossing rays. It turned on an invisible axis, revolving with silent speed. Spinning like a dervish, the head and shoulders of a big man shaped within the hazy edges of the illuminated sphere.

Graham turned his twitching face upward. He whispered to himself, a little queerly: "Nice trick. You do it with mirrors."

He wanted to laugh—or cry. Sweat lay in heavy drops between his fingers. Visual projection always seemed like magic to him.

After all he was only a flabby little man who knew the motions, the incantations, that brought this magic into being. He handled forces he was terribly afraid of within himself. He was always wondering why the chained lighting in the tubes didn't turn and rend him; he thought some day it would refuse to perform its tricks, would swing and destroy him in a sudden burst of coldly coruscating flame.

The gleaming globe still whirled above him, but the spinning slowed, as he narrowed the flow of juice pouring into the A-channel. There were manacled giants in the tubes, but he could make them weak by starving them, by throttling the leaping flow of power that fed them.

The image in the sphere was at first vague and seemed to be upside down. Then the head and shoulders of the projected vision came right side around, the shape of face and neck clarifying first, then the line of lips and jaw slowly sharpening and straightening. Presently Graham had no difficulty at all in recognizing the grim countenance of Jan Garth, Administrator of Star Lines.

"Jupiter supply ship left Mars this date, 12:40, Mars time reckoned in Earth units," Garth said abruptly. "Watched the blast-off through my v-plate here. Record the time for permanent preservation."

"Recorded," Graham said, very low. He had taken it on the absorbent tape.

As soon as adequate projection had been built up, he had switched in the recording spool. Garth didn't say anything for half a minute after that terse exchange of crisp phrases. It was the first time the administrator had used the Jupiter beam personally, and for an instant the harsh voice stumbled, as if the man speaking had suddenly been brought up against reality in his mind; as if he had just awakened to what he was really doing.

He was talking—no; an image of himself was talking—in a little room high up under the room of the interplanetary dome on Jupiter, a room separated from where he stood on Earth by an immensity so vast that the thought of it stunned a man into somber silence.

At last Garth said: "The ship is one of ours. Registered at the Port of Korna, nine thousand tons Earth weight; carrying pilot, navigator, and twenty-eight passengers. The *Star Ship Invincible*. Captain Moran commanding."

"New ship," Graham said succinctly.

"Maiden voyage. It's the first of the new fleet."

"Carrying supplies for the Dome here?"

"Yes."

"We need plenty," Graham said, biting his words.

He shivered, suddenly realizing that he was very cold. Jupiter's atmosphere didn't hold heat, the Sun was very far away; and they had only a little more fuel to feed into the atomic converters. Until the supply ship came, the Dome would be cold.

"I know," Garth said.

"Why did you wait so long to send this ship?" Graham demanded recklessly.

He forgot the power of the other; he forgot that he was only Key Man G-16, Jupiter Station; he thought of how they had to live, here in the Dome, sleeping restlessly in chilly cells, groping through corridors kept dim because light took power and you didn't mind not seeing very well if you could stay at least partially warm. And always the faint ache in their bellies; the ache that came from month after month on the same diet of compressed synthe-food.

Garth said: "This is only a little later than usual. The ship will be there soon. Hold hard."

Graham hunched his shoulders. "You—you haven't forgotten the Sink Hole?"

Garth said: "No."

"The ship's carrying passengers?"

"Yes. Twenty-eight."

"They've been warned?"

"They've been warned."

Graham nodded. "Well, Moran and his navigator know what to expect."

"They're not going to have any trouble."

"You're pretty sure," Graham said softly. "This ship—she's fast?"

The big man shifted his head, raising it with exultance. "I told you; it's the first of the new fleet we've been building on Mars for the Jupiter run. Since the Sink Hole came, we've been working night and day. Now we're ready to take a chance."

The little man sat still, his body humped, feeling the sweat gather in the cold palms of his hands. They were taking a chance, were they? This new ship must be big stuff; at least the lab men thought it was big stuff.

A picture rose in his brain. He glimpsed strained faces, looking into the worried yet courageous eyes of the passengers—passengers who were, he knew, friends and lovers of the people already here in the Dome. They knew what might happen, those passengers; yet they went aboard the *Star Ship Invincible* because the touch of a friendly hand, the pressure of lips and bodies in the physical contact of love, meant more to them than living a safe existence full of the emptiness of fading memories.

They were coming unafraid, risking everything, knowing that the Sink Hole might never close again; because it had closed once before, after an interval of ten yawning years, was no guarantee that it would close now after this reopening. They came, knowing they might be put away forever from the good Earth.

They weren't willing to be cut off from the other planets for ten years, waiting for the Sink Hole to shut together in its periodic pulsation. Ten years was a long time; too long, these faithful ones believed, too long for separation. So they risked more than life for—

"You're not taking the big chance," Graham said after a minute. "Those people aboard the *Invincible* are doing that."

Garth shrugged, "People are always taking chances. That's life, isn't it—taking chances?"

Graham said: "I don't know. Maybe it is."

"They've got everything in their favor," Garth stated. "The Walton Arc is still clear. The Hole's widening slowly this time. And the ship has the speed to make port at the Dome, before the Hole spreads across the Walton Arc."

"I hope you're right," Graham muttered.

All at once a realization came to him, and he went cold in every part of his body. He thought: God, she may have decided to come this trip. Even now she may be on the *Invincible*, not knowing the danger, not sensing fully that the ship rides a race with death. The passenger list—the names of those who were coming on the *Invincible*. He had to know.

He tried to keep the shivering out of his voice, but it was there when he spoke: "You--you'd better let me have the names of the passengers, chief. The people here will want to know who's aboard that ship."

Garth looked at him closely. "All right; I'll give it to you. I've got the record here. Better take this on the tape."

"Yes, sir," Graham said, very low. "The names, sir?"

Garth's hand appeared in the projection, holding a strip of metal-fabric, stamped indelibly with a string of names and numbers; he began to read, his voice low, his eyes now and then glancing at the signal man's face; since the projection had been built on a tight beam operating along a double arc, Graham's body was visible to the man on Earth. The list wasn't long; only twenty-eight passengers. Almost the last in the roll was the name Graham had hoped and feared might be there. There couldn't be any doubt now. The girl had gone aboard the *Invincible*. It all depended now on Moran—on Moran and whatever they had developed in the experimental laboratories on Mars. This ship—there was something about the way Garth spoke of it that gave him hope.

"I've got them all," Graham said, as the harsh voice of the administrator faded out. "Thank you, sir."

Garth stared at him keenly. "Any one you know listed there?"

The little man stammered something incoherent.

"Can't hear you," Garth said, indifferent now. For a moment he had been amused by the taunt anxiety that had crept into the key man's gaunt face, but after all it was nothing to him; he didn't care very much what answer the flabby fellow made.

"Only my wife," Graham said. He choked, and then went on: "Couldn't you tell me what this ship has that the others hadn't, sir? And what--what do you want me to do? There must be something I can do. If I could help to keep her safe it would mean so much to me."

"I understand." Garth softened for an instant; really, the fellow was quite human, with his pleading eyes and twitching little face. "Yes; there's something you can do. You'll connect with the *Invincible* immediately after I've signed off here. Once you've got them, you'll transfer the channel on relay to my operator here, but keep your own key open. Moran is under orders to use the automatic time signal, on a circuit breaker operating every other minute. So long as you hear that signal, you'll know the ship's all right."

"Sure," Graham said. "But suppose it fades?"

"If you think something's wrong, you'll flash my operator and report."

"That's all I've got to do?"

"That's all."

"It's not much," Graham whispered.

Garth turned. "There isn't much we can do if the *Invincible* goes under. I can't believe it will go under."

"Yes," Graham said eagerly. "You said it had a lot of new gadgets. You couldn't—couldn't tell me what they were?"

"It's the best ship we know how to build," Garth said slowly. "I'm not a lab man, so I don't know the jargon or the details, but it's got everything we could put into it. You needn't worry. Moran is the best pilot-commander we have, and Hansen's a navigator; they'll bring this ship through."

Graham shook his head, his lips trembling. "This thing won't be decided by navigating. It will depend on the ship—on speed, on power, on equipment."

Garth straightened, smiling a little. "Well, this vessel is named the *Invincible*."

Graham shivered. "Wrong name. I'm afraid of names like that."

The other threw back his big head and laughed. "Have you got any sensible reason for being afraid?"

"Yes," Graham said.

The heavy-faced man looked at him, suddenly grave. "You'll explain."

"Sure!" Graham said. "I—I've had a lot of time to read the old books here in the station. I mean the old printed books the ancients had before the tape recorder and the film spool. There's a story of a ship of the sea that was built about two hundred years ago, in the twentieth century—"

"Go on," Garth ordered.

"It struck an iceberg—there were icebergs on Earth then; this was before climate control—and it went down. Right under, in just a little while. About a thousand people were drowned, counting the passengers."

Garth shrugged. "What's that got to do with the ship we built on mars?"

"The experts said this ship of the sea wasn't sinkable," Graham said quietly. "Well, they were wrong. They seem to have found then that anything man could make could be easily destroyed. We've had to learn that lesson over and over."

After a silence Garth said: "What was the name of this sea ship?"

Graham answered: "They called it the *Titanic*."

Neither of them moved for a while.

Then Garth shouted: "But you don't know this ship that Moran is commanding. It's made of an alloy, the newest alloy we've yet found; tungsten isotope and C-metal. The hull is split in cylindrical sections twenty feet in diameter over all. The sections are honeycombed with cells; the cells are bulk-headed, shock-proofed, deadened with molecular insulation. The ship is armor-plated in three layers, with vacuum between each layer."

Graham kept thinking of the girl; and not of the girl alone, but of all of them on the *Invincible*; crouching in a little metal bubble that hurtled at inconceivable speed along the Walton Arc, along a plotted curve that passed just beyond the edge of the Hole in Space. Just beyond—maybe. If the Hole didn't grow. And the Hole was growing.

His throat was bitter and dry. "It's no good if you've been preparing against collision. The Hole isn't solid, isn't material or tangible. What the ship's got to have is power—power to pull away."

"You think," Garth said slowly, "the Hole is something like a vortex or a whirlpool? And when a ship comes too near it's sucked under."

"Now you've got it," Graham said.

For a minute they both sat very still, staring at one another with opaque eyes; Graham could hear the sibilant singing of the discharge spark in the R tube behind him. He waited.

"The lab men have given the *Invincible* all the power we knew how to build into her," Garth muttered. "Etheric drive. If a ship's pulled into the Hole, it must come out somewhere. What's on the other side of the Hole?"

"We don't know," Graham said ironically. "I believe it lies in a universe of different dimensional proportions; in a different kind of ether. Somehow that universe, or maybe it was our universe, warped a little out of line, and there's this gap where nothing fits. It begins and ends nowhere."

The other whispered: "The lab men developed an experimental shield—waves generated in a circular blanket that will cover the *Invincible* all over. So the ship can ride in a static ether."

Graham put up his hands suddenly and covered his gray face. "I wish I could feel that you'd gone about this right; that the lab men knew what they were building; but I can't be sure. All I can think about is my wife. We'd only been married a little while when I was transferred here. I didn't want to bring her out to this God-forsaken planet.

"The Hole opened and stayed open, for ten years. I haven't seen her in ten years. But I haven't forgotten. She has been faithful. I know that. Now she's coming to me on a ship that's got a good chance of falling into hell. Maybe I'll never see her again. Maybe I'll never feel her lips against mine again—"

The big man's eyes were hard and unyielding. "You'll see her soon. Don't be a damned fool. You've got a job to do. You can't go soft on me now. None of us can afford to go soft in this game. I couldn't recall the *Invincible* if I wanted to. The ship's gone too far along the Arc."

"No; Moran wouldn't turn back now," Graham said harshly. "I know him, the devil. He's hard as hell. He's like you. You've never been hit like I'm hit now. But wait—it's coming to you. Some day it's coming to you."

Garth laughed; the sound throbbed with immense contempt. This flabby little key man with the face of a rabbit shouting at him, talking like that to him! That was funny. Yes. Damned funny! He roared:

"If I gave the order, even now, Moran would turn back."

Graham grinned, peeling his lips back. "He's after glory. If he went on and made it through, he could laugh at you. He'd be a hero the system over. And if he didn't—what'd be the difference?"

Garth was stung. "You've got your orders, G-16. If the circuit breaker on the *Invincible* stops, you'll ring me in at once."

"Yes," Graham said. "Whatever Moran does, I'll obey orders, chief. I've been obeying orders all my life."

Garth muttered grimly: "You're not after glory, are you?"

"No. Moran can have that."

Garth grinned. "Cut off."

"Cutting off."

The opalescent sphere lost shape and the illusion of solidity; it dissolved like smoke, streaming away in banners of golden glow that vanished in a bright and glittering nothingness. It was gone and Graham sat alone. The stars closed in around him; millions of white orbs watching him. To them he must have been a queer specimen of tormented matter, convulsed by the strange madness called life, wriggling frantically away from the final transfixion that would be his destiny.

Shuddering, he pulled his thoughts from the stars. Before, he had been lonely, but not this lonely; now he ached with the completeness of his isolation. His belly was empty, and his heart was vacant, except for the hunger of a terrible longing; yet these things were as nothing to him. He sat staring down the long slope of fruitless years, seeing before him the shadow of coming bereavement. He felt now that the girl, his wife, still lived somewhere in space; but the warm pulsation of her unique being was burning low. Far away from him she brushed elbows unawares with death. Annihilation was nearer to her than she knew.

His longing and his loneliness, however, were not stronger in him than the lifelong habit of submission to command. Swinging in the chair he began to change the set-up of the power chart.

II.

She stood at the foot of the burnished metal ladder that went up into the control cabin. Hesitantly, she caught her gleaming metal-fabric cloak about her and moved upward; halfway to the top she felt the ladder quiver under added weight, and, tilting her head, she saw a man coming rapidly down. He seemed to become conscious of her presence at the same time and stopped a little above her, staring.

He was a big man, the solid meat of his hard body revealed in muscular outline by the close fit of his space-man's uniform. Blond, burned by the light of suns and stars, he was handsome—an overpowering Nordic.

His lips twisted in a slow frown. "Do you feel the need of exercise, lady? I admit the ship's a little cramped back here, but still—climbing ladders—"

She stammered something. Looking at her more closely and seeing that she was beautiful, his lips twisted a different way and he smiled.

"Didn't you know it's not allowed to go up into the control cabin?"

"Oh, yes," she said lightly, "I knew it." She returned his smile.

He said with a stumbling voice: "You're lovely, but at least you're not a lovely liar."

"Why should I lie?" she asked slowly. "I wasn't doing anything wrong. I was exploring the ship."

"I see," he said, very sober. "First voyage?"

"Almost," she said. "Except for the crossing I made with my father from Earth to Mars. I have no memory of that. I'm Earth-born."

"So am I," he said gently. "Then we'd better be friends. There aren't many Earth-born on this ship."

She nodded. Her burnished golden head moved with an easy grace. Eyes the color of starlit space looked upward into his. She said quietly:

"I've found that. I've had no one to talk to for nearly three days now."

"Hard on a woman," he said, grinning.

She laughed, delightfully.

He moved another rung downward on the ladder. "You've been lonely," he said. "I'm very sorry. Didn't know anyone like you had come aboard—this trip. Should have looked at the passenger list more closely."

"You like me?" she whispered.

He put his head on one side, regarded her carefully, then answered, grave-voiced: "Yes. Definitely."

"I'm glad."

"All right," he said, with amusement. "Now, you like me?"

Her laughter tinkled. "Yes. Definitely."

He looked at her with a glow in his eyes. "I think," he said, "before this goes any further, we'd better get down from this ladder."

"I can't come up?"

"Persistent, aren't you?" he returned. "Sorry, but orders is orders, ma'am."

He laughed again. "Down with you, lady. Or have you a name?"

"I've a name," she said softly. "Tam. Tam Graham."

He felt a sudden keen pleasure in being alive. Three days of monotony, of watching charts and moving keys, hunched in a back-breaking crouch—three days full of overhanging terror were wiped away and he was glad he breathed and could see and smell and hear and taste. He tasted a word now, touching it tenderly with his tongue; the word was "Tam."

"Lovely," he said, without thinking. "It fits. So few people have the right names." She dropped down the ladder in a swift sinuous motion, and he followed her, closed his arms suddenly around her, and kissed the fragrant rosebud of her mouth.

"Some day soon," he said softly, I'll take you up in the control cabin—if you're very nice to me."

He held his arms in the same tight circle, but somehow she slipped easily from his hold, and he stood empty-handed and a little stunned.

Gravely her smooth voice came: "I've a husband somewhere. You may have heard of him. John Graham."

He dropped his hands, the smile fell away from his lips, and his face was covered by a shadow; before this, he had considered himself as not without honor. He was somehow ashamed.

"Yes. Jupiter key man."

"I love him," she said simply. "I'm going to him."

"You're brave," he said. And then: "I'm sorry."

"Forgiven and forgotten," she said, now smiling. "I want you to be a friend to me. You're a friend of John's, aren't you?"

"G-16?" he said. "Oh, yes! My name is Hansen. I'm navigator, in case you didn't know."

"I knew," the girl said.

They looked at one another and laughed together, but the sound of his mirth was strained.

"You're wise. Too wise for me."

"In some ways, perhaps. About ships and space you know things that I shall never know. You're a navigator—that's hard. I've heard John say it was hard."

"Ordinarily," he said, eyes darkening, "it's pretty soft stuff. But not for me this trip. I wish we'd left you back on Mars!"

"Why?" she asked slowly.

"You're taking a long chance. It's fifty-fifty we'll never make Jupiter."

"There's danger," she whispered. "I know."

He glanced at her with admiration. "You have no fear. If you were afraid, I'd feel it. I can feel things like that."

She said softly: "You see, whatever comes, I'll always have the memory of the night we left Mars. The lights crossing in the sky, like pale fingers pointing. The lines of silver ships, and then this ship, a polished cylinder, lying in that immense trestlework—what do you call that?"

"Slip cradle," he answered, looking at her with glinting eyes. "It's the same with me. I remember every blast-off; even to the first trip I took as navigator, on the Mars-Earth run, five years ago. There's something about it."

"The thick Martian night," she said dreamily. "All those confused voices shouting. Monstrous machines and puny people. I'll never forget my first sight of those luminous letters on the side of this ship, stamped on the sleek curve of it: *Star Ship Invincible*."

He nodded, his face strong with exultance. "*Invincible*—that's a proud name. Defiant!"

"Throwing back the light of the stars," Tam whispered. "As if to say—not afraid, not afraid, not afraid of what you can do to me. Not afraid of emptiness, of vastness, of the hard hostility written in the stars."

He shook his head. "The stars aren't hostile. They're indifferent."

"No," she said. "They hate us; I can sense it. They resent our arrogance, our impudence in voyaging out into the colossal sea of space where they have been so long alone."

He grinned. "They're only suns and planets; bright lights along the Broadway of the universe."

"Suns and planets," she repeated softly. "And beyond them?"

He shrugged. "More suns and planets, I suppose."

"Forever and forever?"

"Forever, perhaps," he said, laughing.

"Worlds without end," she whispered, and shivered a little. "I feel small and insignificant. We won't talk of those things."

"All right," he said. They stood silent an instant, then he muttered:

"I suppose you've been all over the rest of the ship?"

"Yes," Tam answered. "I've been exploring. All those cold cells crowded with stellite drums and beryllium cylinders—they hold supplies?"

"That's it."

"For us? I didn't know we'd use so much."

He turned away from her, then swung back. "For us, and for the Dome on Jupiter. We'll use very little. This will be a short trip, if we make it. The ship has a new power source—etheric drive."

The girl looked at him soberly. "Now you talk of things incomprehensible to me. What is it, this etheric drive?"

"You remember your instructions in space school concerning three-dimensional calculations?" he asked. "Well, the drive is possible because we've gone back to the theory of an all-pervasive medium including the universe in its scope. By using a four-dimensional tesseract we are able to exert power directly on the ether.

"Think of the ether as a river in which we are completely immersed; by coming to the surface of the river we are able to ride a current and choose the direction of flow; the motions of the suns and planets are everlastingly stirring currents in the ether—ether drifts. They go in all directions, constantly crossing and recrossing one another. We've found a current Jupiter-bound, and we're riding it. All clear?"

The girl said very low: "You mean, then that at any time we may be hurled away from Jupiter instead of toward it if the drift changes direction?"

He frowned. "No. Naturally we've got a set of Donlin sun engines in reserve. And there's little chance of the direction of the ether flow changing we can choose any drift we want and calculate its probable direction for twenty years to come. That is, we can do that by using mechanical calculators. No man could think that fast—not even me. About all I do is feed the calculators problems. I think up the puzzles, they chew them up, and give me the predigested results."

The girl put one hand on her smooth forehead. "You've given me an ache—here."

He glanced at the little chronometer strapped to one wrist. "Well, you're going to be rid of me now for a while. I've got to back-track to the C cabin. Came aft to take a stroll through this part of the ship and see how things were going. Moran will expect some kind of report. What shall I give him?"

"Tell him," the girl said, "all's well!"

"In more ways than one," Hansen muttered.

His mouth still burned with remembrance of that swift kiss. He was yet stunned with the knowledge that this was the wife of John Graham— this girl married to the flabby little key-man who had been for ten years marooned in the Dome. It wasn't easy to believe, because he didn't want to believe it.

The girl touched his arm timidly. "You'll come back again and talk to me?"

"Sure, I'll come back again. And maybe—I don't know, because Moran's a pretty sour old space-buster, but maybe, I say, I'll be able to take you up in the C cabin. I'll come again as soon as I can."

He made an exaggerated bow, kissed her hand, then smilingly turned away and vanished up the ladder. After he had gone, the girl raised her fingers and slowly rubbed them across her lips.

She went back slowly to the little cell in the ship's hull that had been given to her. It was no better, no worse, than the accommodations offered the other passengers. It was cramped and cold, but it was clean, almost Spartan in its austerity.

There was a wide bed, nearly level with the floor, the smooth silky surface of it shining softly. She sank down in the soft stuff, felt the warm fabric close around her, hold her in a firm yet tender embrace. She was tired with a weariness arising from monotony, yet no desire for sleep came to her.

She was lying very still, half dreaming, half waking, and it seemed only a part of the dream when a spot of yellow light appeared on the wall and a voice spoke to her with exultant eagerness: "Tam, I've found you!"

This was not dreaming. It was real. Too real. With a little gasp she answered, speaking wildly into the cone of saffron light that thickened and strengthened while she spoke:

"John—you can see me?"

His voice came, brokenly, the voice of a man given a rare vision: "Yes; I can see you. And you're beautiful. You're more beautiful than you were so long ago. The years have not changed you, nor time altered you, except to make you more wonderful."

She couldn't move, but her body shivered in a kind of ecstasy.

"This is like magic; like a miracle. John, where are you?"

"The Dome," he said faintly. "Jupiter."

"Let me see you," she said. "Darling, let me see you."

He didn't answer at once. Then: "This beam—works only one way. Hard to keep it narrowed on your cabin. No receiver at your end, no transmitter. Can't build a reverse arc."

She said softly: "It isn't possible?"

"No. It isn't possible."

She thought he seemed glad. That was strange. Yet it might have been only her imagining. She whispered:

"You've changed a little. Your voice is different."

He said: "Darling, I'm still the same, and you're still the same, and our love is as it has always been. And it will be the same through life everlasting."

"Ten years," she whispered. "A long time, John."

"Then you mean—well, I don't deserve you. And no woman could be faithful through ten years."

"But I have been faithful," she answered simply.

He would remember those words all his days.

"The ship," he said, after a silence. "Everything's all right?"

"Yes. In a little while I'll be with you."

His voice shook. "Darling, I can't wait. My arms have been empty so long."

"We waited ten years," she whispered softly. "The years are gone, and we shall not remember them. We have the hours that remain to us."

The shaft of vibrant light quivered and died away, leaving the room full of shadow and the echo of his exultant voice:

"Tam, you're coming to me!"

"Only a little longer," the girl cried to him. "Only a little longer, darling."

The light was gone and somehow a shadow lay over her heart. She had a sudden remembrance of the cold hostility she had seen written in the stars; and the ship still rode the sea of space.

III.

Hansen climbed the ladder into the control cube, feeling like an old man. His joints were stiff and bitterness was in his mouth. All his life he had waited for a woman like the one he had seen below; his eyes had been warmed by the vision of her, and the warmth had gone through his body, lighting torches in his veins. Now that flame was dead, abruptly quenched, and he was blinded by the pain of his spent longing.

He reached the end of the ladder and pulled himself up into the crowded room that had been his whole world during many hours of tense labor. His legs shook under him.

"You've come back so soon?" Moran asked. "Why didn't you do as I said—take an empty cabin aft and sleep a while? You're very tired. So am I—but not so weary as you seem. Your face shows that, sir."

"Does it?" Hansen mumbled.

He rubbed an elbow against a slot in the wall and felt the smooth round surface of a sealing plug slip in place behind him. He stood an instant with his back against that cool metal stuff, unsmiling, his eyes were on the dull gray of the floor.

"I can't sleep back there—with them."

Moran's lips tightened. "You mean, you're afraid the thing we're hoping won't happen, may happen, and you'd be caught with the passengers?"

"Hell, no!" Hansen said, his voice savage. "I'd rather take my place with them than carry this knowledge around with me. They don't know they're doomed. When the thing happens to them, it will be sudden, sharp, complete, like an execution. They haven't been turning the possibility over and over in their minds, fighting the thought of it, then letting the thought sweep in and grow and grow, until it's like a monster devouring a man's thought-stuff. You and I have the joy of that."

Moran came closer to him, walking with tight, clipped steps. The captain put a hand on his shoulder.

"Nothing's gone wrong yet, Hansen. You're borrowing trouble."

Hansen's eyes flamed up at him. "Am I? Am I? So it hasn't been worrying you, eh? It hasn't been worrying you that we've the lives of twenty-eight people in our hands; that maybe we've got to let those twenty-eight people die, because we have our orders, and we obey orders —damned fools, we do what we're told, even when it comes to murder."

The older man didn't move for a minute. The hard, quiet face remained with that curious surface stillness all over it, the mask that had never fallen before Hansen or any other so far as he knew. Then Moran said:

"This isn't murder. They were warned, over and over. They came freely, knowing the chance they took. You and I would be glad to die with them. But we've got a different part to play—a harder part, maybe. I don't know about that. We're men. We'll behave as men."

Hansen straightened. He no longer needed the support of the cold metal slab against his back.

"Hell, you're right! But I—I've seen a woman; not an ordinary woman—she knocked me a little off balance. She seemed to me too beautiful to die. I wanted to save her. I couldn't breathe straight for a little while."

"Some women can do that to you," Moran said, understanding. "You've never taken a wife, have you? And it has come to you that this is the woman for whom you have waited."

"I know it," Hansen said very softly. "but it just couldn't be arranged. She's Tam Graham, G-16's wife, and she happens to love him."

Moran's eyes flickered. "Johnny Graham's wife! On this ship! I remember her. She is—beautiful. I can't forget the way he used to look at her. There's something between them like—like adoration. If anything happens to—"

"Yes," Hansen said. "No good thinking about it. We can't do anything for her. She's only one among many. There are other women riding with us—maybe not so beautiful physically, but beautiful with the same kind of love. It's the same with them as with Tam. It must be the same with them, or they wouldn't have taken this ship. They came with their eyes open. We can't save them all."

"No," Moran said. "You and I didn't make the Hole. We've got our job to do, and we'll do it, the best way we know how. The rest is on the knees of the gods."

Hansen nodded slowly. "Have you checked the chart since I left?"

"Twice," Moran said. "Speed's holding. We're on our course. We've got a good chance of pulling away clean."

They went over to the Danler spatial chart and stood staring at it together. A black smear, twisted like a snake, cutting across the smooth ivory luminosity of the board—that was the Sink Hole.

Swinging across the upper end of that ebony blur they could trace the faint red line of the Walton Arc. A green sliver of glow was the *Invincible*; the ship crawled deliberately, it seemed to them, along the scarlet curve. As it crawled, it came nearer and nearer the blob of unfolding darkness that was the Hole. It seemed as though someone had spilled ink on the white surface of the chart, and the ink was spreading, spreading—

Moran said; "We're doing better than Garth figured. I've balanced the chronometer readings with space-path calculations and made allowances for light distortions due to etheric faults, but still our speed is pretty nearly inconceivable."

"And if anything happens," Hansen said quietly, "we've still a trick in reserve. I don't understand how it's going to be done, but Garth gave you the directions."

"Listen," Moran said impatiently, "I explained it to you once. It's not simple, but you're a navigator with AA rating and dimensional mechanics should be understandable to you. Garth and the lab men believe the Hole is a dimensional warp. Using the etheric drive won't keep us from being pulled into it, or through it, or across it, if a vortex has been formed by the spatial strain caused by the opening of that gap in the void.

"All the etheric currents may be sucked one way, and we're riding an etheric current, you know. If the current we're on goes in the ship goes in. We're hoping against that. We're counting on the strength of the ether stream we're skimming now; we believe this flow will carry us by the Hole before it has fully widened across the Walton Arc. But we may be wrong."

Hansen grinned without mirth. "That's funny. You sound like an expert—'we *may* be wrong.' Hell, it's an odds-on chance the whole damned thing is cockeyed. I don't trust those lab men. Sure—they think up something like this, and then they stay where *they're* safe enough, but they send us space-wranglers out to try it on the dog. If it doesn't work right—that's too bad. Write it off. Unsuccessful experiment. They make a hell of a lot of unsuccessful experiments."

"That's the only way science gets anywhere," Moran said heavily. "Trying and trying and trying. This is a swell ship we've got here, isn't it? It's pretty comfortable, it's clean, it's warm, we've got as good air to breathe as you'll find on any planet, we've got speed and power to burn—not much like the old space boats that used to creep out to the Moon from Earth and then crawl back. There have been improvements; we owe them to the lab men. We owe a lot to the lab men. We've got to take our chances, sure, but they're doing the best they can to make things easier and safer for us.

"Most of them would rather lock the doors of the laboratories and never come out again; they've got what they think is the holy of holies, and the world, our world, the practical world, the world of men and money and machines, is just a damned nuisance to them. We're a lot of childish creatures always begging for new toys, new gadgets, new playthings. We build a civilization, then tear it down, building something different. We don't know what we want."

"I know what I want," Hansen muttered. His fingers twitched. "I want to get this damned ship safe into the Dome at Jupiter, and then I never want to see another damned space-buster again as long as I live. I'm sick of seeing stars; I've got a bellyful of monotony without end."

"You're tired," Moran said. "You've taken too long a trick at the controls. I've felt the same way; world-weariness born of physical weariness. Why don't you trust the automatic pilot when you're on duty? Machines are better than men—for most things."

Hansen swung around, his face contorted. "Damn you, you're not human! You'd rather look at the shine of a stellite stud than see a smile break on a woman's face. You're all wheels and levers and clicking cogs; sometimes I expect to hear a humming and buzzing come from inside you."

Moran laughed with metallic amusement. "I can depend on machines. When you need them, they're there. This ship is a machine. The thing that may save you and me from going into the Hole with the rest of them—that's a machine, too."

"I don't know," Hansen grunted, staring at it. "Maybe it is; sometimes I think it's alive. It's a damned funny-looking thing."

Moran looked across at the dimensional converter with a kind of loving reverence. Smiling, he said: "It's beautiful. Notice! Not a wheel anywhere. That's why you can't believe it is a machine."

The converter was oddly like a flower—a flame flower with metal petals of vivid blue, and a purple cylindrical stalk luminous with an unceasing sweat of cold translucent bubbles that sifted out through a network of tiny apertures on the underside of the petals and flowed downward in a singing stream. It seemed to be covered by a shimmering veil of something shining and smooth and transparent like glass, yet not glass.

Moran whispered: "Try to follow the lines of it with your eyes. You can't. They seem to begin and end nowhere. Yet they have beginnings and endings—not in our universe, not in our dimensional range, but somewhere; somewhere beyond or around or over or under our world. When I think that our laboratory men shaped that mechanism, prisoned free power in it, and gave control of that power to the little cube in the wall there, I'm proud. I'm glad I'm a man. We're only crawling scum maybe, lice infesting the surfaces of dying planets—but by Heaven, we've got a few brains."

Hansen shivered. "I don't like it."

The other laughed. "You're afraid of it, because it's so beautiful and terrible."

"Yes," Hansen said, "I am." Then: "Well, what does the damned thing do?"

"When the time comes that we have to use it," Moran said, "you'll see. I'm trying now to tell you how it works. They've called it a dimensional converter, and that's the right name for it. When I touch that cube in the wall, it will swing, and the angles of its planes one to another will be reversed, and the shape of this room and everything in this room, including your body and my body, will be converted across the dimensions—just for an instant, a fragment of a second, we shall be nowhere. We shall still be in this ship and at the same time we shall be in a million otherwheres.

"There is only one dimension—shape. When we talk about length and width and thickness and existence in relative time, we are only attempting to describe shape. And not even that—what we are really doing is describing size. Size is real, is physical, is solid and touchable. But shape—how can you get hold of that and describe it?

"Shape is the estimation of a thing that we form from the physical and mental impressions and perceptions, sensations and stimulations, that impinge on our receptive mechanisms. We know how a thing looks, but we can't describe it; we can describe some of its physical aspects, and make a few fumbling comparisons with other inadequately described things, and finally we conclude with the generality that everything is relative. This converter is like reality—beautifully incomplete."

"Still what you've said isn't clear to me," Hansen muttered, moving his hands protestingly. "I can't get all this straight in my head. Where the hell will we go when this thing starts working on us—and where will we arrive?"

"We'll come back as nearly as possible to where we were," Moran said, grave-voiced. "Maybe that will be somewhere within the shell of this ship—if the ship exists after passing through the Hole."

His cold glance swung to the spatial chart. The green blob had moved forward: nearly half of the red line had been eaten away, but the arc that remained was very near to the ebony blur of the dead spot. The Hole was widening like a hungry mouth—

Moran nodded toward the space-drive dial. He said, with a kind of savage confidence: "Speed still the same. Course all even. We're not going to have any trouble."

"No," Hansen said. "No; of course not." He looked at the gray metal of the floor. "But I think I'll sleep here. It'll be better if we don't unseal that plug again until we reach Jupiter."

"All right," Moran said, bending over the chart.

Hansen stared at him; absorbed, intent on graphs and dial readings, he seemed indifferent to the existence of human weaknesses, human emotions. With him there could never be a great love. And yet – it might be that he loved his machines with a cold intellectual passion.

Hansen couldn't help shivering. He was thinking of the girl; all that beauty obliterated, sucked into nothingness, destroyed by a devouring darkness. It couldn't be. He couldn't let it be.

Muttering a little to himself, he put his hands up to his head. Looking at Moran's stiff back, he whispered:

"I'm going to do something. I can't let her die without doing something. I can't—"

Moran swung. "Did you speak to me?"

"No," Hansen said in a mumble. "I didn't say anything."

"Thought I heard you talking."

Hansen grinned queerly. "Now you're getting the jitters. Maybe you got 'em from me."

Moran frowned. "You better take a little sleep while you've got the chance. I'll be needing some myself pretty soon and it'll be your trick again; you'll want to be in good shape, if you're not going to use the automatic pilot."

Hansen's face contorted; veins stretched in white tracery under the skin of his cheeks. "Listen, why don't you let me alone? Sure, I'll be in good shape. But let me worry about it, see? I'm sick as hell of your fussing and nagging."

"Sorry," Moran said, with a flush. "Nerves, I guess. Didn't realize how it must seem to you. All right; I'll let you sleep."

The other turned his back again. Hansen stretched himself out on the cool metal of the floor. The cabin was quiet, too quiet; he missed the hum and throb that would have been there if they'd been using the Donlin engines. This etheric drive was ghostly; no sound, no vibration, no crushing sense of acceleration when you were building power.

But he didn't trust it. Too many damned machines nowadays. Machines and more machines all the time. More machines than men pretty soon. Then what? That would be a hell of a fix, if the machines got bright ideas. Thank God, the devils in the dynamos couldn't think. Couldn't they, though? He didn't trust a machine, any kind of machine. Didn't trust them—

A minute later Moran came over and stood looking down at the big blond body stretched on the floor. Hansen slept, restlessly, muttering, voicing stifled groans, rolling a little from side to side.

"A weak sister," Moran said with contempt. "A job like this and they give me a load like him to carry."

He raised his eyes upward, his glance passing through the transparent dome of the control room to touch the steely stars. He saluted them with a lifted fist.

"Hard, aren't you?" He grinned, showing small pointed white teeth. "Hard and secretive and stolid. You don't give yourself away. Me—I'm like you, and I'm glad. To hell with the weak sisters!"

The ship plunked, like a thrown knife, across the empty depths and vacant canyons that gaped between the shaky platforms of the winging worlds. Jupiter loomed close, a haven and a target, but still the Hole stretched like a black wound unfolding in dark flesh. The ship might yet be an unwilling lance forced to probe that wound.

Moran rocked on his two legs, defying and adoring the angry lights that broke the bleakness of those dark skies. Ebony infinity surrounded him, engulfed him, submerged him with a roar of mental surf, yet he remained a rounded entity, complete and unbroken as he had been since he had been cut as a flap from his mother's flesh, since he had emerged as a skein from her skein.

He was a man; he was unique. There were millions very like him, but they were not as he was in all ways. This vision of the void smashed against his eyes, became a part of him, but he was not even now merged with this hungry immensity; like a blind amoeba, the universe extended pseudopodia to take him, to absorb him, but he remained unsoftened and unabsorbed. He was a man; he was unique.

Suddenly he put his head back and laughed, freely and fully, without making any sound.

IV.

Hansen, shivering, suddenly came awake. The shadow of a man's body was over his face; Moran had knelt close to him, was shaking him. He lay still for a minute, frowning, trying to think what it was that seemed so strange. Then he knew; the floor quivered under him in ripples of rhythmic vibration. The Donlin engines were operating. That meant–

Moran, watching him closely, saw realization creep into the half-opened eyes.

Nodding, the captain said somberly: "I thought I'd better waken you. Though there's nothing you can do. Except wait."

Hansen stood up, not straight, because his shoulders slumped and he had the look of an old man again in his face. He groaned. "Why didn't you let me sleep? When I'm awake, I've got to think. I don't want to think."

Moran sneered: "Soft belly! You're afraid?"

"Yes," Hansen said. "Of myself."

He walked slowly over to the chart; when he saw what was mirrored there, he had no need for words. The green sliver of light had left the scarlet arc; slowly the blob of green glow slid toward the edge of the black smear. Hansen covered his face with his hands.

"No good," Moran said softly. "Dance to the music, friend. The ship's going under."

"How long have you known?" Hansen asked; his voice was tired.

"Just saw it now. Everything seemed to be alright until a minute ago. Then something slipped. I could feel it, as if the ship had lurched on one side. The dials didn't register a thing. No warning. But when I looked at the chart—I saw what you saw."

Hansen dropped his hands at his sides. "The Hole—how far away do you think it is?"

Moran thought an instant. Then: "About a million miles, I'd say." He was so cool, so calm, so indifferent; he didn't seem to feel anything at all.

Damn him, Hansen thought. But aloud: "Then we've got about an hour."

"That's it." Moran said pleasantly. "If we keep this speed. But we're accelerating, see. The Hole exerts a definite pull; that bears me out. I always thought it was a kind of vortex, which naturally would develop suction."

"Stop!" Hansen screamed. He was pale around the eyes. "I can't stand much of that. Save your damned drivel for a classroom lecture in space school when you're retired—if you think you'll ever see Korna-on-Mars again."

"I'll see it, all right," Moran said quietly. "So will you, if you hang onto your guts. All we've got to do is sit tight, and when the time comes, I'll turn the cube; we'll take our swing along the dimension line, swing back, and the Hole will be behind us, Jupiter dead ahead. Swell!"

Like a madman, Hansen leaped at him. Without preamble, without words, the navigator sprang. Moran, his mouth gaping in a face suddenly left vacant by complete astonishment, fell backward and went down. His head smacked the stellite flooring of the cabin, the angry glow went out behind his eyes, and his body stiffened to a dead weight in Hansen's frenzied grip.

Hansen laughed, looking at the lolling head, the limp body.

"How's that, eh? Swell, huh! How does it feel to be dead, hard guy? How does it feel?"

Moran didn't answer, because he couldn't. Hansen jumped up, moving with a jerky nervous energy, and crossed the cabin to the seal in the wall. He touched a stud, the gimbaled plug dropped out, revealing the ladder seemingly stretching "down" but really going back into the passenger section. He looked over his shoulder; the automatic pilot held the controls, working smoothly and silently.

He scrambled along the ladder, his legs shaking. At the end of it, a long corridor opened, with numbered cells on either side. He stared at the closed doors blankly; he didn't know what cell she occupied. She hadn't told him, because he hadn't asked her. Before, he hadn't wanted to know; he had been afraid.

Suddenly a door a little distance from him slid into the wall and Tam Graham came into the corridor. She saw him; eyes lighting, she hurried toward him. She was as beautiful as he remembered. For her he had killed; for her he would kill again, if need be.

She came up to him. "Something strange happened," she began breathlessly. "Did you feel it? The ship seemed to go over on one side. There's nothing wrong?"

"Everything's wrong," he said, face grim. "Come with me."

"You're going to take me to the C cabin?"

"Yes."

"But what's wrong? What's happened?"

"I'll tell you when we get forward," he said swiftly. "Are you coming?"

"Of course!"

"Then hurry," he said, his voice strange. "I can't take anybody else, you know. After all, I couldn't save every one of them, could I? Couldn't get twenty-eight people in the C cabin to begin with; silly to think of it. Though there'll be more room when we've thrown Moran out."

He pushed her ahead of him. Going along the ladder, she went first; he followed very closely, his breath puffing. When they were both inside the control room he turned and closed the seal. It seemed to take almost the last of his strength. The blood had been siphoned from his face; he was the color of paper. There was something wrong about his eyes; they didn't seem to focus.

"Here we are," he said. "All nice and cozy. You and I and a dead man."

It was then, looking beyond him, that the girl saw Moran flattened against the floor. Calmly, she stepped a little closer to Hansen and lifted a cool hand gently to his hot face; she covered his eyes in an instant.

"Rest a minute," she said soothingly. "You've been going too fast. Close your eyes. Think straight. Something has slipped away behind your eyes, but it will feel its way back, if you go carefully. Don't get excited."

She took her hand away. Hansen had shut his eyes and had been rocking on his heels, listening to the rhythm of her voice. When he opened his eyes, very slowly, the horrible brightness she had seen before was no longer there.

His eyes seemed a little vacant and washed-out; they looked curiously new, as if he was a child, without experience at all, without many memories, without the impressions and sensations that the years and the actualities of living had recorded on his brain. He said, stumbling with his words:

"Something important happened, but I can't remember what it was. Just a little while ago. Maybe if I take a little time to think, it will come back to me."

She walked past him and stopped, near the chart. She had no knowledge of these things, but the record written in light was plain to read—the ship was slipping into the Hole. Now the meaning of Hansen's queer flood of words was clear to her. They were doomed, and Hansen hadn't been able to face the fact. But he had thought of her, and he had come to her with the purpose of somehow protecting her against the death that loomed for all of them; he had wanted to save her.

But Moran—his silence, his immobility, the crumpled position of his body, the thin trickle of scarlet flowing from his head—that didn't seem to fit in. She knelt, held the captain's head in her lap, wiped away the blood; there wasn't much blood, but the blue bruise at the back of the skull was very ugly. Still he wasn't dead, or dying, and Hansen had spoken of a dead man.

"Is this the man you meant?" she asked softly, looking across at the navigator.

Hansen still stood like a sleeper in a dream, vacantly staring.

"Is this your dead man?"

Hansen jerked around. "He isn't dead, then?"

"No. Stunned."

Hansen laughed a little, very bitterly. "I might have known. You can't kill the devil."

"You—you tried to kill him?"

"Hell, yes!"

"But why?"

"Why?" Hansen muttered. "I had a damned good reason, beautiful lady; he was willing to let you die. He didn't want to let me save you, and I had to save you."

The girl lifted her head and looked at the navigator soberly. "We're all going to die. I've seen the chart. The ship's driving toward the Hole."

"Yes," Hansen said chuckling, "But we're not all going to die. You and I and Moran—we're safe. We're going to live."

"I'm afraid you're a little mad," Tam said softly. "How can that be?"

"We're in this cabin. As long as we stay here, we're safe. Moran knows. Moran knows how to work the gadget. That thing there, against the wall—he calls it a dimensional converter."

The girl turned her eyes toward the sinister flower; it was beautiful and terrible. Fascinated, she asked:

"How does it work?"

Hansen's face drew together in a sudden tight mask. He said heavily: "I don't know. Moran can explain it to you, maybe. He knows. When the time comes, he'll turn that little cube in the niche in the wall, and this thing will shift the C cabin and everything in it across the dimensional line. That will happen just as the rest of the ship strikes the Hole.

"But we won't be in the ship, understand? This cabin is like a ship inside a ship; we'll be in it, and Moran says it will be in a million other places—I've just happened to think. The cube—you've got to know the angles before you can adjust it; like a safe, you've got to have the combination. And Moran is the only one who knows the combination."

He stared stupidly at the man on the floor. "And I've knocked him out. We've only got a little less than an hour, before the ship hits the Hole. I'm a fool."

The girl lifted her bright head. "Then we've got to do something. I don't believe there's any concussion. He's stunned; that's all. We can try to bring him around."

"Sure," Hansen said eagerly. "Sure, that's it. Maybe we've still got a chance, darling."

"Have you got any cold water?" the girl asked; her face was calm, evidencing no emotion.

Hansen said: "I'll get it—to put on his head. That's the thing they always do, isn't it? Sure, we've got some. We've got water, synthe-food, everything. I told you this was a ship inside a ship."

"All right!" Tam cried. "I'll take your word for it. Now get me the water."

He rubbed one hand across the back of his neck, grinning sheepishly. "Yeah; I'm talking too much, I guess. I feel kind of funny. I can't think straight or something."

He went over to the W-generator, returned with a flask full of cold, absolutely colorless fluid. "Synthetic," he said in a queer voice, "but *he* won't know the difference, will he?"

"Give me the flask," Tam said.

He handed it to her like an obedient child, his round eyes adoring her with a vacant intensity. Shivering a little, she commanded:

"Now go sit down somewhere. You're tired; I can see you're very tired, I'll try to bring Moran around. There's nothing for you to do."

Solemn-faced, he saluted her, giving her the full ritual of the space code. "Right, chief!"

He walked to the control board, now ablaze with warning lights futilely signaling that the ship was off course. Buzzers and bells made a subdued clamor at his approach, and as his body came within range of the photo-electric eye, the automatic pilot quietly disconnected itself.

"Damned clever!" he said dizzily, "Damned clever, these machines! Except now they're no good. No good at all. Can't save us, can you? Can't save us, you clever little clicking devils. I better sit down."

He dropped heavily into the pilot's seat and rested his twitching face in his hands. He began to groan softly to himself, muttering over and over: "I'm sick, I'm sick, I'm sick as hell."

It was the wailing of a frightened child.

The girl, leaning close to Moran, rubbed his cold temples with the tips of her fingers. Quiet and steady, her warm hands traveled over his forehead. Then she took the flask of water and let the liquid fall, one icy drop at a time, on the blue swelling at the back of his skull. He shifted his head feebly, whispered:

"Who are you? Thanks, thanks; that feels good. I can't see you yet, but you've got fine hands, soft hands. You're a woman. Get away. No women allowed in this cabin. Get away from me!"

His eyes went wide all at once, blazing like suddenly lighted windows, and his hatred gleamed out at her, mingled with a curious fear. She sensed instantly that he hated her because she was a woman and yet he was afraid, afraid to melt the bars he had welded around him long ago, afraid he might yield to a little tenderness and warm human feeling. He was a scientist first and only human now and then.

"I'm Tam Graham," the girl said simply. "Didn't Hansen mention me?"

He struggled up on his elbow, pulling his head from her lap. He was terribly conscious of the scent of her enveloping him.

"Hansen. I see, I see! He brought you here. He thought he'd killed me, so he was going to put you in my place. You know about the converter?"

"Yes," Tam answered. "I know."

"Then why did you call me back? I was very close to the gate of death. The gate was opening, and suddenly I was pulled away. Something took hold of me and wouldn't let go. That was you."

The girl whispered: "I couldn't let you die. Unfortunately, I'm a Christian. By your creed of scientific savagery, I'm soft. But I couldn't let you die even though I knew you were my enemy."

Strength was returning to Moran's body in a creeping tide. He had his armor on again, all over; he had no weak spots showing. He grunted, the sound full of contempt.

"You're lying, of course. Probably don't realize it yourself, but you are lying. Overlaid with all that careful rationalization of humanity and Christianity, there's a real reason why you revived me. I'll know as soon as

I've talked with Hansen. Hansen can't hide anything from me—that's why he tried to murder my body."

With a grinding effort, he sat up. The room was a broken blur of lights and shadings; he squinted his eyes with a painful concentration and waited, beating down the taut nausea that crept over him. His head ached horribly, but he ignored it.

"Where's Hansen?" he demanded, after an instant.

The girl glanced at him. "Right before you. In the pilot's seat. Can't you see him?"

"Yes; of course," Moran growled. The room began to settle down around him. Pieces fell into place until the shape of the walls, the glow of the lights, the contours of the many mechanisms that crowded the cabin, were no longer a puzzle; things were not quite the same, but he made out a painful semblance of reality.

"Your eyes," the girl said. "They're queer. You're—you're not blind?"

Moran laughed. "You may wish I was before I've finished with you two – but I'm not. I'm in pretty good shape. I can handle you and that murderer. I've just figured out why you brought me around. Hansen remembered that he hasn't got the combination to the cube. He couldn't work my magic. That makes me boss again. He'll do what I say because he has to."

The girl said fiercely: "One thing you'd better consider. He isn't right in his head. If you push him too far he'll go at you again. If you don't want to die—"

"I've been very near to dying," Moran whispered, his eyes receding. "And it isn't bad. It isn't bad at all. In fact, it's quite pleasant. You'll like it."

The girl stood up, tight-lipped. "What do you mean?"

"It's your turn," Moran answered, flat-voiced. "Hansen is going to take you back to the rest of the sentimental cattle who threw their right to live away by coming aboard this ship. You were warned, weren't you? They told you at Korna you could probably expect death."

"I was warned," the girl said, looking down. She stood very still, her breath making a faint little rattle in her throat. "Give Hansen the order. If he obeys your command, I'll go."

Moran got on his hands and knees, then pulled himself to his feet with a jerk. He swayed a little, but remained erect; the muscles in his hard hands knotted together and his veins were big with blood, but he stayed on his feet.

He shouted: "Hansen!"

The man in the pilot's seat turned, ceasing his low mumble. Empty eyes regarded iron eyes:

"Yes, commander?"

"Take this girl to the ladder. She goes aft. You know no women are allowed forward here."

The dazed blond giant stumbled to his feet. "Yes, commander."

The girl shut her eyes; with pale lips she whispered to Moran: "This is your victory, scientist. Glory in it!"

Moran braced his legs wide apart. He regarded her without passion, without animus; his hatred, his fear, were both gone, or pushed far under the surface of his thoughts; unguarded by his will, his brain had experienced a rebirth of emotion, but his control had returned. He was dispassionate. He sat in the seat of his consciousness and touched the studs, worked the levers, turned the switches of the efficient mechanism he had made of his body.

"It isn't a question of victory, woman. We decided on a plan for this emergency. His life is more valuable to me than yours; his brain is better than yours. The cells of his cerebral cortex are stored with intricate technical knowledge upon which I may need to draw. You have nothing; you are only a woman. There are many women."

"There are many men."

"You are pleading?"

The girl bowed her bright head. "I find myself—afraid. I'm sorry. Dying may be pleasant, as you say it is, but life to me is more pleasant. I've got so much to live for."

"How very original!" Moran said softly. "You're unselfish. You're a Christian—yet you're pleading for yourself. You're willing to stay here with Hansen and myself, where you have at least a chance for life, rather than go back there with those who have been your companions. Are none of them your friends? Do none of them mean anything to you?"

The girl tightened her hands together. "Yes, yes! But I can live without them. It's not for myself so much that I want to go on living."

"I see," Moran said. "There's a man on Jupiter. You're going to him."

"Yes," the girl whispered. "After ten years."

"Yours is a great love," Moran said soberly. "I'll grant that. But what about all these others on the ship? Do you think they came on this voyage, risking everything, because they were stirred by a small desire or a puny longing, by faint friendship or light love?"

"Ours is a rare thing," the girl said proudly. "An equal love. His is no greater than mine; mine is no greater than his. He loves, and he is loved. I love, and I am loved."

The vacant voice of the blond giant said, all at once: "The woman stays, commander. Here. With us."

Moran hit him with a gouging glance. "You're noble, all of a sudden. If she stays, we all three die."

"You mean—" the girl cried.

"Listen," Moran said. "Dimensional mechanics aren't like simple arithmetic. The converter is inconceivably delicate. Hansen—you remember the examination, the physical searching and pounding, to which we submitted before we left Korna-on-Mars?"

"I remember," the giant said, wandering in a maze.

"We were weighed, down to the last molecule. The lines of our bodies were measured with calipers. Our uniforms were fitted and shaped to a certain size. Every mechanism in this room was treated the same way; dimensionally photographed. Those dimensional pictures were fed into the calculators while the converter was being assembled and powered. The converter will swing you and me along the dimensional line, bring us back somewhere inside this cabin, maybe a few inches off center, but we'll make allowances for that. The girl can't go. Nobody else can go. The converter is set to handle two bodies of a certain weight, a certain size, a certain shape. See?"

Hansen turned his pleading, bewildered eyes on the girl. "I tried to save you, didn't I, didn't I? But I guess he's right. He's always right. Now I can't do any more."

The girl raised her hands and touched her hair carelessly. Something like laughter pulsed from her white throat. "You've been grand, space man. You've tried to be a hero, haven't you? All right—I won't let you down."

She looked straight into Moran's hard face. "You've saved me in spite of myself, scientist."

"I don't get that."

"I crawled at your feet, begging for my miserable little life. I thought I was important because I was a woman, because I loved a man, because love is a rare thing in the scheme of the universe. But I see it now—love isn't rare. It's common. There are millions on Earth who have the kind of love I thought I shared with one man alone.

"It's glorious to think of that. I'll think of it when I'm dying—back there with those plain little people you called 'sentimental cattle.' I realize now, I'm not important in myself; only what I had was important. And the universe is overflowing with it. If I didn't believe that, if I thought that kind of tenderness would die with me, I'd fight you. But it won't die. It never dies."

Hansen followed her across the room, opened the seal.

He watched her go along the ladder; for a long time he could see her bright head, held high like a torch; then that, too, vanished in the gloom that crept over the back part of the ship.

"Close that seal and lock it home!" Moran ordered with sudden urgency. "We've only a minute longer."

Hansen turned around; his hands were damp with some kind of moisture that had fallen from his face. His blinked his eyes.

"She was glorious!"

Moran was at the chart, muttering calculations and abstruse formulae.

He called over his shoulder: "Take three steps from the seal and lie down on the floor. Close your eyes. The swing along the dimension line is bound to knock us both cold, and we may as well be comfortable. When I've set the cube to reverse itself, I'll be there beside you."

Hansen took three stiff steps into the room, his knees jerking like those of an automaton. He flattened, folded his arms on his chest, shut his eyes. He whispered, hugging himself: "I'm so tired—"

Moran touched the cube in the wall and sprang back from the blaze of burning brightness that seemed to splash outward from the brilliant surfaces. Blinded and reeling, he felt his way along the floor of the cabin, stumbled into Hansen's body, and sank down, bruising his shoulders on something metallic and adamant.

Sensations left him, and perceptions he had no more. His world of being was not black, but blank.

The control cabin became riotous with ropes of light—light visible and invisible, shaded and colorless, warm as flame and cold as space.

V.

When Moran returned to the controls of the mechanism that was his body, he felt like a stranger in an old house; there were so many things that seemed familiar, yet none of them responded to his presence as they might have to a remembered master. He had been gone so long, he had traveled so far away, that his body had forgotten him.

He struggled to get back into his own brain; to crawl within the shell that had been his; grimly he attached himself to nerve centers and dug into the folded convolutions of his cortex. Then he got home—contact! He sent messages, and faint responses returned from the far-reaching periphery of his nervous system. He gave commands, and there were feeble efforts at obedience.

He was very cold. His body seemed to have taken on a frozen rigidity while he had been absent. Now he could sense the fire of awakened life climbing his body, circling dead nerve ends, spanning some still sleeping synapses, moving forward in little aching pulsations. The hot broth of his blood began to circulate, halting an instant to burn some knotted cold spot from his arteries, then booming and roaring through the great valves around his heart.

His heart woke; there was a heavy blow against his chest, racking him all over with dull pain. Something thudded and thundered against the walls of his body cavity, hurled his blood stream outward in spurting fountains that filled his empty veins; then began a regular thumping and pounding, like the beat of compression engines. His heart had begun to throb.

Still he didn't move, because as yet he could not. Caught somewhere in a dusty corner of his brain was the impulse that could tell his muscles his bidding, but it took him a little time to reach into his mind and remember where the nerve spark lay hidden.

He was sure of one thing only—he was alive. He could move. He heard himself breathing. He felt the pound of his heart beating the reluctant blood through his veins. In a minute he would open his eyes and he would see—What?

For a little while he lay where he was, waiting. He did not know what he expected. There was no change. All was quiet. He stopped his breath an instant—complete silence. He could hear nothing except the loud sound of his own heart.

There was something smooth and hard-surfaced under his body, holding him up, supporting him. Then he remembered—he must be lying on the floor of the control cabin. Exultation quivered through him; the cube had worked, evidently; they had gone along the dimensional line and returned. Successful experiment! Write that down. Score another victory for science.

He wrenched his eyes open. For an instant he got the full glare of a bright cold light full in the face. Then he was blind again, and the black dark was so deep around him that he seemed more blind than he had been before. But the darkness fell away, a layer at a time, until he could see again.

Very carefully, because he could hear his muscles creak and groan like tight wire, he put his hands behind him, braced himself first on his arms, then pulled himself to one elbow, and at last sat up.

He looked around. The room was familiar to him, almost the same as he remembered it from the time he had glanced at it last, and yet it was not the same at all. It was still the control cabin of the *Star Ship Invincible*, but he was lying on the floor under the pilot's seat; there had been a perceptible shift, then, in his space-time position. Of course! Couldn't expect the thing to work perfectly. He would probably notice other changes.

The lights were turned on, just as they had been at the instant that ship had gone into the Hole; cold Benson globes, all white, snowy glow, harsh and direct, casting thick black shadows in straight lines. He looked at them steadily for a minute, sitting cross-legged like an Oriental and staring upward.

"Queer effect!" he muttered slowly.

A little shiver went over him. After all, this whole room and everything in it had been subjected to an unprecedented change, taken over by an alien force; he couldn't be surprised at anything, if he was going to be logical. But what an opportunity—he had the chance of making a critical study at firsthand of the results of a unique experimental undertaking. He'd have to be impersonal, dispassionate; even if there had been changes in his own body.

"Record everything on a tape spool," he admonished. "Mustn't forget that."

He couldn't get his eyes away from the lights. All the round white globes had a reddish halo, and the light they gave was shot through with black twisting streamers, impalpable, intangible, like the shadows of shadows.

With difficulty, he took his glance from the Benson globes. He looked at the control set-up. Queer, very queer! The great balanced cylinder of the control base was out of line, slanted wrong; it was the wrong shape. The cylinder seemed to stretch away interminably, gleaming all over with reflected glare that hurt his eyes, as if this brightness was full of little sharp burning spears. The pilot's dais had been touched with the same luminous veneer, gave the same illusion of distortion and distention.

"Elegant!" Moran said. His voice rang hollow, but he wanted to hear himself talk. "Very elegant, indeed—I don't think. I wonder if I'm going to be sick."

He felt that if he sat still any longer he would be. He got on his feet. His legs wavered like rubber stilts under him. Rubbing the back of his hand across his forehead—his hand came away damp—he glanced down at himself; there appeared to be something odd about the shape of his feet, but he couldn't make out exactly what it was.

All at once he was taken about the middle by a hammering nausea; he had hoped to avoid it by standing, no good, evidently. The sensation that shook him was more physical than chemical, he knew that; a mere contraction of his smooth muscles due to shock and nerve tension.

Yet it was odd, very odd. He'd never been sick like this before. An uncontrollable trembling began in his rubbery legs and shot all over his body in vicious recurrent waves. The trembling, the vibration in his legs, the torn soreness of his muscles, had no great significance for him then. Later he was to think strange thoughts.

The first step he took, his left knee gave way, as if the bones had melted. He fell, hitting the floor hard. No sensation at all; that was the queerest thing yet. His body must still be numb from its long freezing.

He got up, feeling stronger. He had better luck the second time he tried walking. Looking at the polished floor of the cabin, which was bright as a mirror, he saw that he wobbled like a duck, yet it was locomotion. He wondered, as he began to take a few steps cautiously, why he wasn't hungry. But how long had it been since they had made the dimensional swing? It might have been a millennium; it might have been only a minute ago.

He didn't think he would want food again for a long while. He felt full and warm inside now, and throbbing with a curious pulse of exultation; he had an unreasoning desire to leap up and touch the "ceiling" of the control room. He actually tried it, but fell back after going upward about five feet, which seemed to prove that the ship's gravity grids were in operation. The ship—was he in *Star Ship Invincible*, or in the control cabin floating free in space? If the cabin had left the ship behind in the Sink Hole, the cabin was now a small ship itself.

He crossed to the visi-plate above the Danler navigation chart. The plate still operated; a faint blue aura surrounded it. He touched a button and the blue became black, the black of outside space. Stars! The plate was speckled all over with perforations of light. In the distance, receding, he saw a web of darkness deeper than infinity; a black hole in the void so dark that it was a purple scar blotting out the stars behind it.

As he stood there, he was conscious of a humming that came through the silence. The automatic switch had jerked along its slot, and the special Donlin engines in the cabin had taken up their beat. He looked down; there was a slight luminescence rising from the gravity grids in the floor plating. Good; the power circuits inside the cabin were unbroken.

There was good air for him to breathe, warm and slightly scented, as it had been before he had gone down into that sea of blackness. It seemed to be all right again everywhere, except for that curious impression his eyes took in every time he stared at anything for very long. There was a scrambling of his vision, so that he briefly thought he could see the air he was breathing, as a white vapor sucked in and out by his lungs. The great glowing panels of the direction board were twisted out of focus, indefinitely extended behind themselves in blurry reflections, as if they were partly shadows and partly real.

Then he saw Hansen, still crumpled on the floor. He took two quick steps, bent down and touched the other. The navigator's skin was so cold all over that it crackled under the tips of Moran's fingers like frozen fire.

Moran turned back the other's eyelids with his thumb and looked at the balls; the man's eyes were turned upward in their sockets and showed all whites.

To any evidence the blond giant was dead. Moran slapped him in the face. He didn't move. Not a muscle jerked or quivered. His jaw didn't even take on any greater color. It remained ice cold and very white—a dazzling ivory pallor. There seemed to be absolutely no blood under the skin of Hansen's cheeks. Moran had seen a man once who had been found frozen in a glacier on Earth, and he had been like that.

Then Moran looked again at Hansen's eyes. The lids had begun to slip shut, as if pulled by springs, but, as Moran watched, Hansen seemed to exert a savage effort, and the eyelids stopped just short of covering the under edge of the eyeballs. Then Moran couldn't believe that Hansen was dead.

Moran bent over him a second time. Very carefully, the scientist took a thumb and held the eyelids back, kept the pressure until when at last he let go, Hansen's eyes remained opened and fixed. Now Moran was sure there was a gleam somewhere in their dazed depths—a spark, grimly struggling upward, attempting to find some way of signaling.

His telepath headgear was still on his body; Moran saw it hanging loose on the belt of his emergency suit. Moran picked up the narrow band of silvery metal and slipped it in a loop around the cold temples. Then he put on his own helmet and concentrated his thoughts in a tight beam of mental energy. Urgently he prodded the inert brain of the limp giant, then waited. If Hansen was conscious enough to will a single labored thought, contact would be made; Moran's alert intelligence could bring him to awakening.

Taut, Moran crouched, waiting. Hansen's mind was dark, calm as a placid pool, so far as Moran could probe into it without the other's will aiding him.

Moran roared, in a great soundless bellow: "Come out of it, space man! I command you!"

And Hansen moved. The eyes turned. Moran leaned very close, glaring into that frozen face.

"You've heard! Now obey!"

Creaking, the stiff lips parted, a little puff of breath came out, a faint groaning whisper: "Yes, commander."

Moran tore off his headgear triumphantly, sprang up, ran to the W-generator, got water. A cold sparkling rain fell in Hansen's face.

"Enough!" Hansen grunted in a hoarse voice. "What the hell are you trying to do—drown me?"

Moran felt better all over. Now he had some one to command, some one to feel superior over, a man to perform obediently at the urge of his will. He warmed; it wasn't good for him to be alone. Even this fool offered a kind of companionship.

"I couldn't drown you," Moran said, grinning. "You've been dead once, to all intents and purposes. You can't die twice—or can you?"

"So the damned thing worked!" Hansen exclaimed with awe. "We've swung along the dimension line, and we've got back, shipshape. That's magic!"

"Magic?" Moran shouted, swelling with anger. "Don't be a superstitious fool. That's science!"

"About the same, isn't it?" Hansen asked.

"No; it isn't," Moran growled. "Don't be an ape."

"Have it your way," Hansen agreed submissively.

Moran stared at him, very sober. For some reason the blond man seemed smaller than he had been, his face was wrinkled and wizened into a dried mask, and his legs were twisted to a queer shape. Moran wondered if he would be able to walk, using those dead legs.

Yet when Moran stared into those strange eyes at close range, he saw a reflection of himself, and *he* seemed to be same as the navigator was—turned and shifted in his body, as if the center of his equilibrium had been reversed. Moran thought, so there have been great changes in us, as in the machines crowding this room. But—how deep did the alterations go? His calm curiosity probed for the answer to that question.

Hansen observed, in a hoarse voice: "Say, you looked damned funny! Like you've had the bends, or something. Been space sick?"

"Listen," Moran said harshly. "You don't think we took that joy ride in the grip of dimensional forces and got away clean, do you? Sure, I look funny. So do you. It's one of the—the changes. You'll notice other things that are—damned funny."

"Maybe I talked too fast," Hansen mumbled. "Maybe the converter didn't work after all. Where are we? Where's the Hole?"

"Behind us," Moran stated, calm-voiced. "We're on course, and close to Jupiter. Take a look in the v-plate."

Hansen got up and went over to the little screen. The Sink Hole didn't show there at all now, nor any trace of it. The sky looked calm, and it was black the way it always had been since Hansen had been aspace, but it was the kind of black a man can look at and understand; there were stars in it, different colors, and the Sun away off in the distance like a red-hot blinking eye put there to watch over you. Jupiter the giant seemed closer, and Hansen thought with sudden hope that they now had at least an even chance of making the Dome.

Moran crossed the cabin and examined the three cylinders standing against the curved wall. That wall was blank, had no glassite porthole, and most of it was covered with a curled mesh of wire, an intricate network of apparatus, because the three tanks carried all the little ship's supplies of air and water and synthe food. If something went wrong in any part of that maze–

Hansen watched him as he tested the tanks. He came around on his heel, face impassive.

Hansen said: "Well?"

"Enough there, if we're careful."

Hansen expelled his breath gratefully. "We're in luck."

"Luck? No. It was calculated how much supplies we'd need before the ship left Korna. The calculations are a little in error, but very little. And I counted on a marginal deviation."

Hansen said: "Oh hell!"

Then for an instant the navigator felt that something had gone wrong in his eyes. Yet it wasn't that. The truth was that Moran was getting smaller.

"Chief!" Hansen whispered hesitantly.

Moran looked up, eyes tight with an inward struggle. "What?"

Hansen stuttered: "I dunno how to say it. But you—you're kind of shrinking."

"Yes; I know."

Moran kept his cold composure. But his body was terribly changed; he was altogether different from the commander who had shipped with Hansen on the *Invincible.* Then he had been a fairly big man, almost as big as the navigator, and strong as stellite; still young, still with the full look of youth and strength in his face. This was a shrunken little old man.

He came close, stood a moment with his face up against Hansen's. He put out a hand to touch the navigator, and the other jerked back, because that outstretched hand looked like a brown and withered claw. He seemed—he seemed to have caved in upon himself.

Hansen shook; his teeth clicked. "What—what's happening to you, commander?"

Moran grinned crookedly. "You'll know soon, I hope. You've been subjected to the same forces. The effects should be very much the same on you."

"How—how does it feel?" Hansen whispered. "What's it like?"

"Wait," Moran answered confidently. "Just wait. You'll get a dose of this medicine soon enough, friend."

His face was chopped in little wrinkled squares by short bitter lines of agony.

"I'll tell you this much," Moran said with a livid smile. "It isn't very pleasant. Not at all."

"Damn you!" Hansen groaned. "You needn't torture me before my time comes. Why are you always throwing little knives into me?"

Moran didn't answer. He was too intent on keeping any sounds of pain from escaping his lips.

VI.

Moran tightened his mouth; as he did so, Hansen could see a plainly visible sifting and sinking that seemed to go on simultaneously all through his body, as if the orbits of the atoms that composed his flesh had abruptly been decreased in the diameter of their paths and closed in upon themselves.

"I'm still getting smaller?" Moran said after a few seconds.

Hansen nodded. "Every minute I'm standing here I can see it happening. You don't come quite up to my shoulder now, commander."

He seemed to stand there considering something abstract, looking very quiet and detached. He appeared to have gone away off and was observing himself as from a reasonable distance. Before then Hansen had hated Moran very heartily, with the deep hatred of an inferior for a superior mind, but something like admiration crept into the navigator now; the commander was so cool and calm, as if he had climbed out of the shell of himself, somehow, and could stand to one side, regarding himself with no prejudice.

"It'll stop soon, I think," Moran said suddenly. "I've had it once before, right after I woke. Then I didn't realize what was happening to me. I just thought I was getting pretty sick. But now it's plain. All clear."

"You're right," Hansen said, "about one thing at least. It seems to be stopping."

In another instant Moran ceased to shrink. The effects remained; his skin hung in loops and folds all over him, and his cold eyes looked too big for his unraveled face. With difficulty he moved, climbed up on the pilot's seat, and sat with his little legs hanging over the edge of the metal-fabric chair.

Hansen couldn't look directly at him. The navigator said: "Well, what's next? What'll happen after this?"

Moran gave a slow shrug. It was queer to see his skin quiver in a ripple along his loose-jointed shoulders.

"That," Moran said, "is what I don't know—yet."

Hansen didn't move. There was silence between them.

Then Moran said: "I know what it's doing to me, and that it will come to you in a little while, but I haven't quite figured out certain things. I haven't found out why it stops once it gets started, and where it will end if it keeps on. Theoretically, I don't suppose there's any limit at all."

Hansen frowned. "You haven't explained a damned thing to me yet."

"Well, the conditions are paradoxical," Moran said thoughtfully. "There's room in this for some beautiful paradoxes. It's plain that the effects you and I have undergone, along with everything else in their room, are due to the distortion caused by the dimensional change. We weren't built to be in a million places at once, see. That's why we can't hold our old shapes; you know, I'm not sure that I'm actually getting any smaller. It's a change in shape, visible to you and me as a change in size."

"Go slow," Hansen said, heavy-voiced. "I'm stumbling along behind you."

Moran grinned. "Our constituent atoms, friend, have been twisted and shuffled around, and they've having a devil of a time finding their places. They've had the most awful wrench they could have got anywhere in the universe; they've been jammed all together, and then stretched structurally outward, and then set free in their old orbits again. But they're not staying put; that's all. They haven't got to a condition of equilibrium yet. That nice balance between attraction and repulsion, between protons and electrons in the nucleus, and electrons outside the nucleus—that balance is overthrown, releasing chaotic forces within the atoms, and naturally the atoms shape the molecules. See?"

"I think so," Hansen muttered. He rubbed a hand across his eyes. "If you're right, and you're always right, time's called for you and me. There's no limit. There's no telling where this thing will stop?"

Moran shook his head. "No. Only there's no guarantee that we'll die, now or later. There was some fault and molecular slippage when I contracted this time. I got out of proportion at least to my eyes and your eyes. That's the reason my skin's loose and I look so queer. If it comes again it may take up the slack. I don't know."

Hansen blinked. "If it stops, maybe we'll be kinds of dwarfs, or something."

"Yes," Moran said. "But I don't think it's going to stop at any imaginable point."

Moran's eyes gleamed; he was fascinated by that thought. He might sink down slowly into a submicroscopic universe. Or if the change was, as he believed, a relative alteration in shape, he might enter a cosmos of different dimensions, a brand-new world, unexplored, opening to his avid gaze, his insatiate curiosity. The possibilities were illimitable for experimental operations. The chance was his.

Then Hansen remembered something. "The ship!" The navigator's voice was hoarse with excitement.

Moran said: "What about the ship?"

"If we keep on getting smaller, and the ship doesn't shrink—how will we eat? What the hell will we drink?"

Moran laughed. "Don't worry about that. Are you hungry now? Fill your belly up then. If you have time to digest it before your contraction begins, you'll be all right."

"Look," Hansen muttered. "If we're eventually no bigger than a drop of water, we're not going to be able to swallow anything of that size. And food—the atoms will be so big they won't go down our throats. Maybe they'll be bigger than we are."

"I've failed to make it clear to you," Moran said. "That's because it's a paradox. We aren't shrinking; we're changing size. The ship isn't shrinking, because it's made of metal; metal's rigid, the atoms are bound tight together. When we came back from the dimensional swing, the metallic molecules fitted together and they've stayed together; but they're not the same. They've changed shape. So have we, only in a different degree."

Hansen didn't say anything, because he couldn't speak. He had begun to diminish in size; at least to Moran's eyes it seemed that he shrank, though Moran's brain accepted it as a relative alteration in shape. An indistinctness seemed to hang about the blond man, like half a shadow.

Even the features of his face, which were close to Moran, so close that the commander might have reached and touched them, were vague and blurred.

The contraction ended. Hansen didn't seem mutilated. His body was more in proportion that it had been; his face was tiny, rather wrinkled but perfectly formed; his legs had lost most of their crookedness; his head was set firmly on his neck, his arms and shoulders flowed together in a smooth line.

Hansen whispered: "I can't take much of that."

Sweat dribbled from the end of his chin. His eyes swiveled wildly. He said, in a high-pitched voice:

"We thought we were pretty damned smart, didn't we? Nothing was going to happen to us. We were safe. To hell with the Hole, to hell with those twenty-eight people we murdered! We'd get through, because we had that damned thing you called a dimensional converter. It's got us— it's got both of us around the throat."

He sucked in his breath. "Listen, I'm going to finish this. Maybe this damned shrinking will go on even when we're both dead, but we won't know it. We won't know it, see?"

Moran slid one hand down his side to the metal-linked belt at his hips and touched the round butt of his ionic projector.

He said: "All right. You've got your I-gun. Pull it out, and we'll fire together. That will end it for both of us."

"Sure!" Hansen said softly.

Moran could see the gleaming in Hansen's belt where his hand projector was, and in his brain the commander had a vision of a bright silver thread, hot and white, spiraling across the narrow space between them, striking death home to them both.

Hansen dropped his fingers to the grip of his little gun, but he had no chance to lift it from where it swung at his waist. Moran had drawn, thumbed a stud, sent an arrow of flame scorching into the blond man's face.

Hansen swayed backward, bending at the knees; he went over, hitting on his shoulders and head. There was a slight thump, like knuckles striking metal; that was the sole sound, except for the snake-like hissing of Moran's flame-thrower.

Moran tossed the little gun away. "I'm ready," he said softly, looking at the stars. "I'm not going to die."

VII.

For three days there had been rain on Jupiter the giant. The rain was scalding hot; it turned to steam as it fell, burned the ground where it struck. The great bronze Dome of the interplanetary station felt the touch of that liquid fire; scales were melted off the outer shell of the Dome, metal ran down in molten waves.

The air above and around the Dome was crowded with tortured flying things, the bizarre creatures that inhabited the upper levels of the great planet. There were strange currents going upward through the atmosphere; the laws that governed the magnetic forces of worlds were seemingly broken.

Over the Red Spot was created a reverse field of gravity. They observed it from the Dome; flying things passing that way were hurled outward at savage speed into the far reaches of the atmosphere. The Red Spot itself remained as always – an enigmatic sea of luminescent flame.

First into the writhing atmosphere above the Red Spot the little ship from space had entered. There was no down pull of Jupiter's immense gravity to increase its terrific speed, but instead was this magnetic repulsion that checked the ship's free fall, wrenched it partly off its course. The controls of the small ship were locked; it traveled along the Walton Arc that had its ending within the interplanetary station.

The little ship fell in a slow bright curve through Jupiter's thick and steamy atmosphere, crumpled its silver shell into the red ground two miles from the Dome.

The electro-telescopes in the station had followed the strange ship in from space. A man came up into the little room at the top of the Dome where John Graham, G-16, sat silently at his key. The man saluted and said in a stiff voice:

"The ship Garth told you a day ago we were to watch for—"

"Yes," Graham said, grim-faced. "I saw it fall."

"You're to take charge of the search party, G-16. The station commander's orders."

Graham nodded. "I obey," he said gently. "I always obey orders."

A day later the rain stopped. Six men ventured out from the Dome, wearing space suits, breathing Earth's atmosphere. John Graham led them. They had taken readings from direction-finders before leaving the station, and they knew about where the ship had fallen. The search was not long.

The little ship was found, almost undamaged, the curious dull metal of which it was fashioned being neither twisted nor broken; where it had given way it had been forcibly torn apart. It was a strange shape for a space ship. It was like a flying cube, oddly distorted along its angles.

There was a seal in one side of the cube. They broke the seal and Graham went in first. He went in, stumbling.

There was nobody alive inside.

One glance told him that.

For a minute he halted there with the blind agony of his unreasoning disappointment mirrored in his eyes; long ago he had believed he had given up hope, yet evidently there had been a spark still left. He shook himself, swinging his hands, and moved forward into the ship.

It wasn't a ship at all. It was the control cabin of the *Star Ship Invincible*. There was a dead man lying on the floor, the body curiously shrunken.

"Hansen," Graham muttered softly. "Moran?"

No sign of the commander. But in one of the curved seats near the control board he found a spool of metallic tape, and beside it a flash tube for recording messages.

The men from the station had come in quietly behind him and stood staring. One of them asked: "What's that, sir?"

Graham turned and pushed past them, unseeing. He flung back over his shoulder a mutter of words. The man who had spoken glanced around the room.

"He's found some kind of a record. He's going back to the station. We're to stay here with the ship until he gets further orders."

Graham traveled fast to the recording room in the Dome. He sat down, put his eyes to the eyepieces provided, fitted earphones to his head. Then with slow careful hands loosened the clip that held one end of the tape from unraveling; he fed the thin metallic strip into the slot of the translator, touched a dial.

A long time later he reached up slowly and thumbed a stud. The narrow tongue of metal ceased to flow into the translator. He took off the headphones he had been wearing, tore away the eyepieces. He put his head in his hands and groaned.

Two men had come into the dim room. One was the station commander.

The commander said: "What have you found?"

Graham grinned queerly. "This is the recording made by Captain Moran. It's all there—what happened to the *Invincible*. But it's not a very pretty story."

"I see," the commander said. "What have you done about the little ship we saw fall?"

"I'm having it brought into the Dome. Are there any orders you want to give me?"

The commander hesitated. "No; I don't think so. Wait! We've got to make some disposition of the bodies."

"Bodies?"

"The bodies of Hansen and Moran," the commander said impatiently. "Didn't you find them in the ship?"

"There was only one body," Graham answered, grim-faced. "Moran is still alive—somewhere. He's gone into a different dimensional universe, but he's alive. He recorded everything that happened until his change in size took him beyond body contact with the tape he was using. He even recorded his murder of Hansen."

"He murdered Hansen?" the commander whispered.

"Hansen and my wife," Graham said, very low. "I'm waiting for further orders, sir."

"No orders," the commander said heavily.

Graham traveled upward to the signal room high on the curve of the Dome. His relief stared.

"You're early, G-16. You've an hour yet."

"Let me take over," Graham said. "Let me take over, will you?"

The other shrugged. "All right with me. You're a fool for work. Why don't you get a little sleep?"

"I don't need much sleep these days," Graham said.

He sat down, closed in once more by sky and stars; he looked at the black, pitiless void that was all around him, and the taste of bitterness was in his mouth.

WITH SOME GAIETY AND LAUGHTER

By FRANK K. KELLY

(From *Story*)

Cold came in with him, and a breath of sterile whiteness without, but no snow except that which clung to the scuffed shoes on his feet, because the wind had died an hour before and there was no snow now driving from the sky. Old Berger, his short-ranging eyes peering from behind the glass walls that hung before his face, went to his counter and stood teetering on his toes.

The young man – he was young, though his face was marked with the shadow of unsweetened bitterness – almost laughed to see the old man waiting amiably for him to speak. It was warm in Berger's shop, and crowded with the presences of many quiet things, and the old man looked so rosy and happy with his apple cheeks and his bright eyes in cozy pockets of flesh, that the young man could not speak for a time, his throat was so choked with tender envy. He stood, taking big breaths of this warm air around him; it sank down with soft hissing into his lungs, and the fragrance of it was sweeter to him than the satisfaction he had once taken in tobacco smoke.

Berger waited patiently, with the expectant quietude of an old man, and didn't press him for facile speech. It might have been that Berger could see how it was with him.

Suddenly he put his hands down on the smooth, shining pane of the showcase. Old Berger's hands were spread up on the counter also, and the young man nearly laughed again looking at the difference between them: Berger's hands were so knotted and old, and still they were well-fed, while good young hands could starve. Good clever hands could find nothing for them to do. Tears did come sourly to the young man's eyes, but he wasn't sure whether this was because of his sudden warmth after great cold, or because he had only now remembered some terrible injustice.

The young man was proud of his hands. They were fine hands, even Berger through his dusty glasses had seen that; but long and slim and clever and strong as they were – and they could do many things well – yet for all that, there was no work for them anywhere in the world.

The young man slowly opened his mouth. Old Berger was frugal with light as with all things, and the loan shop had only what small glitter came of a lamp hanging from the ceiling: in the dimness the young man's mouth was heavy and hard. Berger somehow began to feel a tension about the young man; his head was set too firmly on his neck.

"Yes, what is it, eh?" Berger asked. "A distinguished medal to sell, eh?"

"No."

"Then what do you want here, eh?" Berger said. "It isn't a medal, eh?"

"No, not a medal."

The young man's voice was as unshaken as he looked himself, standing there planted squarely on the soles of his feet. Yet his feet went down through the scraps of leather he had bound them in, and when he walked he felt nothing, whether he walked on stone or on soft ground. The outer skin of him had thickened to a scale over his inner skin. The snow had worked into his dirty shoes; he had known for a long time that his feet were frozen. Yet nothing so real and sharp as that seemed able to reach the cords behind his eyes, and travel up to his brain to tell him what had happened.

It was a long time before he spoke any more after his first five words. At last he said gently:

"I'll tell you how it is with me, friend."

Old Berger nodded in a sort of exasperated patience.

"My name is Gorman. Ray Gorman. I've been an American citizen twenty-seven years. I'm twenty-seven years old. I haven't eaten anything in four days."

Berger made a slow gurgle in his throat.

"Yes, I hunted work, but I could not find any work. There was none of the kind of work I could do."

"Now you're begging," Berger muttered, with just a slight twist to the words.

"Once I begged for a few scraps, but there were not many scraps to be given away in these times. I beg no longer."

"How have you been living, then?" Berger asked, softly.

"I've sold things."

"Your own possessions, of course," Berger said.

"Yes. I've sold all I own, except this one thing I have here. I've brought that to you."

"Yes, let me see it," Berger said, nodding. "Perhaps I'll buy it, eh?"

Berger saw for the first time that the other carried something under his arm. It was a package of some sort, a small flat bundle, carefully wrapped up in soft white paper with a green string tied in a good knot at the middle. The young man carried it very gently, as if it were a thing so valuable to him that he would have walked quietly with death rather than let it be taken from him against his will.

He put it down slowly, on old Berger's counter, as one would handle a precious thing, and left it there a little while, without making any move to open the coverings.

"Ach, I'm glad you haven't brought me any medals," Berger said comfortably. "I have already so many medals."

He pointed one fat old finger and the young man followed the line of that sausage with his eyes, and saw that it was true: Berger had a great number of fine medals, all in one big box divided up into sections to hold them. They were classified according to distinction. The box had contained jewelry once, and there was still some plush to cover the bottom. In a slow way the light of Berger's lamp gleamed on the medals, so that they gave a brave bright shine, and in their rich shiningness seemed to belong there on the plush. It was Berger's best box, because he thought that the medals should be with the plush – being worthy of the good things.

"So," the young man said, clipped. "Fortunately I am not a war veteran."

He smiled, but his eyes in their burning vacancy didn't in the least alter. "My father had one of the best medals, I think. He lived with me till just a short while ago; then he left...I have no bitterness like his bitterness."

Berger coughed in his throat.

"Why did he leave, eh?"

The young man jerked up his head. Now his eyes changed: they took a polish.

"He had somewhere else to go. We were pretty poor, you understand. But he had been honorably to a war and back, and they let him go and enter a Soldiers' Home. There were guns fired at his funeral."

"Then he is dead," Berger said, and held his voice low.

The young man lifted up his wild head again.

"Yes, yes. I thought you'd understand that. I told you, they fire the guns morning and night at the Home. He stays at the Home now. He is not lonely."

"Eh?" old Berger said. "Eh?"

"He has company there. They are all dead where he is."

Berger drew back a little, though it was usually his inclination to approach his customers too closely, and peer at them almost with offensiveness out of his near-sighted eyes.

"Ach, I see," Berger said.

The young man's fingers began to fumble with the string of his package. Berger saw that his fingers had been so cold that even the first blue tinge had gone away from them, and they were left like long sticks of white punk lying loose on the counter. Berger had known the fingers of a few dead men, and this was just the same. He turned his eyes at another angle.

When he looked again, the other had unlaced the knot, and was pushing the wrappings from a round object. Berger stared at what lay on the glass top of the showcase, a circular dark blob shifting under the lamplight in a steady black glow. The thing was a phonograph record of standard size. It seemed in good condition yet, the glaze of the heavy surface still almost unscarred, as if the owner had taken care about the manner of its playing.

"Will you give me a little something for this?" the young man asked softly.

"Well, I don't know where I'd have use for it," old Berger said.

"Even a little money would be good to feel in my hand," the young man whispered. "I've been hungry so long now."

Berger noticed then that when the young man spoke, he kept his lips pressed close together until just before he opened his mouth to let the sound out, as if he used his speech in fear that he had not strength enough to form every syllable that should give his words full meaning. His language progressed on stilts, heavily placed down, perhaps because he thought that unless he took care he would lose footing in his mind, and stumble headlong into a labyrinth of incoherence.

Berger's thick blunt fingers brushed the record slowly, and he bent down to peer at it with his old eyes. There was no title printed on the white inner strip that curled in a circle of stiff paper around the center of the disc. The white ring lay blank.

"What is this, eh?" Berger asked, his glance rising in bewilderment. "It does not say here what kind this record is."

"There is no music on it," the young man said softly. "And no words. It is better than that. You see, it will help you to keep the beast back."

He took a breath, and after the passing of a little time, added:

"It has helped me, when I had need of it."

Berger hesitated, looking at him sideways.

The young man waited two minutes, and then very slowly began to wrap the round black disc in the paper, which had held it before; there was something terrible about the stoop of his shoulders that shook old Berger's brain.

"Wait," Berger muttered. "Did I say I would not buy? Tell me what the record plays, and I will see."

"The record plays nothing. It laughs."

"This beast you speak of – what about that, eh?"

"It laughs," the young man said. "That is all."

"Please," Berger stammered. "I do not understand."

"I've found that if you laugh at the Beast, he won't be so sure you're afraid of him; of course you really are afraid, sick to your guts, but if you put a good laughing face on, with no solemn hollow stuff in you, he'll rage, and charge at you, but he will not overcome you. Only if you flee, he'll turn and follow you to the world's ends…I have no need of laughter to help me now; I am a little beyond that. Do you understand?"

Berger asked slowly: "This beast – where do you find him, eh?"

"He is within you," the young man said. "Oh, and within me. Someone has spoken these fine words: 'With subtlety we can get our hands round the throat of the Beast, and so destroy him.' Wrong, wrong. I have used this record so many times that I know what is right and what is wrong. Laughter is right and sadness is wrong.

You cannot think how good it is sometimes to hear the sound of laughter; it will help you when you think there can be no more help…Wait, I'll show you what I mean. Do you have a phonograph here?"

Berger raised his bony shoulders and let them fall, in the old German way of shrugging that he had kept through these long years in a raw country; he smiled.

"Yes. I think there is everything here. You have seen how many things I have bought that I cannot sell. I am an old man with the heart of a fool. If your record amuses me…"

"Perhaps it will not amuse you," the young man said; a kind of muscular contortion leaped the lines of his face, crossing from one side to the other with such speed that it seemed to vanish in shadow like a thought repulsed. Berger saw that he had struggled a while with some great memories.

"Perhaps it will not amuse you," the young man said again, very softly. "It will do so much more than that. How can I tell you what it has meant to me? I do not think you could know what it means to a man who has not laughed for so long himself, except by forcing a kind of vomit, to hear good laughter when he has need. This is good laughter you'll hear. You couldn't be sad, hearing the voice of it. Nobody could be sad, after such laughter…"

He followed the old man behind the counter. There was an ancient gramophone in one corner of the crowded room. They went to it together. The young man put the record down on the green felt slowly, lifted a needle, set the point on the edge of the black disc; he released the catch that held the voice of the machine to silence.

The black disc hummed, and the light winked back in a moving shimmer from its middle. An echo of all the laughter that had washed the world since it had been shaped out of chaos…rose to them now. There was madness in it, of a kind, and more than madness; it was born to rebirth in a quivering fullness of being that mocked the destiny and the damnation and the death of the Beast. A clean spirit sang in it… A clean spirit singing…

The young man stood as if incapable of lifting the weight of his head while he drank the music of this mirth into him; old Berger couldn't stop looking at him. The laughter rose like smoke leaping into an empty sky.

"Please, that is enough," Berger said. "Shut it off, eh?"

The young man put down one finger and pressed the latch that had power to choke the life from the disc. Now it was quiet again all around them and through them. But the room was not the same room, and the silence was not the same silence: there were remembrances and fragments remaining from the lilt of that laughter.

Old Berger had long ago shut up his soul against these things, and they hurt him now in their renewal of meaning, they were so fresh in their newness and gentle in their cruelty. He put his hands together in the long sleeves of his jacket.

"Will you buy?" the young man said, after a minute.

"Yes," Berger said.

"How much?" the young man asked.

"Five dollars I'll give you for the record."

"Five dollars?" the young man whispered. "That's so little for a priceless thing."

"No more," Berger said. "I can give no more."

The blood ran in a tide into the young man's face.

"Then I'll go now. Good afternoon, friend."

He waited a little time, as if he thought perhaps Berger might have something more to say; but when the old man did not speak, he began to wrap the record again in its coverings. He took it up carefully in his hands, and put it under his arm.

"With some gaiety and laughter," the young man said, "I'll take my leave of you."

He went out. Old Berger watched awhile, and saw the long shadow of that tall body pass by his windows: it dwindled finally into a dim outline against the snow, and at last that too was gone.

"Well," old Berger said. "Well…"

A queer thing, he thought. A queer thing to happen to him of all men; he'd led a quiet life and never harmed a soul.

CROSSING THE VOLTURNO

By Frank K. Kelly

(From *The New Yorker*)

"We never knew until we were across the goddamn bridge," said the staff sergeant with the red sea horse of the amphibian engineers on his jacket. "Then somebody says, 'You crossed the Volturno, boys,' and two guys out of three didn't know what the hell he was saying. It was strictly a psychological deal, strictly psychological."

"What do you mean, psychological?" the technical sergeant asked, smiling at the Frenchwoman behind the bar in the little café. She was small and blonde, and her hair looked bright even in the thickening darkness of the evening. Outside, a rain from the Channel, heavy and cold, was blowing through the chill darkness of northern France.

"Strictly correct, boy, strictly correct," said the sergeant with the sea horse on his jacket. He lifted his foot, encased in a combat boot, and kicked a little white dog into a corner at one end of the bar. "Get in that corner, you little bastard," he said to the dog. He had a high, shrill voice. "Tough little bastard," he said to the technical sergeant. "Wants to fight everybody he sees."

The dog curled up against the bar. The sergeant with the sea horse blinked at the madame behind the bar and waved a short, hard hand toward the technical sergeant.

"Give my friend *la même chose*," he said, opening his jacket and searching for his wallet. "*La même chose pour moi aussi.*"

"*Ah, oui,*" said the blonde French madame, raising an eyebrow at the technical sergeant, who smiled with sober understanding and took a long sip from the glass in front of him

"You speak French?" the technical sergeant asked.

"I was in Africa," the sea-horse sergeant said. "I was in Sicily, Italy, and Normandy. I speak French, Italian, Arab, and Scotch. *La même chose*. My name's Yates, A. C. Yates."

The technical sergeant didn't offer his name. They didn't bother to shake hands. Yates reached over and whacked the dog several times with a hard red palm, pounding the thin head with fierce, drunken gestures of affection.

"Alternating-Current Yates, Always Careful Yates," the sea-horse sergeant said. "Just get that last name right, and you'll get it right. I like you, boy. You got a wicked face. Yates is the name, Sergeant, from Memphis, Tennessee."

A Frenchman with a black cap and a torn raincoat opened the door and came in with a spotted dog, which timidly nosed the floor toward the little white dog.

"You better keep your bitch away from that white dog," the sea-horse sergeant said. He was talking fast and breathlessly. "He's a mean little bastard, *monsieur*."

"He doesn't understand a word you're saying," the technical sergeant said, winking at the woman behind the bar. She put cognac carefully into a clean glass before him.

"Don't he, now?" said Yates. "Look at him pull that dog away."

The little white dog stood on stiff legs and edged forward. Yates reached down and pushed him back into the corner.

"There we was in Italy," Yates said, as if he had heard a question. "We was across the Volturno—that was the toughest river to cross in Italy—and we didn't even know we done it. It was so goddamn dark we couldn't even show a light, and all we had was two little tracks across this pontoon bridge that the engineers built."

"You're an engineer yourself, aren't you?" the technical sergeant asked, looking at the sea horse on the jacket.

"I'm a trucker," Yates said. "I always been a trucker, here and there. Right now I got a bunch of trucks down in the harbor, unloading stuff. You see 'em, going in and out."

"I've seen 'em," the technical sergeant said. He tried to get the blonde woman's eye and couldn't. She flickered her glance over him, and he looked straight back, and missed.

"No, I never been an engineer," Yates said. "But I been attached to the engineers and I know a lot of those boys. I know which engineers built that bridge over the Volturno, all right. I knew it, the way it shook when we went across."

"All those pontoon bridges shake some," the technical sergeant said, rubbing a finger slowly down the side of his glass and smiling at the Frenchwoman.

"There was one more M. P. on the other side of that bridge, and he says, 'Don't show no lights,' and a couple of kraut shells come over, and he says, 'You can see why.' Then we was past the M.P.s and there wasn't anybody ahead but the Joes that was fighting the war."

The little white dog sneaked out and made a dash for the spotted dog, which had gone to sleep on the floor. Yates caught the white dog, and the small head turned, snarling, toward him. He tossed the dog into the air and it slammed against the bar.

"He's a mean bastard," Yates said. "Like me. He'll try to get away with any goddamn thing. You got to watch him every minute."

The technical sergeant dug into a pocket and came up with his wallet. He looked around the café. The Frenchman and the sea-horse sergeant were the only customers there. He nodded to the madame.

"*Cognac pour tout le monde*," he said loudly.

Immediately the Frenchman in the torn raincoat extended his empty glass. Outside, a heavy truck banged along in the rain on the pitted road from the Channel, its headlights glaring into the rusted wreckage of the building across the street. There were no complete houses on that side.

"Look at that, now," Yates said, pounding the bar suddenly with his thick red fists. "You got to have lights. You got to have some kind of lights. Even where we was, over the Volturno. I had the lead truck in the convoy and I couldn't see a foot. So I turned on my lights and drove like hell and the rest come along behind me."

The truck swayed around a curve and disappeared.

"See that?" Yates said, "See that? Now, how could he tell what was on that curve if he didn't have his lights?" He reached for his glass. "I had to turn on my lights. I couldn't see, and we was carryin' ammo, and I had to get there fast, and there was Infantry on that road. I was always afraid of that—runnin' over some doughfoot in the goddamn dark."

"Well, you made it all right."

"Sure, we made it," Yates said, watching the little white dog. "We just made it, boy. We dumped our loads and we got out of our trucks to take a stretch and the kraut shells started comin' over and we hit the ground. They knew where we was and they dropped shells all around there, careful and slow. But they didn't get a one of us. That wasn't their time. They was late."

There was a heavy, thundering crash; it seemed to come from near the harbor. Yates and the technical sergeant turned and stared through the damp window, but in the cold darkness they would see only a blaze of lights in the sheds built by the engineers.

"Sounded like maybe one of your boys might've hit something that time," the technical sergeant said, after a minute.

"There's a lot of crazy bastards that take chances," Yates said, putting down his glass, "I got to go and check up on my goddamn trucks. Look, boy, I think I seen you down in Italy or Africa somewhere."

"No," the technical sergeant said. "I never saw the Volturno."

"I never, either," Yates said. "When I got across, when I got past that last M. P., I turned on my lights. I had to do it. You get to a place where you can't see nothing, you got to have some lights."

He bent over slowly and picked up the white dog and cradled him under his right arm.

"You see Madeleine around tonight?" Yates said softly, speaking to the Frenchwoman. "That black-haired girl?"

The woman shook her head. *"Madeleine? Madeleine?"* she said. *"Non. Ah, non."* "I'm going to take you with me, boy," Yates said sharply to the dog, clasping the shivering white face in his short, tough fingers. "I'm going to take you with me back to Memphis, Tennessee." Then he stopped and cocked his head. "You hear a train, Sergeant?" he asked.

"There's no more trains in or out of this town till tomorrow morning," the technical sergeant said.

Yates turned again, and shaped his lips in an odd way, and a long, shrill moan came from his mouth, like the sound of a train whistle in the night, a fast train whistling at a road crossing or plunging into a tunnel.

"That's the train to Memphis," Yates said. "That's the train I'm going to ride when I get off that boat. Good night, Sergeant. I like you, boy. You got a wild and wicked face. Good night, madame, good night, *monsieur."* He went out into the rainy, pitted street with the dog under his arm, and when he shut the door the glass in it vibrated. As Yates walked down the hill toward the harbor, the technical sergeant heard the quivering whistle, swift and high, of a train hurrying in the darkness of the distant country always remembered, the southern land.

MY INTERPLANETARY
TEENS

By Frank K. Kelly

(From *The Atlantic*)

Certain peculiar experiences I suffered at the age of sixteen, when I was under contract to deal with death rays and rocket ships for several pulp magazines, have prepared me for the day of the robot plane and the flying bomb and other things of the future which burst a little too suddenly on the minds of my friends. Many of them have struggled bitterly to adjust themselves to the possibility of personal disintegration in the atomic age. My mind must have been softened when I was boy, for my main feeling recently has been a sense of wonder that it took the future so long to arrive.

At eleven I had begun to read the fantastic magazines, fascinated first by a cover picture of Martians riding on tripods across London, which illustrated *The War of the Worlds* by H. G. Wells. I brought their issues home and hid them under my mattress, because I knew my father wanted me to read the adventures of Tom Swift, and my grandfather urged me to study the life of Buffalo Bill, who ranked in his affections next to William S. Hart. I stubbornly preferred flights to Mars or trips in time machines.

When I reached fifteen I felt a compulsion to write a strange tale in secret, and I did. I slipped it into a mailbox on my way home from school one day and it was published soon afterward in one of the magazines. I was lost then—words poured out of me by thousands and tens of thousands. A few months later, when I was sixteen, a contract arrived in the mail. My poor mother opened the envelope, and a faraway look came into her eyes. Peering over her shoulder, I saw a magical sentence typed in blue ink on buff-colored paper: —

"Agreement is made on this 3rd day of October, 1931, between the Stellar Publishing Corporation of New York City, hereinafter designated as the Publisher, and Frank K. Kelly, hereinafter designated as Author...."

My mother turned to me. "Oh, Frank! What have you been doing?"

"I couldn't help it, Mother," I said. "I just started writing."

I thought I had climbed the peak of happiness, but my subsequent responsibilities became rather severe. My editors turned out to be extremely critical men. My readers complained that I would not give them joyful endings even on Jupiter or Saturn. My family showed serious doubts about my sanity.

Fighting forward, I sold my dreams of interplanetary war and love among the asteroids month after month—for half a cent her word. But the hardheaded editors were more at home on the airless plains of Mars or in the riotous life of steaming Venus than I could ever be, and they savagely criticized me when I made what seemed to them an obvious error in describing conditions under Saturn's rings or on the moons of Jupiter.

The first letter I received after I signed the contract was dated October 29, 1931, and the editors wrote: "We are accepting your story 'The Man from Earth.' We think it is quite well done, although it contains some scientific errors such as the pool of liquid radium and the fact that water will be transported from Earth to Mars. Your story did have a tendency toward the weird which it might be advisable to avoid in the future."

After these rebukes, they concluded on an encouraging note: "We are looking forward with excited interest to your next contribution."

Their excitement evidently died down rapidly when my contribution landed on their desks. The next letter began plaintively: "We are accepting your story 'On the Mars Run,' as it is substantially better than some of your earlier ones, but why, oh why, did you use such a theme as the invisibility cloak in this story? If such a cloak were known and in use, it could have changed entirely the aspect of the story, for then everybody would be prying into everybody else's affairs with impunity."

The letter continued sternly: "For no reason at all, you drag such a device into your narrative, with an offhand, unconvincing explanation, and thereby give your story an aspect of a bedtime tale. *Not that invisibility is impossible.* But the point is, you drag it in so purposelessly."

In attempting to edge away from the weird and to avoid the "aspect of a bedtime tale," I packed my pages with scientific terms, creating many of the words myself. I was given a brisk rap on the knuckles for this activity:—

"We are accepting your story, 'Exiles of Saturn,' in its revised form. We were not entirely pleased with the revision, since you still keep all of your queer scientific jargon without explaining the terms that you use. You are not fooling the reader by making up new words to indicate scientific apparatus that you do not explain. We wish, in your future stories, that you would keep a little closer to your readers, who do not know just what those terms mean."

I gave the best years of my adolescence, from sixteen to twenty, to the creation of fables of the future. But I never succeeded in giving complete satisfaction to the editors.

While I was struggling to supply the magazines with chronicles of the wanderings of Earth Men through space and time, I tried to creep closer to my readers. They would not take me into their hearts. My vision of the future was too bleak.

In the Reader Speaks departments, I achieved an odd form of fame, if you can call it fame. People wrote in from Australia to suggest that I might choose happier subjects than planetary famines and interplanetary feuds. "Perhaps a happy ending is not possible on this Earth," wrote one philosophical fan of mine, "but how do we know that it is not possible on Saturn or Jupiter?"

The worst blow came from a man in Los Angeles. "Kelly's stories leave me feeling cold and comfortless," he declared from the golden comfort of Southern California. "Is there no hope?"

I kept on writing, because I had compensations for these criticisms—a steady flow of checks, and a few letters praising my work. And one night while I stood on the front porch of my home in Kansas City, a boy rode up on a bicycle. He looked at the iron numbers on one of the porch pillars, and asked me: —

"Could you tell me where I could find Frank K. Kelly, the writer?"

"Right here," I said. "What can I do for you?"

"Would you shake hands?" he said. I was eighteen then, and he was fifteen or sixteen. He seemed to be serious. "I just read 'Evil on Saturn,' and I found out where you live. I've read every story you've ever written, from the first one they printed."

"What was the name of the first one?" I said.

"'The Light Bender,'" he said. "That was the one where you made the Woolworth Building disappear, and nobody knew what had happened to it, but it was there all the time. The scientist had just bent the light around it, so nobody could see it."

He was right. We shook hands. That was the high point of my experience with readers.

My family difficulties increased through the years as my stories grew wilder. I wrote about explorers in glass-topped cities on the moon, duels in the fourth dimension, terrifying studies of scientists who developed living cells in their lonely laboratories and then couldn't stop the multiplication of these cells, which swarmed at last in shapeless masses over the entire Earth.

One magazine featured on its cover a story of mine about a rocket ship bound for Jupiter. The ship had been hurled by cosmic rays into another Universe, where everything seemed to be turned inside out and upside down, in the eyes of the Earth crew. Then they found themselves changing shape, and their thoughts ran backward in their brains.

A few of my finest tales I showed to my grandfather—a tall, straight, pink-nosed Irishman of eighty—and he read them through, his sharp blue eyes frowning. He must have spoken to my father afterward, because I remember my father urged me about that time to take up handball or tennis.

Once when I came home my mother told me she had found my sister crying in the kitchen. "I asked her what could be the trouble," my mother said. "She answered, it was the strange things in your stories."

My mother engaged in months of internal argument before she permitted the neighbors to know that I was a writer. She seldom read any of my stories, and she was a little doubtful about my themes. When I prevailed upon her to glance through several of them and she found that the characters from Earth were of noble mind and had the highest motives—the evil people were usually from Saturn or Jupiter—she was completely converted.

Her early misgivings surged back later, I think. We sat in the kitchen one summer afternoon, having tea together before I attacked my typewriter to finish a serial. My young brother Vincent raced through the back door to join his baseball team. My mother touched my hand, and said finally: "Vincent is worried about you. He was reading one of your stories."

"It's about time he did," I said defensively.

"And he told me, 'Mother, there's something wrong with Frank. In this story I just put down, there's a part where a guy steps out of bed in green pajamas and explodes.'"

Her teacup trembled when she lifted it. "Did you write that, Frank?"

"The fellow had an electronic beam trained on him, that's all," I said. "He was disintegrated by an enemy because he had the plans for a radium plant in his head. I explained the whole thing."

She took a long sip of tea. "Perhaps you shouldn't write any more of those stories."

I couldn't stop. I kept on dreaming of rockets in the night, and sleep, shining ships hurtling through space. Stretched full-length in a soft suspended hammock which relieved my body of the tremendous pressure created by the speed of ten thousand miles an hour, I listened to the drumming of star fragments on the rocket ship's outer shell and I smiled sometimes at the luminous face of Zeletta, the phosphorescent girl who often lay beside me.

My dreams were big and sprawling, and ran to twenty thousand words, including three or four thousand adjectives. With adjectives I bought my brother a baseball glove, and silenced his criticism. My sister got a new hat, my mother got a waffle iron, and I took my grandmother to a Chinese restaurant. She could never get enough of chicken chow mein.

SYNTHETIC SIN

By Frank K. Kelly

(From *The Atlantic*)

Frank K. Kelly is a former Kansas City and New York newspaperman now working in Washington. He is the author of many magazine articles and his novel about the workings of a press association, An Edge of Light, was published in 1949.

When I reached twenty-one, I was hacking out a living by writing about the delights of interplanetary travel. But midway in a tale of a great drought on Mars, I was blocked by a vision of the tanned beauty of the girl next door. I came to a full stop, and I could not start again. The touch was gone, the golden touch which had made my chronicles of war on Jupiter and woe on Mars acceptable to the elastic-minded editors of the science fiction magazines. I stood up, put on a tie, and went out on the porch of my father's house in Kansas City to watch the girls go by.

How did women think? What did they desire, what were their weaknesses, what were the enticing things to say to them? How could I capture one? These questions flickered through my troubled mind. The bright face of Zeletta, the phosphorescent girl of my teens who had shared my adventures on the far planets, became a small and faded image in my memory.

When my first fumbling efforts to capture a few women were repulsed, I turned to my submissive typewriter and produced a flood of love stories. The stories were always poignant and passionate. The women in them were vigorous, outspoken creatures. Not certain of how women should talk in tales of love, I made them speak as forthrightly as men—not with rocket pistols or death rays, but with harsh words and fists when necessary.

"Caveman stuff doesn't go any more," scribbled one manuscript critic on the back of a rejection slip. "Tone it down." Another advised me crisply: "You may be all right when you learn restraint." One man warned me: "You get to the point too abruptly. Winning a woman is not always done by direct action." When I got a story printed in a love pulp periodical, a feminine reader commented: "No woman would act like that." Most of the complaints hit the same note: I was too brutal.

When I wrote savage stories of burning love, I was rejected by a flock of blondes, brunettes, and redheads. One girl explained to me that I had an irregular occupation, and no girl would marry a man who carried his love stories as far as I did. Another said she loved me a little, but not enough. My knowledge of women grew slowly, and my stack of stories became higher and higher.

A friend of mine glanced over a dozen manuscripts one night. He lingered on a sardonic tale of an impetuous man rebuffed by women who were frightened of his despairing style of love-making. "Why don't you try this on a confession magazine?" he asked. "If you put a moral on this, it would sell."

I stared at him. "It isn't exactly taken from life," I muttered. He regarded me with wonder. "The stories in those magazines are dream stuff," he said. "All you need for them is a heated imagination, and you've got it."

"But I've never overwhelmed any women," I said. "I've never fallen in love with a friend's wife. I've never been caught in a tragic triangle."

After he had gone I threw my manuscripts into a cardboard box under my desk, and I decided to get a steady job. I became a newspaperman, and I tried to forget my elegies on love. But I kept adding to the tall heap of stories in the brown box, and one New Year's Day I abandoned my job to go to Manhattan, determined to become a sophisticated freelance and to savor the tempestuous freedom of Greenwich Village.

Before I boarded the train that cold and rainy day, my friend slipped a letter into my overcoat pocket. He explained that he had composed a few lines of introduction for me to a confession magazine editor, and urged me to use the letter if I found myself absolutely on the rocks. I didn't want to get into an argument, but I silently resolved that before I would turn to confessing synthetic sins for a living I'd sink back into the newspaper business.

In New York I hoped to encounter the adventures I had not been able to find in my own hometown, yet somehow they eluded me. For six months I lived in dingy furnished rooms on West Seventeenth Street with a fellow refugee from Kansas City, a taciturn reporter. He roamed the bleak Manhattan streets by day in search of jobs while I paced the gray rooms or pounded my portable typewriter.

At night the horns and whistles of ships in the Hudson River haunted our fitful frustrated sleep. We seldom met any girls, and when we did we had just enough money to take them to the movies, so we didn't make much progress. My savings dribbled away in expenditures for English muffins and coffee, and at the end of six months I had sold only one story, a short and powerful piece about a French cabin boy on a merchant ship, who had been saved from drowning by a talisman given to him by a Breton girl.

On a rainy night when my reporter friend returned to the rooms dripping moisture and melancholy, I announced my intention of seeking a spot on a newspaper. He simply shook his head. "Then I'll use my letter of introduction," I said. "If I can't sell anything else, I can sell confessions."

Bill sighed deeply and removed his wet shoes. "We're doomed," he said. "As far as I can see, you haven't got anything to confess."

I went to the bare cupboard, and then turned. "I've never been to Mars, but I sold a lot of stuff about Mars," I said.

Bill shook the water from his shoes.

"Try it," he said. "Okay, try it."

The next day I donned my last gabardine suit and rode in the subway to the offices of the Morality Publications on Forty-second Street. When I walked into the reception room I noticed that it was decorated in crimson and cream, colors richly symbolic of sin and forgiveness.

My letter gained for me a quick admittance into the spacious office of Mr. Snow, the editor of *True to Life*. He studied me for several seconds, and nodded. "You've got that tormented look," he said. "I think you're going to write things for me. I'll tell you what we want, now. We want straight stuff, stories pulsing with the heartbeat of life, quivering with the warm blood of human experience."

I hesitated. "What is your word rate?"

"If I like your stuff, you'll get four cents a word. Later you'll get more. Now I'll tell you what I want you to do first. Here are copies of some back numbers of my magazine. Take them home and read them and come back to see me a week from today." He scratched a pencil across a calendar pad. "Next Thursday, at three o'clock." He came around the rim of the desk, carrying a pile of thick magazines. I took them, and the weight made my arms sag.

Before I could continue the conversation he caught my arm and led me along a corridor to the reception room, talking about our mutual friend in Kansas City.

"He told me you were an evangelist," I said.

Mr. Snow stopped. He looked a little touched and a little pleased.

"In a certain way, I am an evangelist," he said. "My magazine has done more to win decent treatment for unmarried mothers than any other in the country. All our publications have high standards of morality. You've loved long enough to know that sin leads to sorrow, and redemption brings rejoicing. Remember that."

He squeezed my shoulder and retreated toward his office. I went past the pale receptionist, took an elevator to the lobby of the building, and stepped into the glare of Forty-second Street, shaken and confused.

Back in the gloomy furnished rooms down in the Village, I studied the magazines. NIGHT OF DISILLUSION was featured on one blazing cover; MY MOTHER WAS MY RIVAL was splashed on another. There were stories of luckless brides, lost girls, unhappy bigamists.

I didn't have the background, the range of experience, to produce such tales, but the next day Snow called me. "I need a 5000-word piece to fill out my next issue, and I need somebody not long out of college to handle it," he said. "There's a young professor, teaching at a college for women. He takes advantage of his position, he's a cruel heartbreaker. Then he falls in love with one of his students, really in love, and she treats him with cold contempt because of his reputation. He pays the penalty of loose living."

"But he gets her in the end," I said.

"No. Our stories are true to life. We don't have to force a happy ending. She goes away, and he keeps her enshrined in his heart, and becomes a great teacher, a fine influence on all the girls in the college. He becomes a living proof that faithful love does exist."

"Do you think I can handle it?" I asked.

"Certainly you can," he said. His voice became softly persuasive. "I'll give you a break. Tell it from the man's angle. We don't usually take it from that angle, but it'll be easier for you. Later you can try the woman's angle."

I wrote it, and he bought it. He took me to lunch at a hotel to discuss the future. Before we ate, he spread the pages of the story on the tablecloth. "It's good," he said. "Fine, except for a few things. You don't get enough *bone* in your love scenes. *Bone*, that's what you need. And your plot needs more of a motor. You've got to have an engine to make it go. What drives this guy? Why does he go from woman to woman, when he secretly believes in one big love? Can it be that he's seeking the tender affection his mother didn't give him? Or maybe there's some other reason. But get it in. Get it all in."

He seized one of the pages. "Now this scene in the woods needed some juice. I touched it up. Listen to this: 'Call it wisdom, call it madness, call it what you will! Pearl and I were lifted up to the heights of ecstasy, and all the dull world fell away from us.' That gives it more *zip*. You've got to have *zip*, you've got to have *zing* in these scenes.

Campaigning Against Prejudice: Anti-Discrimination Commission Handles 1000 Cases in New York

Law Which Requires Equality of Employment Opportunity
Is Said to Be Accepted by Employers, Employe[e]s
After 2 1/2 Years' Trial.

By FRANK K. KELLY

A Special Correspondent of the Post-Dispatch

New York, Dec. 20

A few weeks ago the chairman of the New York State Commission Against Discrimination, which has been successfully campaigning against racial, religious and national group prejudices for two and a half years, announced a triumph of conciliation, which had effects far beyond New York's borders. Chairman Charles Garside disclosed that the AFL Brotherhood of Railway and Steamship Clerks, Freight Handlers, Express and Station Employe[e]s had repealed regulations which had restricted Negroes to membership in local auxiliary lodges.

Regular local charters are now being issued by the brotherhood throughout the country to replace the limited auxiliary chapters under which the lodges with Negro members had operated. This action follows a step taken by the Brotherhood at its last national convention held last May in Cincinnati. At that time the union eliminated from its constitution all provisions restricting membership to white persons.

These changes in the policies of the Brotherhood resulted from a series of conferences conducted between the New York Commission Against Discrimination and officers of the union. Out of those conferences came the establishment of Negroes as full-fledged members of the Brotherhood, with the right of equal participation in all affairs of the union.

Ives-Quinn Law Has Teeth for Enforcement.

The case of the Brotherhood was one of more than 1000 handled by the Commission since it began work under the Ives-Quinn Law in July 1945. In this particular instance, 23,000 Negro workers gained recognition of the equality granted to all American citizens as a civil right. In other cases, involving various types of employers from shoe shop owners to university trustees, the Commission has won important gains for thousands of employe[e]s. The number cannot be accurately estimated, but it is undoubtedly large, because more than 2000 employers have asked the Commission to review their employment practices to make certain that they have complied with the law.

In the steam railroad industry alone, national and international unions with hundreds of thousands of members have changed their constitutions to eliminate discriminatory clauses. Other unions have formally agreed, at the request of the New York Commission, to waive union rules where they are in conflict with the Ives-Quinn Law. The New York Commission regards revised rulebooks and printed alterations in existing rulebooks as satisfactory evidence of co-operation by the unions.

Although the Ives-Quinn Law has teeth, providing that any person, employer, labor organization or employment agency willfully resisting the Commission or willfully violating a Commission order shall be guilty of a misdemeanor punishable by a year's imprisonment or a $500 fine or both, representatives of the Commission have not yet been forced to use those teeth to secure compliance. Skillful use of conciliation and persuasion has proved to be an extremely effective policy.

When the act against discrimination was passed with the approval of both the Democratic and Republican parties and signed by Gov. Thomas E. Dewey in 1945, there were gloomy predictions that dozens of employers would leave the state and set up factories elsewhere, that white workers would refuse to work alongside Negro workers, that public resentment would cause a loss of trade in stores where employe[e]s of mixed races dealt with customers. So far, these dour predictions have not come true.

Some Cases Dismissed After Being Investigated.

The law requires that consideration be given to all employe[e]s and applicants for employment on the basis of their qualifications as individuals regardless of race, creed, color or national origin. The employer's right to set the qualifications for any job has not been taken away form him, but be must apply the same standards of qualification equally to all persons.

Since any individual may file a sworn complaint of discrimination and obtain an investigation by the Commission, the investigators have been drawn into a number of strange cases. A white man of American ancestry charged that the company he worked for had refused to pay him for a V-J day holiday and had paid all other workers who were said to be of German extraction. It was brought out that the worker was absent on the day before the V-J holiday and company rules were against holiday payment to employe[e]s absent immediately prior to a holiday. The complaint was quickly dismissed.

A young Negro woman applied for a position as a skilled bookkeeper with experience in a plant holding government contracts. She reported that she was not considered by the personnel director, and yet advertisements for experienced bookkeepers appeared for the next three days in newspapers. Investigation showed that the salary asked by the young woman was $400 over the top salary paid by the company for that type of work. The company had another Negro girl doing the same kind of work, and the personnel director offered to hire the complainant if she would accept the salary offered. The case was closed.

Acting on charges made in letters, Commission representatives looked into the employment practices of a large concern which asked job applicants discriminatory questions on application blanks. The company employed a number of Negroes and Jews but did not put them in positions which would bring them into direct sales contacts with the public. After a few conferences with Commission officials, members of the firm agreed to change their interviewing policies as well as their printed application blanks. Owners of the concern were informed that the Commission would make a follow-up investigation within six months to be sure that these changes were carried through.

One Violator Forced to Pay $92.73 in Wages.

A Negro man went to a union local, seeking a job as a night elevator operator. The union sent him to a midtown apartment house in Manhattan. The building superintendent told him: "All our night elevator operators here are white." He filed a complaint with the Commission, on the advice of union leaders. The owners of the apartment house told investigators that the superintendent had been instructed not to reject any applicant because of color. The superintendent assumed all responsibility and was advised by the Commission to pay the Negro applicant $92.73, which represented three weeks' pay covering a period when the complainant was unemployed.

Miss A, a Negro girl, was sent by an employment agency to apply for a job as a clerk in a stock room. The agency had just telephoned the stock supervisor and had been assured that the position was open. When Miss A appeared, the personnel interviewer seemed to be shocked, put both hands to his head and cried: "The job is taken." Miss A filed a complaint with the Commission and the usual investigation followed. The company insisted that the job had been filled in the 15-minute period between the phone call made by the employment agency and the arrival of Miss A. Finally the owner admitted that a Negro girl had never been hired as a clerk, acknowledged that there was a vacancy and declared he would be willing to hire the complainant. In the meantime, she had obtained another job. The company owner did, however, eventually hire a Negro girl and the Commission accepted his assurances that he intended to change his policy to conform with the law.

Commission Adopts A Policy of Persuasion Instead of Using Its Police Power to Achieve Compliance With the Ives-Quinn Law.

In a large department store on Fifth Avenue, an employment manager frankly asserted that the store was reluctant to employ Negroes as saleswomen. He said there would be a marked resistance by customers, since the saleswomen performed such personal services as fitting dresses, bathing suits, and other articles of clothing. The similarity of such services to those performed by Negro maids, long accepted by women in many homes, was pointed out to him. After considerable discussion and [and] after the provisions of the Ives-Quinn Law were explained to him, the manager yielded. He hired a qualified Negro girl, and promised to give equal opportunity in the future to every qualified applicant.

An experienced Negro cook, a woman of fine appearance and excellent references, complained to the Commission that a restaurant chain had informed her that no Negro women cooks were employed in the kitchens. She was told by the dietitian in one of the restaurant branches that the company felt that if they hired a Negro in that branch the four white kitchen workers would quit and the chain would loose valuable employe[e]s. Commission representatives conferred with the owners, and the Negro woman got the job. The four white women did not resign, but welcomed her and all of them worked together amicably.

An unexpected angle was found in one case. A disgruntled employe[e] accused the partners of a small firm of discharging him for discriminatory reasons. Commission investigators found no discrimination, and discovered that the partners had in fact headed anti-discrimination committees in their community. The employe[e] appeared to be suffering from a persecution complex. A study of his record showed he had not been able to hold any job for more than a week for the past three years.

An Employment Agency Eliminates One Question.

A German-born worker of Jewish descent, who left Germany when Hitler came into power and became a naturalized citizen of the United States, declared he had applied for a job as a welder in a New York plant and had been asked where he was born. When he stated Germany as his birthplace, he was informed that he was ineligible. An investigation brought out the fact that the plant was part of an atomic energy project and that the Federal Government required all workers to be native-born citizens. The case was dismissed.

An employment agency which aroused the Commission's interest was extremely selective in handling applicants, and an investigation was launched. The Commission representatives soon learned that the emphasis of the agency was placed almost entirely on the qualifications of individual applicants and that very high positions with high rates of pay were involved. The only objectionable question on the application blank was one requesting the birthplace of the applicant. This was deleted after a series of conferences. The initial resentment of agency executives changed to an attitude of good-will when it was made clear that the inquiry was not conducted with any desire to stir up charges or to pillory anyone. The agency placed all its files at the disposal of the Commission and explained all notations made on application blanks by interviewers.

In hundreds of cases since the Ives-Quinn Act went into force, the Commission has turned up the fact that many discriminatory practices have arisen from fear on the part of employers, rather than from any deeply rooted prejudices against minority groups. Fear of losses, in the form of trade or public support, and fear of labor trouble due to the attitudes of employe[e]s who might object to working with members of other racial groups are the two principal fears encountered.

Persuasion Has Been Most Successful Method.

Once the hurdles of these fears have been overcome, however, many employers have been astonished by the relative ease with which different groups have worked together. Negro bus drivers, salesgirls, switchboard operators and stenographers, Polish clerks, Italian bookkeepers and Jewish supervisors have adjusted to one another with few clashes. One large employer who made the changes requested by the Commission with the feeling that unnecessary difficulties were being created later said to one of the commissioners: "Some of the new people I've hired are outstanding. I'm glad I hired them. You ought to point out to employers the benefits they get from an increased labor market when they have access to so many more qualified workers."

The law applies to all employers who have six or more persons on their payrolls, but does not cover non-profit organizations of a fraternal, religious, charitable, exclusively social or educational nature; domestic help, or persons who employ members of their families. It covers hiring and firing, upgrading and promotion policies, conditions of work, application forms, practices of employment agencies, membership in labor unions, and discrimination by fellow employe[e]s.

The conciliatory methods used by the Commission and its success in obtaining results through persuasion instead of police power have led to general acceptance of the law by employers, labor unions and almost all sections of the public. At the present time, there is little or no agitation for its repeal or modification, even from those who declared that it would be impossible to get employers to abandon discriminatory practices through legislation.

One of the most useful means of public education created by the Commission is the formation of local community councils, drawn from business groups, labor, the clergy and civic organizations. Some members of the Commission believe that in the long run these councils may accomplish more than legal sanctions.

Councils have been set up in Albany, Troy, Buffalo, Syracuse, New York City, Westchester country and Broome county and many others are in the process of formation. The local council is the body, which stands between the enforcement machinery of the state and the problem requiring solution. Where direct use of the authority of the state might fail to break down prejudice, "neighbor talking to neighbor" on the local level often succeeds.

'To Secure These Rights'

The President's Committee on Civil Rights, headed by Charles E. Wilson, president of General Electric Co., recently recommended:

"The enactment of a federal Fair Employment Practice Act prohibiting all forms of discrimination in private employment, based on race, color, creed or national origin," and "the enactment by the states of similar laws."

Six states already have laws against discrimination in private employment. They are New York, New Jersey, Massachusetts, Connecticut, Indiana and Wisconsin. Some cities, including Chicago, Minneapolis, New York and Cincinnati have enacted ordinances to prevent such discrimination.

This trend—to prevent discrimination by government action—began with the establishment of the Fair Employment Practice Committee by President Roosevelt in 1941. That committee has not operated since June, 1946, when Congress failed to appropriate funds for its continued support. The report of the Committee on Civil Rights, however, has brought the entire issue before the country on the broad principle that it is our obligation, in furtherance of the "American heritage," to "build social institutions that will guarantee equality of opportunity."

Since that report points to the example of the State of New York, the Post-Dispatch has sought to discover how legal action to prevent discrimination actually works in practice in that state. That is the subject of Mr. Kelly's report presented here.

AN EDGE OF LIGHT

By Frank K. Kelly

In the central wire room of the Consolidated Press building, in the long white-walled room filled with the hammering of teletypes and the ringing of small bells, James Hammill sat in the slot of the general desk where the main wires met. His shirt sleeves rolled to his elbows, an old cigar in his mouth, his thin face circled by a cloud of smoke, he marked messages and bulletins and night leads from Chicago and Rome and Moscow, Tokyo and Bombay and Berlin. He didn't think of what he had done or where he might be going, he leaned over the scarred green desk and let his fast hands run.

Hammill knew that if he lost a minute he couldn't get it back. If he dropped a minute, World Press or Globe might beat him to the next broadcasts and take the top lines of the next editions. He kept his score on a yellow sheet of ruled paper. He noted down the exact minute when a bulletin hit the wires with a rush of loud bells, and Consolidated bureaus over the country gave him the exact arrival times of bulletins sent from the WP or Globe wire rooms in New York. Consolidated led in two bulletins out of three. That was the standard of the night desk, and Hammill held the standard.

The clustered ceiling lights glared through the smoke around him, the teletype printers clattered, the small urgent bells rang. His hands throbbed, his fingers ached, the smoke hurt his eyes. When he turned his head in any direction, he saw the black-rimmed clocks on the white pillars in the wide room. He sat surrounded by the faces of time. If he didn't slow a little, if he didn't steal a minute now and then, he might not last another year. He might have a stroke like Joe Landell, he might fall on his face under a desk like Al Dwyer. If he did slow a little, if he stole a minute when he needed it, he might not last a month. One night Brenden would come around and show him the record, the count of headlines on the sixty big front pages, and Brenden would quietly replace him. He hummed a Duke Ellington tune in his throat, a melody of blues.

He wrote the time of a bulletin received in Cleveland, and the yellow paper beneath his black pencil suddenly reminded him of Derry's smooth bright hair and he remembered her hair falling against his face and the look in her eyes. He knew he should never feel low, he should never hum the blues. "Nobody breaks until he gets ready to break," he could hear her saying with her sure smile. "And you're an armored man. You'll be around for years and years."

Nothing could break him, he could handle anything that came. It was nearly eight o'clock, the stories that had to go on the high wires would be finished soon, and the lull would come. He stretched his arms. Then he hunted the dangerous errors in the night leads, he fought the threat of libel, he shouted and argued, he ripped the pieces of pink and blue and yellow paper that showered from the teletypes. He answered the three muffled telephones that tormented him, scribbled "F-Cables" or "Local Desk" on strips torn from his note pad, slapped the strips on a black iron spike at his left elbow, and called for copy boys.

This was a heavy night, this might be the night when he blew apart, when the cracks in him opened too far to close. At any minute he might begin to mumble like Bryan, the A wire man who sat across from him. He might drive the copy spikes through his hands and leap on the desk. He might grab the tangled telephones and throw them on the floor.

Yet he made it. He reached eight o'clock with hands that trembled only slightly, and if he had begun to bleed it wasn't noticeable.

Around eight the rhythm of the night's news began to shift to a slower place, the revised stories slated for the early morning papers had gone dwindling along the wires, and there came the periodic pause that saved him. If anybody ever asked him whether he had been saved, he could cite a hundred heavy nights when he had been.

He settled in his chair and rubbed his throat. The Ellington tune died down in him. He felt the scrape of metal and he looked at his left hand and saw the gold ring. He had forgotten the drastic difference in his life. In the ring an image of Derry flickered, and her challenging smile rose before him.

Why did he think of her as challenging and defiant, when she had never really challenged him, never defied him? Because she had taken him, because she was the one who had tied him to her, because he had wakened the morning after their quick marriage with the feeling that she would demand more and more from him day after day and night after night as long as he lived with her. And he wanted to live with her as long as he lived.

Bryan muttered across the desk: "I've got a thirst, Jim. Have a 'Coke'?"

"I owe you one," Hammill said. "I'll buy."

He beckoned to a boy, produced two nickels, and sent the boy to the Coca-Cola machine in a distant corner of the huge room. He crushed his cigar in an ashtray and swung his head toward the window. He had a clear view of the lighted avenue and the plaza in the next block, the bare little park below the Press building. Along the paths of the plaza, the small figures of people moved on hidden errands. He felt as though he sat on the ledge of a crumbling wall above them.

One of the telephones near him buzzed. He wanted to knock it to the floor and let it lie there squawking. His hands pulled the receiver to him and he shouted automatically: "General desk. Hammill speaking."

Lila's voice, hushed and faint, called to him: "Jimmy?"

"Lila," he said. "Where are you? I can barely hear you."

"I can hear that noise," Lila said, her voice lifting a little. "It must be a bad night. I just wanted to ask whether you'd seen a story from Chungking, or if you'd heard from Steve."

"Nothing so far tonight," he said. Her voice troubled him. "But it's still early. Lila, when are we going to see you? Why have you been keeping away from us? We've missed you."

"I'm sure Derry misses me. How late will you be there, on the desk?"

"Two o'clock. Lila, you're wrong about Derry."

"Of course I'm wrong. I've been wrong from the beginning. I don't know how to be anything but wrong."

"You're lonely," he said. "There's no need for you to be. Come over to our place. You can't stay in that apartment by yourself."

"You hate to be alone," she said. "I like it. I can see things. I can put things together. Jimmy, I'm going to ask you something and I don't want any lies. You're sweet when you try to lie, Jimmy, but you can't do it. You get hoarse and you talk too fast. Now tell me. When did you last get a letter from Steve?"

"I haven't heard from Steve for months."

It was the question he had expected and he had practiced his answer, he had repeated that answer until he could give it flatly and calmly. He had received a letter every week since Steve had been in China, until three weeks ago. Then the letters had stopped. He had carried the final letter with him for days, reading it and trying to understand what had happened to Steve. Afterward, he had burned the envelope and the sheaf of paper covered with writing that looked like Steve's scrawls. But the Steve he'd known could not have written that letter.

"I thought he'd always write to you," Lila said. "I didn't expect him to write to me. But you were so much closer to him."

"I can't hear you," Hammill said. "There's too much racket here. Lila, I can't figure what's bitten him. I can't figure why he went to China, I can't figure why he stays there."

"You know why he stays there. Because Brenden won't let him come home. You go to Brenden and ask him why he keeps Steve in

China. Will you? Tell him to let Steve come back, because I need someone around. Will you?"

"I'll see Brenden," Hammill said. "Lila, why haven't we heard from you before tonight? All these weeks --"

"Jimmy, you know why you haven't heard from me. You know damned well."

"There's one thing I can tell you, let me --"

"I'll try you later."

The receiver clicked. He had lost her. He knew why she hadn't called him, he knew why she stayed alone.

The copy boy returned from the "Coke" machine with two paper cups full of dark liquid. Hammill took a cup and passed the other to Bryan. Hands fluttering, Bryan raised the cup and spilled some of the fluid. Bryan had been on the desk a year beyond the margin. The next time Brenden made a tour of the wire room, Bryan would be shifted to a quiet spot.

Hammill reached into the copy boxes in front of him, the three-tiered boxes where he kept copies of messages, stories sent and received, and stories which had not been transmitted. He found items for the A wire, items he had delayed during the heavy hours, and he tossed them to Bryan, who glowered. He had stopped getting drunk with Bryan, and Bryan hadn't forgiven him.

"I got a night lead on Churchill due from Washington," Bryan said. "I haven't got room for this fodder."

"Think the Churchill lead will be hot?"

"It'll be hotter than this stuff," Bryan said.

"Hold the fodder then. Let me see the Churchill lead when you get it."

He remembered Bryan saying to him, on the final night when they had been drunk together: "Why the hell do you chase widows, Jimmy? Lila and Derry, both widows. Both choice pieces, but both widows." He'd answered: "Lila's not a widow." Bryan had laughed. "You think she still counts on Steve? Steve will never come home any more, not to her. He's left her to you, with his blessing." He had smacked Bryan from a bar stool and then he had lifted Bryan to the stool and he had left the bar.

He thumbed stories from the local bureau, thrust the carbon-smeared pages on the black spike at his elbow, and tossed his pencil in the air. He wanted to take a phone and surprise Derry, he wanted to urge her to call Lila. She would have to say the things to Lila he was afraid to say.

"Here comes Churchill," Bryan said.

"Throw him over," Hammill said. What would Derry be doing now? She believed she had all the time in the world, she thought every minute could be stretched and filled with pleasure, and one minute was as good as another. She might be lounging on the red couch in the living room, swinging her round legs and listening to music now, the slow swirling music she liked, or she might be sitting in the shaded bedroom, peering into the narrow private street at the alley cats stalking under the iron Village lamps.

Bryan tore the sheet of flimsy from the teletype and flipped it toward him.

"It's medium hot," Bryan said.

Hammill read the first paragraphs and he remembered the implacable face of the old man in London and he remembered that Churchill would run any risk in the cause for which Churchill fought. He was afraid then. Derry would die and he would die in this town, in two or three years. In four or five years, at the extreme limit. If they were lucky, they would be in the same room, in their own street, in their bed.

The memory came to him of the Englishman standing in a smashed London street in the worst summer of the war, the summer of 1944 when the V-bombs blazed over London. That was the worst summer because the signs of coming victory were everywhere and people hated the chance of death just before victory; the last ones killed were the most deeply mourned. In the eyes of the watchers in the wrecked street, he saw the shuddering sorrow. Churchill had halted near a ruined house, and the massive head had drooped for a moment. Yet when the head tilted, the wide face of Churchill was a face of defiance, the face of a fighter who could go on fighting forever.

NIGHT LEAD CHURCHILL-INTERPRETIVE

WASHINGTON, MARCH 7 (CONSOLIDATED PRESS) – THE HARDENING U.S. POLICY TOWARD RUSSIA TONIGHT INDICATED THAT PRESIDENT TRUMAN APPROVED WINSTON CHURCHILL'S "IRON CURTAIN" SPEECH TWO DAYS AGO IN FULTON, MO., WHICH CALLED FOR A VIRTUAL ANGLO-AMERICAN ALLIANCE TO BLOCK SOVIET EXPANSION.

IN A STERN NOTE TO MOSCOW MADE PUBLIC TODAY BY SECRETARY OF STATE BYRNES, THE U.S. ASKED RUSSIA TO FULFILL THE TERMS OF THE ANGLO-SOVIET-IRANIAN TREATY OF 1942 AND THE 1943 DECLARATION OF TEHERAN, BY PULLING ALL RED TROOPS OUT OF THE LITTLE COUNTRY OF IRAN.

CHURCHILL'S SPEECH, THE BYRNES NOTE ON IRAN, AND THE ANNOUNCEMENT THAT THE 45,000-TON BATTLESHIP "MISSOURI" WOULD BE SENT TO TURKEY, REPORTEDLY THREATENED BY RUSSIA, HAVE CREATED AN ATMOSPHERE OF TENSION.

THE CHANCES OF WAR THIS SPRING ARE REGARDED BUST IT BULLETIN COMING

BUST IT BUST IT BUST IT BULLETIN COMING

TLR 801 PM EST

"Something sighted," Hammill said. He got to his feet. "Get the key channels open and keep them open. This bulletin may be hot."

"It won't be," Bryan said. "Bet you a buck it won't be. Trying to scare Uncle Joe, that's all. He's a rugged boy, he won't be scared."

"Maybe not," Hammill said. "Then what?"

"We'll make a deal."

He stared at Bryan. If he had never left New York, he might have talked like that. In another year he might be another Bryan, he might be as wise and empty as Bryan. If he had another year, if anybody had another year. Hell, if people could never learn anything except bombing and burning, it might be better if they didn't have another year.

"You've got it figured," he said to Bryan.

What did he have against making a deal, why was he so angry?

There had to be a deal eventually, why did he kick about Bryan's smug smile? Why not make the deal before the war broke, and save these streets and these buildings and give the people in the plaza a chance to keep on carrying their heads on their shoulders? He knew why he was angry. He was angry because he was frightened that he might be like Bryan. He wouldn't be like that if Derry kept demanding more and more from him, if Derry kept him free of the old grooves, the easy lines he had followed.

"Oh, there'll be fireworks," Bryan said with the flickering smile, the rapid smile of the insider.

"Plenty of fireworks," Hammill nodded. "Have you ever heard a rocket bomb, brother? Have you ever seen one?"

"Sure. I saw plenty of them in the newsreels. They make some racket, and they've got red-hot tails."

They do more than that, Hammill thought. If that was all they did, anybody could stand that. Men around him sliced stories from the East wire, the West wire, the South and the State wires, the Metropolitan, the B and the C wires, and boiled the stories down for relay to other bureaus, or boosted an item from the C to the B, or shoved night leads on the B to Chicago for the Middle West.

He stood there, waiting in silence. He didn't know why he had risen to his feet with the Churchill copy in his hands, why he didn't sit in his chair. The teletype machine beside Bryan began to clatter.

"Bet it won't be hot," Bryan said. "Bet a buck."

"I'll take a dollar of your money."

He forced himself to settle in the swivel chair. Bryan would probably win the bet. It was too soon for that kind of trouble. Maybe the old man's speeches would clear the poisoned air. Nothing could happen this year. Nothing could happen next year, or the year after. The armies had been sent home, the people weren't ready.

Suddenly he had an urge to leave the desk, to duck across the street below the building and have a double Martini at Tony's. Any night at Tony's he could see safe people smiling and talking at a bar, people who had never heard a bomb falling in their lives. Except in the newsreels.

"Where's Radford?" he said. "Churchill or no Churchill, I've got to eat."

Radford usually dawdled over dinner and had to be dragged in from Tony's or Laverty's by a copy boy. Hammill swiveled around, searching for the big man, looking for the firm solid face of Radford. Radford was tall, and thick in the arms and legs, built for brawling and drinking, but Radford didn't get into bar fights, Radford shrugged trouble away and went home nearly sober.

"The wonder boy's on his third piece of pie," Bryan said.

Hammill thrust a hand in one pocket, scraped the four dollars he had there. He might ask Derry to meet him. He could feel hopeful under her glance, he could take her hands and make her believe that he hadn't tapped his reserves, he hadn't wavered.

He heard a jangle of bells, and Bryan said in a raw voice: "Bulletin from Washington, Jimmy, and I owe you a buck."

"Here we go again," the fat teletype operator said, leaning against a pillar.

"Give it." Hammill put an arm over the barrier of the desks and pulled the torn bulletin from Bryan's fingers.

> BULLETIN
> WASHINGTON, MARCH 7 (CONSOLIDATED PRESS) –
> THE UNITED STATES WILL SEEK DRASTIC ACTION BY
> THE UNITED NATIONS TO EXPEL SOVIET TROOPS FROM
> NOTHERN IRAN IF THAT BECOMES NECESSARY, A HIGH
> GOVERNMENT OFFICIAL REVEALED TONIGHT.
> TLR 802 PM EST

He smoothed the scrap of flimsy paper. It didn't rock him. This wasn't the signal for the armies to leave home. He had seen the shuffling of these cards in other games. He had been at the League, and he knew the United Nations had no more weight than the League. How many tanks and how many planes did the UN have? Where were the international generals, and the world Army?

Drastic action. There wouldn't be any drastic action. He had been in Geneva when Mussolini had sent the Italian divisions through the Suez Canal to massacre the Ethiopians, and he had heard the diplomats scream, he had seen them wave their arms in overwhelming gestures. But they took no action until the action was too late. And the UN had less power than the late lamented League.

"I was here Pearl Harbor day," the fat teletype operator said in a wounded voice that made the men at the other desk swing their heads in brief surprise. "I opened the channel to Washington and the flash came right at me, WHITE HOUSE SAYS JAPS BOMB HAWAII. I had a hell of a hangover. I got the flash and the bulletin on the A, then I went in the washroom and tossed my lunch."

Bryan slapped both hands on the steel desk. "Shut up and take it easy. There's more coming."

"This isn't another Pearl Harbor," Hammill said. "It won't come to anything."

"Okay," the operator said. "Okay. You guys know everything."

The teletype machine throbbed, the metal keys reached forward, the warning bells rang.

> BULLETIN MATTER – XXX REVEALED TONIGHT
> THE OFFICIAL, WHOSE NAME COULD NOT BE DISCLOSED, DECLARED THAT IRAN WOULD TAKE THE CASE TO THE UN SECURITY COUNCIL ON THE GROUND THAT THE CONTINUED PRESENCE OF SOVIET TROOPS CONSTITUTED A THREAT TO THE SMALL NATION'S INDEPENDENCE AND FULL SOVEREGNTY.
> IN THE 1943 DECLARATION OF TEHERAN, SIGNED BY THE UNITED STATES, BRITAIN AND RUSSIA, THE

THREE GREAT ALLIED POWERS PLEDGED THEMSELVES TO GUARANTEE AND RESPECT THE EXISTENCE OF IRAN AS AN INDEPENDENT AND SOVEREIGN NATION. THE U.S. WOULD BACK IRAN IN THE CONTENTION THAT IF RUSSIAN TROOPS REMAIN IN THE COUNTRY THE U.S.S.R. IS GUILTY OF VIOLATING THIS DECLARATION.

(MORE COMING – CHANNELS CLEAR)

TLR 804 PM EST

Hammill lifted a telephone. "Somebody'll have to go back in the short-wave room and start listening to those Moscow broadcasts, to help out the regular boys there. This ought to draw some sparks from the Kremlin."

"The boys in our Moscow bureau will get the stuff," Bryan said.

"Maybe they will, maybe they won't. They've got censors on their necks."

"It won't be long," the teletype operator muttered. "We're on our way."

"Relax," Hammill said, turning to him.

Bryan asked: "Figure Byrnes is trying a bluff?"

"You tell me. You weren't worried a while ago. You had it figured."

"I don't see how those Russians can act tough when they haven't got anything except a mob of farmers with uniforms and rifles," Bryan said, picking up a message from a side wire. "Cleveland is thrilled because our Iranian bulletin was four minutes ahead of World Press, six minutes ahead of Globe."

"They're always happy in Cleveland," Hammill said, shaking the phone. "Where the hell is that local bureau desk man?" The Cleveland message tickled him. He thought of Cleveland on the big lake, and he thought of the lake at Geneva, the tailored men at the League, who stood and argued while Mussolini's ships went through the canal loaded with troops.

The local bureau at last responded. The night desk man there agreed to send a reliable reporter into the short-wave room for emergency duty. The teletypes began to hammer again, and another strip of paper fell before Hammill.

WASHINGTON – IRANINAN CRISIS – FIRST ADD XXX THIS DECLARATION

THE DISCLOSURE FOLLOWED PUBLICATION TODAY BY THE STATE DEPARTMENT OF A STERN NOTE TO MOSCOW, AND THE FEELING OF CRISIS HAS MOUNTED HERE IN RECENT HOURS.

THE AMERICAN NOTE ASSERTED THAT UNDER THE 1942 ANGLO-SOVIET-IRANIAN PACT THE RUSSIAN GOVERNMENT HAD A SOLEMN OBLIGATION TO WITHDRAW ALL MILITARY FORCES SIX MONTHS AFTER THE END OF WORLD WAR II. THE SIX MONTHS EXPIRED MARCH 2, 1946,

JUST FIVE DAYS AGO. BRITISH TROOPS HAVE WITHDRAWN UNDER THE TREATY, BUT RUSSIAN FORCES REMAIN.

(MORE COMING)

TLR 806 PM EST

"It's tapering off," Hammill said. "I'm going to grab some dinner. I can't wait for Radford."

He rolled down his shirt sleeves, took his baggy coat from the back of his chair and shrugged into it. He couldn't ask Derry to meet him at Tony's, he didn't have the money to buy her the right number of drinks. He looked through the broad window at the bare garden in the plaza.

"Everything's in shape," he said. "Watch the phones until Radford arrives, Dan."

"You want to see the end of this Iranian stuff?" Bryan coughed.

"We won't see the end of it for a long time," Hammill said. "You juggle it for a while. I'm hungry and I'm thirsty."

He was really thirsty but he wasn't really hungry. He was seldom hungry for food, he was losing weight and he was glad of it, he had enough weight to carry around. He buttoned his coat and turned, and there came Radford, huge and young and guilty-looking under the wire room glare. He could see the awareness of crime mingling with rebellion in the wary eyes, the tight face, the long jaws.

"Anything breaking?" Radford asked.

"Strawstack of messages here," Hammill answered. "Where've you been?" He swung at Radford, and Radford dodged like a boxer. "Columbus is worried about a story on Miss Columbus of 1946, who brought greetings from Columbus to the Mayor of New York at the City Hall this morning. The boys at the Hall skipped it. The local bureau is checking. Schenectady wants to know about a General Electric conference held here today --"

He took a breath and he glanced at the shining emblem in the lapel of Radford's thick tweed coat, the miniature bronze eagle caught within a circle, and he added: "And maybe we've got a war cooking."

That was rough, that was pretty rough on Radford. But the wearing of the emblem irritated him and he couldn't help it. He had been bombed, he had been hit, he had scars on his arms and his hands and all through him, and he didn't have the emblem to wear because he hadn't been on the military payroll. He'd heard more guns than most of the men who wore the button, he had a right to be sore, to take a swing at somebody. Yet he was sorry when he had spoken, when he saw the havoc in Radford's face.

"A war?" Radford said. "You've been putting rum in those 'Cokes' you and Dan Bryan drink all night."

"Go through those Washington bulletins and see what you think, brother."

Radford glanced at the bulletins on the desk, and sat heavily in the vacant chair. Hammill looked at his hands.

"This time we'll stop it," Radford said. "By God, we'll stop it. There are plenty of guys like me, and we'll stop it."

"Sure," Hammill said. "March in some peace parades. Get out and make some speeches. It's fun. I tried it, fifteen years ago. You might as well try it. You might have luck."

Radford bent over the desk. "I've got luck, or I wouldn't be here. I had five years in the Navy, and I had to have luck to get home. You know that."

"Well, you'll need it," Hammill said. "You'll need it. I'd like to give you some of my luck. I've had plenty, too. I'm one war ahead of you." He saw the damage he had done and yet he had to keep on, he didn't know why. He knew Radford thought of him as one of the tough and futile men, one of the cynics and scoffers of their trade.

"Give the UN people a chance." Radford said. "Maybe they'll do better than the League. They've got more of us behind them."

Hammill nodded. "Major Bryan has it analyzed. He'll tell you what we have to do. If anybody wants me, I'll be at Tony's."

Hammill had to pivot around to keep himself from placing a hand on Radford's shoulder, to stop himself from gabbling: "It won't come to anything, Tom. I've been through a couple of wars and I know how they start." How did he know it wouldn't be different this time? He couldn't make a sure promise. He could throw words at Bryan, but not at Radford.

He went through the wire room, entered the lavatory and washed his smudged hands, spilled some water on his face, massaged his forehead with his fingers to dull the ache there, used a paper towel, and hurried to the row of elevators in the corridor. He punched a button on the corridor wall.

He had survived Ben Martin, the best man he had known in his life. He had survived Dick Ganey, who might have been a great man. He had survived all of his friends except Steve Parelli, and he didn't know why. If he couldn't find the reason for it, he couldn't blame Radford for considering him a tough rooster too mean to die.

The elevator came. As he rode to the lobby, Hammill knew how much he missed Ben and Steve. The three of them had gone through misery and none of them had cried or caved, they had never admitted that they had seen enough. Ben would never be around again, and Steve was dying in China. The Steve he'd known had begun to die in those crazy letters, the letter he had burned. He couldn't go down a street again in his life with Ben on his left and Steve on his right. He could never stand between them anymore; he couldn't lean on them and let them lean on him.

But Steve might be back, Steve might change again to the Steve he'd known. He hated to think of the night Bryan had bet fifty dollars that Steve wouldn't come back. Bryan thought a bet could decide anything. "Steve told me he couldn't live with people who had the whole damned world begging at their doors and went around scared of their shadows," Bryan had said. "He told me he thought New York had a terrible smell, he thought the country had a terrible smell. He told me the smell in China was better. He was wilder than ever. I was in China once, and no country could smell any worse." Hammill hadn't seen a story from Chungking for a dozen nights, and the letters had ended three weeks ago.

The elevator door opened.

"Kind of foggy in the street," the elevator man said.

"They ought to build a tunnel to Tony's for nights like this," Hammill said.

"Lot of people would go to sleep in that tunnel."

Hammill left the elevator and went to the side door of the building. Beyond the revolving door, the street gleamed with mist and the neon signs of taverns were pink and yellow blurs in the night. Taxi horns honked and policemen on horses blew silver whistles. The tide of taxis and cars rumbled between the curbs, carrying the evening crowd toward Broadway and the theaters.

Blocked by traffic, he watched the men leaning toward the women in the cab seats, he saw the flaring of matches and cigarettes, and he caught the comfortable purring voices of the women. There were the poised and handsome people, the ruling people in the ruling city of the world, the smart and secure people from the tall apartments and the decorated houses in the rich and careless city. The voices of the women drew him. He knew them, the New York girls, the ones who liked to dance and drink and secretly squeeze their thighs together, the girls who could kiss desperately and bite hard and laugh.

Then he heard the engines of a plane in the mist, a plane flying in the cold high darkness above the choked street, and he flattened against the building, shaken by a trembling he couldn't control. This was New York, this wasn't London. He knew where he stood and the pavement was solid beneath him. This was a quiet night in March between wars and there was still a truce, the truce had not been abandoned.

Still he couldn't keep himself from trembling. He had been bombed too often, he had seen too many wars. He remembered the way the ground shook under rockets that couldn't be seen or heard until the explosions came, and he was afraid the luck of the people in the taxis and in the packed streets couldn't last. Luck didn't run forever, in any country, in any city.

He put his hands in his pockets, and tried to step from the shelter of the building and his legs wouldn't swing along. With a gradual movement, knowing he had to do it or admit that he had been broken, he tilted his head to look toward the plane off there in the fog above the city. It was a passenger plane bound for La Guardia Field, it couldn't be anything else.

LITTLE GUY WHO SHOOK THE WORLD:

HARRY S. TRUMAN

BY FRANK K. KELLY

FRANK KELLY was a reporter on the Kansas City Star *before coming to the Associated Press in New York. Author of a novel on newspaper life, he has also been a Nieman Fellow at Harvard and taught journalism at Boston University. In 1948 he was Assistant Director of the Research Division of the Democratic National Committee.*

In a decisive hour of history, while the world swings from crisis to challenge, a plain president from heart of the United States stands at the head of the dominant nation on earth. He holds the enormous powers of the Presidency in his vigorous hands, and he smiles upon the whole world with a bright look of supreme confidence.

Throughout the earth, the friendly face of the president is now a familiar image. His firm chin, his determined mouth, his heavy glasses which make him seem so mild and humble, are as well known to millions of people in many countries as the features of their neighbors. His countenance is open, his glance is very direct, his brisk appearance declares that here comes a man who is exactly what he seems to be.

Harry Truman is regarded by his fellow Americans as a "little guy," a man easy to measure and easy to describe. He is like the fellow next door, the John Q. Public who keeps the democratic way of life full of sparkle and zest. He is called Mr. America—the genial, jaunty, generous citizen who has the sturdy qualities every American hopes to have. He is admired and respected as the Chief Executive of the United States, and he is cordially greeted as "Harry" by truck drivers and society matrons.

Yet there is a mystery about this man from Missouri, the citizen from the town called Independence, who races through his demanding days and nights while humanity stumbles forward into the glaring dangers of the atomic age. It is the astonishing mystery of a man who is always what he seems to be, and often more than he seems.

"There must be at least thirteen men named Truman," one of his associates said, watching him stride along in the morning sun toward the White House. "It would take more than a dozen men to do the things he does."

Where does he get his limitless endurance, the stamina which few men can match? How can he take blow after blow from his political enemies and bounce back, triumphant in the last round of so many struggles? Where does he get the stubborn daring that staggers politicians and delights people in his own country and the world? Where did he get the wisdom which guided him in his big decisions, which have changed the course of history?

Although he knows he has made a good record as president, he is not fully aware of his own stature. After his victory in the election of 1948, he was portrayed by his critics as a cocky and arrogant man. But not long after his re-election, he declared publicly that there were a million Americans who could handle his job as well as he did.

There are many Americans who applaud him when he makes such statements, who praise him for his modesty and his sense of proportion, and have no conception of the real miracle of Truman.

No one has really explained the mystery of this president, who rises and declines rapidly in apparent prestige yet never loses the warm affection of his fellow citizens, the president who admits his mistakes yet has still managed to be right in most of the important actions he has taken in the field of foreign policy.

It is very doubtful whether there are a million men in America or the world who could equal Truman in his achievement as president. It is very doubtful whether any man alive could equal him as a symbol of successful democracy.

"He is a living proof that it's a bad mistake to underrate the plain people of a free country," a foreign correspondent said, after attending a press conference at the White House. "He is a man of quick wit, and he knows where he is going." The simple facts of the president's background do not explain his achievement as a world leader. He has stunned the skeptics at every stage in his career. His inner growth in knowledge has gone on steadily and quietly through the crowded years of his active existence. He has drawn upon the deep reserves of strength which many men possess but few are able to release.

Blithe and beaming, Harry Truman walks in the constant glare of the Presidency, and he grows taller as he moves. The sources of his growth, the silent stretching of a human being under the pounding pressures of his time, are hidden from his friends and his foes.

Most men cease to grow when they are forty or fifty years old. Their resistance to change becomes greater than their desire to take in what is new. Truman has continued to develop, as a man and as a leader, and he shows no sign of stopping. "I've had to work so hard all my life that I've kept out of mischief," the president told the minister at his church, when the clergyman congratulated him on his sixty-fifth birthday anniversary.

He was born in 1884, into a world that appeared to have permanent landmarks and a stable structure, the world of Queen Victoria and Grover Cleveland, the world held together by the British Navy and the gold standard. He worked on a farm, fought in World War I, ran a haberdashery store in Kansas City, served as a county judge and as a United States senator. He was just folks, a little guy who had made good. Then he was catapulted into the White House. He became in 1945 the man who shook the world into a new age, an age of infinite promise and infinite danger. He made the decision to use the atomic bomb, and in so doing he shook the world.

Since that April afternoon in 1945, when death claimed the tired body of Franklin D. Roosevelt in the cottage in Georgia, he has carried on his shoulders the huge weight of responsibility for the fundamental decisions the president must make.

No man in history stepped into the executive office under harder circumstances. Roosevelt had been the president for a whole generation of Americans, the father in the White House, the laughing leader who could conquer war and disaster, the man in the wheel chair who had beaten illness and fear. Roosevelt had flouted so many precedents that people had begun to believe F.D.R. could flout the precedent of death.

Millions of families felt as though a father had left them forever. Sailors wept on ships at sea, and soldiers fighting in Europe and the Pacific spoke of Roosevelt as a casualty of war. Colored people walked the streets of Washington, crying and staring at the sky in search of him, repeating his name. Even the enemies of Roosevelt acknowledged his magic, and could not believe that F.D.R. was dead.

It was a lonely hour for Harry Truman. He took the oath as Chief Executive in the cabinet room of the White House, surrounded by the mournful faces of the men who had looked to Roosevelt as their leader. He could not tear his glance from the clock above the mantel, and he has never forgotten the moment when his voice ended the recital of the oath and he knew that the time of testing had arrived for him.

He was uprooted from the pleasant, convivial, relaxed life of the vice president and thrown straight into the tidal wave of the war then roaring toward a climax. The momentum of world events swept him along successfully in his first months as president. He pledged himself to follow the policies of Roosevelt, and his earnest, folksy voice on the radio reassured the people that Roosevelt had left an heir.

Gradually, a picture formed in the minds of millions of Americans. Here was a plain citizen from the breezy state of Missouri, a blunt American from the Midwest who had been summoned to the White House to carry out the wishes of the departed leader. Here was a modest, mild man, very determined to do his best and well aware of his limitations.

"He's a swell guy and he's in a tough spot," the people said. "He takes advice. He doesn't claim to be another Roosevelt. He deserves a helping hand."

It was a picture which had elements of truth, and yet it became so fixed in the public mind that it obscured the growth of Harry Truman as the new leader of the United States. Truman did not follow the pattern of Roosevelt. Truman became a leader of a different type who gained his goals by a direct approach, who did not use the complex techniques of Roosevelt.

Truman gave the first sign of his development in the White House a few weeks after he took his oath. The conference to create the United Nations, which began in San Francisco on April 25, 1945, bogged down in a disagreement with the Soviet representatives. Truman sent Harry Hopkins to Moscow to find a satisfactory compromise, and Hopkins came to terms with Stalin.

So the United Nations got under way with a minimum of delay, thanks to Truman. The man from Missouri was a fervent believer in the principle of a world organization to maintain lasting peace. As a member of the United States Senate before his nomination for the Vice Presidency, he had been a strong advocate of international cooperation in every field.

One of his associates declares that two of the major influences upon the president seem to be his devotion to the ideals of Woodrow Wilson and his religious convictions as an adherent of the Baptist faith. Wilson made him an internationalist, and the prophetic element in his religion convinced him that there were appointed times for men and nations to fulfill their missions upon the earth.

"He often talks about the tragedy of the League of Nations," this friend said. "He feels that in 1919 and 1920 we had a great responsibility to lead the world into an era of peace. We wouldn't accept it—then. Our failure contributed to the downfall of the League and the eventual outbreak of another war. With the United Nations, we got a second chance to build a solid peace."

His experiences as a front-line fighter in France, as a crusader who enlisted under the banner of Woodrow Wilson to make the world safe for democracy, released the inner power of his strong nature. As an officer, he discovered he could lead men under fire and hold their loyalty, because he had the courage and the endurance he needed in the hours of danger.

Before President Wilson called Americans into World War I in 1917, Harry Truman had spent nine years on his family farm near Independence. He plowed a straight furrow on the broad acres along the western edge of the state that lies close to the center of America. He listened to his mother, a sturdy and sensible woman whose life went back to the pioneer years in the 1850's, and he learned the value of firm honesty. He did his work capably and was well liked, but he was not considered as a man marked for any special role in the records of his country.

As an American soldier overseas, Truman was lifted from the provincialism of the Midwest. He was eager for experience, had a warm sympathy for people of every kind, and began to understand the problems faced by the countries of Europe for centuries. He had been a student of history in his youth, and he fitted his knowledge into the background of history.

When he came home to America from that war, Truman followed the debates in the Senate over the fate of the League with intense interest. He was one of the millions of Wilsonian Democrats who supported the League, and he knew that the association of nations could not thrive without American participation.

After he entered politics and himself became a member of the Senate, he widened his study of international affairs. In 1938, when it became evident that the League was collapsing after its failure to halt the aggression of Italy in Ethiopia and Japan in Manchuria, Truman assigned a member of his staff to prepare a full report on what had happened.

"He told me to go beyond the League," this man recalls. "He wanted a summary of all the attempts that had been made to create federations of nations, all the ideas and plans put forward by men who had dreamed of world organizations."

So Truman was better equipped to take over the Presidency in the tremendous year of 1945 than many of his fellow Americans realized. He knew that the United States must not shrink from its responsibilities of leadership in the United Nations. He knew that he must secure the advice and consent of the Senate at every stage. He acted with the passionate sincerity of a religious man who felt certain that his country had been given a rare blessing—a second opportunity to join other nations in establishing a permanent peace.

The United Nations started in a blaze of hope. The European phase of World War II came swiftly to an end. The popularity of Harry Truman rose to unparalleled heights. He had not aroused the enmity of any large group in his own country, and he had touched the right chords in foreign policy.

He went to Potsdam in July of 1945 as the man who represented the resourceful, optimistic, benign American people. He was welcomed with flowers and cheers in Belgium, storms of oratory and tears of genuine gratitude. He did not receive the frenzied adulation given to Woodrow Wilson in 1919, because Europeans were more exhausted and fearful than they had been in that year, and Harry Truman was not the remote Olympian figure Wilson had been.

At Potsdam, he gained the respect of two fiercely conflicting leaders, Josef Stalin and Winston Churchill. He sat between them during the long arguments over the disposal of defeated Germany. When Clement Attlee replaced Churchill after a British election, Truman got along successfully with the new Prime Minister.

In his attempts to find a middle ground between the position taken by Churchill and the position of Stalin, Truman made some concessions at Potsdam. But those were the days when the heads of the Allied Governments still met in mutual cordiality, and adjustments were the order of the day. There was confidence in all camps that there would be a continuous meeting of minds in the postwar years, that the Russians as well as the other Allies had committed themselves to a course of compromise and amicable adjustments.

When Truman rode through the devastated cities of Germany, he saw what modern war had done to a great nation. He remembered the fire power of artillery in World War I, and he recognized the menacing development of the destructive forces available to industrial countries. He surveyed the wreckage of Berlin, walked through the rubble of Hitler's Reichchancellery, turned to an aide and said: "This is what happens when a man overreaches himself."

While the Potsdam conference was in progress, Secretary of War Stimson arrived from America and informed the president that the explosion of an atomic bomb in New Mexico had given the United States a weapon which would rock the world. Grave and solemn, Truman called in his close associates.

"You'd better sit down," the president said, indicating some chairs. "I've got to tell you a terrible secret."

No president before Truman had confronted the decision he had to make, there in the ruins of Germany. He was isolated then upon the pinnacle of presidential power. He could not share his accountability for the consequences, could not divide it with any friend, any adviser or associate. He knew that the American Constitution named him as the man who had to choose, and all mankind would demand reasons for his choice.

He did not make the decision lightly. Sometimes he had been condemned by his enemies as a man who spoke too quickly, acted with a rush, shot from the hip. He came from the wide center of the United States, where people believed in being forthright. His conscience pressed him to drive through to the heart of the matter. He had to decide whether to use this awesome weapon upon the populated cities to bring the people of Japan to their knees, or hold it in abeyance whiled Allied divisions fought their way into the Japanese islands in an invasion which might cost a million lives. He could not risk dropping one of the few bombs available into a barren place, where its effectiveness would not be burned home to the Japanese.

"Truman handled it the way he handles all his problems," a man who was there recalls. "He gathered the evidence, he listened to the experts, and he thought about it in terms of people. Every day the war lasted, thousands of good men were dying, families were being wrecked, homes were being blasted. Stimson and the military chiefs estimated we might lose half a million men if we landed in the Japanese islands, and the Japs would lose half a million or more. Nobody could tell how long the fighting might continue."

With hard honesty, Truman faced the truth about total war. Women and children were in it, civilians as well as men in uniform. The evidence indicated that the atomic bomb might shock the Japanese government into surrender and stop the carnage. He made his choice. Two cities with the greatest concentration of war industries to Japan were picked as the targets: Hiroshima and Nagasaki. But before the bombs were hurled upon them, the Japanese were given a drastic warning by the governments of the United States, Great Britain and China, in a declaration as threatening as the diplomats could devise without revealing the existence of the new weapon. Truman offered them a last opportunity to get out of the war.

After he had determined what seemed to him the correct course, the president's conscience was clear. In the years since then, he has not suffered from any pangs of self-condemnation. The blinding flashes of the bombs brought Japanese pleas for peace, and finished the slaughter in the Pacific. That proved to him the wisdom of his decision. "Now I believe we are in a position where we will never have to make that decision again," the president tells his friends. "But if it has to be made for the welfare of the United States, and the democracies of the world are at stake, I wouldn't hesitate to make it again." He feels that the obliterating force of atomic energy has been emphasized too much. From the beginning he has regarded it as a God-given instrument which would bring about gigantic strides in medicine, industry and agriculture, and would eventually transform the world for the benefit of all nations.

In 1945, after the collapse of Japan, the president and those around him felt sure that there were no large obstacles in the path toward peace. Secretary of State James F. Byrnes was positive that the difficulties with the Russians could be smoothed over, by a policy of peace.

Ten million Americans were discharged from the armed services in the months after the Japanese surrender. Lend-lease was terminated. Truman and his advisers turned their attention to domestic problems, to the maintenance of full production and full employment in America.

The main responsibility for restoration of war-devastated areas was turned over to the United Nations Relief and Rehabilitation Administration, known as UNRRA. This organization drew heavily upon American supplies, and the United States continued to send a steady stream of goods to stricken countries; but the Truman government concentrated on the vast task of shifting the American economy from the needs of war to the needs of peace.

Then in March 1946, only a few months after the guns had become silent in the Pacific, a sudden international crisis occurred. Soviet Russia refused to withdraw troops from the northern provinces of Iran, occupied under an Allied agreement of 1942. The agreement called for the removal of all Allied troops six months after the conclusion of hostilities in World War II. British and American units pulled out, but the Russians stayed.

Millions of people all over the world saw the specter of a third world conflict rising from the Middle East. The Iranian crisis reached its climax shortly after Winston Churchill declared in a speech at Fulton, Missouri, in the presence of President Truman, that the Soviets were ruthlessly seeking domination of the earth.

But the Soviet Union backed away, withdrawing its divisions from Iran, and the nations felt a returning surge of confidence in the establishment of a settled peace. Secretary of State Byrnes altered his policy after a consultation with Truman, changing it from faith in long patience to faith in patience plus firm determination.

Through the clouded year of 1948, the president clung to his conviction that the Soviet leaders did not really intend to divide the world and disrupt the progress of the United Nations. He permitted Henry A. Wallace, then Secretary of Commerce, to make a public address which explained away the obstructive tactics of the Soviets. This apologia conflicted with the views of Secretary Byrnes, who asked the president to clarify his stand.

Reluctantly, the president came to the conclusion that the Soviets would not cooperate in strengthening the United Nations and working for world recovery. He dropped Wallace from his cabinet. He began to search for methods of containing the Soviet drive for world control.

"The decision to launch the Truman Doctrine in 1947 was the turning point," one of his friends explained. "The British notified him that they couldn't carry the load of keeping Greece from going Communist. Greek rebels, armed and aided by the Communist governments in Albania, Bulgaria and Yugoslavia, threatened to turn Greece into a Soviet state."

Truman talked it over with General George C. Marshall, who had succeeded Byrnes as Secretary of State. Marshall pointed out that Communist seizure of Greece would give the Soviets a springboard for domination of the whole Mediterranean area, and would outflank Turkey. At some point, the march of Communism had to be deflected or blocked.

The president delivered his decision at a joint session of both houses of the Congress. He was very serious, his face was lined and drawn, and his infectious grin had vanished.

There were two ways of life contending for the allegiance of men, he said. One was based upon the democratic rule of a majority, with free elections, independent courts, and guaranteed rights for individuals. The other was based upon the dictatorial rule of a minority, with rigged elections, controlled courts, and all individuals dependent upon the State. He promised that the people of America would go to the aid of free people who were threatened by aggression. Greece, torn by civil war, and Turkey, under severe pressure from a Russian government seeking the

Dardanelles, were immediately threatened. So he called for assistance to those countries.

His proposal was bitterly attacked by Wallace and some members of Congress, as a program which would drag the United States into another war. But Truman called it "an investment in world freedom and world peace." He insisted that if the United States faltered in its leadership "we may endanger the peace of the world—and we shall surely endanger the welfare of this nation."

The newspapers gave his program the name of the Truman Doctrine. He did not use that title when he enunciated it, and he never refers to it by any designation except as "the plan to help Greece and Turkey." His "doctrine" is seldom mentioned, and seems to have receded into distant history, and yet it was the forerunner of the European Recovery Program, the North Atlantic Treaty, and "the bold new program" to give American technical knowledge to underdeveloped countries, which the president brought forth when he began his second term.

Development of the "doctrine" astonished the experts in the State Department. These men drew up a memorandum for the president, outlining the conditions in the Mediterranean which made action seem urgent. After discussing this memorandum with Marshall and his advisers, Truman went far beyond the relatively simple issue of aid to two small countries and laid down an unprecedented principle of American foreign policy.

The European Recovery Program of economic cooperation, called the Marshall Plan, was a logical extension of the Truman Doctrine. No one realized more clearly than the president the necessity for a concerted effort by the European nations to speed their own recovery and alleviate the misery that was stirring discontent among the people.

Secretary Marshall gave his invitation to the countries of Europe in June of 1947 to get together on a program for lifting the living standards of the whole continent, after discussing it with the president. The plan captured the imagination of the American people and the non-Soviet world; and the leaders of both major parties, awake to the peril of the rising Communist tide in France and Italy, pushed it through Congress.

"Some day the historians will paint the picture of what vision and imagination this program required," a friend of the president said, not long ago. "Then the part Truman played in it will be fully understood."

Imposition of a blockade around Berlin by the Russians in the spring of 1948 led to the president to take another step. He stood firm in a situation full of danger, and approved the daring idea of flying supplies into the beleaguered Western sectors of the German capital. "It was the second hardest decision I've had to make," Truman told a friend. "Some of the military experts felt it involved the risk of immediate war. Even if that risk existed, I knew there was only one decision that could be right."

There were gloomy prophets in 1948, who believed that the air lift was a gamble which might pull the United States into a war which would mean the end of civilization. There had also been gloomy prophets in 1947, who had predicted that the Truman Doctrine spelled disaster and the European Recovery Program could not possibly succeed.

But in 1949, Allied trains again started moving into Berlin. The blockade had been removed, the deep faith of Harry Truman in the strength of free nations had been justified again, and the world looked brighter.

"The world is going to be all right," the president assures his visitors in his executive office. He leads the callers over to the globe given him by General Eisenhower at Potsdam in 1945, and his energetic fingers drum rapidly on the painted sphere.

"We are going through the gateway into a wonderful age," he says, looking back at four years of struggle and progress. "I'd like to be a young man again."

And he nods his head, beaming like a little guy who holds a big secret.

THE PRESS LOOKS AT THE PRESS, IN THE FIELD OF FOREIGN NEWS

By Frank K. Kelly

What does Britain look like—reflected in the huge mirror of a large group of American newspapers? What does the United States look like—reflected in the British press, the German press, the Italian press?

What does India look like in the British papers, and Britain in the press of India? What kind of news flows back and forth between India and the western world?

As part of the most comprehensive study of world news in the history of journalism, the International Press Institute is preparing world-pictures of ten countries as they appear in the flow of the news—and asking editors in those nations to comment on the accuracy and quality of the pictures.

An organization of editors with members in 34 countries, the IPI is sponsoring a study of the press, and by the press. The study, financed by a special Ford Foundation grant, examines for the first time the nature and the extent of the news flow, and asks working members of the profession to say what the implications of that examination may be. Editors, news agency executives, and foreign correspondents have been enlisted in a trans-oceanic exchange of ideas and information, with the IPI serving as a channel of communication.

The press has been poked and prodded by many types of researchers in the past. People of all types have expressed their opinions about what the press should or should not do. But never before in history has there been a hardheaded examination of the activities of the press in an important field conducted by members of the press for their mutual benefit on an international level.

That is why the IPI study has no parallel. That is why it has aroused the interest and drawn the wholehearted assistance of leading editors, agency heads, and correspondents. That is why its reports are expected to have practical value in improving the flow of news among the free nations.

The IPI has no connection with the government of any country. It has no affiliation with the United Nations, or any other international body. It is a voluntary association of editors, dedicated to four main purposes—"the furtherance and safeguarding of the freedom of the press…the achievement of understanding among journalists and so among peoples…the promotion of free exchange of accurate and balanced news among nations…and the improvements of the practices of journalism."

It was first sponsored in April of 1949 by the American Society of Newspaper Editors, at the urging of the brilliant Sunday editor of the *New York Times*, Lester Markel. In October, 1950, thirty editors from fifteen countries decided it was a desirable and feasible organization, and in April of 1951 the Ford and Rockefeller Foundations made grants totaling $270,000 to cover the costs of the first three years of operation. It was formally organized in Paris a month later, with Markel as chairman of the executive board. Headquarters were established in Zurich, Switzerland a few months later.

In the spring of 1952 the Ford Foundation authorized a special grant for a survey of international news. The study got under way in September, when staffs were organized in Zurich, New York, and Madras, India. W.

MacNeil Lowry, associate director of the Institute, formerly chief Washington correspondent for the Cox newspapers, was given operating responsibility for the entire project. Directors with extensive newspaper experience were appointed for the American phase and the other phases of the survey.

Arrangements were made with a group of ten leading researchers in U.S. journalism schools, headed by Dr. Ralph Casey of the University of Minnesota, to handle the task of measuring the amounts of foreign news printed in American papers. The news flowing on agency wires was measured by the IPI staff in New York. These tasks were assigned in Zurich to a number of skilled researchers with newspaper background, working in the IPI office there.

Four separate weeks—one in October, one in November, one in December of 1952, and one in January of 1953—were chosen for the measurement part of the project. One hundred and eighty-one newspapers—105 in the U.S., 76 in other countries—were placed on the study list. The wire reports of all the major news agencies were made available by the agencies for study during the same weeks.

Ninety-three of the American papers were put on the list through a statistical sampling method used by Dr. Chilton Bush, head of the Institute for Journalistic Studies at Stanford University. Under this system, every daily paper in the United States had an equal chance to appear on the list. The list gave fair representation to morning and evenings papers, papers in different regions of the country, papers representing a cross-section of American journalism. For purposes of comparison with this list, a separate list of twelve papers were made up, composed of leading papers such as the Washington *Star* and the St. Louis *Post-Dispatch*, which had not been included in the Bush statistical sample.

The papers in Europe and India were selected by the IPI staff in consultation with editors in the countries involved, in order to get representative lists for each country. Forty-eight papers in Western Europe and 28 in India were chosen for examination.

Coding manuals were prepared by the IPI staff in New York and Zurich—with coordination by Dr. David M. White of Boston University in the U.S. and H. Sinding-Larsen in Europe—classifying foreign news into 14 categories: war, politics, foreign relations, defense, economic, cultural, education and science, religion, crime, judicial-legal, disasters, human interest, social, and sports. Using these manuals, the researchers in Europe, the United States, and India measured the newspapers and the wire service reporters, tabulating the amounts of news in each category printed by the papers and sent along the wires by the agencies.

At the same time, the newspapers were studied to see how much foreign news was supplied by the major news services, how much by special or staff correspondents, and how much by syndicates. During the same weeks, editors handling foreign news—including a group of 35 telegraph editors in the U.S.A.—were asked to make reports on the daily editing problems occasioned by the flow of the news and to give indications of why they printed some stories and rejected others.

All of these activities were designed to show the sources and the nature of foreign news—the extent of its volume, the origin of it, and the use of it.

To tackle the difficult problem of estimating the value of such news, the IPI developed two instruments—the composite picture of one country in the press of another, and the case history of a news event occurring in one country and reported in another.

The composite picture was defined in a reportorial, objective summary of the facts concerning the life of Country A in one month's file of representative newspapers of Country B. For example, such a picture would present a summary of the facts brought to British readers by the British press about life in India, or a summary of the facts presented to Indian readers by the Indian press about life in Britain.

The case history was defined as a chronological, objective summary of the facts concerning a news event in one country as reported over a period of three days or more in a majority of the representative newspapers in another country. Such a history would deal with the coverage given to the British atomic explosion in the U.S. press, or the coverage given to General Eisenhower's cabinet appointments in the British press or the press of another country under study.

These word pictures and case histories were prepared by the IPI staff members, on the basis of clippings drawn from newspapers in the countries being examined. The US staff was assigned the job of preparing nine pictures—one each of India, Britain, Holland, Belgium, France, Italy, Switzerland, Western Germany, and Sweden—and 18 case histories, two from each of these nine countries. The Zurich staff and the Indian staff prepared other pictures and case histories, using Western European and Indian papers.

After completion, these summaries were scheduled to be sent to editors to obtain their comments on their accuracy and completeness. The editors also were requested to comment on the case histories of specific news events.

Twenty-seven correspondents of other countries stationed in the U.S. were asked to prepare reports done in specific terms in answer to this question: "Do you think the American press is giving an accurate picture of your country?" A composite picture of his country, based on one month's flow of the news, was sent to each correspondent, to help him make his report specific.

The third phase of the IPI survey was designed to cover suggestions for improvement. Many editors were directly interviewed by members of the IPI staff, both in the United States and Europe. More than 450 editors were sent questionnaires, seeking their views on the gathering and handling of foreign news at every stage.

Two questionnaires were prepared for news agency executives—one for the top men in the agencies, and one for agency editors and bureau chiefs. They were asked to give their opinions on the use made of agency dispatches by the papers, the influence of editors' demands on agency reports, and any suggestions they might have for the improvement of foreign news presentation in general.

Both in the direct interviews and in the questionnaires, the editors and agency executives were invited to express their ideas on the training required by foreign correspondents and foreign desk men in the modern world, and for their analysis of the ways in which correspondents and desk men did or did not measure up to their standards.

Under the IPI project, plans were also made to reach the readers of newspapers. Questionnaires were prepared for readers, and readers were asked for their views on possible improvements that might arouse greater interest in foreign news.

When all these phases of the flow of the news survey have been completed in the spring of 1953, the IPI will have the largest assemblage of facts and ideas about handling of foreign news ever gathered together. It will be published in a series of reports next summer, after the annual meeting of IPI members of London.

Lester Markel summed up the objectives of the Institute, in the project and its other activities, in a statement he made early in December of 1952.

"The main objective of the Institute is to bring about greater world understanding through a better flow of information," Markel said. "In this project, the objectives are the compilation of the first comprehensive analysis of the nature and extent of the news flow, the discovery of areas of ignorance in one country about another, indication of possible causes for these areas, obtaining suggestions for improving the flow of news, and promoting cooperation among editors and news agencies."

YOUR FREEDOMS:

THE BILL OF RIGHTS

THE STIRRING STORY OF THE BATTLE
FOR CIVIL LIBERTIES IN AMERICA

Part I   How Your Rights Were Won

You take it for granted that you are an individual person. You have a name, an identity, a sense of being somebody different from everybody else. You have clothes, books, records, other possessions that belong to you. Looking at the world through your own eyes, you see things in a way that is different from the way other persons around you see things. You are a separate person.

As an individual, you have rights. In most of the countries of the world today, there are laws on the books guaranteeing the rights of individual human beings. Even in Communist countries, where the governments are extremely powerful, recognition is given in principle to the idea that every human being has certain basic rights that must be protected and respected.

In practice, of course, these rights are often impaired or violated by governments and other powerful organizations which claim control over their members. In totalitarian nations, the state comes first and the individual must be ready to sacrifice his rights whenever the sacrifice is demanded.

If you live in the United States, in Western Europe, or in countries where the principle of individual freedom is strong, you have many liberties. You know that your ancestors suffered and fought for these liberties. You are not quite sure of your knowledge of how your rights were won. You may think that your liberties cannot be lost, because these freedoms were established nearly two centuries ago in America and the countries with many liberties have dominated the world in the twentieth century.

Actually the development of individual liberty came about through a slow process of extending over thousands of years. Liberties have been won and lost; over and over again. In your time, you may lose your freedoms if you do not think about them and care about them.

The awakening of individual consciousness—the idea of every person as a separate person—grew slowly through the countless centuries of man's development. Primitive tribes generally considered men and woman as parts of the tribes, not as free and separate beings.

In the countries around the Mediterranean Sea, a belief in the dignity of man as an individual gradually arose. The great thinkers and philosophers of China and the Far East had considered man as a river of humanity flowing into the enormous ocean of life in the universe. But the Greeks and the Jews considered man as an individual—as a single person, wondering where he had come from and where he was going.

In keeping with the Jewish tradition, Christianity asserted that every person was significant in the eyes of the Creator. Every human being had an eternal future. Every human being had been given an enormous gift of freedom by a God who was a personal God, a God interested in the fostering and full growth of every single person.

As the Christian culture spread, emperors as well as slaves accepted the idea that the essential worth of a man or woman did not depend upon his or her position in the material world. Even a slave had a soul, and that soul had a value beyond measure. Slaves were mistreated, slaves were compelled to live in poverty and servitude, yet every slave was a person and could not be regarded as a commodity like gold or iron.

The revolutionary ideas of Christianity led to the fall of the Roman Empire, the rise of new kingdoms, and finally to the spread of republics and democracies where the people were regarded as the sovereigns. The ideas of the Greek philosophers, which were close in many respects to the ideas of Christianity, helped to advance the cause of individual rights.

At the cost of many lives, men and woman struggled through the ages to define and at last establish the list of rights to which they believed they were entitled. Many were punished with the whip and the rack, many were killed, many were sent into exile, but the cry for liberty could not be stifled.

These were the rights that came to be regarded as fundamental:

• The right to free speech, and with this was the right to be silent, not to be forced to testify or accuse one's self.

• The right to exercise freedom of belief and worship—this was closely associated with freedom of speech, and it came to mean that no one church should be given the endorsement or support of the government.

• The right to assemble, to discuss grievances, and to seek changes in government or society.

• The right to protection of life and property against seizure by rulers.

• The right to a fair trial by a "jury of peers"—that is, by a group of persons of the same standing.

• The right to be protected against cruel and unusual punishments—outlawing physical tortures such as burning, blinding, and mutilation of limbs.

• The right to have independent counsel when facing charges brought against an individual by rulers.

These ideas flourished in all the countries affected by the Judeo-Christian scriptures and the philosophy of the individualistic Greeks. In three Western countries—England, France, and Germany—the ideas finally sparked a series of rebellions against princes and nobles. The demand for individual freedom led to bloody fighting, the beheading of kings, the slaughter of thousands in fierce combat.

In England there arose a movement called Puritanism. It was composed of people who left the Church of England because they felt that church had not been sufficiently purified from corrupt practices. Dissenters in religion and in politics, some of the Puritans were driven from England. Some of them fled to Holland and then went to North America, where they founded colonies on the shores of Massachusetts Bay.

These Puritan colonists felt that the rights of Englishmen, won in earlier generations, were being destroyed in England by monarchs who despised Parliament or would not call the Parliament into session. In the twenty years between 1620 and 1640, the Puritans transferred more than 25,000 selected men and woman to what became known as New England. In 1640, after Parliament had again assembled in old England, many of the Puritan colonists returned to the motherland. But those who remained in Massachusetts and other colonies developed ideas of independence which later flamed in the American Revolution.

During the period of colonial settlement, Catholic immigrants under the leadership of Lord Calvert formed a community in Maryland with an atmosphere of freedom. Under Calvert's charter, a representative assembly was established. This body, like the House of Burgesses in the neighboring colony of Virginia, soon asserted its rights to pass legislation for all free men within its area.

In Colonial Virginia, the settlers claimed the rights and privileges of Englishmen—which included free speech and the right to a jury trial. The House of Burgesses, as the assembly was called, declared in 1624 that it had the right to control taxation in the colony.

Harsh and intolerant as they were in some ways, the Puritans in New England cleared the way for the growth of American ideas of individual freedoms. The pioneers in Maryland and Virginia, in Rhode Island and other colonies also made it clear to their governors that they felt entitled to the rights assured to every freeholder in England under "the common law."

Every free man in England claimed that the sovereign ruler had a responsibility to protect his life, his liberty, and his property from arbitrary assaults. These rights were traced back to the twelfth century. The use of juries was first mentioned in 1166, in connection with a criminal case, although there are some records indicating that juries were used a century earlier in civil cases.

It was in the twelfth century, however, according to historians, that the right of accused persons to have "learned counsel" was recognized. Statutes in 1275 and 1444 were aimed at prohibiting excessive fines and excessive bail bonds. Sheriffs were ordered to give prisoners every opportunity to be released on bail unless their crimes were very serious.

During the 150 years which followed the landings in Massachusetts, Virginia, Maryland and other colonies, the settlers in the new land had to keep up a constant struggle against attempts by the English kings and royal governors to bring them under absolute control. In Virginia, an influx of royalists overthrew the colonial democracy of the early days and power shifted into the hands of the governor and his council. In New England, royal governors fought to control the rising tide of popular democratic government.

When James II came to the throne of England late in the seventeenth century, he consolidated all of New England into one province and appointed Sir Edmund Andros as governor-general. Andros was already in control of New York and New Jersey; these colonies were brought into the New England province. King James took out of the new charter all provisions for popular representation, and Andros had the powers of a dictator.

After the English revolution of 1688, the colonists regained their old forms of government. Under bold leaders, the people of Boston and neighboring towns took Andros a prisoner and captured the royal fort in Boston harbor. A new charter was granted to Massachusetts in 1691.

The revolution of 1688 in England foreshadowed in some ways the American revolt which came nearly a century later. James II lost his throne because he violated the rights that Englishmen were determined to maintain. In 1689 the Parliament adopted a declaration of rights and liberties, asserting that it was illegal for a king to suspend laws without Parliament's consent or to levy taxes without Parliament's approval.

Indicating the principles that were to be embodied in the American Bill of Rights, the Declaration of 1689 said that British subjects had the right to petition the king freely, that freedom of speech and debate in Parliament could not be questioned, and that the raising or keeping of a standing Army in a time of peace without the consent of Parliament was not legal. The Declaration specified that elections of members of Parliament should be freely held, and Parliament should be frequently convened.

In this Declaration, Parliament said that excessive bail should not be required of any person accused of a crime, excessive fines were not permitted, and cruel and unusual punishments were prohibited. A person under a criminal charge was guaranteed a trial by "impartial jurors," and fines and forfeitures of accused persons before conviction were not lawful.

Many historians rank the Declaration of 1698 with the Magna Carta as the most important statements of rights and liberties in English annals. The Magna Carta, signed by King John in Runnymede in 1215, secured the rights of barons and nobles, whereas the statement of 1689 provided for the rights and liberties of a great many Englishmen. Before William and Mary took over the royal powers in England (after the fall of James II), they had to acknowledge the validity of the Declaration.

The colonists in New England, Maryland, Virginia and other areas in America were certain that the statement of 1689 applied to them as well as to residents of England. Chief Justice Holt of the highest court in England affirmed their position when he ruled in 1694 that the rights of Englishmen extended to those in the colonies. "All the laws in force in England are in force there," Justice Holt said. And twenty-six years later, in 1720, Attorney General West gave an opinion that the common law of England was the law in the colonies unless there was "some private Act to the contrary."

When King George III came along in the 1760's and undertook to force the American colonies to pay increased taxes without giving the colonists the right to be represented in Parliament, an explosive situation developed. "No taxation without representation" became a battle cry, and by 1775 the colonies were in a state of rebellion.

In 1776, American leaders took the drastic step of asserting their independence. Saying that they spoke for the people of "the United States of America," these leaders appealed to the world for support against the British king, vividly describing their grievances against him. In effect, they found George III and his ministers guilty of un-British activities: the king and his councilors had failed to apply the Declaration of 1689 to free men in the colonies.

The tremendous sentences in the Declaration of American Independence rang forth for all mankind to hear: "When, in the course of human events, in becomes necessary for one people to dissolve the political bands which have connected with one another, and to assume, among the powers of the earth, the separate and equal station to which the laws of nature and of nature's God entitled them, a decent respect to the opinions of mankind requires that they should declare the causes which impel them to the separation.

"We hold these truths to be self-evident—that all men are created equal; that they are endowed by their Creator with certain inalienable rights; that among these are life, liberty, and the pursuit of happiness. That, to secure these rights, governments are instituted among men, deriving their just powers from the consent of the governed...."

The men who signed the Declaration of 1776 knew they were risking their lives, their fortunes, and their honor. But they were prepared to take the risks. Behind them stood long lines of ancestors who had risked all for liberty in other centuries.

"Whenever any form of government becomes destructive of these ends, it is the right of the people to alter or to abolish it, and to institute a new government, laying its foundation on such principles, and organizing its powers in such form, as to them shall seem most likely to effect their safety and happiness," the American Declaration said.

Those were bold words in the eighteenth century, when the earth was dominated by the might of kings. Those are still bold words today, when many people shiver at the revolutions occurring in Asia, Africa, and Latin America. The men who founded the United States knew what they were doing, and they knew it was an awesome thing. They proclaimed "the right of the people to alter or to abolish" any form of government.

The signers of the Declaration were not a bearded rabble of anarchists or bomb throwers. They were sober, solid, substantial gentlemen. Many of them had sizable estates. Some of them thought they might be hanged for what they were doing.

But they went ahead, because they were moved by the spirit of liberty. And the spirit of liberty has prevailed in the nation they founded. In spite of fits of fear and in spite of the dire predictions of those who distrust the people, the nation has survived and grown under God to a towering height of prosperity and power.

The Declaration of Independence, the Constitution, and the Bill of Rights—these are the sacred documents of America. These are statements revered and respected wherever freedom thrives.

Let us now consider the Bill Rights, the charter of our fundamental liberties.

Part II   The American Revolution and Our Charter of Liberties

The American Revolution was fought and won by a loose organization of states—the thirteen colonies, linked together by the Articles of Confederation which were ratified between 1778 and 1781 while George Washington's Army was carrying on the struggle against the British. Without the aid supplied by France and other allies, it is doubtful whether Washington's forces could have triumphed. The Continental Congress lacked the power to raise taxes, and without tax revenues the soldiers could not be paid regularly and the rapid depreciation in the value of the United States dollar could not be controlled. The states ignored many of the resolutions passed by the Congress, participated in tax and trade "wars" among themselves, and conditions were finally so chaotic that foreign diplomats wondered whether the United States should be regarded as one nation or thirteen.

Alarmed by the rebellion led by Captain Daniel Shays in 1786, the inflation of the currency and other signs of approaching anarchy, a convention of businessmen gathered in Annapolis that year and suggested that Congress call an assembly of citizens to revise the Articles of Confederation. Congress acted on the suggestion, and a Federal Convention met in 1787 to see what could be done. The delegates were not authorized to draw up a new constitution, but decided to do so under the leadership of Washington, Benjamin Franklin, James Madison, George Mason, Oliver Ellsworth and other men of property and power. Thomas Jefferson and John Adams were overseas on special missions, and did not take part; but both believed that the establishment of a stronger federal government was necessary.

The Constitution of 1787 is the one under which we are living today. It has lasted longer than any other written constitution drawn up by the leaders of any other major nation. It has been hailed for many years as a masterpiece of political wisdom.

Yet it was subjected to strife when it was submitted to the original thirteen states for ratification. In several important states, only a few more votes were cast for the Constitution than were cast against it. Some historians have contended that it would have been defeated if it had been placed before the people in a referendum. As it was, approval was given by states legislatures after stormy debates.

The attacks on the Constitution came principally from two sources—those who felt that it weakened the states too much, and from those who wanted a Bill of Rights. Jefferson, the author of the Declaration of Independence, was one of the leaders who felt that a charter of personal rights and protections for the states had to be added to the basic document as quickly as possible.

In the First Congress that assembled after the Constitution had been adopted, Madison proposed a series of twelve amendments. The First Amendment as we have it today was actually the third one on Madison's list; his first two amendments dealt with the number of Representatives to be elected and with the compensation to be paid to members of Congress. He wrote his Bill or Rights on the basis of proposals offered by a number of state legislators during the conflict over the Constitution.

Many of the states had already developed Bills of Rights. The most notable was the Virginia Declaration of Rights, which was largely composed by a wealthy planter, George Mason. Its first section placed property rights high among the "inherent rights" with which men were endowed "by nature." This section declared: "All men are by nature equally free and independent and have certain inherent rights, of which when they enter into a state of society, they cannot by any compact deprive or divest their posterity; namely, the enjoyment of life and liberty, with the means of acquiring and possessing property, and pursuing and obtaining happiness and safety."

Life, liberty and the pursuit of happiness were generally accepted as among the fundamental rights of man. Madison and the others who pushed the federal Bill of Rights through the First Congress, acting under the Constitution, evidently felt that property rights were adequately protected by the Constitution and by the American tradition of regarding the possession of private property as an essential element in man's happiness. The Americans had moved a long way from the closely regulated economic system, which had prevailed in England, and were determined to preserve the individual's free access to property.

The provisions of the Bill of Rights were affected by the debate in Congress and by the views expressed to Madison by Thomas Jefferson in letters from Paris. Jefferson declared: "A bill of rights is what the people are entitled to against every government on earth, general or particular; and what no just government should refuse or rest on inference." He asked for plain words "providing clearly, and without the aid of sophism, for freedom of religion, freedom of the press, protection against standing armies, restriction of monopolies, the eternal and unremitting force of the habeas corpus laws, and by trials by jury in all matters of fact triable by the laws of the land, and not by the laws of nations."

Jefferson was impatient with the ideas of James Wilson, a Pennsylvania lawyer who had taken part in the Constitutional Convention of 1787, and felt that a charter of rights and liberties was not necessary. Wilson claimed that the framers of the Constitution had reserved many rights to the people. The Constitution did not say that any branch of the federal government had power to take away freedom of religion, of the press, or any of the liberties Jefferson was so eager to preserve. So Mr. Wilson thought that Mr. Jefferson had no cause for alarm.

"I consider all the ill as established which may be established," Jefferson told Madison in a strongly phrased letter. "I have a right to nothing which another has a right to take away; and Congress will have a right to take away trials by jury in all civil cases." And Jefferson said again that he wanted a federal Bill of Rights "to guard liberty against the legislative as well as the executive branches of the government."

Alexander Hamilton, one of the most ardent defenders of the Constitution, saw no need for the inclusion of a charter of liberties in the document, and gave his reasons eloquently in No. 84 of *The Federalist* papers, one of the statements issued by those who advocated its ratification.

"Bills of rights are, in their origin, stipulations between kings and their subjects," Hamilton wrote. "Such was Magna Carta, obtained by the barons, sword in hand, from King John. Such were the subsequent confirmations of that charter by succeeding princes. Such was the Petition of Right assented to by Charles I in the beginning of his reign. Such, also, was the Declaration of Right presented by the Lords and Commons to the Prince of Orange in 1688, and afterwards thrown into the form of an act of parliament called the Bill of Rights.

"It is evident, therefore, that according to their primitive signification, they have no application to constitutions, professedly founded upon the power of the people, and executed by their immediate representatives and servants. Here, in strictness, the people surrender nothing; and as they retain every thing they have no need of particular reservations."

Hamilton pointed out that the preamble to the Constitution proclaimed: "We, the people of the United States, in order to...secure the blessings of liberty to ourselves and our posterity, do ordain and establish this Constitution for the United States of America." Nothing could be clearer than that, Hamilton believed.

"Here is a better recognition of popular rights, than volumes of those aphorisms which make the principal figure in several of our State bills of rights, and which would sound much better in a treatise on ethics than in a constitution of government, Hamilton continued.

"I go further, and affirm that bills of rights, in the sense and to the extent in which they are contended for, are not only unnecessary...but would even be dangerous. They would contain various exceptions to powers not granted; and on this very account, would afford a colorable pretext to claim more than were granted.

"For why declare that things shall not be one which there is not power to do? Why, for instance, should it be said that the liberty of the press shall not be restrained, when no power is given by which restrictions may be imposed? I will not contend that such a provision would confer a regulating power; but it is evident that it would furnish, to men disposed to usurp, a plausible pretense for claiming that power. They might urge with a semblance of reason, that the Constitution ought not to be charged with the absurdity of providing against the abuse of an authority which was not given, and that the provision against restraining the liberty of the press afforded a clear implication, that a power to prescribe proper regulations concerning it was intended to be vested in the national government. This may serve as a specimen of the numerous handles which would be given to the doctrine of constructive powers, by the indulgence of an injudicious zeal for bills of rights."

Hamilton insisted that the liberty of the press, as well as other freedoms, must altogether depend upon the support of public opinion and "on the general spirit of the people and of the government." He wrote: "Here, after all, must we seek for the only solid basis of all our rights."

"The truth is…that the Constitution is itself, in every rational sense, and to every rational purpose, a bill of rights," Hamilton concluded. "Is it one object of a bill of rights to declare and specify the political privileges of the citizens in the structure and administration of the government? This is done in the most ample and precise manner…. Is another object of a bill or rights to define certain immunities and modes of proceeding, which are relative to personal and private concerns? This…has also been attended to, in a variety of cases, in the same plan."

In one sense, Hamilton was certainly right. The Constitution had been written by men who were determined to form a government with limited powers, controlled by the people. (The people, in their minds, were persons of education and substance, capable of considering the problems of government rationally and rather objectively.)

But Thomas Jefferson raised the great questions. In one of his articles, Jefferson said: "Is the spirit of the people an infallible, a permanent reliance? Is it government? Is this the kind of protection we receive in return for the rights we give up? Besides, the spirit of the times may alter, will alter. Our rulers will become corrupt, our people careless. A single zealot may commence persecution, and better men be his victims. It can never be too often repeated that the time for fixing every essential right on a legal basis is while our rulers are honest and ourselves united."

Jefferson foresaw that the high and noble enthusiasm of the revolution would not last. He was aware of the fact that the generation which had achieved so much was a rare generation. He wanted that generation to place upon the scrolls of the nation a clear and simple statement of fundamental rights, so that congressmen and presidents and judges of the coming generations would have stated before their eyes a list of the liberties regarded as fundamental by the Founding Fathers of the American nation. He was afraid that the people would be forgotten and their rights might be disregarded. In an article on the administration of justice, he wrote: "They will forget themselves, but in the sole faculty of making money, and will never think of uniting to effect a due respect for their rights." He rallied the forces for a federal Bill of Rights, and his friends and followers entered the fray with passion and persistence.

Jefferson, Madison and other advocates of a written Bill of Rights triumphed. Hamilton, Wilson and others who honestly contended that the very spirit of the Constitution was the spirit of liberty were acknowledged to have much in favor of their arguments, but most of the people who could vote one way or another decided that the basic freedoms should be spelled out in unmistakable terms.

Deep questions related to man's nature and the workings of human society were at issue in these struggles. Was freedom a matter of the spirit or did it have to be established, identified and protected by the law? Was it a good thing to depend upon public opinion for final sanctions of what could and could not be permitted? Or were there some "inalienable rights" beyond the power of the people to give or to take away?

In the eighteenth century, many men believed in a "natural law." Men felt that there were certain principles of human life which had been laid down by the Creator of the universe. These principles were above human governments, and men could appeal to them with the expectation that their rational fellows would pay heed to those principles.

Many of the men who shaped the American Revolution and fought for the Bill of Rights believed that John Locke, the English philosopher, was correct when he asserted that "to understand political power aright, and derive it from its original, we must consider what state all men are naturally in—and that is a state of perfect freedom to order their actions and dispose of their persons and possessions as they think fit, within the bounds of the law of nature, without asking leave, or depending upon the will of any other man...." They also thought Locke was right when he added: "But though this be a state of liberty, yet it is not a state of license...which obliges everyone; and reason, which is that law, teaches all mankind who will but consult it, that, being all equal and independent, no one ought to harm another in his life, health, liberty, or possessions."

Governments were created to preserve those principles, the American leaders believed. The "positive law," which could be derived from the "law of nature," could be expressed in constitutions and in bills of rights. So the basic liberties of the individual, although not given by the government, could be defined and protected in charters supported by the people acting through the government.

In the minds of the men who framed the Constitution and the Bill of Rights, liberty and law were linked. Rules of fair conduct, prescribing the procedures to be followed by Congress, the president and the courts, were bulwarks of liberty. To maintain freedom, men had to make sure that the power of the government was positively on the side of freedom, not simply enforcing negative prohibitions.

The government established by the United States was a new kind of government—it was to be limited, it was to be a servant of the citizens, and it was to do its utmost to encourage all generations of Americans to secure the blessings of liberty for themselves and all those coming along in the stream of history.

XIII Could We Lose the Bill of Rights?

The story of America's development as a constitutional democracy is one of the great stories in history. It has been described from many aspects. It has been studied from many angles by Europeans, Asians and Africans as well as Americans. It is not fully understood—and it will never be completely comprehended because it involves the tremendous mystery of how people learn to govern themselves.

All historians agree that one vital factor in keeping America free is the preservation of the Bill of Rights. According to surveys, most Americans believe in the Bill of Rights, yet relatively few know what it contains or what would happen to them if it should be lost. Few of us relate to the Bill of Rights to our personal lives—and yet every one of us, young and old, depends upon those rights for our freedom to speak without fear, our opportunity to belong to the church of our choice, our liberty to work where we please and to vote for any leaders we choose to represent us.

Under the Constitution originally adopted by our Founding Fathers, we had no specific charter of liberties. It wasn't necessary to spell out the rights of Americans, Alexander Hamilton said. As long as the love of liberty flourished in American hearts, no tyrants could enslave us. Other leaders who wrote the Constitution agreed with Hamilton.

As we have noted earlier, it took strenuous efforts by Thomas Jefferson and James Madison to get the Bill of Rights adopted. It has taken strenuous efforts and strong devotion by many Americans to keep the principles of the Bill of Rights alive in times of war and uneasy peace. In the present age of social, economic, and scientific revolutions, the meaning of the Bill of Rights requires new thinking and new dedication.

Much depends upon the knowledge and the attitudes of the young people of America. There are indications that many young people do not have an ardent love of liberty in their hearts.

Polls taken not long ago on five college campuses in Southern California, covering 1,100 students, revealed that many of them were hazy about the Bill of Rights. Many were willing to limit the individual freedoms of their fellow citizens in various ways. They did not seem to realize that their own freedoms might disappear if our constitutional protections were weakened.

Nearly half of these students approved of "double jeopardy"—that is, the trying of a person twice for a serious crime; yet the Bill of Rights provides that a person once acquitted in such a case cannot be tried again for that offense.

About 49 percent said they would support the internment of "suspicious persons" in government camps in the event of a national emergency, and were vague about how they would attempt to decide whether persons were "suspicious" or not.

Nearly a third of them were willing to give the police authority to use wiretaps on private telephone conversations. (The Supreme Court has ruled that wiretapping is forbidden under federal law, and evidence obtained by wiretapping is not admitted in federal courts.)

Fifty-three percent of them would not allow a labor leader to invoke the protection of the Fifth Amendment in an investigation. (The Fifth Amendment in the Bill of Rights declares that no one can be compelled to testify against himself.)

Substantial support for censorship measures was expressed by these students. A third of them felt that a government investigating committee should have the power to question any newspaper editor who criticized the committee's work. About a fifth of them believed that the Postmaster General should have the power to ban books which he considered immoral or obscene.

In general, the attitudes of these students indicated that many young Americans regard the views of the community or the desires of government officials as paramount above the ideas of individual persons. Other surveys have indicated that American young people are confused about the Bill of Rights or do not see why the protections and guarantees stipulated in the Bill are needed in the twentieth century.

Former President Dwight D. Eisenhower, Chief Justice Earl Warren, and other leaders have expressed alarm over the erosion of American liberties. Through indifference and ignorance, our fundamental rights might be lost.

In an address at Defiance College, Ohio, in May of 1963, General Eisenhower urged Americans to renew their devotion to self-reliance, independence of spirit, and love of liberty. He said that the framers of our Constitution could not know that "in less that two centuries the immensity of domestic and international affairs would tend to create in us a feeling of individual helplessness...."

Eisenhower declared that some citizens had given way to "an unthinking abandonment of personal and local responsibility to a few men in government, giving to them a frightening power for good or evil—and almost certain to invite error or abuse."

In the same month, President Robert F. Goheen of Princeton University denounced the students who participated actively in a riot which damaged homes and other property there. In a letter to Princeton's undergraduates, Dr. Goheen said: "The collective surrender of selfhood by otherwise responsible individuals, and the inconvenience, danger and damage it worked against others, seem to be equally deplorable.... Its sheer wantonness and irresponsibility stood, of course, in particularly sharp juxtaposition to the deeply somber struggles [of the Negroes] in Birmingham."

Dr. Goheen said he was not disposed to take a gloomy view of the new college generation in America. He declared: "The unhappy madness of the night of May 6 has not changed my conviction that most of you will make fully as worthy contributions in the future as has any preceding generation of Princetonians. This letter, then, has not been written in despair. It is offered in the hope that we can all profit from searching and responsible reflection over issues of this sort."

Chief Justice Earl Warren chided the lawyers of the nation for their failure to debate the issues presented by three proposed amendments to the Constitution. One amendment would permit state legislatures to amend the Constitution themselves without concurrence of Congress; one would create a Court of the Union, composed of the chief justices of each state, with power to review and override decisions by the U.S. Supreme Court; and a third amendment would deny federal courts the power to rule on the apportionment of seats in state legislatures.

"If proposals of this magnitude had been made in the early days of the Republic, the great debate would be resounding in every legislative hall and in every place where lawyers, scholars, and statesmen gather." The Chief Justice said. If the amendments were adopted, he felt that "the United States as we know it would be at an end."

He expressed astonishment and dismay at the fact that so little attention had been given to the dangers in these amendments. Supported quietly by a hardcore group of believers in state sovereignty, the amendments had been approved by legislatures in a number of states. Twelve states had approved the proposal to change the method of amendments in an address at the National Press Club in favor of the Court of the Union, and four had approved the proposal to take away the federal power to determine the apportionment of seats in legislatures.

Governor George Romney of Michigan, a proponent for strong state governments, attacked the proposed amendments in an address at the National Press Club in Washington. The amendments went much too far, Romney felt. If adopted, the proposals would change our federal union into a weak confederation of the kind which had proved to be unworkable in the early days of the nation.

"Mutilation of the federal government will not strengthen the states," Governor Romney declared.

How could such amendments get approval by state legislatures without a thorough public discussion? How far has an attitude of irresponsibility sunk into the fiber of the American character? How many of us have fallen into the condition that General Eisenhower called "an unthinking abandonment of personal and local responsibility"?

Some signs indicate that millions of Americans have done so. The loss of our fundamental liberties has become a real possibility.

If we lost our Bill of Rights, what would happen to our way of life? Here are some of the things that could happen:

The government could keep young men in the military services for indefinite periods, without giving any explanation or justification for this policy.

Young men and women leaving school could be assigned to jobs in industries where the government asserted that workers were needed. Young people could be forced to take these jobs.

Students protesting against government policies—including those who recently picketed the White House—could be thrown into federal prisons by order of the president.

Americans, young or old, could be required to give up their property for public use without compensation if local, state or federal authorities decided that such property was needed for public projects.

The books available for reading in American homes could be censored by the Postmaster General or local committees under city, state or federal ordinances. Since the First Amendment protections for free speech would be gone, there would be no legal grounds for objecting to the censorship.

The names of persons writing critical letters to their Congressmen might be turned over to the police, and such persons could be arrested and imprisoned for "bringing disrepute upon the federal government or federal officers."

Editors who printed articles in their newspaper criticizing the government would be subject to arrest at any time, night or day.

The programs of television and radio broadcasting stations would be governed by rules dictated by the federal agencies regulating the stations.

If appeals were made to the courts, the judges would not be able to use the precedents established since the foundation of the United States—because these precedents, in civil liberties cases, are largely built upon the Bill of Rights.

The very quality of American life would be gone.

The independence, the willingness to speak out, which mark the true American everywhere, would be crushed.

The eager exuberance, the lively restlessness, of Americans—noted by all foreign observers, cited by many as evidences of the creative atmosphere in America—would give way to cringing manners, fear of the police, fear of informers, fear of freedom itself.

Could we lose our Bill of Rights?

Could we come to a day in America when a military patrol could come to the White House and take the president away?

Could we come to a day when military chiefs could declare elections null and void—as they have done in many countries?

Could these things happen here?

The answer rests in the minds and hearts of the rising generation of Americans. Certainly this generation—and the generations before us— have tried to hold on to the basic freedoms written into our Constitution more than 175 years ago. Let us hope that this generation cares enough about these liberties to understand them, to defend them, and to see their priceless value.

COURT OF REASON

By Frank K. Kelly

Prologue

Pursuing Jefferson's vision

In the generations since Thomas Jefferson and a few other revolutionaries proclaimed the independence of the American Republic, many men and women have tried to uphold his bold idea that we are all endowed by our Creator "with certain unalienable rights"—and among these rights are "life, liberty, and the pursuit of happiness.'" It is a vision that endures even in times of terror and despair. The story I present in this book—the stormy history of the Fund for the Republic—rises out of that vision: the dream of freedom and justice for all.

In 1976 we Americans hailed the 200th anniversary of Jefferson's great document, the Declaration of Independence. We celebrated with fireworks and frolics, with prayers and parades and pageants, with tall ships sailing up the Hudson River. That time of joy and confidence seems far behind us, but it reminded Americans and the world of the lofty dream on which this nation was founded.

To me, the best parts of the celebration were Jefferson's words, occasionally quoted in speeches, on radio stations, in television broadcasts. For me, they still vibrated with the promises that had stirred people for 200 years. I agreed with Robert Hutchins, the head of the Fund for the Republic, who once said: "Justice and freedom; discussion and criticism; intelligence and character—these are the indispensable ingredients of the democratic state. We can be rich and powerful without them. But not for long."

Enjoying that celebration, I was glad that I had served as an officer of the Fund for nineteen years in its struggle to keep Jefferson's vision before the people in an age of violence and revolutionary change—an age in which the survival of democratic institutions seemed very much in doubt. The Fund had never achieved what Hutchins and its directors hoped it would: a full public understanding of the vital necessity of maintaining the "unalienable rights" at the heart of American life. Yet it had fought a good fight, and the fight had to go on.

The Fund was launched in 1952, in a bitter time of division in America, when Senator Joseph McCarthy, the House Un-American Activities Committee, and other self-anointed patriots were hunting "spies" and people with "Communist connections." Blacklisters, bigots, censors, and right-wing organizations were active. The Jeffersonian tradition was overshadowed by another old American tradition—the tradition of witch burning.

In that year I had resigned from my job as staff director of the Senate Majority Policy Committee, disgusted by the fear and paralysis in the United States Senate. I was in New York when the Fund's creation was announced, working on a study of world news for the International Press Institute. I was impressed by the fact that the Ford Foundation's trustees had felt it necessary to establish an independent fund to preserve and advance the principles of the Declaration of Independence, the Constitution, and the Bill of Rights.

The directors of the Fund—whose names were disclosed by the Ford Foundation—were eminent in their fields. I knew that their eminence would not keep McCarthy and his cohorts from attacking them, but I believed they could withstand any attacks. With the $15 million provided to the Fund by the Ford Foundation, they could certainly help the civil liberties groups, the women's organizations, leaders in the churches, and others who were striving to support the Bill of Rights in the era of McCarthyism.

As an assistant to the Senate majority leader, I had witnessed McCarthy's rise to power. In the afternoon of February 20, 1950, I had been with Senator Scott Lucas of Illinois—then the majority leader—on the Senate floor when McCarthy shouted accusations that "Communists" known to the Secretary of State were shaping policies of the Truman administration. I had been a speech writer for President Truman in the campaign of 1948, and I knew and admired Secretary Acheson. I urged Lucas to challenge every statement McCarthy made. I could see reporters in the press gallery making notes, and I knew his charges would produce big headlines.

"I'm not going to get into a spraying contest with a skunk," Lucas muttered to me. Lucas was a tall, elegant man with an air of melancholy disillusionment. He was not ready to engage in a fight with any other senator, but he did stir in his chair when McCarthy declared that he would cite 81 "cases" of people in the State Department with "Communist connections."

In Wheeling, McCarthy had spoken of 205 people. In Reno, a few days later, he had talked about "57" cases. How many "cases" did he claim to have?

Lucas rose reluctantly to his feet and asked McCarthy what relationship the 81 "cases" had with the 205 or the 57 previously mentioned by the Senator. McCarthy shrugged.

"I do not believe I mentioned the figure 205," McCarthy said. "I believe I said over 200." He did not explain how that figure had dropped to 57 in Reno. He said that the 81 "cases" he had brought to the Senate included the 57 he had cited in Reno, plus 24 additional "cases."

Lucas asked him what he meant by "cases." Frowning impatiently, McCarthy said, "I am only giving the Senate cases in which it is clear there is a definite Communist connection." A few minutes later, he said that some of the "cases" did not refer to communists and "some of these individuals…are no longer with the State Department."

McCarthy searched through the piles of papers he had placed on his own desk and the desk of a senator who sat near him. He dropped some of the papers. When he came to what he called "case 72," he said, "I do not confuse this man as being a Communist. This individual was highly recommended by several witnesses as a high type of man."

McCarthy held the floor for nearly six hours, waving papers, contradicting himself, his voice rising and falling. Lucas interrupted him sixty-one times and was finally told by McCarthy that he would not respond to any more "silly questions" from the majority leader. Senator Herbert Lehman, of New York, asked McCarthy to clarify his language. McCarthy indicated that Lehman, who had been governor of New York for several terms, was not capable of understanding what he was talking about.

Senator Brien McMahon of Connecticut, who had been an assistant attorney general of the United States before he was elected to the Senate, made thirty-four efforts to pin McCarthy down. McCarthy brushed him off, waving and shouting.

Just before midnight, with a gesture of disgust, Lucas moved that the Senate should adjourn. The turbulent session was over. The fires of McCarthyism had proved beyond the power of the Senate to control.

Lucas and I were exhausted, but we clung to the hope that McCarthy's demagoguery would backfire against him. We did not realize then that McCarthy was on the verge of becoming one of the most powerful men in America.

In later years, after I had become an officer of the Fund for the Republic—which had really been created to combat the evils of McCarthyism—I realized that the clash between Lucas, McMahon, and McCarthy was a collision between two attitudes with roots in the early days of the American nation. There was a Jeffersonian heritage of reason and tolerance for radicals. And there was a heritage of conformity, of heresy hunting, of witch burning.

McCarthy had a deep undercurrent running for him—the undercurrent of distrust, the cynicism of many Americans. That current had been strong since the angry divisions of the American Revolution, when those who stayed loyal to the British king regarded the revolutionists as "traitors" and the revolutionaries denounced the royalists and drove many of them into Canada. American politicians had exploited the suspicions of many people since the founding of the Republic.

McCarthy turned the "Communist issue" against the Democratic senators who ran for reelection in 1950. When Lucas and other senators defended Truman and Acheson, they were asked why they had not purged the government of people who had charges of "Communist connections" in the "loyalty files"—dossiers that had been established under Truman's own "loyalty program." They were accused of "coddling Communists."

As the majority leader of the Senate, Lucas was a prime target for the McCarthyites. Traveling with Lucas through Illinois that autumn, I heard people say, "Lucas is in with that crowd in Washington. He's not one of us any more. Maybe he's soft on the Reds." His role in the Marshall Plan, which had pushed back communism in Western Europe, was largely ignored. The Chicago *Tribune* attacked him day after day. Many people, including those who doubted McCarthy's charges, were swayed by McCarthy's diatribes.

At that time the United States was the most powerful nation on earth. But fears of a communist threat to American security had flared after the explosion of a Soviet atomic bomb in September 1949, three years ahead of the predictions of American scientists. People in Illinois asked Lucas why Truman had not kept the Russians from "stealing" the "secrets" of atomic bombs. They asked why Acheson had not denounced Alger Hiss, who was suspected of being a spy. They wanted "dangerous aliens" and "radicals" to be deported or jailed. They seemed to have little confidence in the democratic institutions established by Jefferson and the other founding fathers of the United States.

There was one man in Illinois who did speak boldly in the Jeffersonian style. That was Robert Hutchins, then the head of the University of Chicago, who had told an Illinois commission investigating "subversive activities" that "the policy of repression cannot be justly enforced." He had announced that he would not dismiss any teachers because of their ideas or associations, and the trustees of the university had stood by him. In the miasma of McCarthyism, Hutchins seemed to be a shining figure.

Lucas and other senators smeared by McCarthy were defeated. I found few exemplars of the Hutchins brand of Americanism in Washington when I returned there. The new Senate majority leader, Ernest McFarland, of Arizona, asked me to stay on as his research assistant, but I soon discovered that he was not willing to tangle with McCarthy under any circumstances.

The atmosphere in Washington and in the rest of the country deteriorated month after month. It seemed to me that the confident era of Roosevelt and Truman was being overwhelmed by an age of hate. I left the Senate staff in the spring of 1952, depressed and disturbed by the state of the country.

For a few weeks that summer I felt a surge of hope. Averell Harriman, encouraged by Truman, sought the Democratic nomination for president. I served as the Washington director of his campaign, because I knew that Harriman had many of the traits of leadership needed by the nation.

A man with an astonishing range of knowledge and experience, Harriman had been secretary of commerce, ambassador to Britain, ambassador to Russia, director of the Mutual Security Administration. With Paul Hoffman, he had administered the Marshall Plan with brilliance and enormous energy. He was cool, aloof, an aristocrat in many ways. Yet he believed in the Jeffersonian tradition. I thought he could become a president in the brave style of Franklin Roosevelt.

Harriman, of course, did not get the nomination. Soon after the Democratic convention opened in Chicago that July, Governor Adlai Stevenson of Illinois declared that he would accept a draft, although he had previously assert that Harriman was the man best qualified to be president. Stevenson was nominated on the third ballot with Truman's backing. Stevenson offered me a place on his staff, but I had already accepted an appointment as the United States director of the International Press Institute study of world news.

After Harriman's withdrawal I took no part in the electoral battle of 1952. Eisenhower and Nixon, with the bruising participation of McCarthy and his friends, campaigned against "communism, corruption, and fumbling in Korea." Stevenson tried, as he put it, "to talk sense to the American people." His speeches were magnificent, but my experience in the Lucas disaster gave me a feeling that he was headed for defeat. Many Americans were not in a mood to listen to a man speaking in the Jeffersonian manner.

Stevenson's efforts were crushed in the Eisenhower-Nixon landslide in November 1952. McCarthy swaggered around the country like a military hero, claiming much of the credit. It seemed to me that the United States was sinking deeper into a quagmire of fear.

The Fund for the Republic gave me another surge of hope. Its directors seemed to know that they had to face controversy. When Robert Hutchins was chosen as the Fund's president in 1954 to succeed Clifford Case, who had resigned to run for the Senate in New Jersey, I was sure that the Fund would be a strong champion of civil liberties.

In 1954 and 1955 I watched with admiration while the Fund went into one battle zone after another. The Fund financed a report that showed the injustices in the government's loyalty program. It started an investigation of blacklisting in motion pictures, radio, and television, raising the hackles of the House Un-American Activities Committee. It financed a series of authoritative books on communism, provided money for an effort to strengthen the right of freedom of conscience, gave support for an exposure of the spreading fear among teachers, and aided many civil liberties groups. No other foundation in America had ever plunged so far into dangerous areas.

Attacks on the Fund increased, despite the prestige of its directors and the endorsement of the Ford Foundation. The national commander of the American Legion excoriated it. Fulton Lewis, Jr., and other right-wing broadcasters and columnists slashed at it. Lewis predicted that it would feel the full fury of the Committee on Un-American Activities. I noted these attacks, but did not believe they would get anywhere. I thought the Fund was impregnable.

After the completion of the International Press Institute study, I took a job with the Stephen Fitzgerald Company, a public relations agency with headquarters in New York. I was astounded when Hutchins came to the agency's office in December 1955, asking for help.

Hutchins told Fitzgerald and me that the Fund's directors were worried about its future. He said he had been instructed to find an agency and a public information specialist who could make the public more aware of the Fund's value. He had received good reports on us, he said, from Martin Quigley of the Ford Foundation and Louis Lyons, curator of the Nieman Foundation at Harvard.

In March 1956, after I had been interviewed by several members of the Fund's board, I was elected a vice president of the Fund. The Fitzgerald agency was employed to give public relations advice. Before I moved to the Fund's headquarters, I was warned by friends in Washington that I had made a blunder. I was told that the Fund was marked for destruction.

Among the board members who had talked to me, only Jubal R. Parten, an independent oil producer who had served as chairman of the trustees of the University of Texas, seemed to have great confidence in the Fund's future. Parten had asked me what I thought of Hutchins. When I told him that I admired Hutchins for his record at the University of Chicago, Parten had said, "So do I. Of course, he shocks some people. He talks straight. That always shocks some people."

My conversations with other directors—who saw enemies closing in, and were sharply critical of Hutchins for "alienating possible supporters of the Fund"—made me wonder whether I had overestimated the Fund's strength. The possibility of its destruction no longer seemed utterly ridiculous to me.

Parten and Hutchins had reinforced my own conviction that the Fund was worth defending. I thought I had to do what I could, I believed that the Fund might still be able to rally many of the people who believe in the Jeffersonian tradition. The American Civil Liberties Union, the American Friends Service Committee, some noted lawyers, women's organizations, and church groups were valiantly defending civil liberties and civil rights—and the Fund could work with them.

So I entered the most exhilarating, exhausting, frustrating, rewarding, and wounding experience of my life. I stayed with the Fund and its creation, the Center for the Study of Democratic Institutions, for nineteen years, from the time of Eisenhower to the time of Jimmy Carter. The Fund proved to be much more durable than any of its foes had expected it to be—and more vulnerable to internal battles than its friends had envisioned.

When the Fund created the Center in Santa Barbara in 1959, it went through a sweeping transformation. It was no longer a grant-making foundation. Its remaining financial resources were devoted to the Center. The board's role diminished. The Center was run by Hutchins with the assistance and advice of the other officers of the Fund and the counsel of fellows picked by him.

Hutchins frequently referred to the importance of the directors and the significance of the Fellows, but nearly everyone knew that the Center was a monarchy. Hutchins was a king who wanted to save democracy. He was also a judge who reviewed the world's problems. He was intrigued by a proposal once made by a Center consultant, Gerald Gottlieb, for the formation of a Court of Man, a world tribunal with power to render judgments on those who misused authority. Hutchins would have relished being the Chief Justice of such a court.

Before he became president of the University of Chicago, Hutchins had been the dean of the Yale law school. President Roosevelt had once talked about appointing Hutchins to the Supreme Court of the United States. Hutchins studied that court and its opinions. He frequently led discussions of the court's rulings.

In the 1950's, Hutchins had described the Fund as "a small island of sanity in a McCarthyite world." He actually operated it as a court of

494

reason, decided what project to undertake, what issues to examine, what organizations to aid. When he established the Center he called it "an intellectual community," yet his dedication to the law, his interest in the judicial process, made it a court of reason, too.

Sadly, Hutchins and his fellows—even after the drastic reorganization of the Center in 1969—were not able to devise a constitution for the Center that might have made it a truly democratic place. Hutchins and the directors of the Fund could not solve the problem of passing on his power to a successor while he lived.

In 1975, when the Center was split again by dissensions over its administration and its future, Hutchins wrote a rueful letter to my wife, who had proposed a continuous dialogue focused purely on the Center's internal problems. She had hoped that the Center could show what thinking could do to bring a solution. Hutchins said, "I'm afraid our experience shows that the achievement of an intellectual community can be thwarted by all kinds of apparently trivial factors and that it is possible only if luck is added to the basic requirements of character, commitment and intelligence."

Two months after he wrote that letter—and after Malcolm Moos, his temporary successor, had been removed and Hutchins had returned to the Center's helm—Hutchins decided to try again, perhaps hoping for better luck. Aware of his own faults and failings, aware of the limitations of his chosen colleagues, Hutchins kept on trying until he died in 1977.

I talked with Hutchins almost every day for nineteen years. I learned something in every encounter with him. He was challenging, astonishing, witty, ironic, sometimes very warm, sometimes cold, sometimes humble and exhausted, sometimes imperious, yet always searching, always learning. Sometimes he appeared to be Zeus on a mountain called Olympus. Sometimes he viewed his life as an avenue of ruined monuments.

That he managed to bring his vision of a community into being and to maintain it as an independent entity for twenty years is in itself a testament to his tenacity, resourcefulness, and intellectual vigor. His tragedy, and that of the institution, was that he could not keep it free of the insidious factionalism, the warring ambitions, the overbearing obsessions, and the backbiting that afflict all human communities, no matter how lofty their ideals. In a sense, Hutchins' Center belongs to that continuous tradition of Utopian ideas that have burst upon the American landscape throughout the history of this nation of pilgrims and immigrants.

A true community of minds, a court of reason, may be valid only as an idea to be cherished and reached for—not as a reality to be developed here on earth. To me, there were signs through all the years that Hutchins was seeking a heavenly city, a fellowship of kindred minds—like the fellowship of the saints in a hymn he loved, a hymn his father had taught him to sing: "Blest Be the Tie That Binds."

With the aid of many people who have opened their thoughts and their records for me, I have tried to describe in this book how the Fund and the Center developed and changed. No one will ever encompass the whole story and the connecting stories with the main tale. So many projects were conceived, so many ideas were offered and argued, so many meetings were held, so many publications were issued, so many conflicts occurred, so many notable people were involved—and the story expands and extends into the future.

The Fund started with the Jeffersonian idea. It made major contributions in the first phase of its existence, but it could not put an end to heresy hunting in America. McCarthy is dead, and the House of Un-American Activities Committee has been abolished. Yet federal, state, and local agencies keep files on millions of Americans: the seeds of suspicion, the viruses of McCarthyism live on. In 1981, members of Congress began to talk of re-establishing committees to expose "subversive" people.

The Center lives on, too, although it is no longer the completely independent entity Hutchins and other founding fellows (including myself) established in 1959. It was taken over in 1979 by the University of California at Santa Barbara and its headquarters were transferred to the university campus. The dialogues on Eucalyptus Hill were ended—and new dialogues were begun. It is now called the Robert Maynard Hutchins center for the Study of Democratic Institutions.

If this planet does not become a radioactive cinder in a nuclear war, this center may be a place of controversy and insights for a long time to come. It may excite many minds in the future, as Plato's academy has excited human minds in all the centuries since the Greeks tried to discover through illuminating dialogues what the potentials of human beings are, what ought to be done to foster freedom and justice and how to build a better world.

Chapter 1

A father's voice, and $15 million for democracy

When he was five years old, his father woke him in the middle of the night to tell him that Theodore Roosevelt had been elected president. He never forgot the note of exultation in his father's voice. Roosevelt was a bold and brave man, his father said: a fighter for justice, a leader with strong moral fiber. That was what the country needed.

He never forgot the early mornings when he knelt beside his father on a bare floor, praying for God's guidance and the courage to do what was right. The evil in the world had to be opposed. True men had to stand up straight and speak up plainly against oppressors and exploiters, against persecutors, against those who were corrupt and spread corruption.

As he grew older, Robert Maynard Hutchins no longer believed that the answers to all the world's problems could be found in the Bible or in his father's wisdom. He felt the suffering men inflicted on men when he served as an ambulance driver at the front in Italy in the First World War. He encountered frustrations as a student at Yale, as a teacher in a boys' school, as dean of the Yale law school, as head of the University of

Chicago. He grew more and more angry at the power and persistence of evil in the world, in others, and in himself.

On a day in February 1953, when he walked into the conference room of the Ford Foundation in Pasadena, California, Hutchins burned with rage against the spreading tide of McCarthyism. He was carrying on his father's work in his own way. As an associate director of the Ford Foundation, he had helped to spend $75 million on projects he considered to be for "the common good" of humanity; now he hoped that Henry Ford II and the other trustees could be persuaded to take another $15 million dollars from Ford's treasury to strengthen American democracy. He believed that the decision to be made that day might be a crucial factor in the battle to save the American Republic.

He was a tall, ruggedly handsome man whose features conveyed a rather awesome dignity. He was aware of the impression he made on other people, and he habitually kept in check the inner rage and deep depression that gnawed at him. He wanted to change the world, and he found that the world was hard to change. He had reformed the Yale law school, but he wasn't sure the reforms would last. He had remodeled the University of Chicago, but the university was already reverting to its old patterns.

That day in Pasadena, he was particularly disturbed because his friend and backer, Paul Hoffman, had been forced to resign from the presidency of the Ford Foundation. Hoffman had brought him into the foundation, telling him that the Ford organization had "the biggest blank check in history." His years with Hoffman had been years of great hopes and high visions. Without Hoffman, his own position in the foundation was precarious. He knew that Henry Ford II was perplexed by his wit and felt uneasy in his presence.

Paul Hoffman came into the conference room, shaking hands with the trustees who had driven him from the presidency. Hoffman had promised to come to the trustees' meeting as a representative of the Fund for the Republic, and Hoffman kept promises. Hutchins greeted him warmly.

Soon after the Fund had been created by the Ford trustees and announced to the press in December 1952, the directors of the Fund had invited Hoffman to serve as its first chairman. Hoffman had long advocated the creation of just such an organization to uphold essential freedoms. The Ford trustees had approved the election of Hoffman as the Fund's chairman. All of them liked and admired Hoffman as a person.

The question to be settled by the Ford trustees at the February meeting was whether the Fund would be given a large grant to enable it to operate in difficult and dangerous areas. Hutchins and Hoffman—and W.H. Ferry, Ford's public relations counselor—had urged Ford and the trustees to provide enough millions to enable the Fund to function effectively on a national scale. From the beginning, Ferry had played an important part in the development of the Fund idea.

Hutchins moved quietly around the conference room that day. He felt that the future of the Fund depended largely on three of the Fund's directors who were there to present the Fund's plans. These three men—like all of the Fund's board—had been chosen by Hutchins and Hoffman. Hutchins believed that the months he had spent with Hoffman in going over a list of 200 possible directors had been well used.

He had known each of the three men for a long time. Erwin Griswold, the dean of the Harvard Law School, had received a bachelor's degree and a master's degree from Oberlin College, where Hutchins' father had taught for many years. Jubal R. Parten and Hutchins had been friends for eighteen years, ever since they had worked together to establish an astronomical observatory. William H. Joyce, Jr., a successful manufacturer who had been brought up on the Bible and William Shakespeare, had been one of Hoffman's assistants in the Marshall Plan.

Griswold, who had served as chairman of the Fund's planning committee, was dedicated to the Bill of Rights and had been horrified by the behavior of Senator Joseph McCarthy. He had been on the faculty at Harvard for nineteen years and dean of the law school since 1946. Before going to Harvard, he had practiced law in Massachusetts and Washington and had been a special assistant to the attorney general of the United States under Presidents Hoover and Roosevelt.

Griswold was a solid, square-shouldered man with a Republican background and the sober manner of a legal expert, and he impressed Ford and the trustees as a man who would keep the Fund on a steady course. Behind Griswold sat Bethuel M. Webster, of the Wall Street law firm of Webster, Sheffield, & Chrystie, who had been retained as the Fund's counsel on Griswold's recommendation. Webster was dapper and confident, widely known and respected.

Griswold reviewed the first three meetings of the Fund's board. At the initial meeting on December 10 and 11 in New York, nine of the fifteen directors were present. They had elected the planning committee and had approved a grant of $50,000 to the American Bar Association's Special Committee on Individual Rights as Affected by National Security. At their second meeting, the directors had selected Paul Hoffman as their chairman and had decided that the Fund would need between $15 million and $25 million to finance its work over a period of five years. At their third gathering, they had approved a nine-page prospectus prepared by Griswold's planning committee.

While Griswold presented the prospectus in blunt terms, Hutchins watched the faces of the Ford trustees. He was not sure how much candor they could take. One of the most important trustees—Frank W. Abrams, chairman of the Standard Oil Company of New Jersey—had tried to get him to have the whole idea of the Fund reexamined by a panel of five notable people outside the Ford Foundation. In the summer of 1952, while Hutchins had been pushing the trustees toward a decision, Abrams had written to him: "Perhaps the most difficult of the programs to be certain about is the Fund for the Republic. I know of no topic that is of more fundamental importance—yet I know of none where the possibilities of inadvertently doing harm rather than good are more real." Hutchins had not accepted Abrams' suggestion. He felt that the Fund had to be launched as soon as possible.

The prospective program outlined by Griswold that day emphasized that the Fund would rely on research and educational methods, but the subjects to be explored would undoubtedly be hard to handle and might be hotly disputed. That was why the Fund's directors felt that they had to be completely independent—and why a large grant from the Ford Foundation was necessary, to assure the Fund's existence during years of controversy.

Under the prospectus, the Fund proposed to tackle "the extent to which information obtained by wiretapping, third degree interrogations, unlawful searches and seizures, had been gained by illegal police methods." This was a matter of particular concern to Dean Griswold and other legal defenders of the Constitution, who felt that the people's rights were being undermined by such violations of the Constitution's fundamental guarantees.

The Fund also planned to examine "the rights of witnesses in quasi-judicial proceedings, including availability of counsel, opportunity for cross-examination, etc.; the use and misuse of the Fifth Amendment privilege against self-incrimination; the availability of qualified counsel for indigent or unpopular defendants; and the extent to which the press influenced judicial or quasi-judicial decisions by giving unequal coverage to sensational accusations and subsequent denials."

These were all topics that had concerned Hutchins for years. He was enraged by wiretapping, unlawful searches and seizures, beatings of accused people, and the use of torture by the police. He was anguished by the obvious injustices in the federal loyalty procedures, which did not provide opportunities for cross-examination of accusers. He was troubled by wild stories in the press, which made it difficult for many people to be tried fairly in the courts.

In another section, the prospectus discussed by Griswold on that day in February referred to the possibility of "a study of the activities of the House Un-American Activities Committee, the Senate Internal Security Committee, and other Congressional investigating committees." The

Fund was not going to flinch from examining some of the most powerful groups in American life.

Other thorny issues raised in the prospectus were the influence of communism in the United States—with a sharp sentence declaring that "communism will find in the Fund for the Republic no haven for its subversive activities"—blacklisting in the movies and in broadcasting; government secrecy provisions; immigration laws; equal voting privileges for minorities; released time for religious activities in the public schools; freedom of expression for teachers; discrimination in restaurants and transportation facilities.

In presenting that grim catalogue to the Ford trustees, Griswold showed no doubt that the trustees would be convinced of the absolute necessity of providing the Fund with money enough to become a resplendent champion of civil rights and civil liberties. He indicated that the Fund's directors were willing and able to take the heat that would certainly be generated by the projects he had outlined.

Jubal R. Parten of Madisonville, Texas, then spoke to the trustees. He was a tall, straight, slim man with a military bearing and had been called Major Parten by his friends since he had attained the rank of major as a young officer in World War I. In a letter to a friend, soon after Parten had agreed to be a director of the Fund, Hutchins had referred to him as "the best man on the Fund's board."

Parten had become an independent oil producer after he returned from his Army service in 1919. He had earned a law degree from the University of Texas, and he had once thought of practicing law or entering the diplomatic service, but he had decided that seeking and finding oil offered more excitement and more opportunities to lead a productive life. He was a man of many interests, active in education and philanthropy. He had been chairman of the University of Texas regents and had served as chairman of the Federal Reserve Bank in Dallas for eight years.

Although he was a wealthy Texan, shrewd in business, persistent in pursuit of his aims, Parten did not conform to the pattern of hard-driving

Texans who distained ideas and intellectuals. He was a reader of history. His home town, where he had lived all his life, was named for James Madison, one of the founders of the American republic. He shared the visions of Madison and Thomas Jefferson. He was alarmed by the reckless behavior of Joseph McCarthy and the House Un-American Activities Committee.

His first invitation to join the Fund board had come from Hoffman. He had told Hoffman that he was already on too many boards. Then Hutchins had called him. "This is going to be a rough ride," Hutchins had said. "We need battlers. You don't want to miss this." Parten hadn't been able to resist that challenge.

The light of battle was in his eyes when he addressed the Ford trustees. Like Griswold, he stressed the requirement for complete independence for the Fund. He foresaw that Ford dealers would put pressure on the foundation when the Fund got into trouble. If the Fund had complete independence, it could take full responsibility for its projects.

Parten supported Griswold's request for a grant of $15 million. With that much money available, Parten felt the Fund could make a substantial impact. A grant of that size would make it possible to find a first-rate man to serve as the full-time chief executive of the Fund, and Paul Hoffman had already indicated that he could not give much of his time to the actual operations.

William Joyce spoke as fervently for the Fund as Griswold and Parten had. Joyce had started a shoe manufacturing company with a small loan from his father, and his products were sold in many countries. He had been a speaker at conferences of businessmen, urging them to encourage their employees to participate in the development of their companies. He asserted that the advances of the American people were due to acceptance of "the idea of freedom and the idea of equality." He thought that the Fund could demonstrate to the world that Americans were really committed to those ideas—and the tide of McCarthyism would recede.

Bethuel Webster then offered a few comments to the Ford trustees. He did not speak for long. His presence in the room with Dean Griswold was evidence enough that he would be available to provide the advice of an experienced Wall Street lawyer whenever the Fund required it.

Ford and his trustees thanked the Fund directors and Webster for their statements. Watching them, Hutchins felt his confidence rise. He thought that the odds were in the Fund's favor, but he waited for the verdict of the Ford trustees with impatience. He believed that the Fund should have been started in 1951, when the spread of McCarthyism had first become shockingly evident.

Hutchins had been struggling to master his impatience since his years at the University of Chicago, when he had tried to reform the university at a breakneck pace and had aroused the implacable opposition of many faculty members. This time, his patience was not severely tested. The Fund directors were called back to the conference room after a brief interval, and Ford announced that the trustees—on a motion Ford had made himself—had authorized the transfer of $14.8 million to the Fund, with $2.8 million to be given at once and the balance to be provided when the Department of the Treasury certified the Fund as a tax-exempt foundation.

"I think we should turn you loose and let you do the job," Ford said.

Recalling the moment of decision later, Parten emphasized that there were two points the Fund directors had to accept. They were not to make any grants that would endanger the Fund's status as an educational foundation. They were not to hire a card-carrying communist as a staff member. Parten said, "Since we didn't regard the two conditions as tying our hands in any major way—because we didn't intend to do either of those things—we accepted."

It was a high moment for Hutchins. He had been pleased when the trustees had appropriated large amounts for two other projects he had pushed—the Fund for the Advancement of Education and the Fund for Adult Education. But it had been harder to get the Fund for the Republic through the foundation's labyrinth, so the taste of triumph that day in 1953 was sweeter.

Hutchins and Hoffman expressed their appreciation to Griswold, Parten, Joyce and Webster. The Fund had won the full backing of the Ford trustees at last. The struggle to win that approval went back to January 1951. At the urging of Hutchins and Ferry, Hoffman had first asked the trustees to consider a national commission to protect democratic principles in an era of international conflicts. Hutchins had talked with Hoffman several times before Hoffman had presented the proposal. It was discussed and put aside by the trustees.

In August 1951 Hutchins had tried to move the project forward with a two-page memorandum entitled "A Fund for Democratic Freedoms." In September of that year, W. H. Ferry had sent a statement to Ford and his associates, calling for "bold experimentation." Admitting that such a policy mighty sometimes "prove irritating" to some of the Ford Motor Company officials and might "embarrass temporarily members of the Ford family," Ferry asserted: "In the long run it will bring more credit to the Ford name than the easy and innocuous course of making impressive contributions to established activities.... Here it should be remembered that the reputation of the Ford Motor Company largely centers around Henry Ford's lifelong preoccupation with experimentation and pioneering ventures." (Hutchins said later: "W. H. Ferry and I worked out the plan for the Fund for the Republic....")

Henry Ford II and his trustees were willing to put money into "pioneering ventures" if they were sure that the men engaged in such ventures were solid men with excellent reputations. Griswold, Parten, Joyce, and the other directors of the Fund had been personally approved by every one of the Ford trustees. In the action the trustees took on that February day in 1953, they felt that they were placing approximately $15 million of the foundation's money in very safe hands.

Ford and the trustees had been pleased by the generally favorable response of newspaper editors to the announcement of the Fund's formation with an initial grant of $200,000 in December 1952. The

Christian Science Monitor had declared: "Spokesmen for these philanthropic trusts have given a House committee and the American public some excellent lessons in the courage and intelligence necessary to sustain progress." Other newspapers had carried good headlines: "Foundation Will Seek to Protect Thought in U.S." and "Ford Foundation Fights for Freedom."

The list of the Fund's directors was reassuring. In addition to the three men who had spoken at the Pasadena meeting, the members were James F. Brownlee, legal partner in the J. H. Whitney firm; Charles W. Cole, president of Amherst College; Eleanor B. Stevenson, wife of the president of Oberlin College; George N. Shuster, a leading Catholic educator, president of Hunter College; Meyer Kestnbaum, president of Hart, Schaffner and Marx; Richard Finnegan, editor of the Chicago *Sun-Times*; Malcolm Bryan, president of the Federal Reserve Bank at Atlanta; Huntington Cairns, a noted lawyer in Washington, D.C.; Russell Dearmont of St. Louis, president of the Missouri Pacific Railroad; Elmo Roper, public opinion analyst; M. Albert Linton, president of the Provident Mutual Life Insurance Company, Philadelphia; James D. Zellerbach, president of the Crown Zellerbach Corporation of San Francisco; and Paul Hoffman. (Bryan, a man who sought to avoid controversies, had resigned after attending the Fund board meeting on December 10, 1952, where he had learned that the Fund planned to go vigorously into civil rights). But the other board members were apparently ready to face the strife ahead of them.

Hutchins hoped that the quick resignation of Bryan did not mean that the board would disintegrate under fire. He had examined the character of all the prospective directors. Hoffman and he had tried to find as many staunch conservatives as possible in order to show that civil liberties and civil rights had the support of intelligent conservatives as well as liberals. Yet he knew that every director could be shaken to some extent by the bludgeoning that might come from McCarthy and his allies. He had written to a friend: "It is a pretty good group, worried about civil liberties, and also worried about its respectability. I do not know which worry will win."

In the months following the Pasadena meeting, Hutchins began to show impatience. The Fund's board seemed to move very slowly. The Fund had received a "temporary" certificate of tax exemption on March 20, 1953, and the Ford Foundation promptly provided $2.8 million, with an assurance that the remaining $12 million would be given when the fund had a regular certificate. But the Fund directors were preoccupied with finding exactly the right man to serve as president.

The uproar that had followed the Fund's first allocation of money— $50,000 to be given to the American Bar Association's Special Committee on Individual Rights as Affected by National Security—had made the directors doubly determined to find a president acceptable to leaders in the Congress and the Eisenhower administration. Some members of Congress had labeled the Bar Association project "an investigation of investigations" and felt that it was an invasion into the prerogatives of Congress.

When the $15 million grant to the Fund and the election of Hoffman as its chairman were announced to the press, many newspapers commended the Fund and the Ford Foundation. The St. Louis *Post-Dispatch*, for example, praised Hoffman in an editorial on March 1, 1953: "Fortunately Paul Hoffman…is continuing as chairman of the board to administer the Fund for the Republic. This is fortunate because pressures of many sorts will be brought against a full inventory of our civil rights. It will take Paul Hoffman to stand up against these influences." But the Washington *Times-Herald* and the Chicago *Tribune* were skeptical and critical. The *Times-Herald* said: "All we have to say is that 15 million dollars would be a high price to pay to 'get' Senators McCarthy and Jenner and Representative Velde (of the Un-American Activities Committee)."

McCarthy seemed ready to pounce on the Fund. He wrote to Hoffman on March 31, demanding information on what the Fund planned to do and asking Hoffman when he could "appear in Washington" to explain the Fund's program. On May 1, after Hoffman had informed him that "both the executive staff and the program of the Fund are still in the process of organization," McCarthy asked for a complete list of the Fund's staff as soon as members were appointed.

Nixon, who had been elected vice president under Eisenhower, also kept an eye on the Fund. In response to an inquiry from Nixon, Hoffman assured him in a letter on March 24 that the Fund's initial research would be "directed toward as accurate a determination as possible of the extent and nature of the internal communist menace and its effect on our community and institutions."

Aware of the close scrutiny to which the Fund was being subjected, the directors had decided that a scholarly study of communism would be valuable in showing the facts about its impact and might reduce the hysteria induced by the McCarthyites who saw "communists" or "communist influence" everywhere. Hutchins doubted whether any number of studies would pacify McCarthy and Nixon, but he knew that the Fund had to sponsor such studies for its own protection.

Among the nominees for the Fund's presidency in March 1953 were Governor Earl Warren, of California; Justice Robert Jackson, of the United States Supreme Court; and Erwin Canham, editor of the *Christian Science Monitor*. Jackson did not with to leave the Court. Warren was appointed chief justice of the United States. Canham was committed to his work as an editor.

While the search for a president continued, two committees on the board began to function. One, headed by Elmo Roper, tried to discover the best methods for conducting a broad study of domestic communism. The other, chaired by Huntington Cairns, delved into procedures for reviewing and publicizing "the legacy of American liberty."

In the middle of April 1953, Paul Hoffman found a Congressman who was willing to be considered for the Fund's chief executive position: Representative Clifford Case. Hoffman asked five of his fellow directors to talk with Case as soon as they could.

Case, described as "winsome but tough" by a colleague in Congress, was an energetic, affable man who had been in the House of

Representatives for eight years. He had taken definite stands for civil rights, had vigorously supported Eisenhower in the presidential election campaign of 1952, and was respected by the Washington correspondents of the major newspapers. He had been endorsed in his congressional campaigns by the American Federation of Labor and the Americans for Democratic Action, a liberal group, but he was not a target for the right-wing organizations. He had the friendship of Nixon and the admiration of some Democrats.

Case impressed Charles Cole, and made an equally good impression on Huntington Cairns, Albert Linton, and George Shuster. John Lord O'Brian, a noted Washington attorney who had replaced Malcolm Bryan on the Fund's board, thought that Case might be just the right man. David Freeman, a lawyer who was serving as the acting president of the Fund during this interim, was also enthusiastic about Case.

At their meeting on May 18 in New York, the directors elected Case as a member of the board and as "president of the Fund for the Republic," subject to the negotiation of satisfactory terms of employment. Case accepted a few days later, saying that he would leave his seat in Congress early in August and would begin his duties as the chief officer of the Fund in September. Freeman agreed to become secretary of the corporation as soon as Case took over.

Hutchins was pleased by the selection of Case. He was known to be a congressman dedicated to the Bill of Rights. Case was quiet, discreet, patient, willing to listen to advice. He was ready to leave the public pronouncements on the Fund's policies to Chairman Hoffman and to carry forward the programs developed by the board's committees. He was a prudent man, who would not act in haste. He satisfied the board's desire for respectability, but he was likely to stand up to McCarthy.

At the May 18 meeting, the board appropriated $25,000 for "summer studies" on the legacy of American freedom, and $10,000 for Samuel A. Stouffer, a professor of sociology at Harvard, to compose a questionnaire and an outline of a survey on "popular attitudes on the extent of domestic communism and its impact." Another $10,000 was provided for studies of the records of congressional committees, trials of communists, and revelations of admitted communists, to be directed by Arthur E. Sutherland, of the Harvard law school.

When the board met again a month later, Case was welcomed as a director and as president-elect, but Paul Hoffman presided. The board granted $55,000 to the American Friends Service Committee for its extensive efforts in race relations, gave an additional $19,500 to Professor Stouffer for a "trial run sampling of his questionnaire," and another $2,500 to Dr. Sutherland. Hoffman proposed a "study of nonconformity," without any notable reactions from his fellow directors.

Although the directors were apparently satisfied with Case, a mood of caution still prevailed. The board members did not act on a suggestion that Case should have contingency funds to be "dispensed with the advice of a committee of the Board." Until Case had shown what he intended to do, his freedom as an executive would be limited.

Observing the Fund's first steps, Hutchins grew more restive. The House Un-American Activities Committee, headed by Harold H. Velde, of Illinois, was rampaging through the country, investigating teachers and spreading fear in schools. J.B. Matthews, a member of McCarthy's staff, claimed that 7000 Protestant clergymen were tainted with communism. McCarthy was branding people who invoked the Fifth Amendment protection against self-accusation as "Fifth Amendment communists." Hutchins hoped that the Fund would do more than just talk about "the legacy of liberty" and collect questionnaires on "popular attitudes."

In July the Fund established an office in New York. Requests for grants poured in from civil liberties organizations and educational institutions, but the board did not act on them at its August meeting, spending much of its time in discussing future policies. At the September session, the Fund board granted $40,000 to Columbia University's Bicentennial Committee for a film, radio broadcasts and pamphlets entitled *Man's Right to Knowledge and the Free Use Thereof,* and $35,000 to the Voluntary Defenders Committee of Boston, a group formed to aid indigent defendants. Case was given authority to employ consultants and several assistants.

Hutchins wrote to Parten in November, chafing at the Fund's ponderous pace: "How about getting started at the local level? For example, we could organize a corporation with the same base as the Fund for the Republic, but limited to Southern California. We could raise money locally to match a grant from the Fund....I am inclined to think that the Fund will eventually find that it will have to work through local and regional groups. I talked about this with Joyce and Hoffman. Bill was enthusiastic. Hoffman seemed primarily interested in other matters, such as getting your tax exemption and the balance of the money due from the Ford Foundation." Hoffman was eager to get the Fund under way, but he felt that it was essential to get a permanent certificate of tax exemption from the Treasury and the full Ford grant before the Fund began a large-scale program.

Hutchins also prodded Elmo Roper, asking him what he thought of the Fund's plodding course. Early in December 1953, as the Fund approached the end of its first year of existence, Roper wrote to Hutchins: "I think it is probably fair to state that progress is being made, but frankly, it is being made at what to me is a discouraging rate. But I think it is fair to add that no judgment ought to be passed for another three months' period."

That did not sit well with Hutchins, who saw the erosion of civil liberties in the United States proceeding at a rapid rate. He continued to be an associate director of the Ford Foundation, and he was frequently consulted by officials of the Fund for Adult Education and the Fund for the Advancement of Education as well as by directors of the Fund for the Republic. That was not enough for him. He yearned to be in the thick of the fight against McCarthyism.

The evil in the world seemed to be growing. The Fund for the Republic had a vital mission to fulfill. To Hutchins, there was no time to be lost.

Chapter 31

The Fund and the Center:

What was accomplished? Were the achievements worth the cost? Could anybody tell? What could the future hold?

In the vast complexity of modern society, with hundreds of organizations striving to exert an influence on the course of events, with change in every field occurring at an enormously rapid rate, it is extremely difficult to estimate the importance and value of an educational foundation. Showered with money by the Ford Foundation, the Fund for the Republic was ushered into the world with a flourish of trumpets— proclaimed to be a champion of civil liberties and civil rights, with a board of directors composed of famous and powerful people. The Fund set out to preserve the American Constitution and to defend the Bill of Rights against demagogues and hysteria.

During the first five years of the Fund's existence, the directors spent or appropriated more than $11 million from the $15 million provided by the Ford Foundation. In the process of making grants to dozens of groups seeking to maintain the vitality of the rights and liberties of the American people, the Fund enraged the chairman of the House Un-American Activities Committee and others who felt they had a monopoly on what was patriotic and what wasn't.

In those highly active years—from 1952 to 1957—the Fund generated support for peaceful desegregation of American schools, exposed the influence of communism in American life in a series of books written by experts, financed an analysis of American attitudes on conformity and dissent, aided a study of wiretapping and secret surveillance methods used against citizens, fostered an epoch-making report on racial integration in housing, established a Commission on the Rights and Liberties of American Indians, analyzed the government's security system and the pressures against academic freedom in colleges and universities, took a hard look at censorship movements, and financed an explosive report on blacklisting in the entertainment industry—a report that shook Hollywood and the broadcasting systems.

The 1950's were years in which people generally kept their heads down and avoided controversies. The Fund plunged head-on into one controversy after another.

The reports and recommendations of the studies financed by the Fund in its first five years produced more tangible results than the publications later generated by the "basic issues" projects and the Center for the Study of Democratic Institutions, which grew out of these projects. The assault to which the Fund was subjected by the House Un-American Activities Committee was so outrageous that Sam Rayburn, Speaker of the House of Representatives, set in motion a movement among Democratic congressmen to abolish the committee—and that movement finally succeeded. The Fund's exposure of blacklisting was used by John Henry Faulk, a CBS commentator who had lost his job, to win the largest libel suit in history—and led to the breakup of the blacklisters.

The Fund's aid to interracial groups in the South was a factor in the gradual acceptance of desegregation in that region. The Fund's reports on communism dispelled much of the hysteria about the extent of communist influence in America.

It was virtually impossible to measure the success or failure of the Center, which Hutchins and his colleagues founded in 1959. What are the measurements of "success" in a series of endless dialogues? Who could tell what effects were being evoked in the minds of the hundreds of people from many fields who took part in Center conferences and international convocations? Or how far the repercussions spread?

When Supreme Court Justice William O. Douglas was chairman of the Center's board, he repeatedly advocated the establishment of Centers in all the major cities of the United States and in other countries. He called for an enormous continuing education program to stimulate the flow of new ideas and the presenting of such ideas in terms that would awaken millions of people to the need for reforms to meet the requirements of human survival. But the money necessary for the Douglas proposals could not be obtained.

In the 1960's, the concerns of most citizens were focused on the cold war with communist antagonists, the maintenance of economic growth, the technological competition with the Russians, "containing" the Chinese Maoists, and preventing the spread of communism in Asia and Europe. The arms race grew more horrifying year by year, but no one seemed to know how to slow it down or stop it. The power of the Pentagon expanded, and so did the industrial complex related to the gigantic military forces considered necessary for national security.

From its inception, the Center gave much attention to the impact of the arms race and the cold war on American society. Two Center pamphlets by the noted military historian Walter Millis—*Individual Freedom and the Common Defense* and *The Constitution and the Common Defense*—were widely circulated. Millis described what he called "the war system" and declared that it would have to be dismantled if humanity wished to survive. He predicted that the devastating power of nuclear weapons would force the great nations to avoid a nuclear war. Thus far, his predictions have proved to be accurate.

Nuclear war was avoided, but the United States plunged into a disaster in Vietnam under Presidents Kennedy and Johnson. The Vietnam War disrupted the world's economy and contributed to the raging inflation that brought poverty and hardship to millions in many nations. President Nixon took four years to sanction American withdrawal and continued the huge budgetary deficits that slashed the value of the dollar and brought the United States to the verge of economic collapse.

The scholars at the Center did not ignore these developments or retreat into an ivory tower. The Center published a series of warnings, urging the American people to get their leaders to consider more constructive policies.

In 1965 the Center issued a booklet entitled *How the U.S. Got Involved in Vietnam*, outlining the dictatorial nature of the Saigon government and the corruption that infected the whole regime in South Vietnam. In 1967, two directors of the Center—Harry Ashmore and William Baggs—went to Vietnam and returned with proposals that could have ended the war in that year, saving many thousands of American lives and preventing the expenditure of many billions of dollars.

While the Vietnam tragedy went on, the center brought together groups of experienced people who suggested alternative policies for American relations with Asian nations and released a series of taped discussions that revealed the misconceptions, misinformation, and miscalculations of American officials. George Kahin of Cornell University, a visiting fellow at the Center, widely recognized as a leading specialist on Indochina, insisted that Vietnam was only a small part of far thornier problems confronting the United States in Asia. He also pointed out the mistakes and misunderstandings of the Soviet Union in that area of the world.

The publication of the so-called Pentagon Papers later confirmed the accuracy of the criticisms made by Kahin and others at Center meetings. The warnings from the Center were heeded by some senators and endorsed by many citizens but were brushed aside by Presidents Johnson and Nixon.

The Center tried in many ways to build foundations for peace through realistic exchanges of ideas and proposals by leaders from many countries who participated in the convocations based on Pope John's statement "Pacem in Terris" (Peace on Earth). No other educational institution brought together so many leaders to examine the requirements for international order. The Center convocations helped to pave the way for better relationships between the United States and the Soviet Union and helped to create an atmosphere in which new relationships were established with Mao's China.

But the Center was active in many other fields at the same time. Scholars at the Center issued warnings on the decay and disarray of democratic institutions long before the Watergate scandal appeared in the headlines. Other Center publications warned of the creeping pollution of the planet, long before millions of people realized that the web of life might be destroyed by such pollution.

Far in advance of actual developments, people at the Center revealed the thinking of radical students, the changing attitudes of the young toward the whole society, the implications of the changes in race relations, and the demands of ethnic minorities. The Center showed the defects and the power of the mass media at a time when many people were not aware of the pervasive impact of the press and broadcasting industries on every aspect of modern life.

Six years of discussions, involving dozens of meetings and the thoughts of 200 consultants (including historians, judges, political scientists, economists, and many others), went into the Center's model for a new American Constitution, published in 1970. The principal drafter was Rexford G. Tugwell, a former member of President Roosevelt's "brains trust." But the man who pushed the project along was Robert Hutchins, who had repeatedly cited the fact that the Constitution of 1787 made no mention of political parties, labor unions, corporations, ecology, education, technology, or other areas with which modern government had to deal.

The model Constitution was not conceived as a document to be presented to the people for ratification and implementation, but as an instrument for thinking about the issues of the 1970's. At a time when American institutions did not seem to be functioning effectively, the Center scholars hoped that the model might awaken hope in millions of apathetic citizens and bring new vitality to a sagging democracy.

But the development of that model Constitution turned out to be one of the most controversial projects in which the Center had ever engaged. It was regarded as foolish, futile, and possibly dangerous to the American system. It stirred some discussions for a couple of years but it did not produce the long-range effects Hutchins had tried to evoke.

When internal strife occurred at the Center in 1969 and in 1975, it became evident to people outside the Center that the scholars on Eucalyptus Hill were not able to solve their own constitutional problems. From 1959 to 1969 the Center did have some of the characteristics of a community. While there were many disagreements among the staff members, there was a feeling that everyone had an assured position under the benevolent reign of Hutchins. The expulsion of Ferry, Hoffman, Seely, Bishop Pike, and others in the spring of 1969 destroyed that feeling of security for those who remained as well as those who were evicted.

The fierce factional fighting, which damaged and eventually destroyed the administration of Malcolm Moos, showed again that the struggle for power overrode the devotion to dialogue. Hutchins, who had been largely responsible for the installation of Moos, finally decided that Moos had to be removed and that determined the outcome.

Personal attacks made by members of the opposing camps upon one another revealed the passionate feelings of those involved in the civil war. These explosions of anger saddened me and disturbed many people who regarded the Center as a citadel of reason. But people with keen intellects have engaged in angry disputes all through history. The people at the Center were as vulnerable to their emotions as other people in other places and other times.

In spite of its own internal failures, in spite of the defects and limitations of its own projects, in spite of the distortions in purposes and programs forced upon it by the necessity for a perpetual fund-raising campaign, the Center has undoubtedly had an impact on scholars, editors, broadcasters, political leaders, lawyers, economists, and others in many fields in many countries. As the principal program of the Fund for the Republic, it was an important factor in the survival of the principles of freedom and justice in a technological, bureaucratic, fast-changing society.

Were the projects of the Fund and the Center worth what they cost? It is difficult to make a final judgment. In the years between 1952 and 1977, the Fund obtained and spent about $42 million. Over a twenty-five-year period, this means an average annual expenditure of about $1,680,000. Most of this money went for salaries, consultants' fees, payments to people. Hutchins believed in living well himself and in paying his associates good salaries. Some of them earned what they got, and others didn't. Hutchins was not deeply concerned about administrative details or deficits.

Undoubtedly some of the money received and spent by the Fund might have been put to better uses. But Admiral Hyman Rickover, who took part in several Center conferences and once donated $1,000 to help keep the Center going, told me that he thought the Center's budget was very small for an institution performing such a significant service. He referred to the billions he could easily get for nuclear submarines, and he said he thought that the Center's work was more vital for the future of humanity than submarines or other weapons.

Paul Dickson, in his authoritative book on American research organizations, entitled *Think Tanks*, described the Center in these terms: "The Center's particular form of megalomania is an accompaniment of its own style: fierce independence, chronic optimism, and iconoclasm. Its singular dedication to clarification of existing issues and to the attempt to give early warning to those issues that will crop up in the future is a task of ever-increasing difficulty. If dialogue—rather than war or revolution— ever becomes the vehicle by which the nation and the world cope with present issues and face future ones, then the Center will have made an impact."

There have been some signs in the 1970's and 1980's that the idea of the dialogue—often neglected, often praised, and often abandoned—still appeals to some of the leaders and many of the people in the world. As long as people have minds and voices, they will attempt to communicate with one another. Whether the Center—without Robert Hutchins—will be able to make major contributions to the thinking and planning of humanity in the coming years remains to be discovered.

The Center's new president, James Miller, declared in the July-August issue of the Center Magazine that he hoped "to add something to the Center's tradition—a greater emphasis on science." He said that the Center will "continue to conduct an unbiased forum, one committed to no cause except—as Robert Hutchins often said—the causes of justice and democracy."

The terrible problems of the nuclear era still loom over us. The death of humanity may be imminent. The darkness is immense around us. Whatever light the Center can shed in the future will be needed, as it was in the past.

CREATING A NEW INSTITUTION

By Frank K. Kelly

The work of the U.S. Commission on Proposals for the National Academy of Peace and Conflict Resolution gave the movement to establish a national peace academy new energy, visibility, and confidence. Its balanced final report, *To Establish the United States Academy of Peace*, is now the basic statement for building a national peace institute. The commission's primary purpose was to explain why and how to create a national peace academy; its analysis remains durable and important to thinking about peace. *The Hundred Percent Challenge* concerns the idea's future. Our excerpts from the commission's report cover the academy's design; research perspectives; and negotiation, mediation and conciliation as seen through the eyes of a diplomat seized by Colombian guerillas, an advisor on the Camp David accords, and a minister active in the Iran hostage crisis.

When you enter the Thomas Jefferson Memorial in the District of Columbia, you read his words:

> **I am not an advocate for frequent changes in laws and constitutions, but laws and institutions must go hand in hand with the progress of the human mind. As that becomes more developed, more enlightened, as new discoveries are made, new truths discovered and manners and opinions change, with the change of circumstances, institutions must advance also to keep pace with the times. We might as well require a man to wear still the coat which**

fitted him when a boy as civilized society to remain ever under the regimen of their barbarous ancestors.

Jefferson's experience taught him that one of the hardest tasks in American life, and in the life of any nation regardless of its age, is the changing of old institutions and the creation of new ones. The ringing statements of the Declaration of Independence – that "all men are created equal," that they are "endowed by their Creator with certain unalienable rights," and that governments are instituted "to secure these rights" – were not accepted by many Americans as self-evident. Jefferson, Washington, Mason, Madison, Hamilton, and all the other founding citizens did more than debate these truths; they set out to make them part of America's daily life.

Having experienced governance under the Articles of Confederation, Americans decided to change institutions. A stronger national government was needed, so the new Constitution did not refer to a union among the states but instead declared, "We, the people of the United States, in order to form a more perfect union, establish justice, promote the general welfare, and secure the blessings of liberty to ourselves and our posterity, do ordain and establish this Constitution." The Constitution was an instrument for peaceful resolution of conflict – between the executive, the legislative, and the judicial branches of government; between the states and the federal authority; between the economic interests of the country's various regions; and between government and the individual as reflected in the Bill of Rights.

Dr. Benjamin Rush, a signer of the Declaration of Independence, and Benjamin Banneker, a mathematician, architect and designer, publisher, and black American, tried to convince Congress to add a provision on peace. In an article published in *Banneker's Almanac and Ephemeris for the Year of our Lord 1793*, they called for the Constitution to include a "peace office," for the United States on a government level equal to that of the War Department. Although not espousing the anti-federalist barrage of criticism of the Constitution, they wrote that "it is much to be lamented that no person has taken notice of its total silence upon the subject of an office of the utmost importance to the welfare of the United States, that is, an office for promoting and preserving perpetual peace in our country."

In the United States, perpetual peace was not preserved. Jefferson and others had known that the poison of slavery could tear the republic apart, but they were unable to repudiate that wretched institution of "barbarous ancestors." Nor could they see how to incorporate their secession into their "more perfect union." The bloody Civil War – viewed by the South as the War Between the States – changed the Constitution and abolished slavery, but left deep wounds still felt today. Nineteenth-century Europe, too, was violent and events seemed to prove the maxim of Charles Darwin – "the struggle for existence goes on everywhere" – and the incompatibility of biology and religion.

Yet a poet from that time spoke to men who made decisions about violence, death, justice, and peace. In "The Golden Year," Alfred Lord Tennyson wrote, "Ah! when shall all men's good/Be each man's rule, and universal peace/Lie like a shaft across the land?" And in 1842, his poem "Locksley Hall" foresaw changes in technology and institutions:

> For I dipt into the future, far as human eye could see,
> Saw the Vision of the World, and all the wonder that could be;
> Saw the heavens fill with commerce, argosies of magic sails,
> Pilots of the purple twilight, dropping down with costly bales;
> Heard the heavens fill with shouting, and there rain'd a ghastly dew
> From the nations' airy navies grappling in the central blue...
> Till the war-drum trobb'd no longer, and the battle-flats were furl'd
> In the Parliament of Man, the Federation of the World....

These hopes were shared by President Woodrow Wilson, whose presentation to Congress in 1918 of a fourteen-point program for durable peace included a new institution that became the League of Nations. Despite the League's collapse (heralded by its impotence in the face of Haile Selassie's 1935 plea for intervention to stop the Italian war on Ethiopia), Wilson's idealism had a strong impact on the people of later generations, including Presidents Franklin Roosevelt, Harry Truman, and

Dwight Eisenhower. Truman, in fact, carried a copy of "Locksley Hall" in his wallet for many years, and he told a biographer: "Now Tennyson knew there were going to be airplanes, and he knew there was going to be bombing and all of it. And some day there would be a parliament of man. It stands to reason, and that's what I was doing when I went ahead with setting up the United Nations…. The UN is the first step."

Yet for two centuries, the Rush-Banneker idea of a national institution in the United States devoted to improving the ways of peace had proponents but little success. In his 1969 booklet "Why a Department of Peace?" Dr. Frederick L. Schuman reported that "the proposal was later echoed during the course of the 19th century by various publicists and legislators, [but] their efforts were without result." One could date the modern era back fifty years to 1935 when Senator Matthew Neeley of West Virginia introduced a Department of Peace bill similar to the Rush-Banneker peace office and Congressman Fred Bierman of Iowa proposed a "Bureau of Peace and Friendship" for the Department of Labor to do sociological research on peace and war. Between 1935 and 1976, more than 140 bills were introduced to establish a department of peace, a national peace agency, or standing committees of Congress.

World War II prompted a number of Cabinet-level proposals. In 1945, Senator Alexander Wiley of Wisconsin proposed creating a small high-level Department of Peace with the Secretary's responsibilities to include the position of United States Representative on the United Nations Security Council. That year, too, Congressman Jennings Randolph of West Virginia, who later became a senator and continued his constant and steady advocacy of a national peace institution, introduced a Department of Peace bill that for the first time incorporated the proposition that the international exchange of people and ideas would be an effective way to promote peace. In 1945 and 1947, Congressman Everett Dirksen of Illinois, also later a senator, introduced bills for a peace division in the State Department, and in 1947 Senator Karl Mundt of South Dakota urged a Department of Peace.

In 1955, Senator Mike Mansfield of Montana and Congressman Charles Bennett of Florida proposed the creation of a Joint Congressional Committee for a Just and Lasting Peace, and Congressman Harold C. Ostertag of New York introduced a bill that included the concept of a national peace college. One of the most significant accomplishments occurred in 1961, when President John Kennedy signed the legislation promoted by Senator Hubert Humphrey of Minnesota to establish the Arms Control and Disarmament Agency, a semi-independent agency located in the Department of State that would formulate policy, conduct negotiations, disseminate public information, and undertake research on the control and reduction of armaments.

The idea of private citizens also promoting such a national effort began with the Rush-Banneker proposal. In our time, Dan and Rose Lucey of Oakland, California persuaded members of the Christian Family Movement in the 1960's to support the formation of a peace academy, and in 1969 Thomas C. Westropp took out a full page newspaper ad in Cleveland to outline reasons for a national peace academy. In 1976, Senators Vance Hartke of Indiana and Mark Hatfield of Orgeon introduced Senate Bill Number 1976, to create the George Washington Peace Academy. When the Hartke-Hatfield bill was introduced, a parallel effort to support that action was developed among private citizens. Dr. Bryant Wedge, a Washington psychiatrist and a teacher concerned with mediation and conciliation, Dr. Jerome Frank, a Johns Hopkins University psychiatrist, and Nachman Gerber, a Baltimore businessman, formed the Ad Hoc Committee for a National Peace Academy. This committee launched the National Peace Academy Campaign (NPAC).

NPAC set out to examine the scope of public support for a national peace academy, and it was at that point that I became involved with the movement. Dr. Wedge persuaded Henry Burnett (a direct-mail specialist) and me to develop materials about the peace academy idea for mailings to several million citizens. Burnett's work led to a special project of the Anacapa Fund of Santa Barbara. The response showed Americans from coast to coast were ready to consider such a new institution to "keep pace with the times." NPAC was poised to begin its drive that ultimately would expand membership from the initial three thousand supporters to an active constituency of more than forty thousand people. The combination of S.1976 and the establishment of NPAC marked the beginning of today's organized movement to establish a national peace academy.

Senator Claiborne Pell of Rhode Island chaired hearings of S.1976 by the Senate Labor and Public Welfare Subcommittee on Education, but the committee took no action. Senator Pell and others concluded that, although public interest was strong, the peace academy idea needed further development. The route would be a federal study commission. In 1977, Andrew Young of Georgia and Helen Meyner of New Jersey introduced a national peace academy commission bill in the House, and in the Senate the measure was introduced by Mark Hatfield, Jennings Randolph, and Spark Matsunaga of Hawaii. Hearings were held, but progress again stalled as the House measure failed in 1978. The Senate, however, amended the House-passed Elementary and Secondary Education Bill with a provision to establish the Commission of Proposals for the National Academy of Peace and Conflict Resolution. The amendment was accepted in conference, the bill became law when signed by President Jimmy Carter in November 1978, and appropriations became available in 1979. In December 1979, commission appointments were completed: President Carter appointed Arthur Barnes, Elise Boulding, and James Laue; House Speaker Thomas P. O'Neill, Jr. named William Lincoln and Congressmen John Ashbrook of Ohio and Dan Glickman of Kansas; and the Senate President Pro Tempore Warren Magnuson chose former Congressman John Dellenback, John Dunfey, and Senator Spark Matsunaga, who was elected commission chairman.

The law directed the commission to study the theories and techniques of peace and to examine the existing institutions involved in resolving conflicts among nations. From these analyses, it was to determine whether there should be a national academy of peace and, if so, its size, cost, location, and relationship to institutions of higher education and the federal government. These evaluations were to be transmitted in "a final report to the president and each House of the Congress."

The commission worked for a year-and-a-half. In addition to its study of theories and techniques and its examination of institutional strengths and limitations, it held more than 50 private meetings with educators, representatives of religious, ethnic, scientific, and academic groups, and practitioners in the arts of conflict resolution. Commissioners undertook a number of special visits, including ones to military service academies and the United States Mission to the United Nations. The commission conducted "public seminars" (expanded versions of public hearings) at sites around the nation: Boulder, Portland, St. Louis, Columbus, Los Angeles, Boston, Dallas, New York, Atlanta, Tallahassee, Honolulu, and Washington D.C. Approximately ten thousand people were specifically invited to participate in these two-day meetings. The public seminars produced over six thousand transcript pages. Questionnaires were sent to two hundred people with experience in community, national, and international mediation, and to two hundred and fifty students enrolled in peace and conflict study programs as well as their faculties. The commission also received thousands of unsolicited communications. Commissioners held two half-day and six day-long public meetings to organize their work, determine findings, debate conclusions, and develop recommendations.

The commission's principal recommendation was that "the president and Congress of the United States of America should establish the United States Academy of Peace." In its report, the commission emphasized the appropriateness of the federal government creating this new institution, especially in such precarious times of frequent breach of peace among nations and threats to global survival. The commission pointed to the enormous resources of the United States, drawing particular attention to our democratic history and to the practical lesson from our heritage that the ways communities and nations resolve their disputes must be incorporated into any examination of peace among nations. The commission emphasized that the academy should serve people outside of government as well as those in government, that it should be structured so its independence is protected from undue influence, whether private or government, and that it should not participate in government policymaking or intervene in ongoing disputes. Finally, as part of its report, the commission included draft legislation that incorporated its recommendations. This proposal became the measure to establish the United States Academy of Peace that was introduced in the Senate by Senators Hatfield, Randolph, and Matsunaga, and in the House by Congressman Dan Glickman.

Among the many leaders who supported the academy idea, General Andrew Goodpaster – former Superintendent of West Point and former Supreme Allied Commander of the NATO forces in Europe – offered some of the strongest reasons for considering it a necessary institution.

> It has long seemed to me that there is a place as well as a need for a carefully designed institution, additional to all that now exists, devoted to the serious study, both theoretical and practical, of peace and conflict resolution. From many years of service in peace and war, it is my conviction that a clearer, deeper understanding of the issues that bear on peace and the processes that support it can be of great and lasting value.
>
> There is widespread failure, I believe, both in the government and in the population at large – including, in particular, its opinion-leading elements – to understand how peace relates to the other fundamental values, needs and aspirations of our people, and how peace together with these other values can best be safe-guarded and sustained.

GLORIOUS BEINGS:

WHAT WE ARE AND WHAT WE MAY BECOME

BY FRANK K. KELLY

It is a tremendous joy for me to be here tonight – to share with you my visions of humanity's future. I have great expectations for this gathering, because I see glorious beings all around me. You are glorious because you are connected to the starry skies that shine beyond this hall. You have radiating through you the glory that fills this marvelous universe. It is vast; it extends far beyond our sight, and yet we are closely related to it. Dr. Brian Swimme, a noted physicist, says: "The vastness of the universe couldn't have been otherwise... This universe, which is 30 billion light years across, is the smallest universe we could fit into... The universe had to expand at this rate to enable our existence... We belong here. This is home. This has been our home for 15 billion years... If you altered the origin of the universe even just slightly, none of us would be here. That means, then, that our existence is implicit. We don't only stand on our feet... We stand on the original fireball; we stand on the expansion of the universe as a whole..."

When I gaze at your luminous faces I am convinced the physicists are right. I am also sure that Albert Einstein was right when he said that if we could understand what we really are we would know that we are glowing fields of electromagnetic energy. We are also collections of vibrating molecules composed of dancing atoms filled with positive and negative charges. And yet we are more than all that. The physicists can describe what we are but they cannot describe who we are.

I know that there are auras of light around your amazing bodies, and your immortal souls are shining through your eyes. Look at one another. Listen to one another. Touch one another. Become aware of what marvelous beings you are. You are far more involved in shaping the future than you have begun to realize. You know that humanity is in a tragic situation. You are surrounded by more dangers than any generation before you – and yet you have more strength, more technological knowledge, more allies to help you than you have begun to realize.

How do I dare to make such statements to you? I dare because I have lived in this body for almost ninety years – and in my long life I have experienced many miracles. In my science fiction I became a pioneer of wonder. I leaped from planet to planet. I predicted some of the transformations through which humanity has already passed. I had glimpses of many more.

One world has never been enough for me. When I was a child I was drawn to the stars. I imagined that I came from another galaxy. When I walked at night in my father's backyard and gazed at those blazing lights, I did not feel dwarfed by them or overcome by their immensity. I wanted to look over the horizon, to search for the hidden marvels, to see the unseen, to hear the signals that might be coming from other forms of life. I did not regard the stars as menacing or as solar centers for alien creatures more powerful than human beings. I saw them as playgrounds for my mind and spirit – and I still do.

I believe that we human beings will triumph over all the horrible problems we may face and over the bloody history which tempts us to despair, because we pray and we play. Through prayer we connect with the grace that pours in an endless stream from the Spirit, we discover what Einstein and other great beings discovered: "Everyone who is involved in the pursuit of science becomes convinced that a spirit is manifested in the laws of the universe – a spirit vastly superior to that of man, and one in the face of which we... must be humble." Yes, we must be humble but we must rejoice in our awareness of that Spirit moving through us, acting through us, shaping the future with us.

Through play we discover our kinship with the Almighty Being who brought us into life. God laughs and dances, God gave us the power to find endless joy in singing and dancing, in celebrating birthdays and holidays, in creating the Olympic Games and all the other games developed by people all over the earth. Scientists play with ideas and equations and make discoveries that enable us to go farther and faster than we have ever gone before. Some of those scientists brought us into the Nuclear Age and made us realize that we must find ways of living in peace or confront unparalleled catastrophes.

I grew up in a praying and playing family. I was born during a thunderstorm in an old house in Kansas City to a young mother who was dazzled by the flashes of lightning around her. My father was a firefighter, with dragons tattooed on his arms and enough nerve to try anything. Before he became a fireman he had been around the world as a sailor – and he had a variety of experiences to show him that human beings were enticing and frightening, sometimes loving and sometimes savage, builders and destroyers. As a child I loved to see him drive a big red truck from the fire station – a truck pulled by four white horses. I thought he was glorious and saw my mother's radiant beauty as a sign of glory, too.

I went to Catholic schools where I was taught that I shared in the creative mightiness that had shaped the stars. I believed that I was made by an Omnipotent One who delighted in making things new – who was present in every bird and tree, every dog and cat, every whale and walrus, every tiny insect and every towering elephant, every field and forest, every man and woman. I was assured that I was made in the very image of that creator, who spoke through every song and swayed in every dance, who felt every joy and every pain, who panted with every runner in a long race, exulted in every batter who smacked a home run, who was sad with every one who struck out.

And I had a special teacher, a nun named Sister Mary Alacoque, who treated me and all of her students with deep respect. "I see God in you," she said. She spoke freely of the spark of divinity she glimpsed in us. We were great, we were full of grace, we were headed for the heights of heaven.

When I began to write science fiction stories, she did not laugh at me. She encouraged me to let my mind run without limits. She told me that God had given me some of his creative gifts, some of his daring, some of his cosmic imagination.

She also warned me that I would be tested, that I would go through trials and tribulations. Everybody had to endure sorrows and to bear pain: That was inherent in being human, in going through the crucible of creation and shaping the future. That was her message – and the message I also received from other teachers. At every stage in my existence, that message of being tested and challenged came to me with messages of confidence and courage – most often from women but sometimes from men who demonstrated to me the strength of friendship when I was almost ready to abandon hope.

While I was writing my interplanetary tales in the 1930's, the world around me was full of agonies. Millions of people were starving to death in dire poverty, and other millions fought for bread and jobs. The Nazis in Germany murdered Jews, Christians, and all their opponents; Fascists led by General Franco took over Spain, Stalin ordered the deaths of peasants in the Soviet Union; Japanese militarists invaded China. National Guardsmen prepared to put down revolts in the United States, where millions of men and women were jobless and desperate.

The Suffering of Humanity

The sufferings of humanity were reflected in my stories. I described the plight of people who fled to dark cities on the moon. I wrote about people who were exiles on Mars and other planets in the solar system. I depicted the hunt for scientific solutions to social problems, the surge of technological inventions, the mechanization of life, the slaughter of revolutionaries. In one story I predicted a Japanese military attack on the United States, occurring in 1940. In another, I described a possible war between the Soviet Union and America, in which both sides used long-range rockets to obliterate cities. I saw the future coming then in blood and terror, but I kept on believing that the people on this strange planet would evolve toward higher levels of compassion and develop many ways to care for one another.

When I entered the University of Kansas City in 1935, I encountered a professor who urged me to abandon science fiction and to grapple with the realities of my own time. He asked me to submit a story to a new magazine which offered prizes for serious fiction by college students. I wrote one called "With Some Gaiety and Laughter" which brought me to the attention of people in Europe and Latin America, and opened a way for me to enter the field of journalism.

The story was about a man whose only possession was a recording of human laughter – the laughter which kept him from committing suicide, the laughter which assured him of the ability of human beings to endure everything and to triumph over the tribulations they encountered. The acclaim given to that story, its translation into several languages, and its use by a commentator on the National Broadcasting Company's main radio network, impressed editors at the *Kansas City Star*. I was offered a job which altered the direction of my life.

I spent my first ten months on the Star's staff primarily on death notices. As a young man I had not given much thought to death. In those ten months I gained a deeper appreciation of the significance of each human life and its boundaries. An editor told me: "People read death notices more carefully than any other pieces in the paper. Any mistakes you make will be painful." I was given a list of morticians and I called them every night. Then I had to talk to family members and friends of the persons who had died. Every detail in every story had to be thoroughly checked.

The mystery and the complexity of being human came home to me in those conversations. I learned about the qualities most cherished by sons and daughters, by wives and husbands, by grandchildren and associates. I was informed of the achievements of young people in studies and sports, and of the many gifts people had displayed in their active years; the endurance of sickness and suffering, the capacity for humor in the worst of circumstances, the instances of hospitality and generosity, the kindness extended to strangers and servants, the efforts made to serve those who needed help. I heard about people who became more exuberant as they advanced in years, who confirmed the truth of Pablo Picasso's statement that "it takes a long time to become young," and I listened to the praises of those who struggled with crippling diseases, those who dealt cheerfully with handicaps, and those who were heroic in peace and war.

The people whose lives and departures were reported to the Star were generally in the middle or upper classes. Blacks were seldom mentioned. Kansas City was a segregated place in those years. Blacks and other minorities were in the background, living in their own atmosphere, covered by their own publications. They had their own activities, their own churches, their own doctors and ministers, their own hospitals, their own cemeteries.

During my months in the field of obituaries, I came to believe that there were many good and generous people in the community. If everybody behaved as well as the people whose lives were described to me, then humanity was evolving in the right direction. I was disturbed by the fact that I knew little about the black people and the many poor families existing in my city, but I assumed that they had the same good values as the hundreds of persons I wrote about in the columns of the Star. I hoped that I would get to know people of different colors and different ethnic backgrounds as I went on with my work as a reporter.

After I became an expert in briefly describing many lives, I was suddenly taken from the hushed atmosphere of the morticians into the hectic atmosphere of the General Hospital. I rode in ambulances with drivers and doctors to the scenes of accidents, explosions, fires, murders, and domestic violence. I saw people lying in the streets or bleeding in the back rooms of apartments and boarding houses. I discovered that many men were brutal. Men shot one another, strangled one another, attacked one another, stabbed their enemies and sometimes their friends, tried to destroy one another. They beat their wives and their children. Often under the influence of alcohol and other drugs, they crashed into one another with their automobiles, ran over pedestrians, and exploded with rage when they were frustrated. They often had to be shackled or restrained by tough policemen.

An Important Lesson

I noted that women were often subjected to physical injuries by men, but rarely engaged in violent acts themselves. I had always been grateful for the kindnesses of women, for their tenderness and nurturing affections for their parents, their sisters and brothers, their lovers and husbands, their children and their friends. I knew that they had human faults and failings; I knew they could be angry and speak harshly about other people; they could be dominating and vindictive, and occasionally inflict blows on other women and men; but they were rarely killers. They seldom inflicted the severe physical wounds that men did. I became convinced that the future of humanity depended partly upon the civilizing influences of women.

My estimates of men were strongly affected by my experiences as a reporter at the General Hospital. Before that, I was influenced by my father's adventurous nature. He left home at 16 to see the world and he had been in many countries. He expected me to be as active and restless as he was, and I tried to fulfill his expectations. In my science fiction I had shocked and surprised him.

When I was three years old, in 1917, he had responded to President Woodrow Wilson's call for a declaration of war against Germany. He had rushed off to enlist in the Army. He was eager to crush the German Kaiser, to make the world safe for democracy, and to fight in a war to end war. I had to wear a little soldier's uniform and salute him when he came back from an officers' training camp. He became a captain in the Infantry and went into combat in France. He returned eventually with a large wound in his neck and nightmares from hand-to-hand struggles with Germans in the trenches over there. He often woke up screaming, believing that he was confronting a German who was trying to rip him open with a bloody bayonet. He made me realize the basic savagery of war.

In war, men sought glory by wounding or killing one another and by proving their willingness to sacrifice their lives for their countries or their causes. The young Germans my father encountered in the trenches in the 1914-1918 war were as brave as he was, as sure as he was that what they did for the Fatherland was right. Millions of men died in that war, striving to demonstrate their manhood.

I remember the Armistice Day in 1918 – that faraway November day when the slaughter stopped. I remember the ringing of church bells, the screaming of sirens, the tumultuous noise of celebrations. I also remember the weeping and wailing of a woman in the boarding house where my mother and I were staying while my father was in France. I clung to my mother and tried to hide my face from the awful sounds of grief. That woman had received a telegram telling her that her husband had been killed in one of the last battles. I will never forget her cries and her anguish.

Why did glorious beings destroy one another? Why did young men, full of health and vigor, use knives and guns to kill one another in bloody holes in the ground? I begged my mother to tell me why, but her answers did not calm my heart or stop the howling of that woman in torment. She said the Kaiser's armies had to be defeated, to save the world from his evil rule. Then there would be peace and joy for freedom loving people.

When I had to go into the American Army in World War II, to eliminate the evil Fuehrer Hitler and the Japanese militarists who had attacked my country, I was assured that there would be peace and joy when those monsters were exterminated. They were smashed and those of us who had fought against them celebrated wildly, but then we learned that the evil Stalin and his minions, who had been America's allies in that struggle, had to be removed, too. The battle against Stalin and the communists was called a "cold war" because it required different methods of combat but it had to be waged with all the resources available because the future of humanity was at stake.

In 1948, I was asked to write speeches for a president, Harry Truman, who had been compelled to make the most horrendous decision in history – the decision to use atom bombs against Japan to end the Second World War. I discovered that he had given much thought to the creation of a global organization to save humanity from the scourge of war. He carried in his wallet a visionary poem by Alfred Tennyson, written in 1842, predicting a final war involving aerial navies, which led to the formation of a Federation for the World, a Parliament for humanity.

Truman had helped to create the United Nations and he had determined to make it effective in enabling humanity to enter an unprecedented era of lasting peace and enduring prosperity for everyone. The success of the Marshall Plan, carried out under his leadership, had saved Western Europe from economic chaos. He wanted to see the rich countries devote some of their knowledge and tremendous resources to aid the poor nations to reduce or eliminate poverty all over the planet. He believed that a "decent, satisfying life" was "the right of all people."

US Leadership in Post-War World

The campaign Harry Truman ran in 1948 was based on the conviction that "the destiny of the United States is to provide leadership in the world toward a realization of the Four Freedoms." Those freedoms were described in an address to the American Congress in 1941 by Truman's predecessor, Franklin D. Roosevelt. Roosevelt asserted that the nation stood for four basic freedoms vital to human progress: Freedom of speech and expression; freedom of worship; freedom from want (by assuring to every nation a healthy, peaceful life for its inhabitants); and freedom from fear, by reducing military arms everywhere.

Roosevelt and Truman accepted the generous idea that the United States must help people everywhere secure an abundant life after the carnage of World War II. The United States had emerged from that horrifying struggle with a booming economy – and the future seemed full of unlimited possibilities. They did not want the American people to fall back into the isolationism, which had caused the country to retreat from its responsibilities after the first global war. They felt that the future of humanity depended upon the ethical behavior of a giant nation, which had attained amazing heights of power and prosperity – and had no real rivals.

I shared the hopes of those leaders. I had lived through the transformation of the United States from a country with millions of unemployed and desperate citizens into a place with dazzling opportunities in every field. The United States was far ahead of other countries in scientific and technical advances. It had absorbed millions of immigrants and refugees from other parts of the world. It had become a glorious place.

The political experts and the pollsters in 1948 failed to see that Truman's program and his hard-hitting speeches appealed to the American people. All of them said that he would lose, but he won. The editors of the Atlantic Monthly Press in Boston, who had accepted my first book, thought that I had made a mistake in becoming a speech writer for Truman. They persuaded Boston University to appoint me as a professor in the school of communications. I was glad to get that position because I did not want a government job in Washington. I enjoyed working for Truman but I did not seek a federal appointment. I was primarily a writer, not a politician.

When Truman triumphed, however, I was asked to become a special assistant to the Majority Leader of the Senate. In that place, I was expected to have a role in getting Truman's proposals enacted into law. I shared his vision of what humanity needed and I returned to Washington with enthusiasm. I served there for four years – years of conflict and frustrations, years of fear and turmoil in which Senator Joseph McCarthy frightened many Americans into believing that the Truman administration had been infiltrated by communists.

I saw powerful senators succumb to fear when they were attacked by McCarthy. Truman's proposals for a national health insurance plan were defeated by medical lobbyists. His civil rights bills and other important measures did not get much support in the Senate. The Marshall Plan did move forward, however, with the backing of Arthur Vandenberg and other far-sighted Republicans. I made my office in the Capitol available for use by Paul Hoffman, Averell Harriman, and others involved in the administration of the Marshall Plan.

On many votes in the Senate, I was struck by the significant impacts of lobbyists who shaped many of the bills that passed and defeated others. I asked Wayne Morse of Oregon one night, while a vote was occurring: "How many senators will vote in accordance with their consciences?" Morse replied slowly: "About twenty of them, I think. All of the others have strings on them." I saw then that it was virtually impossible to get the Senate to support Truman's position that the United States should provide leadership in the world toward a realization of the Four Freedoms.

Truman seldom showed any signs of depression in those turbulent times. I learned later that he frequently repeated a prayer he had used since he was 18 years old: "Almighty and Everlasting God, Creator of Heaven, Earth and the Universe, help me to be, to think, to act what is right because it is right; make me truthful, honest, and honorable in all things; make me intellectually honest, for the sake of right and honor and without thought of reward to me. Give me the ability to be charitable, forgiving, and patient with my fellow man – help me to understand their motives and their shortcomings, even as Thou understandest mine! – Amen, amen, amen."

Truman's prayer showed that he felt a connection to the Creator of the universe. As a human being, he had tremendous freedoms and tremendous responsibilities. Like Einstein, he believed there was a creative spirit in the universe, far above him and beyond him, and he was humbled by that belief. He asked for help from the Everlasting God, but he acknowledged his own duty to decide what was right and to do what was right.

I had an opportunity to talk with him about his major decisions as president. In an interview in the White House, he spoke candidly about how he had reached those decisions. When I asked him about the decision to use atom bombs on Japan, I saw anguish in his eyes. He made it clear that he felt the weight of what he had done.

"You remember what old General Sherman said about war," Truman reminded me. "He said that war was hell. And he was right. We were in hell when I made that decision. We were firebombing Japanese cities, killing thousands of Japanese men, women and children. We were preparing to invade Japan, and that invasion would have cost many thousands of lives. I wanted to stop the killing. I wanted to stop the war. I knew the atom bombs would destroy many people, but I was told that they might shock the Emperor into an act of surrender."

Truman looked at me and then he said: "You know, Frank, the Japanese are just as human as you and I are. I wanted to save Japanese lives as well as American lives." His decision will always be controversial because the war might have been ended without the atom bombs, but I was convinced that he did what he thought was right. He knew that the Japanese people were members of humanity – and every human life was precious.

In that interview – which I conducted in preparation for a chapter about Truman in a later book – he spoke with confidence and hope. He predicted that the Soviet system would collapse and that Americans and Russians would work together in a future parliament for humanity – a federation for the world. The success of the Marshall Plan encouraged him to believe that people everywhere could eventually take positive steps to end poverty.

I left Washington in 1952, to become the United States director of the International Press Institute's study of world news, financed by a grant from the Ford Foundation. My experience in the Truman era indicated to me that the American people were not well informed about what was really going on in other countries and in the United States. The International Press Institute study showed clearly that Americans were not getting enough information from the press and broadcasting companies to make good judgments on the major developments affecting the future.

The Center for the Study of Democratic Institutions

Four years later I became vice president of the Fund for the Republic, an educational foundation dedicated to upholding the American Constitution and the Bill of Rights. In 1959 the Fund established in Santa Barbara a Center for the Study of Democratic Institutions, a unique organization which brought together people from many backgrounds to examine the conditions necessary for the survival of human freedoms in an age of revolutionary changes.

The Center blazed across the world's horizons for twenty-two years. It helped to prevent a war between the United States and the Soviet Union. It fostered efforts to end the tragic conflict in Vietnam. It was a pioneer in the environmental movement. It shed light on the political and economic activities of corporations and labor unions. It sponsored discussions of the significant role of religion in a free society. It called attention to the deficiencies of the mass media and the destructive potentialities of commercial television. It published a model for a new American Constitution, designed to protect human liberties and to indicate human responsibilities for a constructive future. It brought together thousands of people in dialogues and conferences in Santa Barbara, San Francisco, Chicago, New York, Washington, Malta, and Geneva. It became an "early warning" system for humanity.

In my sixteen years of participation in the Center's work, I gained a full appreciation of the value of long-range thinking. I heard the ideas of brilliant people from every field of human endeavor – atomic scientists, philosophers, anthropologists, diplomats, bishops, theologians, psychologists, novelists, poets, artists, peace activists, Supreme Court judges, senators, governors, presidential candidates, playwrights, labor leaders, university administrators, state and local legislators, economists, and others. I argued with Nobel Prize winners and questioned scholars who were employed by the Center to make major revisions of the Encyclopedia Britannica. Groups of these scholars examined the future of law, economics, philosophy, religion, and politics.

On the Center staff, we planned meetings on science and world affairs, on the systematic study of technology, on the prospects for democracy in the new nations that had arisen after the collapse of the European colonial empires, on the possible changes in the American character in an affluent society, and the inescapable connections between the American problems and world problems. We had an insatiable thirst for knowledge about everything that was going on in every area of human activity – and we were intensely concerned about the effects of current events on the lives of coming generations. We were accused of inventing a new sin – "intellectual gluttony." I was among those guilty of that sin. I wanted to know all there was to know about everything.

The preamble for our proposed model for a new Constitution contained a declaration that it was designed "to welcome the future in good order." We thought that every human being should be concerned about that. We could see that the future had menacing aspects as well as glorious possibilities.

A National Peace Academy Campaign

I left the Center in 1975 after it went through a drastic reorganization. After several years of writing books and articles, I had another chance to engage in a project with repercussions on humanity's future. I was invited to join the board of directors of the National Peace Academy Campaign, which had been created to get Congress to approve an idea which had been around for almost two centuries – the formation of a federal institution to "promote and preserve perpetual peace."

In 1793, when George Washington was president, two glorious beings – a black mathematician named Benjamin Banneker and Dr. Benjamin Rush, one of the signers of the Declaration of Independence – deplored the fact that the new nation had a War Department but no Peace

Department. They launched a proposal to create a "Peace Office for the United States." They didn't get much support.

In the 19th century, various members of Congress and others tried to bring a Department of Peace into existence, but they weren't able to get enough public backing for the idea to be seriously considered. Yet it was revived in various forms in the next century. In the 1970's, in connection with the Bicentennial Celebration of the American Republic, Senator Hartke of Indiana and Senator Mark Hatfield of Oregon sponsored a bill "to establish an educational institute" to promote understanding of "the process and state of peace." The United States had been involved in many wars, and they thought it was time for this country "to consider the dimensions of peaceful resolution of differences."

Senator Claiborne Pell of Rhode Island, an old friend of mine, held hearings on the Hartke-Hatfield bill and suggested the formation of a national commission to examine proposals for a Peace Academy. The commission came into existence in 1980, conducted public hearings in locations ranging from Hawaii to Massachusetts, and finally endorsed the establishment of such an academy. In 1984, through an amendment attached by Senator Hatfield to a huge Defense Department appropriation, a few million dollars were made available for what was then called the U.S. Institute of Peace. That achievement came almost 200 years after the proposal offered by Benjamin Banneker and Benjamin Rush.

The institute had the support of majorities in both branches of Congress, largely due to the activities of the National Peace Academy Campaign. When I got into the Campaign I recruited Henry Burnett of Santa Barbara, a direct-mail expert, who managed to increase our membership from 3,000 to more than 30,000 persons, who brought immediate pressures upon Congress. We were delighted by the triumph of the idea after such a long struggle.

It is my belief that the Peace Institute will have many constructive impacts upon humanity's future. It has been steadily supported by the Congress for the last eighteen years. Plans for a headquarters building near the Lincoln Memorial in Washington are now under way. The building will provide space for many activities, including a laboratory for "leading edge research on issues of peacemaking"; a "central venue for convening parties engaged in ongoing conflicts"; a "training ground for diplomats, military personnel, international relief agency professionals, economic development officers and other practitioners working in areas of continuing, recent, or potential conflicts"; a "classroom for educating generations of international relations and foreign policy professionals and specialists in the skills of conflict management"; a "public relations information hub for disseminating relevant materials and information on issues of international conflicts and peacemaking"; a "focal point for heightening public awareness and understanding about the nature of international conflicts" and "a national and international clearinghouse where ideas and initiatives can be aired, exchanged, and promoted."

For the first time in the history of this nation, in a tragic time when the country needs to become aware of the many methods for resolving conflicts without military action, a Peace Institute will become a visible presence in the nation's capital. Millions of visitors from all over the world, as well as millions of Americans, will have continuing opportunities to take part in the programs of that Institute.

The idea of a Department of Peace is also being pursued. Representative Kucinich of Ohio recently introduced a bill in the House of Representatives to authorize such a Department. I believe the time will come when a Secretary of Peace will sit in the president's cabinet. The Secretary of Peace, as well as the Peace Institute, will keep the chief executive and all officials continuously reminded of the necessity for building a Culture of Peace to replace the Culture of War, which has dominated humanity for so long.

When the Peace Academy Campaign was at its height, I was invited to become a founder of another organization with a vital mission – the Nuclear Age Peace Foundation. That Foundation – launched by David Krieger, Wallace Drew, Charles Jamison, and myself in 1982 – initiates and supports worldwide efforts to abolish nuclear weapons, to strengthen international law and institutions, to use technology responsibly, and to empower young people to create a more peaceful world.

The Foundation now has thousands of members. It is a non-profit, non-partisan organization, in constant communication with hundreds of other organizations. It publishes a journal and occasional books and distributes information in many ways. It sponsors and cosponsors meetings, dialogues, and conferences with schools, colleges, universities, and other peace groups. It has consultative status to the United Nations Economic and Social Council, and is recognized by the UN as a Peace Messenger Organization.

I am grateful to be connected to this inspiring foundation. Its vision is a world full of joyful activities, free from the threats of weapons of mass destruction. We try to foster an atmosphere in which human beings realize how glorious they are, how many gifts they have, how the future may unfold with beauty and unconditional love everywhere. We work daily to make that future possible. We honor people who have demonstrated leadership in advancing peace and justice. We have presented awards to educators, scientists, religious leaders, artists, and others. Among them are Jacques Cousteau, Bishop Desmond Tutu of South Africa, Theodore Hesburgh of Notre Dame, Mairead Maguire of Ireland, the Dalai Lama of Tibet, Linus Pauling, Elisabeth Mann Borgese, Dr. Helen Caldicott, Carl Sagan, Paul Ehrlich, Yehudi Menuhin, Queen Noor of Jordan, Admiral Gene La Rocque, Senator Claiborne Pell, and many others.

The terrorist attacks in the United States on September 11 in 2001 produced a wave of fear. People from 80 countries died in the wreckage of the World Trade Towers. Everyone now knows that terrorists may strike again at any time, anywhere. There are reported to be terrorist groups in 65 nations. The war in Afghanistan destroyed one such organization, but there are many more. People everywhere are now fully aware of the vulnerability that has to be faced.

We Are All Connected

Yet that atmosphere of vulnerability has made us realize that we are all connected. We have to deal with the roots of terrorism in cooperation with the United Nations and other international organizations. Our Secretary of State, Colin Powell, told participants in a World Economic Forum that the United States and its allies must engage in a campaign against poverty, saying that those tempted by terrorists must be shown that "there is a better way" to correct the injustices existing on our planet. Powell said: "We have to go after poverty. We have to go after despair. We have to go after hopelessness ... We have to put hope back in the hearts of people."

A great meeting was held in Santa Barbara last November by the Nuclear Age Peace Foundation, which stirred hope in the hearts of the 500 people who took part in it. Two Peace Leadership Awards were presented at that assembly. One went to Hafsat Abiola, a dauntless advocate for human rights on the African continent, who founded the Kudirat Initiative for Democracy on the African continent. The other was given to Craig Kielburger, founder of the Free the Children organization, who started a movement that led to the liberation of thousands of children from slave labor.

When those two young leaders described what they had done, the people there gave them spontaneous ovations. It was evident that they were Glorious Beings – and they had been sustained by their awareness of the goodness and generosity existing in so many members of the human species. Bursts of admiration and affection flashed through the audience in wave after wave. They had demonstrated how constructive all human beings could become.

There were hundreds of students in that gathering – students from high schools and colleges, students with a wide range of gifts and capabilities, students from many ethnic backgrounds. Their young faces were shining. They were clearly inspired by the young woman from Nigeria and the young man from Canada. And the people there – people of all ages – were radiant with happiness. There was a surge of renewed confidence in humanity's future.

I thought then of statements made by Brian Swimme, a mathematical scientist, who has expressed his belief in a "cosmic generosity" pouring through the universe. He said that all human beings faced a cosmic challenge "to become generosity in a new form – the human form."

A tremendous manifestation of generosity occurred after the devastation of the World Trade Towers. People lined up to give blood; the Red Cross was deluged with gifts. People from other cities went to New York to be helpful in any way they could think of. The glorious qualities of humanity were evident there.

In my years on this planet, I have seen one transformation after another. I saw the world recover from the terrible depression in the 1930's. I saw the League of Nations fall and the rise of a new organization, the United Nations. I saw a Europe torn by centuries of national antagonisms evolve into a European Union. I saw totalitarian regimes in Spain, Italy, Germany, Russia, Africa, Asia, and South America give way to governments more responsive to the needs of the people. I saw women attaining their rightful positions in many places. I saw the leaders of many religious organizations working together. I saw the development of a world communications system through the Internet.

A Center for Humanities Future

To serve the global community now arising through the efforts of Glorious Beings all over the world, I advocate the creation of a Center for Humanity's Future. Such a Center could be a place of light and listening, a place of exploration and encouragement for people to become even greater than they are now, a launching pad for ideas from everywhere. It would enable all of us to become more aware of what marvelous capacities we have and stimulate us to become more creative than we have ever been. In the coming centuries, in which we will face more complex problems than ever before, it will be essential to evoke the godlike qualities inherent in every person. To act with the unconditional love transmitted to us by our Creator, we will take joy forever from a full appreciation of what we really are – embodiments of the cosmos, each of us aware of the strength we can draw from the universe, each of us absolutely original and limitless in our range of growing. As we become what we were intended to be, we will act upon our understanding of the fact that what we think and what we do will have repercussions through the whole future.

That is why the Center should be dedicated to celebration – to foster the release of everyone's finest thoughts and everyone's dancing spirit. Celebration means more than a never-ending party, although it does include all aspects of joy, because human beings are at their best when they are joyful, feasting and frolicking.

The Center would spread the light of eternal sunrise over our beautiful earth. It would honor all the wonderful works of compassion going on in many places, sparking many dialogues and loving exchanges, inviting everyone to open up and communicate through many languages through electronic translations, encouraging everyone to feel equally loved and respected, drawing everyone to "welcome the future in good order."

The Center could have its headquarters in Santa Barbara – in this vibrant community, which has hundreds of educational and philanthropic organizations. Its initial sponsors could be the Nuclear Age Peace Foundation and La Casa de Maria, the conference and retreat place where thousands of persons each year experience spiritual growth.

Another organization which could be connected to the Center is the PAX 2100 group, which is working on a road map that could lead to a broad structure for peace in the next hundred years. This group was brought into existence by the late Walter Gray, a visionary business man, and William Allaway, former director of the Education Abroad program of the University of California in Santa Barbara. The Center could also collaborate in projects with the Future Traditions Foundation, which was created in Santa Barbara by Misa Mandigo Kelly, a dancer and choreographer, with other young artists. These artists described their objectives in these terms: "Art is our vehicle. Peace is the destination. We merge traditions of the past with innovations of the present to develop a future of peaceful, compassionate lifestyles."

The Center could draw upon the results of studies conducted by the Foundation for the Future, established by Walter Kistler and his associates in Bellevue, Washington. That Foundation was formed to sponsor research into the critical factors that might have the most impact on the long-term survivability of humanity. Looking ahead to the Year 3000, it has brought together brilliant thinkers from many fields in a series of seminars and workshops.

The board of advisors to that Foundation includes Brian Fagan of the University of California in Santa Barbara; Robert Muller, former Assistant Secretary General of the United Nations; and Barbara Marx Hubbard, leader of the Foundation for Conscious Evolution, also based in Santa Barbara. These distinguished persons would certainly be invited to participate in dialogues at the Center.

I mention these organizations and these gifted people because they are among the many elements that support my faith in humanity's future. There are many persons here tonight who are leaders in many fields. I look forward to the dialogues we will have in the coming years – dialogues that will give us greater understanding of how we are linked together in a growing community on this marvelous planet.

Tonight I have taken you with me through the long journey of my life. That journey has kept a feeling of hope alive in me, even in times of deep pain. I have heard the cries of the wounded and I have seen men dying in agony near me in the Second World War. I have been tempted to fall into despair, but despair leads nowhere. I believe that Einstein was right when he acknowledged his awareness of the "spirit manifest in the laws of the universe" – a spirit filled with cosmic generosity, a spirit that never dies.

In my office I have a luminous painting by John August Swanson entitled, "Festival of Lights." It shows two wide streams of human beings descending the slopes of green mountains, carrying candles that illuminate their faces. Above the dark mountains are cascades of stars – stars extending through endless distances. It is evidence that the stars and mountains and the people with their candles are all connected. The Spirit is in them all.

A Global Celebration of Creativity

When I look at that painting, I am stirred again to advocate an Annual Report on the State of Humanity, to be presented with a global Celebration of Creativity. Artists of all kinds – painters, singers, dancers, poets, musicians, mystics, healers, prophets, sculptors, architects, philosophers, mediators, meditators – could lead community celebrations which would be linked together around the world. All human beings are artists. That Celebration would recognize the creativity of everyone. It could be videotaped and used on television and the Internet to bring delight into the lives of people everywhere.

That celebration could make us aware that we have come into existence to be Celebrants, to explore the wonders of all the worlds, to travel through many universes, to dance to the stars – and beyond the stars.

In the future, I see a World Parliament in which every human being will be represented by a process of free elections. That Parliament will base its decisions on the ethical principles developed by the Earth Charter Commission. It will foster a Culture of Peace in which war will be unthinkable. It will promote an increasing awareness of the spiritual dimensions of human beings.

We are glorious beings, but we will become more glorious as we unite ourselves with the flood of creativity pouring through the universes around us. We will grow UP forever – UP and UP, higher and higher. The poet William Blake said: "That one who kisses joy as it flies lives in eternity's sunrise." We will celebrate each moment and celebrate each other and all the forms of life – the other animals, the trees, the flowers, the ants, the butterflies, and every living being – and so we will live in a never-ending sunrise.

THE POWER OF WOMEN IN SHAPING A GOOD LIFE

By Frank K. Kelly

How grateful I am for the warmth and love I have received from women from the days when I emerged from the dark comfort of my mother's womb to the embrace of her warm arms and the kisses she showered upon my face and other parts of my body.

My first experiences of women's generosity came, of course, from my plump and sweet smelling mama. She was a girl with smooth skin and soft blue eyes delightful in the dancing beauty she had received from Irish and English ancestors. She renewed the world for me every time she laughed. She taught me that the big thing I had to fear was fear itself.

Yet she was tormented with fears herself. She had married an Irishmen who believed that life should be filled with gaiety and laughter —a man who had gone around the earth as a young sailor, who had fondled girls in every port and drank too much whiskey when night came on.

She knew that I was like my father in many ways. I wanted to hug every girl in sight and yet be faithful to the ones who were special, the ones I called "my beloved."

As an Irish mother she encouraged me to appreciate girls, but her highest ambition was to have me become a Catholic priest. She thought the best role for a big man was to be "a holy Father." She had priests over to our house for dinner and asked them to talk about the wonders of the priesthood. There was a desire in me to bless people and to free them from their sins, but when I told the holy fathers that I wanted a family of my own, with children from my loins, the churchmen rejected me. I was already in love with girls in my neighborhood, and I wanted the romps and rollings I expected to get from a lawful wedded wife.

I got the wife I wanted when I was 27—a glowing woman with big eyes and long legs, a social worker who was trying to help the poorest people in Kansas City. We had two enchanted evenings when I was there, and then she came to New York to marry me.

We were married in the Episcopal Cathedral of St. John the Devine at 5 o'clock in the evening of December 5, 1941. We set that date because it was her birthday. We went to the Cathedral because my beloved knew a priest, the Rev. James Pernett DeWolf, who had become the Dean there.

My best man was a Jewish guy from Kansas City— Bill Kalis, who had become my closest friend at the university in the years before our graduation. Bill and I had shared an apartment in New York, and he had a romance going with a sexy blonde named Mabel McCallum. He married her a few months later.

We had a party on the night of December 6 that rollicked on to the morning of the 7th. The party ended for me when Kalis took a full glass out of my hand. "You're on your honeymoon," Kalis said. "Get on home and make love. You'll never have a better time in all your life."

We went back to the Patchin Place and soared sky-high together. Barbara whispered as we hit the bed: "I'm not a virgin. I hope you didn't expect one." I answered: "Why should I? I'm not one either." As we came up for air, I asked her if she remembered what the king said to the queen on their first night: "Do the common people do this? I've heard that they do." And the king muttered: "Too good for them." She almost choked with laughter. "Your mother took care of you," she said. "She made you a king." My full name was Frank King Kelly. She had given me her name— that was true.

Arm in arm Barbara and I fell asleep after I had discovered that night that she had more places to kiss than any other girl I'd ever known.

We wakened with the sun in our eyes. I turned on the small radio next to our bed, and we heard a man's voice saying: "This is NBC. The White House has just announced that Japanese planes have bombed Pearl Harbor. We are at war."

"War?" I said, "Did he say we're at war?" Barbara mumbled: "To hell with it! It's not for us."

"But it is," I said. "I've got to call the AP." I had been given a week off from my job at the AP in Rockefeller Center.

I phoned the AP office and Norman Lodge, who had been a war correspondent in Europe, answered crisply, "Start building your air raid shelter."

"Do you need me?" I asked. "I can come back to work if you need me."

Lodge had been to our wedding party. He snapped: "You just got married, Kelly. Go back to bed."

Barbara took the phone and clicked the receiver. She muttered: "If you try to get out of this bed, I'll break your right leg. You aren't going anywhere."

I discovered then that love meant more to a woman—at least the one I married—than any war. We both knew that war would sweep over us—but we couldn't let it destroy us.

I remember how my mother had not shared my father's patriotic fervor in World War I. He had rushed out and enlisted in the Army after President Wilson had committed us to a crusade to wipe out war and save the world for democracy. He went to an officers training camp in Kansas and later into battle in France as a captain in the 89th Division. He came home with an ugly hole in his neck made by a piece of German shrapnel. His experience in hand to hand combat gave him nightmares for the rest of his life.

He had seemed pleased by the little soldier's uniform I wore for a while in that war, but he never encouraged me to join the Army in the Second World War. He hoped that I could stay out of it.

My wife did not forgive me easily for wanting to go back to the AP after the Pearl Harbor attack. She treated it as a burst of insanity and I later regretted it myself.

It took me a long time to realize that women often had more wisdom than men. I grew up in a time when women were expected to be housekeepers and children raisers but not be executives or leaders in any field.

I knew that the woman I married—Barbara Allen Mandigo—was widely admired for the help she gave to suffering people as a social worker in Kansas City. When she came to New York to be my bride, she was qualified for many jobs available there. I was making $65 dollars a week and our apartment cost $45 a month under rent control rates regulated by the city.

"You can probably make more than I'm getting from the AP now," I said. "But I don't want you to feel that you have to take a full-time job to give us a good income. I'm going to sell some stories that will bring us enough money to go to the Rainbow Room or Café Society Downtown or any other place we want to go."

"What kind of a life do you want?" she said, sitting on my lap. "Do you want to make love every night—or only on Saturdays and Sundays? Do you want to have a house on Long Island, possibly full of children— or continue the way we are in Greenwich Village, in our little love nest in Patchin Place?"

"Right now, I like to enjoy our nest," I said. "I like to come home at two or three in the morning and find you naked, with a ribbon in your hair. I'd like to have our honeymoon go on forever. I'm always hungry for you. You'll be beautiful and sexy for at least sixty years. After that we might settle down."

She laughed. "I think I can love you as long as I live," she said. "You bring home the bacon and I'll cook it."

"We'll never have buckets of money," I said. "I hope you won't feel deprived if I don't buy you a fur coat."

"You'll keep me warm," she said. "What more can I ask for?"

I remembered that my father had earned a good salary at Sears after he came home from the First World War. He could afford a mink coat. My mother confided in me that she hadn't expected to get such a symbol of material success. "I would have preferred another child," she said. "I wanted four but we only had three."

My father was proud to have three although he hadn't been eager to have any. He lavished gifts on us when he was sober, but had bursts of wrath when he was drunk. He disappeared for several days at a time when he was hitting the bottle.

He blamed his heavy drinking on his Irish heritage and urged me to drink as little as possible. Lighting cigarettes and blowing smoke at me, he'd say: "don't be like me, son. I'm going to die early. You might live to be 100 if you stay away from booze and smoking."

"I'm Irish too," I said. "And I'm proud of it."

"But your middle name is King," he said. "And your mother had some English ancestors, as well as some Indian blood. She insisted that her full name was Martha Oneita King, and she had you baptized as Francis King Kelly. I called you Frank King Kelly."

I liked the idea of having three names. Kelly was too common, just by itself. There were thousands of Kellys in the Dublin phone book. They were a vast throng—priests and farmers, saloonkeepers, beautiful girls, wonderful women, famous fighters.

I was linked to them all. But through my mother's strength, I was also a King. I had a right to a royal manner. My grandparents on my mother's side were named Alf and Constance King.

My mother also had connections with the Farrells of Nebraska. My uncle was president of the Lincoln Insurance Company. He was a tall rich man. When he came to Kansas City to see my mother, he always brought gifts for all members of the family. He liked the fact that I was a writer. When he died, he left me $1,000 in his will. That was a lot of money in those days.

So it gave me a sense of importance to be a King as well as a Kelly. I found that many of my friends were impressed by my full name. So the power of a woman—Martha Oneita King—attached me to the Kings and the Farrells, and perhaps to the Indians who had lived around Kansas City before I was born there. My mother never explained how she got the name of Oneita. But I liked it. As a boy I gave out war whoops at school and made wild claims.

My mother saw that Barbara had become a dominant person in my life. Barbara's full name was Barbara Allen Mandigo, plus Kelly. Her mother was an Allen of New England, and an Allen reportedly had come to America on the Mayflower, a ship, which had been an early arrival. Her mother was a member of the D.A.R. (Daughters of the American Revolution) a women's group dedicated to freedom and justice.

Her father's name was Clark Rogers Mandigo. He went to Harvard and was successful in business until the stock market crashed in 1929. He died a few years later.

When I returned from France in World War II, I took my wife to Kansas City for a short visit. My mother welcomed us with open arms and gave us the front bedroom upstairs in her house—the room she had enjoyed with my father before he died.

On the third day of our visit, my mother shocked Barbara by saying to her: "You must give your man a rest. You mustn't make love every night. You're going to break that old bed."

Barbara didn't back down at all. She answered, smiling; "You and Frank's father must have overloaded it."

I intervened: "I was overseas for a long time, mother. I had a lot of invitations from those English and French girls. They were lovely."

I remember the girls in Paris, who greeted us as liberators in 1944 when we drove out the Germans. They slipped their arms around us and whispered in our ears.

My mother nodded: "I read about those girls. Like your father you were probably eager to flirt with them."

"I flirted," I said. "But I told them I had a wonderful wife at home. I was faithful."

My father had boasted about having a girl in every port when he had gone around the world as a young sailor—but he hadn't been married then. He hadn't taken vows of fidelity—and I had made pledges to Barbara in the Cathedral of St. John the Divine. Barbara was the center of my life.

Some of my friends in the Army were faithful to their wives, and some weren't. Some of them had children overseas, and some were infected with venereal diseases. I was glad that I could get home without those burdens on my conscience.

I had a deep respect for the women who entered a marital relationship with a lifelong commitment. There was something divine about it.

One of the elements in my feeling of permanence with Barbara was my awareness that she had been gifted with psychic abilities like those my mother had.

In the spring of 1918, my mother put me into a little soldier's suit she had given me, and called a taxicab to take us to Union Station. She persuaded one of the railroad people to take us down to one of the main tracks. We sat on a bench. My mother looked far along the tracks and said in a loud voice: "There's a troop train coming and your father is going to be on it." A porter standing close to us said: "No troops coming today, lady. We haven't been notified of any troop trains."

We sat down on the bench any way and we heard a train whistle. It came rattling into the station with soldiers waving at us from every window.

My father dropped from one of the cars and lifted me into his arms. "You look after your mother," he said to me. "I may be gone for a long time."

I couldn't understand how my mother had been so sure of his appearance. Later I thought he must have told her in a letter or a phone call. But he denied that he had tipped her off. He would have been severely reprimanded if he had leaked any information. He had become a captain in the training camp and he stuck strictly to the Army's rules.

"You'll get back safely," my mother said in her firm voice. "You're named for St. Francis, and he's praying for you."

"I'm praying for you, too," I said.

"We're going over there to throw out the Kaiser and his men," my father said, swinging me into my mother's arms. "Then I'll be back and we'll go to the ballgame together."

My father was badly wounded in one of the first battles in France. But my mother counted on St. Francis and the prayers of the nuns who ran the school where I studied. And he did come home alive.

We also counted on St. Michael the Archangel; because my father's full name was Francis Michael Kelly. For some reason my mother didn't give me another saint's name. She insisted on linking me to her ancestors. She called me Francis King Kelly. Her mother's name had been Constance King.

I liked being a King as well as being a Kelly. When I became a writer, it gave me a special recognition. There were many Kellys in the world, but relatively few Kings.

When my father came back to Kansas City he did not have a kingly bearing or the laughing look of a lucky Kelly. A piece of German shrapnel had torn a hole in his neck and pulled the left side of his neck down in a grim grimace.

He horrified me. I did not want to go close to him—or let him close to me. But I couldn't prevent it.

He forced me to hear his description of what it was like to lie dying on a battlefield.

"I had fallen into a deep hole," he said. "And a soft rain was falling on my face. It was my own blood, spurting in a fountain out of my neck. A medic slid into the hole and shoved a piece of mud-covered metal into my torn body. And I began to realize that I was dying."

I tried to stop him from telling me any more, but he wouldn't shut up. He had to tell me something he considered to be very significant.

"There was no pain—no pain at all," he said, grabbing my arm. "I felt that I was sinking into a deep warm bed, the most comfortable bed I'd ever found. And then the medic pulled me up and took me to a field hospital—and the bleeding stopped. I was back in the turmoil of life."

My mother didn't want to hear about his war experiences. She said, "Women are not made for war, but for love. We'll never have peace until women rule the world."

I decided, based on the experience of my own life, that we must liberate the feminine qualities within all of us to be appreciated and supported. I shared the views of William Sloan Coffin, pastor of a huge church on Riverside Drive in New York, who declared: "The woman who most needs liberating is the woman inside each man."

Dr. Sherwin Nuland, a noted surgeon who has written valuable volumes on the history of doctors, has found a great change in the medical profession with the entry of women into all fields. He wrote: "Our young men are learning from our young women. Our juniors are teaching our elders. We are no longer afraid to nurture ..."

All my life I have been nurtured by creative women. In addition to my amazing mother and my brilliant and beautiful sister Kitty—I had marvelous girls in college, girls who taught me to dance all night, to savor the ecstasies of exploring young bodies in the back seats of cars, to see the beauty of a full moon and the sparkling of the stars through their perfumed hair.

I'll be forever grateful to Mary Harbord who shared hours of mouth-to-mouth fun with me on a long couch in her parent's living room while they were away. She came close to surrendering her virginity to me but never quite lost it. We read poetry together, listened to music with the lights out; we spent hour after hour entwined together, we camped on that couch and she let me enjoy the secret garden between her long legs.

After Mary decided she wasn't ready for marriage, I fell in love with a red-haired girl who had invited me to her high apartment in a tall building downtown. Rachel Maddox was a writer who was drawn to me after she read some of my mystery stories. She was an imaginative storyteller herself. Her *Turnip's Blood* won a prize in a story magazine and her novels, *The Green Kingdom* and *A Walk in the Spring Rain*, were mystical and moving.

I hoped that Rachel would be in my embraces forever. I went to see her almost every night. I bought her gifts, including nightgowns. She was willing to go to bed with me naked but I thought she looked more beautiful in a transparent blue gown. She wore the gowns for me.

She encouraged me to believe that I could be a famous writer. She told me that I might rank with Hemingway and Faulkner and other writers we both admired. I never achieved the stature she had expected me to reach. Yet I did appreciate her high hopes.

I think she was shocked by my reaction when we broke up. She told me that she was going to marry another man—a stockbroker in Kansas City. She had a whole group of admirers around her, but I thought I had a special place.

The next night, she had a party in her apartment. I got drunk and ran toward the balcony, screaming my intentions to jump from it to my death. One of my closest friends, Shelby Storck, tackled me and sat on my chest. I had been the best man at his wedding. He growled at me: "Don't be a damned fool. I'll sit on you all night." Later he took me home, lecturing me all the way: "I don't think Rachel will ever want to hear from you again."

We arrived at my parents' house at 3 in the morning. My parents had retired, and Shelby got me into my room without waking them up. "Stop your bawling," he said. "Rachel wasn't the right woman for you. My wife has a friend who'll give you a better break than you deserve."

His wife's friend was a girl named Barbara Allen Mandigo. I married her and we had 54 years of glorious times together. I never heard a word from Rachel after that night. I heard that she was afraid of me and I could understand why.

Barbara helped me to make the best decision of my life. She encouraged me to apply for a Nieman Fellowship at Harvard and sent them a collection of my articles that led the Neiman Committee to award me a Fellowship.

That Fellowship opened many doors for me in subsequent years. Robert Hutchins consulted Louis Lyons, then the curator of the Nieman Foundation, when he was seeking a communications officer for the Fund for the Republic. Lyons gave me a strong recommendation, which led to my election as a vice president of the Fund.

At the time that election occurred, I had a job as an officer of the Fitzgerald Company, a public relations agency on Madison Avenue in New York. The agency's clients included the National Association of Electric Companies and the Standard Oil Company of New Jersey, with particular service for the Creole Petroleum Company in Venezuela. I was uncomfortable about being involved with those huge corporations. I wanted to be a crusader for human rights.

I had been the associate director of a Ford foundation study of world news, and a consultant against censorship for the American Book Publishers' Council. I had felt that those jobs were really challenging.

A few days before Hutchins telephoned me about the Fund for the Republic, Barbara had urged me to be hopeful about the future. "You're going to get a hot spot at one of the big foundations," she said. "It's going to give you a chance to be a fighting Irishman." I hadn't taken her prophecy very seriously. I didn't know anybody at the Ford Foundation except those involved in the report on the handling of international news.

When Hutchins telephoned me and asked me to have lunch with him, I was astounded. When he asked me what I thought of his public statement that he would hire a Communist if the Communist had high qualifications for a particular job—a statement which had evoked calls for his resignation as head of the Fund— I expressed my admiration for his courage and his honesty. I said I was delighted to be working with the people on the Fund's board (who included Oscar Hammerstein, Paul Hoffman, Elmo Roper, and others who were outstanding leaders).

When I went to the Fund's headquarters on the 55th floor of the Lincoln Building in the center of Manhattan, I found that I had been given an office next to Hutchins. He carried a portable typewriter into my office, saying: "I've heard you might find this useful." Barbara urged me to work closely with Hutchins, and I did.

I was not received warmly by the first vice president of the Fund—W. H. Ferry—who had aroused antagonism in the board due to his abrasive statements. Ferry had been an advisor to Henry Ford and he had urged Ford to give the Fund an initial gift of 15 million dollars. He regarded himself as one of the founders of the fund. He claimed to have a close relationship with Hutchins, but I noticed that Hutchins was irritated by some of the public speeches Ferry made.

One of the board members—Erwin Griswold, dean of the Harvard Law School—asked me to give him private reports on what Hutchins and Ferry were doing. I angered Griswold by saying that I couldn't be a secret agent for any member of the board.

I persuaded my friend Hal Boyle, who had become a columnist for the Associated Press, to do an admiring interview with Hutchins. Boyle's article pleased the board but did not placate the right-wing radio columnist, Fulton Lewis, Jr., who was working with the House Un-American Activities Committee in a campaign to deprive the Fund of its status as a tax-free educational institution.

The Fund came under a savage attack from Senator Joseph McCarthy and the Un-American Activities Committee when we published a report on blacklisting in the movies and the broadcasting companies. The report was written by a friend of mine, a Catholic journalist named John Cogley, who had been an editor of a magazine called *The Commonweal.*

When Cogley was summoned to testify before the Committee, I told him that I would be there with him. Hutchins was gloomy when the Congressmen went after Cogley. He said to me: "We're going to lose our status as a philanthropic institution by Christmas." I refused to believe that. I said then: "It's hard to label a good Catholic as a Communist. If we put up a good fight, we'll win."

J. R. Parten, a wealthy Texas oil man, who had been attacked by racists when he supported civil rights for black people and other minorities, had become chairman of the Fund's board. He was a close friend and backer of Sam Rayburn, the Speaker of the House of Representatives, who had been personally smeared by political extremists.

When I learned from Clyde Doyle, a member of the Committee, that the Fund was considered to be a subversive organization because it had distributed copies of Edwards R. Murrow's CBS program entitled "Harvest of Shame"—exposing the bad treatment given to American farm workers—I transmitted the information to Mr. Rayburn. He was enraged and declared: "I know Ed Murrow. He's no more of a Red than I am. It's time we closed down that committee."

When Cogley came before the Committee he defended the findings of the report on black listing vigorously. At the end of the day, Cogley said: "I wrote a book. Is the Committee trying to deny my rights to do that?" Chairman Walters snapped: "We called you for the purpose of ascertaining what your sources were, in order to determine whether or not yours are the conclusions we would have reached had we embarked on this same project."

By that remark, Walter confirmed Cogley's contention that the Committee's action in summoning him had basically challenged freedom of the press.

After the Cogley hearing, the Committee came under fire from many leading publications, including the *New York Times*, the *Washington Post*, the *Times Herald*, and the *London Observer*.

Largely due to the integrity of its leaders—including Hutchins, Parten, Paul Hoffman and others—the Fund defeated the Committee and it receded from the headlines and lost much of its power. The attacks made by Senator McCarthy and other demagogues were also repulsed.

The victory of the Fund over its enemies could also be attributed to the stanch character of the wives of its staff members, who spoke for it in social gatherings on many occasions in all parts of the United States. The Fund and its subsidiaries—such as the Center for the Study of Democratic Institutions—never lost their respectability even in a time of vicious assaults on persons who tackled controversial issues.

Like many men of the 20th Century, I expected to die before my wife departed from this plane of existence. She had the same expectation, and our plans were made accordingly. In my will, I left every one of my earthly possessions to her— and she did the same for me.

Bur she died of cancer on December 4, 1995 in the Santa Barbara Hospital. I was with her, sitting close to her and holding her right hand. On the other side of her hospital bed was a woman who had become her closest friend—actually more than a friend, a soul sister, someone who had prayed with her everyday, someone who had shared her charitable activities, who had been a follower of St. Francis of Assisi, who had dedicated her life to the joys of giving.

A few moments before she passed away, Barbara spoke to her sister: "Christine, I think Frank will be very lonely when I'm gone. We have a union deeper than I ever expected to have. Will you look after him? Will you be his helpmate as I have been?"

I sat stunned between them. I was not prepared for life without Barbara—or to have another person at the center of my life. Christine had come to Santa Barbara a few years before Barbara was stricken. She was a tall, beautiful woman with a brilliant mind, a quick laugh, an immediate sympathy for people who needed help.

Soon after Barbara had given me into the hands of Christine, my son Terry arrived from his home in Madison, Wisconsin. I had telephoned him a few days earlier to tell him: "Your mother is close to departure. Seeing you would bring her much joy." When Terry came into the room, her face filled with delight. "I just made the right connection on the airlines," Terry said. "I hope you'll get better soon." She spoke in a whisper. "Oh Terry," she said. "I'm not going to get any better. Give me a hug." He embraced her—and then she was gone. A nurse took her wedding ring off her hand and gave it to me. Memories of our fifty-four years together rushed through my mind.

We had lived through war and peace together, through hard times and good times. I thanked God that Terry and Stephen, our two sons, had been there. Christine, her "soul sister," had been in the hospital room many times. Mark Asman, the pastor of her church had been with us when I had brought her by ambulance to the hospital. Her friends from Trinity Episcopal Church had sent her flowers and had come to visit her in her final hours. I was sure that she had gone into the arms of angels and that she would intercede for us at God's throne.

I went into the hospital corridor and called Steve Gibson, a friend who worked in a funeral parlor. I knew he would give Barbara's body reverent care.

When I got home—in the old house on Padre Street where we had experienced many years of love—I asked Christine to join me in prayers and in reading of the Persian poet Rumi, which we had read so many times with Barbara. She responded swiftly and warmly.

"I didn't expect Barbie to put me into your hands," I said. "I hope I won't be a burden for you. I know you already have many things to do."

I saw the grief in Christine's face and she saw the sorrow in mine.

"It doesn't feel like a burden to me," Christine said. "We three had a deep friendship. Barbara will be with us as long as we live. We know that God is love, and God has brought us together. We can be grateful for that. If we have strong faith, that will sustain us together."

So the love that grew between us gave us a new understanding of how the worst wounds could be healed. Christine refused to become my lawful wedded wife, but she accepted my companionship in many days and nights in partnership. She was my beloved and I was hers.

My family members gave us their approval and her parents and her children by previous marriages accepted us happily in their lives. We told them all that Barbara had blessed us.

Barbara and Christine, like my mother and my sister and other great persons I have known in a life of more than 90 years, have led to my conviction that human beings are glorious beings, capable of transforming the world in the future.

The future beckons and threatens all of us. The horizon that stretches before us in our swiftly changing world is higher and wider than any we have glimpsed before. The future pulls us, shapes our dreams, and opens many paths. The liberation of women has released enormous waves of creativity in many fields.

We are being carried into new dimensions in which the nurturing strength of good women is released through men as well as feminine leaders. Let us welcome the future with topless expectations, realizing that one world is not enough to fulfill the powerful dreams that burst through us.

Every year we must have worldwide celebrations of humanity transformed—with new men and women dancing and singing in luminous embraces.

Every year we must have a Global Celebration of Creativity. Artists of all kinds—painters, singers, dancers, poets, musicians, mystics, healers, prophets, sculptors, architects, philosophers, dedicators, mediators, astronauts, and others—could lead community celebrations which would be linked together around the world. All human beings are artists. That Celebration should recognize the creativity of every one.

We are glorious beings, but we will become more glorious as we join the flood of creativity pouring through the universes around us.

The poet William Blake said: "The one who kisses joy as it flies lives in eternity's sunrise." We will celebrate every moment and live in a never-ending sunrise.

We shared the ideas expressed by Brian Swimme, Director of the Center for the Story of the Universe.

"We are the first generation to live with an empirical view of the origin of the universe," Swimme declared in one of his books. "We are the first humans to look into the night sky and see the birth of stars, the birth of galaxies, the birth of cosmos as a whole. Our future as a species will be forged within the story of the world."

Science now teaches us that we are connected with everything in the universe and the universe is pouring forth new forms of life in countless ways.

The universe is filled with a glorious light—and our minds are filled with that light. Now that the energies of women are being fully released, we will share in a glorious future. We will see ourselves, and all life with a majesty beyond our wildest imaginings.

We will be aware at every moment that one world is not enough!

"It is always inspiring to visit with Frank Kelly, a man who served in four presidential administrations during some of the most challenging and exhilarating moments of the last 80 years. My husband Walter and I first met Frank through the Center for the Study of Democratic Institutions in Santa Barbara. We have been strongly influenced by his deep wisdom, his principled yet compassionate ideals, and his unwavering dedication to global peace."

— Congresswoman Lois Capps

"In Kissing Joy as it Flies, Frank King Kelly at his modest but articulate best demonstrates his deep understanding of the human condition. He finds good, if not greatness in everyone he meets in a career that spans two World Wars, journalism and Washington politics, and a Santa Barbara think tank. Once again he celebrates each of us as 'Glorious Beings'. A must read."

— Bill Allaway

"Frank Kelly has lived an extraordinary life that covers most of the 20th century. His spirit of optimism has touched the lives of countless people. He has been a science fiction writer, a reporter, a citizen soldier, a speech writer for President Truman, an assistant to the Senate Majority Leader, a vice president of the Center for the Study of Democratic Institutions, and a founder and senior vice president of the Nuclear Age Peace Foundation. In his tenth decade of life he continues to be a fount of new and innovative ideas. He believes that humanity has a great future if we can put aside our differences and grasp the essential miracle of life. His life and spirit inspire confidence that a better, more peaceful world is possible."

— David Krieger, President, Nuclear Age Peace Foundation